The Aftermath

RHIDIAN BROOK

VIKING
an imprint of
PENGUIN BOOKS

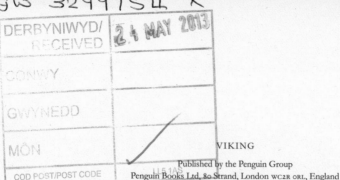

VIKING

Published by the Penguin Group

Penguin Books Ltd, 80 Strand, London WC2R 0RL, England

Penguin Group (USA) Inc., 375 Hudson Street, New York, New York 10014, USA

Penguin Group (Canada), 90 Eglinton Avenue East, Suite 700, Toronto, Ontario, Canada M4P 2Y3
(a division of Pearson Penguin Canada Inc.)

Penguin Ireland, 25 St Stephen's Green, Dublin 2, Ireland (a division of Penguin Books Ltd)

Penguin Group (Australia), 707 Collins Street, Melbourne,
Victoria 3008, Australia (a division of Pearson Australia Group Pty Ltd)

Penguin Books India Pvt Ltd, 11 Community Centre,
Panchsheel Park, New Delhi – 110 017, India

Penguin Group (NZ), 67 Apollo Drive, Rosedale, Auckland 0632, New Zealand
(a division of Pearson New Zealand Ltd)

Penguin Books (South Africa) (Pty) Ltd, Block D, Rosebank Office Park,
181 Jan Smuts Avenue, Parktown North, Gauteng 2193, South Africa

Penguin Books Ltd, Registered Offices: 80 Strand, London WC2R 0RL, England

www.penguin.com

First published 2013
001

Copyright © Rhidian Brook, 2013

The moral right of the author has been asserted

Set in Garamond MT Std 13.5/16pt
Typeset by Palimpsest Book Production Ltd, Falkirk, Stirlingshire
Printed in Great Britain by Clays Ltd, St Ives plc

A CIP catalogue record for this book is available from the British Library

HARDBACK ISBN: 978–0–670– 92112–6
TRADE PAPERBACK ISBN: 978-0-670-92291-8

www.greenpenguin.co.uk

ALWAYS LEARNING   **PEARSON**

This book is dedicated to Walter, Anthea, Colin,
Sheila and Kim Brook

'You will be called the repairer of broken walls.'

Isaiah 58:12

'It doesn't seem to make any sense – one family in a place this size.'

Brideshead Revisited, Evelyn Waugh

September 1946

I

'The Beast is here. I've seen him. Berti's seen him. Dietmar's seen him. With his black fur like a fancy lady's coat. And those teeth like piano keys. We have to kill him. If we don't, who will? The Tommies? The Yankees? The Russkies? The French? None of them will, because they're too busy looking for other things. They want this and they want that. They're like dogs fighting over a bone that's got no meat on it. We have to do it ourselves. Get the Beast before he gets us. Then everything will be better.'

The boy Ozi readjusted his headgear as he led the others through the pulverized landscape of the Tommy-bombed city. He wore the English hard-helmet he'd stolen from the back of a truck near the Alster. Although it was not as stylish as the American or even the Russian helmets he had in his collection, it fitted him the best and helped him swear in English when he wore it, just like the Tommy sergeant he'd seen shouting at the prisoners at Hamburg's Dammtor station: 'Oi! Put your fucking hands up. Fucking up, I said! Where I can see them! Dumb bloody fucking Huns.' Just for a moment those men had failed to raise their hands; not because they didn't understand, but because they were too weak from lack of food. Dumb-Bloody-Fucking-Huns! Below the neck, Ozi's clothes were a hybrid fashion of make-do invention where rags and riches jumbled together: the dressing gown of a dandy; the cardigan of an old maid; the collarless shirt of a grandfather; the rolled-up trousers of a storm trooper tied with the belt of a clerk's necktie;

and the shoes, shredded at the toe, of a long-gone station-master.

The ferals – the whites of their eyes wide with fear and accentuated by dirty faces – followed their leader through the shattered scree. Weaving around the moraines of brick-rock, they came to a clearing where the conical rocket of a church spire lay on its side. Ozi raised a hand to halt the others and reached inside his dressing gown for his Luger. He sniffed the air:

'He's in here. I can smell him. Can you smell him?'

The ferals sniffed like twitchy rabbits. Ozi pressed up against the lopped-off spire and inched towards its open end, gun out, guiding him like a divining rod. He paused and tapped the cone with it, indicating that the Beast was prob-ably within. And then: a flash of black as something bolted from inside out into the open. The ferals cowered but Ozi stepped out, took a wide stance, closed one eye, aimed and fired.

'Die, Beast!'

The shot was muffled in the low, muggy atmosphere, and a tinkling, metallic ricochet threw back the message that he'd missed his target.

'Did you hit him?'

Ozi lowered the gun and pushed it into his belt.

'We'll get him another day,' he said. 'Let's look for some food.'

'We've found a house for you, sir.'

Captain Wilkins stubbed out his cigarette and placed his yellowed finger on the map of Hamburg that was pinned to the wall behind his desk. He traced a line west from the pin-head marking their temporary headquarters, away from the bombed-out districts of Hammerbrook and St Georg, over

St Pauli and Altona, towards the old fishing suburb of Blankenese, where the Elbe veered up and debouched into the North Sea. The map – pulled from a pre-war German guidebook – failed to show that these conurbations were now a phantom city comprised only of ash and rubble.

'It's a bloody great palace by the river. Here.' Wilkins's finger circled the crook at the end of the Elbchaussee, the road running parallel to the great river. 'I think it'll be to your taste, sir.'

The word belonged to another world: a world of surplus and civil comfort. In the last few months, Lewis's tastes had narrowed to a simple checklist of immediate and basic needs: 2,500 calories a day, tobacco, warmth. 'A bloody great palace by the river' suddenly seemed to him like the demand of a frivolous king.

'Sir?'

Lewis had 'gone off' again; off into that unruly parliament inside his head, a place where, more and more, he found himself in hot debate with colleagues.

'Isn't there someone living in it already?'

Wilkins wasn't sure how to respond. His CO was a man of excellent repute with an impeccable war record, but he seemed to have these quirks, a way of seeing things differently. The young captain resorted to reciting what he had read in the manual: 'These people have little moral compass, sir. They are a danger to us and to themselves. They need to know who is in charge. They need leadership. A firm but fair hand.'

Lewis nodded and waved the captain on, saving his words. The cold and the calories had taught him to ration these.

'The house belongs to a family called Lubert. Loo-bear-t. Hard "T". The wife died in the bombings. Her family were bigwigs in the food trade. Connections with Blohm and Voss.

They also owned a series of flour mills. Herr Lubert was an architect. He's not been cleared yet but we think he's a probable white or, at worst, an acceptable shade of grey; no obvious direct Nazi connections.'

'Bread.'

'Sir?'

Lewis had not eaten all day and had taken the short leap from 'flour mill' to bread without thinking; the bread he pictured in his head was suddenly more present, more real, than the captain standing at the map on the other side of the desk.

'Go on – the family.' Lewis made an effort to look as if he was listening, nodding and setting his jaw at an inquisitive tilt.

Wilkins continued: 'Lubert's wife died in '43. In the firestorm. One child – a daughter. Frieda, fifteen years old. They have some staff – a maid, a cook and a gardener. The gardener is a first-rate handyman – ex-Wehrmacht. The family have some relatives they can move in with. We can billet the staff, or you can take them on. They're clean enough.'

The process by which the soul-sifters of the Control Commission's Intelligence Branch assessed cleanliness was the *Fragebogen*, or questionnaire: 133 questions to determine the degree of a German citizen's collaboration with the regime. From this, they were categorized into three colour-coded groups – black, grey and white, with intermediate shades for clarity – and dispatched accordingly.

'They're expecting the requisition. It's just a matter of you viewing the place then turfing them out. I don't think you'll be disappointed, sir.'

'You think they will be disappointed, Captain?'

'They?'

'The Luberts? When I turf them out.'

'They're not allowed the luxury of disappointment, sir. They're Germans.'

'Of course. How silly of me.' Lewis left it there. Any more such questions and this efficient young officer with his shiny Sam Browne and perfect puttees would have him reported to Psychiatric.

He stepped from the overheated British Military Detachment Headquarters into the premature cold of a late-September day. He blew vapour and pulled on the kid gloves that Captain McLeod, the American cavalry officer, had given him in the town hall at Bremen the day the Allies had announced the division lines of the new Germany. 'Looks like you get the bum deal,' he had said, reading the directive. 'The French get the wine, we get the view and you guys get the ruins.'

Lewis had lived among the ruins for so long now he had stopped noticing them. His uniform was fitting garb for a governor in this new, quadripartite Germany – a kind of internationalized mufti which, in the midst of post-war disorientation and re-regulation, passed without comment.

The American gloves were prized but it was his Russian-front sheepskin coat that gave him the most pleasure, its provenance traceable back via the American to a Luftwaffe lieutenant who had, in turn, taken it from a captured Red Army colonel. He'd be wearing it soon enough if this weather kept up.

It was a relief to get away from Wilkins. The young officer was one of the new brigade of civil servants that made up the Control Commission, Germany, a bloated force of clipboard men who saw themselves as the architects of the reconstruction. Few of these people had seen action – or even a German – and this allowed them to pronounce and theorize their way to decisions with confidence. Wilkins would make major before long.

Lewis took a silver-plated cigarette case from his coat and opened it, catching the light from the sun on its clear, buffed surface. He polished it regularly. The case was the only material treasure he had with him, a parting gift from Rachael given to him at the gates of the last proper house he'd lived in – in Amersham, three years ago. 'Think of me when you smoke' was her instruction, and this he had tried to do, fifty, sixty times a day for three years; a little ritual to keep the flame of love alive. He lit a cigarette and thought about that flame. With distance and time it had been easy to make it seem hotter than it was. The remembrance of their love-making and of his wife's olive-smooth, curvy flesh had sustained him through the cold and lonely months (her flesh seemingly growing smoother and curvier as the war went by). But he had grown so comfortable with this imagined, ersatz version of his wife that the imminent prospect of actually touching and smelling her unsettled him.

A sleek black Mercedes 540K with a British pennant on the bonnet pulled up in front of the steps of the headquarters. The Union Jack at the wing mirror was the only thing that looked out of place. Despite its associations, Lewis liked this vehicle, its lines and the silky purr of its engine. It was appointed like an ocean-going liner, and the ultra-careful driving style of his driver – Herr Schroeder – added to the impression of it being like a ship. No amount of British insignia could de-Germanize this car, though. British military personnel were built for the bumbling, bulbous Austin 16, not these brute-beautiful, world-conquering machines.

Lewis walked down the steps and gave his driver a half-salute.

Schroeder, a reedy, unshaven man wearing a black cap and

cape, leapt from the driver's seat and walked briskly round to the rear passenger door. He bowed once in Lewis's direction and, with a flourish of his cape, opened the door.

'The front seat is fine, Herr Schroeder.'

Schroeder seemed agitated at Lewis's self-demotion. '*Nein*, Herr Kommandant.'

'Really. *Sehr gut*,' Lewis repeated.

'*Bitte*, Herr Oberst.'

Schroeder clunked the rear door shut and held up a hand, still not wanting Lewis to lift a finger.

Lewis stepped back, playing the game, but the German's deference depressed him: these were the motions of a defeated man clinging to patronage. Inside, Lewis handed Schroeder the scrap of paper on which Wilkins had scribbled the address of the house that was probably going to be his home for the foreseeable future. The driver squinted at it and nodded his approval of the destination.

Schroeder was forced to steer a weaving course between the bomb craters that pocked the cobbled road and the rivulets of people walking in dazed, languid fashion, going nowhere in particular, carrying the remnant objects of their old lives in parcels, sacks, crates and cartons, and a heavy, almost visible, disquiet. They were like a people thrown back to the evolutionary stage of nomadic gatherers.

The ghost of a tremendous noise hung over the scene. Something out of this world had undone this place and left an impossible jigsaw from which to reconstruct the old picture. There was no putting it back together again and there would be no going back to the old picture. This was *Stunde Null*. The Zero Hour. These people were starting from scratch and scratching a living from nothing. Two women pushed and pulled a horse cart stacked with furniture between them, while a man carrying a briefcase walked along as

9

though in search of the office where he once worked without even a glance at the fantastic destruction that lay all around him, as if this apocalyptic architecture were the natural state of things.

A smashed city stretched as far as the eye could see, the rubble reaching as high as the first floor of any building still standing. Hard to believe that this was once a place where people read newspapers, made cakes and thought about which pictures to hang on the walls of their front parlours. The facade of a church stood on one side of the road, with only sky for stained glass and the wind for a congregation. On the other side, apartment blocks – intact except for the fronts, which had been completely blown off, revealing the rooms and furniture within – stood like giant doll's houses. In one of these rooms, oblivious to the elements and exposure to watching eyes, a woman stood lovingly brushing a young girl's hair in front of a dressing table.

Further along the road, women and children stood around piles of rubble, scavenging for sustenance or looking to save fragments of their past. Black crosses marked the places where bodies lay waiting to be buried. And, everywhere, the strange pipe-chimneys of a subterranean city protruded from the ground, pouring black smoke into the sky.

'Rabbits?' Lewis asked, seeing creatures appear from unseen holes in the ground.

'*Trümmerkinder!*' Schroeder said, with a sudden anger. And Lewis saw that the bobbing creatures were 'children of the rubble' and that the car was drawing them out of their holes.

'*Ungeziefer!*' Schroeder spat with an unnecessary vehemence as three of the children – it was hard to tell if they were girls or boys – ran straight in front of the car. He gave them a warning toot but the approaching black bulk of the

Mercedes did not deter them. They stood their ground and forced the car to a stop.

'*Weg! Schnell!*' Schroeder screamed, the veins in his neck pulsing with a thick rage. He tooted the horn again but one of the children – a boy in a dressing gown and English helmet – marched fearlessly to Lewis's side of the car, jumped on the running board and started tapping on his window.

'Vat you got, Tommy? Fucking sandvich? Choccie?'

'*Steig aus! Sofort!*' Schroeder's spittle sprayed Lewis's face as he leant across the colonel and raised a fist at the child. Meanwhile, the other two children had climbed on to the bonnet of the car and were trying to pull off the triangular chrome Mercedes emblem.

Schroeder turned back and leapt from the car. He lunged at the children as they tried to scamper across the bonnet to safety and managed to catch the tail of a nightshirt. Schroeder yanked the waif towards him; he held the child by the neck with one hand and began to thrash him with his other.

'Schroeder!' It was the first time Lewis had raised his voice in months, and it cracked with the surprise of it.

Schroeder didn't seem to hear and continued to beat the child with a vicious force.

'*Halt!*' Lewis got out of the car to intervene, the other children backing away for fear they'd get the same. This time, the driver heard, and he stopped, a curious expression of shame and self-righteousness on his face. He let the child go and came back to the car, muttering and panting from his exertions.

Lewis called to the children: '*Hierbleiben!*'

The eldest boy stepped back towards the car, and his pals followed him tentatively towards the Englishman. Other ferals were now coming over to pick up scraps, children camouflaged by filth. Close up, they gave off the oedemic stench of the starving. All of them put out hands in supplication to this kindly English god passing in his black chariot. Lewis fetched his haversack from the car. It contained a bar of chocolate and an orange. He offered the chocolate to the eldest boy.

'*Verteil!*' he instructed. He then gave the orange to the smallest child, a girl maybe five or six years old – her life a war-span – and repeated the order to share. But the girl immediately bit into the orange as if it were an apple and started to chew, skin, pith and all. Lewis tried to indicate that the fruit needed peeling, but the girl shielded the gift, afraid she was going to have to give it back.

More children were pressing in now, hands out, including a boy with one leg who leant on a golf club for support.

'Choccie, Tommy! Choccie, Tommy!' they called.

Lewis had no more food to give, but he did have something more valuable. He took out his cigarette case and tapped out ten Player's. He handed the cigarettes to the eldest boy, whose already distended eyes bulged at the sight and feel of the gold in his hands. Lewis knew that his transaction was illegal – he had both fraternized with Germans and indulged the black market – but he didn't care: those ten Player's would buy food from a farmer somewhere. The laws and regulations that the new order had imposed had been concocted in a mood of fear and revenge by men sitting at desks, and for now – and until an unknown time in the future – he was the law in this particular bit of the land.

Stefan Lubert stood before his remnant staff – the hobbled gardener, Richard, the breathless maid, Heike, and the obdurate house cook of thirty years, Greta – and gave them a final set of instructions. Heike was already crying.

'Be respectful, and serve him as you would serve me. And

Heike? – all of you – if he offers you work, you must feel free to accept. I will not be offended. I will be glad to have you here, keeping an eye on things.'

He leant forward and wiped a tear from Heike's round cheek.

'Come. No more tears. Be grateful that we don't have the Russians. The English may be uncultured, but they are not cruel.'

'Do you want me to serve refreshments, Herr Lubert?' Heike managed to ask.

'Of course. We must be civil.'

'We have no biscuits,' Greta pointed out. 'Only the cake.'

'Fine. Make tea and not coffee. Although we don't have coffee. So this is just as well. And serve him in the library. It's too bright in here.' Lubert had hoped the officer would come on a dull, grey day, but the early-autumn sun was sending its best light through the art deco stained glass that decorated the high window opposite the minstrels' gallery and on to the floor of the hall, making it all the more inviting. 'Now, where is Frieda?'

'She is in her room, sir,' Heike said.

Lubert steeled himself. The war had been over for more than a year, but his daughter had still not surrendered. He needed to suppress this little putsch now. Wearily, he climbed the staircase. At Frieda's bedroom door, he knocked and called her name. He waited for an answer he knew wouldn't come then entered. She was lying on her bed, her legs raised a few inches off the mattress. A book – a signed copy of Thomas Mann's *The Magic Mountain* which his wife, Claudia, had given him for his thirtieth birthday – was balanced across her feet. Frieda did not respond to her father's presence but continued to concentrate her efforts on keeping her weighted legs in the air. They were beginning to tremble with the strain.

How long had she been in this position – one, two, five minutes? She started to breathe furiously through her nose, trying to disguise the effort, refusing to show weakness. Her strength was impressive, but it was joyless, another of those Mädel routines she had religiously kept up since the war.

All strength, no joy.

Frieda's face began to flush and a tiara of sweat formed at her forehead. When her legs began to sway from side to side, she did not let them drop; instead she lowered them in a controlled way, as of her own will.

'You should try the Shakespeare – or perhaps the atlas,' Lubert said. 'That would test your strength better.' Although his jokes tended to ricochet back with redoubled velocity, lightness was still his preferred weapon against her fierce and humourless moods.

'The books are not important,' she said.

'The English officer is coming.'

Frieda sat up suddenly, without using her arms. She swung her legs athletically to the floor and wiped the sweat back over her braided hair. The ugly, defiant look she had adopted in these last few years pained him. She stared at her father.

'I would like you to greet him,' he said.

'Why?'

'Because –'

'Because you are going to give up Mother's house without a fight.'

'Freedie. Please don't talk that way. Please come. For Mutti's sake?'

'She wouldn't leave. She would never let this happen.'

'Come.'

'No. Beg.'

'I would like you to come now.'

'Beggar!'

Unable to stare his daughter down, Lubert turned and walked away, his heart pounding. At the bottom of the stairs he caught himself in the mirror. He looked gaunt and sallow and his nose had lost some definition, but he hoped this would help. He had dressed in his most moth-eaten suit. He knew he would be giving up his home – it was one of the finest on the Elbchaussee and more than any luxury-starved, middle-ranking officer from England would be able to resist – but it was important to make the right impression. He had heard stories about the Allied forces purloining all manner of treasures since the surrender, and the imperialist, philistine English were known abusers of people's cultures – he was particularly nervous about the paintings by Fernand Léger and woodcuts by Emil Nolde which hung in the main rooms – but he had the idea that if he could deport himself in the right way the English officer might think well of him and be less inclined to abuse his possessions. He poked the ashes of the previous evening's fire and rearranged them slightly to show that they had been burning furniture. Then he took off his jacket, loosened his tie and struck a pose somewhere between dignified and respectful: hands at his sides, one leg slightly askance. This felt too casual, too informal, too confident, too close to who he really was. He pulled the jacket back on, tightened his tie, smoothed back his hair and stood more erect, his hands clasped meekly in front of his trousers. That was better: the demeanour of a man who was ready to hand over his house without rancour.

Lewis and Schroeder did not speak for the rest of the journey. Lewis could see Schroeder's lips moving as he replayed the encounter with the ferals and recited silent expressions of disgust and irritation, but he elected to say nothing more about it. The car soon reached the outer limit of the city and the edge of all that the British and Americans had bombed so comprehensively three years before. The road was now smooth, with plane trees lining the verges and whole houses lying behind high hedges and gates. This was the Elbchaussee, and these were the homes of the bankers and merchants that had made Hamburg rich and its port and working districts such a desirable target of Bomber Command. They were grander, more modern, more impressive than any residence Lewis had seen outside of London or any house he might have expected to live in.

The Villa Lubert was the last house on the road before it turned away from the River Elbe, and when he saw it for the first time Lewis wondered if Captain Wilkins had made a mistake. It lay at the end of a long drive lined by poplar trees: a great, white wedding-cake structure built in the grand style, with porticos and a large, semicircular, colonnaded balcony. The ground floor of the house was raised several feet from the earth and split by an imposing stone staircase climbing to a lower-level balcony. Pillars wreathed in wisteria supported an upper balcony from which the residents could watch the Elbe flow some one hundred yards away. Lewis was shocked by the bright elegance and size of this house. It was not quite a palace, but it was still a residence more suited to a general or a chancellor than a through-the-ranks colonel who had never owned his own home.

As the Mercedes turned into the circular drive, Lewis could see three figures – two women, and a man he presumed to be the gardener – forming a guard of honour. Another figure – a tall gentleman in a loose-fitting suit – came down the staircase to join them. Schroeder eased the car round the drive and stopped right in front of the welcoming committee. Lewis didn't wait for the driver to open his door; he let himself out straight away and made for the man he presumed to be Lubert. Lewis was half into a salute when, at the last moment, he redirected his hand to shake that of his host.

'*Guten Abend,*' he said. 'Colonel Lewis Morgan.'

'Welcome, Herr Oberst. Please. We can speak English.'

Lubert clasped Lewis's hand with friendly strength. Even through the gloves, Lubert's hand felt warmer than his own. Lewis nodded to the women and the gardener. The maids bowed, and the youngest of them gave him a curious look, as though he were a member of a lost tribe. She seemed amused by him – by his accent or perhaps by his odd uniform – and Lewis smiled back at her.

'And this is Richard.'

The gardener clicked his heels and stuck out an arm.

Lewis took his bare, calloused hand and let that lever-arch arm yank his own up and down like a piston.

'Please – come in,' Lubert said.

Lewis left Schroeder sitting in the driver's seat with his legs resting on the running board of the Mercedes, still sulking after being reprimanded, and followed Lubert up the steps into the house.

The house revealed its true self inside. Lewis did not much care for its style – the angular, futuristic furniture and the awkward, difficult artworks were too modern, too outré for his tastes – but the quality of the build and the skill of the design were to a standard superior to anything he had seen in an English home, including that of the Bayliss-Hilliers, who lived in the manor house at Amersham and whose home Rachael coveted and believed to be the acme of all residences. As Lubert walked him through the house, graciously explaining the function of various rooms and the history of the place, Lewis began to project ahead to the moment when Rachael would step into this house for the first time and he could see his wife taking in the light, clean lines of these rooms and her eyes widening at the grandeur of it all – the marble window seats, the grand piano, the dumb waiter, the maids' bedrooms, the library, the smoking room, the fine art – and as he imagined this he had a sudden, unexpected hope that this house might in some way make up for the lean and distant years the war had laid between them.

'You have children?' Lubert asked as they climbed the stairs to the bedrooms.

'Yes. A son. Edmund.' He said the name as if reminding himself.

'Then perhaps Edmund would like this room?'

Lubert showed Lewis into a room that was full of children's – mainly girls' – toys. A rocking horse with bulging black eyes and a china doll perched side-saddle on its back stood at the far end. A doll's house as big as a kennel and built in imitation of a Georgian town house had been placed at the foot of a small four-poster bed. Several mid-sized dolls sat on its roof, their legs dangling over the tops of the bed-rooms, a line of porcelain giants squatting on someone else's home.

'Your son will not mind the girls' things?' Lubert asked.

Lewis couldn't say for sure what Edmund would like or dislike – his son had been ten when Lewis had last seen him – but few children could object to such space and treasure.

'Of course not,' he said.

With every beautiful room and every intimate piece of information – 'This is where we liked to watch the boats'; 'This is where we liked to play cards' – Lewis felt more uncomfortable, as if Lubert were heaping hot coals on his head. He would have preferred some hostility, or at least a brittle, silent resistance – something, anything, that might harden him enough to make this task easier – but this civil, almost quaint, tour was making the whole business worse. By the time they arrived in the master bedroom – the eighth bedroom on this floor, with its high and narrow French-style box bed and oil painting depicting the green spires of a medieval city hanging just above its headboard – he felt wretched.

'My favourite German city,' Lubert said, catching Lewis staring at the spires, trying to work it out. 'Lübeck. You should try to see it if you can.'

Lewis looked but didn't linger. He moved towards the French windows and looked out across the garden and the River Elbe beyond it.

'Claudia – my wife – liked to sit out here in the summer.' Lubert went to the windows and opened them out on to a balcony. 'The Elbe,' he declared, stepping out and sweeping his arm in a 180-degree arc from end to end of the vista. It was a proper, great European river, wider and slower than any in England, and here, at the bend, it was almost at its widest – perhaps half a mile across. This river and the cargo it carried had built this house and most of those along the northern bank.

'It flows into our Nordsee. Your North Sea?' Lubert asked.

'It's the same sea in the end,' Lewis said.

Lubert seemed to like this, and he repeated the phrase. 'The same sea. Yes.'

Others might have seen Lubert's performance as an attempt to make Lewis feel bad, or they would have detected in his upright poise all the haughtiness and arrogance of a race that had sought the world's destruction and now had to face the consequences, but Lewis did not see things that way. In Lubert, he saw a cultured, privileged man humbling himself and clinging to the last cliff of civility in order to limit the damage to a life already ruined. Lewis knew this whole show was an attempt to win him over, to lessen the blow in some way, perhaps even persuade him to change his mind, but he could not condemn Lubert for trying, nor could he summon up the faux anger with which to play the aloof, decisive man of expedient.

'Your house is wonderful, Herr Lubert,' he said.

Lubert bowed in gratitude.

'It is more than I need – more than my family needs,' Lewis went on. 'And . . . certainly much more than we are used to.'

Lubert waited for Lewis to finish, his eyes brightening, sensing a surprise retreat.

Lewis looked out across the great river that flowed out to their 'shared sea' – the sea that was carrying his own estranged family towards him now. 'I'd like to propose a different arrangement,' he said.

2

'"You are about to meet a strange people in a strange enemy country. You must keep clear of Germans. You must not walk with them, or shake hands or visit their homes. You must not play games with them or share any social event. Don't try to be kind – this is regarded as weakness. Keep Germans in their place. Don't show hatred: the Germans will be flattered. Display cold, correct and dignified curtness and aloofness at all times. You must not frat . . . ernize . . .'"

Edmund repeated the word: '"Fraternize"? What does that mean? Mother?'

Rachael had just started to drift at the 'cold, correct and dignified' part and was picturing herself displaying these characteristics to unknown Germans. Edmund was reading 'You are Going to Germany', the official information booklet that every Germany-bound British family were given as part of their travel pack, along with ample bundles of sweets and magazines. Getting her son things to read out loud had become Rachael's tactic, a simple way of encouraging him to learn about the world outside while at the same time giving her space to think.

'Mmmm?'

'It says we must not fraternize with the Germans. What does that mean?'

'It means . . . being friendly. It means we are not to enter into relationships with them.'

Edmund considered this. 'Not even if we like someone?'

'We won't have anything to do with them, Ed. You won't need to make friends with them.'

But Edmund's inquisitiveness was a Hydra: just as Rachael cut off the head of the last question, another three appeared to replace it.

'Is Germany going to be like a new colony?'

'A bit, yes.'

How she had needed Lewis over the last three years to bat back the constant questions. Edmund's bright, curious mind needed a foil and a sounding board. With Lewis away and with her old, attentive self temporarily absent without leave, Ed's questions had largely been met with faraway, preoccupied nods. Indeed, Edmund had grown so used to his mother's delayed reactions that he repeated everything twice, as though she were an old, deaf aunt who had to be humoured.

'Will they have to learn to speak English?'

'I imagine they will, Ed, yes. Read me some more.'

Edmund continued:

'"When you meet the Germans you will probably think they are very much like us. They look like us, except that there are few of the wiry type and more big, fleshy, fair-haired men and women, especially in the north. But they are not really as much like us as they look."' Edmund nodded, relieved to hear it. But the next part threw him. '"The Germans are very fond of music. Beethoven, Wagner and Bach were all Germans."' He stopped reading, confused. 'Is that true? Bach was a German?'

Bach had been a German, but Rachael could barely bring herself to admit it. Beautiful things surely belonged on the side of the angels.

'Germany was different then,' she said. 'Keep going. It's interesting . . .'

The booklet stirred a primitive and reassuring emotion in

Rachael. She could feel herself affirming its essential message: when all is said and done, Germans are bad. This idea had served the general purpose of getting them all through the war, bringing a consensus that stopped them from blaming anyone else. Germany could be blamed for almost everything that had gone wrong with the world: bad harvests, the cost of bread, lax morality in the young, a fall in church attendance. For a time, Rachael had gone along with it, letting it serve as a catch-all explanation for her various low-grade domestic dissatisfactions.

Then, one day in the spring of 1942, a stray offloading of an unreleased bomb from a Heinkel He 111 returning from a raid on the refineries of Milford Haven killed her fourteen-year-old son Michael, destroyed her sister's house and hurled her across the floor of the sitting room like a rag doll. Even though she herself had walked from the wreckage unscathed, some spirit shrapnel lodged itself deep inside her, beyond the reach of surgeons, poisoning her thoughts and causing her to think with a limp. That absurd bomb shattered her faith in the essential goodness of life and blew it into the ether like so much dust, leaving a ringing in her head that had got louder with the war's end.

Even though, within the narrow circle of her own acquaintance, she'd been outdone in statistical loss – the Blakes had had two sons killed in the D-Day landings; George Davies had returned from a POW camp to discover that his wife and children had been killed in a bombing raid on Cardiff – Rachael could find no solace in other people's tales of woe. Pain was uniquely one's own, and undiminished by a democracy of suffering.

Blaming Germans brought only temporary remission, though. In the aftermath of the blast she had looked to the skies through the still-smouldering, roofless rafters and imagined the airmen laughing as they flew back to Germany, but it felt empty blaming men who were doing their duty. She had, for a second, thought of their leader's culpability, but thinking about that man seemed degrading to her son's memory.

After a few weeks, feeling returning, she found herself unable to pray, as she had always done, and with this came the unexpected sensation of wondering if God was there at all. This God, whom she'd always imagined to be on her side, felt suddenly as remote and generalized as a Führer. Her response was not the engaged anguish of someone who believed (to shout at God required faith); it was more the silence of someone who wondered if they ever really had. The words of Reverend Pring, that 'what we learn from sorrow will increase us', served only to compound the strange sensation of divine absence. When the priest tried to console her that they believed in a God who had also lost a son, she replied, with unexpected sharpness, that 'He had at least got His back after three days.' The startled priest let this hang in the air for several moments before telling her, in the most reassuring cadence he could muster, that all who believed in *that* resurrection shared the same hope. Rachael shook her head. She had seen her son's broken body, pulled from beneath the beams, his blameless face white with dust and death. There would be no resurrection for Michael.

In austere times, self-pity was a heavily rationed commodity, a thing no one should be caught indulging in public. And yet, Rachael's sense of having had a bad war, of being more sinned against than sinning, did not diminish. Without a God to blame she returned to earth in search of a culprit, and she found one. It was not who she expected, and at first she tried to suppress the idea, thinking it further proof of her 'fragile nerves', as Dr Mayfield had put it. Lewis – who had had a good war, a heroic war – had been miles away, training recruits in Wiltshire, when it happened, and even though it was his idea that they head from Amersham to the safety of the west, 'far beyond the reach and interest of the Luftwaffe', and he who had insisted the boys go with her, he could not possibly have anticipated this lazy unfurling of bombs by a German aircrew just trying to get home quickly. But grief, stirred with other unspoken resentments, can set loose a flock of squawking thoughts which, once out of the cage, are hard to put back. It was Lewis's face that loomed largest when she railed loudest, and his absence had served only to compound his guilt. If she blamed anyone, she blamed him.

'Mother? Who are you talking to now?' Edmund asked her. The reverie had taken her off again, and again it was poor Edmund, her youngest and only surviving son, who had to call her back. The taboo of her grievances had driven everything inside, to the private realm, taking her so far from the world that she sometimes lost all sense of time and place. Rachael tried to relocate herself.

'No one, Ed. I'm just thinking . . .' she said. 'I was just thinking . . . that I have another card for you.' She reached for the packet of Wills in her handbag and lit the cigarette which Dr Mayfield had suggested would be 'good for her nerves'. She handed the cigarette card to Edmund, who took it enthusiastically then rejected it.

'I've already got that one,' he said.

Rachael looked at it. It showed an illustration of how to protect a window against a blast. 'Those still have all the boring war-information cards,' Edmund explained. 'Can't you smoke different ones?'

'Your father will have new ones. I think he still smokes Player's.'

Rachael flicked the ash into the ashtray and brushed some

flakes from her tweed skirt. Today was the first time she had dressed herself with Lewis in mind in over a year; the first time, in fact, since she had seen him for those three brief, peculiar days after VE Day, when she had felt like the only person in all of Britain unable to let herself go. She was wearing the tweed which he had, uncharacteristically, said she looked 'gorgeous' in, as well as the Je Reviens Worth ('a bomb') perfume he had brought back from France. After years of curtains for coats and beetroot juice for lipstick, her get-up felt almost ostentatious.

As Rachael caught her reflection in the train's carriage window, she noticed the woman and child – a girl of about ten – sitting opposite her, respectively reading booklet and comic. The woman seemed to be tut-tutting with her eyes.

'I think this is important, Lucy,' she said to the girl. 'It's a message from Prime Minister Attlee.' The woman read from the booklet: '"British wives will be looked upon by the Germans as representatives of the British Empire, and on their behaviour and that of the children, far more than that of the armed forces, the Germans will judge the British and the British way of life." We must remember that,' she said, and although she looked at her daughter as she said it, Rachael felt the words were directed at her. No doubt this exemplary British wife had come to the conclusion that the overdressed, self-absorbed and distracted lady opposite, who barely seemed to register her son's presence and muttered arguments to herself, must be a selfish wife, a very bad mother and quite the worst kind of person to represent her country.

'After the bomb landed there was a sort of delay when everything stood still . . .' Edmund paused for effect. 'And then all the sound and air was sucked away and my mother was thrown . . . thirty feet across the house.'

Edmund was an eleven-year-old boy living in exciting times: riding a converted German troopship across the North Sea to be reunited with a father who was a living war hero, to live in a land that once contained the most powerful and evil regime in history; better still, he was a boy armed with war stories that were more than a match for anyone's.

The bomb that had killed Edmund's brother had also thrown his mother – ten, twenty feet (thirty, if he had the right audience) – across his aunt's sitting-room floor. The incident might have left her with a slight tremble and quick tears (she cried at the slightest thing – a piece of classical music on the wireless, a limping bird in the garden), but he could forgive her these tics. They had an obvious source in Michael's death and her own narrow escape. Her dodging of death had given him a sort of pride and a good story to embellish.

And he was embellishing it now to what he felt was a sure-fire 'thirty-foot audience' consisting of a girl of about thirteen with a beauty spot, a red-headed boy who looked about eleven and an older boy, maybe sixteen, in a dogtooth sports jacket. While class distinctions had been temporarily neutralized by the excitement of transit, it was impossible not to mentally calculate one's relative place in this new society, and even before the disclosure of their fathers' ranks, Edmund had guessed that he was at least equal to Red Hair and Beauty Spot in class, and almost certainly superior to Dogtooth, who sat apart, feigning disinterest in Edmund's mother's survival story, tapping a cigarette end and brushing back his Brylcreemed satin hair.

Despite the boy's showy indifference, Edmund could feel his story drawing him in. He had just described the moment the bomb had hit the house, complete with 'the crump' of the impact, the strange 'push-pull' sensation of the explosion which his mother had tried to explain to him. It was accurate in most respects, except for the *'wam! wam! wam!'* of the anti-aircraft gunfire that hadn't actually existed in the rural Welsh market town of Narberth. Nor did he feel the need to mention that he was at a neighbouring farm the day the bomb had hit.

'Thirty feet? That's nearly . . . three times as long as this cabin.' Red Hair traced the imagined arc of the Flying Mother with a rotation of his head and punctuated her landing somewhere beyond the deck with a confirming 'Gosh'. Edmund, as if seeking to seal off any doubts, ended his story with the indisputable fact of Michael's death, the details of which needed no amplification:

'My brother was not so lucky.'

Having won their respect with How His Mother Defied Death, Edmund had their sympathy with And His Brother Died.

It was said that everyone had 'a bomb story', but Edmund had not yet met anyone who could match his. He waited to see if any of the three would make their move. Red Hair cleared his throat and tentatively mentioned a cousin who had died while watching *Gone with the Wind* at the Alhambra Cinema in Bromley along with ten other people, but he hadn't known him very well. Dogtooth stayed silent, but Edmund guessed his smirking look indicated that he was now going to trump his tale with one of his own: Death by Doodlebug? German Pilot Caught in a Tree? No matter. He had another story up his sleeve if he needed it.

Edmund produced his pack of playing cards. 'You know how to build a house of cards?' he asked. He spread the cards and set out the foundational pyramid on the pull-out table. The pitch and roll of the ship would add an extra challenge.

'We have to share our cabin with another family,' Beauty

Spot said. 'My father is only a captain.' She had already noted the layout of Edmund's quarters, a space commensurate with his father's rank. 'But my mother hopes he will become a major soon, then we will get a better house in Germany. What rank is your father?'

Edmund glanced quickly at Dogtooth to make sure he was listening. Here was an easy, modest way to play his best hand. If How His Mother Defied Death was a full house, How His Father Won a Medal was his royal flush.

'At the start of the war he was just a captain. He quickly made major and won a medal and got promoted again. Jumping from major over lieutenant colonel straight to colonel.'

'What did he get a medal for then?' Dogtooth was hooked and Edmund noted the accent: aspiring grammar school. No amount of elocution lessons could disguise it.

Hardly needing encouragement, Edmund told them how his father had jumped into the River Ems to save two sappers trapped in a lorry and how he had to fight off the attentions of a German sniper to do it. It wasn't the first time he'd told the story, and he had learned to pause just before the part where his father, having dived beneath the surface and freed the trapped men, managed to resurface and take out the sniper with a grenade. Afterwards, there was awed silence, until Dogtooth asked:

'What medal did he get?'

'The DSO. The Distinguished Service Order.'

'Did Something Ordinary, you mean.' Dogtooth tutted a laugh and, with that, doubt seeped into the room like water filling a truck in a river. Edmund felt his story sinking. Beauty Spot restored some unity with a statement all could agree on:

'The only good German is a dead German.'

Edmund and Red Hair nodded, while Beauty Spot offered

more insights into the true nature of Germans, as learned at her grandmother's knee:

'My grandmother said that if you look into their eyes you can see the devil . . .'

Red Hair had done his research, too:

'We can't talk to them or even smile at them. And they must salute us and do as we say.'

'And we can't fraternize,' Edmund added, pleased to use this new word.

Dogtooth lit up and shook his head. Edmund secretly admired the way he blew the smoke through his nostrils and believed absolutely nothing anyone said.

'Listen to you lot. You've got no idea, have you? There's only one thing you need to know about Germany . . .' He held out his cigarette. 'Just one of these buys you a loaf of bread. One hundred will get you a bike. Enough of these and you can live like a king.'

And, with this, he took an exaggerated drag and blew smoke at them, forcing everyone to blink, except for Edmund, who kept his eyes wide open long enough to see his house of cards collapse.

The Wives of the Men Already in Germany had gathered in the ship's lounge. Much effort had been made to disguise this vessel's provenance; any trace that it had once carried Waffen SS to the newly conquered ports of Oslo and Bergen had been erased with lime and cream paint and cheery bunting. Only the most eagle-eyed passengers would have noticed an old graffito still on the deck railings telling the world that Private Tobias Messer had stood there long enough to knife his name into posterity.

The SS *Empire Halladale* was the showboat of Operation Reunion and its cargo representatives of a still-great global power, a nation that, even in lean times, was capable of providing perks for its citizens. As far as the 'cargo' was concerned, it was a good time to be sailing away from England, away from Potato Pete and Dr Carrot, gravy stockings and relentless parsimony. This little floating corner of the Empire seemed to mock all that and suggest a life of largesse ahead.

Rachael sat with three officer's wives, comparing household inventories. As she was a colonel's wife, her list ran to three pages; Mrs Burnham's (major's wife) ran to two and a half; Mrs Eliot's and Mrs Thompson's (captains') to two. It was testament to the miracle of British bureaucracy that even in these bankrupt times it could find within its broken and bust self the wherewithal to decide that a captain's wife did not need a four-place tea set, that a major's needed a full dinner service, and that only commanding officers' wives should have a port decanter.

Rachael was the 'senior-ranking wife' in this party, but Mrs Burnham was the natural leader here and Rachael was happy to defer. This confident, glamorous woman was something of a know-all, quick and crude, but she brought a sense of the conspiratorial to the gathering that made them all feel that going to Germany was an adventure, an opportunity to be grabbed with both hands. Mrs Thompson, a clipped snob of a woman, was hanging on her every word. Only Mrs Eliot seemed uncomfortable. She had been sick ever since the ship had set out from Tilbury and her pallor matched the routine grey-green of their cups and saucers.

'Feeling better?' Rachael asked her.

'This tea is helping.'

'Make the most of it,' Mrs Burnham said. 'The Germans may well be experts with coffee but they don't know the first thing about making tea.'

Mrs Burnham had already scanned her list, noted the lack

of condiments, napkins and goblets, and she now turned her attention to Rachael's.

'Everything there?'

Rachael had few complaints, but Lewis's double-rank promotion had elevated her into new and unfamiliar realms of entitlement and there was pressure to show that she was to the manor born.

'Sherry glasses would have been nice.'

Mrs Burnham launched into a mock-serious complaint: 'Well, I don't know what to say! The governor's wife simply must have sherry glasses, or there will be questions in the House!'

All of them laughed, and Rachael felt glad to have someone make her laugh. Mrs Burnham articulated what Rachael felt but could not express. All that was drab and restrained and stiff was to be left behind in grey, burnt-out England. Back there, Mrs Burnham might well have been classed as brash and vulgar, but here, free of protocol and in unknown territory, she could talk with the unchecked confidence of a New World explorer.

Sensible Mrs Eliot's question went against the mood. 'Is it true there's a shortage of suitable family housing because of the bombing? George wasn't sure where we were going to live when he last wrote.'

Mrs Burnham quashed the doubts. 'They've started requisitioning houses. There'll be plenty of room.'

'I hear their houses are well made,' Mrs Thompson chipped in. 'Especially the kitchens.'

'It's not the kitchen I'm worried about,' Mrs Burnham said, 'it's the bedroom. And I'm rather counting on a large, comfortable bed.' As she laughed, Rachael noticed a red flush at her throat like a wanton brooch.

But Mrs Eliot was still worried about the ramifications of the housing shortage.

'But where are they going to put *them*?'

'Who?'

'The German families . . . the ones whose houses are being requisitioned?'

'Billets,' Mrs Burnham said, shooting the word out like a pellet.

'Billets?'

'Billets,' she repeated.

Mrs Eliot tried to picture billets and German families living in them. 'How awful,' she said.

'I hardly think we should be feeling sorry for them,' Rachael said, with surprising force.

'Quite right,' Mrs Burnham applauded. 'They can jolly well move over and make room. It's the least they can do.'

'I think so, too,' Mrs Thompson concurred. And with this majority decision reached, the unpleasant subject of the German families and their billets was dropped. As the women started to chat among themselves, Mrs Burnham turned to Rachael, lowering her voice in confidence.

'So. When did you last see your husband?' Mrs Burnham's flush seemed to glow and Rachael could smell her skin beneath her perfume's sickly disguise; it had a sweet, almost spicy, odour.

'VE Day. For three days.'

'Well, you two have some catching up to do then.'

'I fear I've got a little too used to having the bed to myself these last few years.' Rachael surprised herself with this admission, but this buxom, vivacious woman seemed to demand such frankness.

In truth, Lewis had become a chimera to Rachael: half

man, half idea. Of course, they had been intimate once. But it had never been a question then; it just happened. It was always straightforward and uncomplicated and – she was sure of this – enjoyable and equal in the giving and the taking. Despite this, she could not recall the intimacy – not even picture it – and this made Mrs Burnham's question all the more troubling. Rachael was heading to a hostile land to start an uncertain, new life but the thing she was most uncertain of was not the enemy but her husband. It had been over a year since they had 'had a moment' (as he had liked to call it when they were newly married) or 'made love' (as she had ventured, enjoying the discreet depth of that phrase), but the event was now vague and crepuscular, a clinch lost in the disappointment of the war's end.

'Well, I don't know about you, but I intend to make up for the stolen years,' Mrs Burnham said, and with that she took a deep, suggestive drag on her cigarette, leant forward and dropped an extra sugar lump into her tea. Even though Rachael had not taken sugar in her tea for five years, she took two lumps and dropped them in the cup.

3

Lewis watched the British servicemen gathering on the platform of Hamburg's Dammtor station. They were nearly all here to meet a wife and, for some, the train from Cuxhaven was about to bring an end to a separation that had lasted months, even years.

For him, it had been seventeen months since those strangely deflating three days of victory celebrations in London; seventeen months since he had looked at Rachael in the flesh, smelt her ferny breath, heard her play the piano. He would no longer have to rely on the snapshot of her – taken on a belting July day on a beach in Pembrokeshire – which he'd kept tucked behind the elastic strap of his cigarette case. She seemed to be at her own height of summer in this shot: the loose-fitting flower-press dress; the breezy tilt of her head – even in black and white her cheeks seemed to bloom. He was not a visual man, but he had surprised himself with the images and memories he had been able to conjure during their time apart. They were less the stylized, posed perfection of romantic cinema, more the intimate, unscripted moments film was unable or not allowed to show. Most frequently he had returned to the first time he had introduced Rachael to his family – his sister, Kate, stunned at the quality of his catch and instantly approving – and their spontaneous and naked midnight swim in Carmarthen Bay, with slimy kelp lapping their limbs.

Her imminent incarnation threatened all this, and, as he stood there, smoking, he began to think about the person who would step from the train. How would real Rachael compare to the easily pocketed and admired photo Rachael who had smiled back at him throughout the war, in all weathers and circumstances?

Lewis tucked her image back behind the elastic and over the smaller photo of Michael and snapped the case shut. He took one last drag of his cigarette and flicked it into the tracks below. Above him, in the glassless frame of the station roof, birds were making homes where they could. A sudden exclamation of delight made Lewis look down at his feet, where, standing in the tracks, an emaciated man, maybe sixty years old, stood pawing Lewis's still-smoking cigarette end, inspecting it for tobacco and muttering, '*Danke, danke, danke,*' over and over. In normal times, the man's enthusiastic thanks for this most minuscule of windfalls would have sounded like sarcasm; in *Stunde Null*, a tossed fag end was manna from a godforsaken sky. Pity and disgust tugged at Lewis's guts and, once again, pity pulled the stronger. He took three cigarettes from his silver case, bent down and gave them to the man. For a moment, the man stared at the fresh cigarettes, hardly daring to take them in case they proved to be a mirage.

'*Nimm Sie! Schnell!*' Lewis said, conscious that most of the gathering servicemen would take a dim view of his benevolence. The man took the cigarettes and cupped them in his palm before squirrelling them away inside his coat.

As Lewis straightened he saw two men coming up the platform towards him. One was Captain Wilkins, clearly animated by the anticipation of seeing a wife whom he had constantly and unashamedly referred to as 'my petal'. Lewis, who found it hard to articulate his affection for Rachael to Rachael, let alone to others, secretly admired this uxorious tendency in his number two. Wilkins was perfectly jejune about it, sharing intimacies like a young lover unable to contain himself, including, once, a poem he had written, 'To

His Petal', which contained the line 'I will water you, my flower, and flood you with my love.'

The man with Wilkins had the crown of a major on his epaulette. He was exotic, unEnglish-looking, with silky black hair, pretty-eyed but alert, and Lewis immediately felt the need to up his game in his presence.

'Sir, this is Major Burnham,' Wilkins said. 'Intelligence Branch. Here to sort out the blacks from the whites and greys and what-have-yous.'

Rather than salute, Burnham shook Lewis's hand. Intelligence had their own hierarchy and were quick not to show any deference to the regulars, whom they regarded as ill-equipped for the task of rebuilding a shattered state. Lewis didn't care about the lack of a salute, but he immediately detected, in Burnham's efficient movements and precise declarations, a man on a mission.

As Burnham glared at the emaciated scavenger, Wilkins jumped into the silence. 'We found the major a house only yesterday. Not far from you, sir. On the Elbchaussee.' Lewis's number two was becoming sensitive to his superior's un-orthodoxies, likes and dislikes, his tendency to speak his mind. He was already sensing a clash. 'You'll almost be neighbours,' he added.

Burnham was still distracted by the man, who had now clambered up on to the platform and extended his hand, no doubt hopeful that the colonel's friends would be as benevolent. The major spoke to him in impeccable German:

'If you don't move on, I will have you arrested.'

The man put up his hands and backed away, bowing and scraping, as fast as his weak legs would carry him.

Burnham grimaced. 'The smell of these people.'

'It's what a diet of 900 calories a day does for you,' Lewis responded.

'At least they're less trouble when they're hungry,' Burnham said, offering a mirthless smile.

'Good point,' Wilkins said, trying to diffuse things. Burnham nodded, while fixing Lewis with a well-practised, interrogative stare. The resonant whistle of the incoming train saved Lewis having to explain to Burnham that he was wrong about that. Quite wrong.

'Why are all those children running after us?'

Edmund was leaning over the half-open window of the carriage. Outside, hordes of German children ran with outstretched hands alongside the incoming train, which had now slowed sufficiently for them to keep pace with it. The children called out the names of the holy trinity – 'Choccie, ciggies, sandvich' – but the passengers on this train were not familiar with the expected and accepted ritual of tossing rations, and no bounty was thrown.

'Perhaps they want to see what we look like' was all Rachael could muster. 'We're nearly there.'

'Are they Germans?'

'Yes. Now come. Get your coat on.'

'They don't look very German.'

Rachael straightened Edmund's tie, licked her finger, rubbed a mark from his cheek with it and flattened down his hair.

'Look at the state of you. What will your father think?'

Porters, outnumbering passengers, were on hand to take luggage and free the arrivals to look for husbands and fathers. Having passed her case to an eager, grey-looking old man, Rachael stepped from the train into a bustling river of tweed, hats, powder and lipstick which flowed towards the waiting men. She could already see reunited couples embracing in the steam. As she had promised, the major's wife was already making up for lost time. Mrs Burnham walked up to her husband, cupped his chin and kissed him with an open mouth. It was brazen, and Rachael shivered with a covetous thrill. She would never kiss Lewis in such a way in public; even in their salad days, this would have been risqué.

Before he saw her, Rachael saw Lewis – holding back from the crowd and standing apart, his expression, in that moment, slightly fearful, vulnerable – and her heart did exactly what the stories in *Woman's Own* said: it leapt, intensifying the pulse at her throat and her breathing. For a second she felt intense affection, but it faded as soon as he saw her, offering only a quick expansion of his eyes then a smile for Edmund, who had run ahead to greet his father. Lewis met his son with a ruffle of his just-tidied hair and a nervous acknowledgement of time passed:

'Look at you. Like a runner bean.'

'Hello, Father.'

Lewis continued to look at Edmund, speechless at the changes which always seem so surprising to adults and so prosaic to children, until, no longer able to use his son as decoy, he looked at Rachael and gave her a pecked kiss which landed half on her lips, half on her cheek.

'Good journey?' he asked.

'The crossing was a little rough.'

'Let's go and have some tea. We might have some strudel if we're lucky.'

'Germans can't make tea,' Edmund chipped in, trying to please.

Lewis laughed. It was one of the few clichés about the Germans that happened to be true.

'They're getting better at it.'

Edmund was all saucer eyes, taking in every detail around him. He suddenly became animated by something happening across the tracks.

'What are they doing?'

'Oh my God,' Rachael whispered.

Two children were dangling a boy upside down over a bridge in front of an oncoming train. The dangling boy was holding a golf club and for a moment it looked as though the engine would strike him, but the train passed under him, with feet to spare, and as it passed he knocked some coal off the top of the tender for the waiting women below to catch in their skirts.

'Are they allowed to do that?' Edmund asked, full of admiration.

'Not officially,' Lewis answered.

'Aren't you going to stop them?'

Lewis winked conspiratorially at his son. 'I see no ships,' he said, and with that he steered his family towards the exit gate before more difficult questions surfaced.

Hamburg's grandest hotel, the Atlantic, had survived the war and was an oasis of extravagance in a desert of thrift. This impression was magnified by the palm court in the main lounge, where musicians played among the potted palms to tea-drinking British who, for a few hours, were able to forget the grey years and imagine this to be the most colourful of postings. Lewis was trusting that the faded grandeur, the serving of tea, the antiphonal sounds of clinking cutlery, and the thick carpeting would create the ambience of comfort and reassurance he required for his difficult announcement. But he was not happy about the music. The musicians here usually performed the jaunty, popular tunes preferred by the English; today's players – a male pianist and a female singer – were putting their all into a melancholy song in German which was a counterpoint to the tune Lewis had anticipated. Difficult news needed a happy soundtrack; whatever it was they were performing, it had to change.

Rachael recognized the piece immediately as one of Schubert's *Lieder*, and she gave herself to its deep current. Her strudel lay untouched in front of her as she fed, instead, on the music, listening with an intense and, in this room, unique concentration. Next to her, Edmund wolfed his strudel and fired question after question at his father. He had a whole war's worth stored up and they were in need of immediate answering. Lewis smoked and did his best to give answers, while waiting for the right moment to ask for the tune to be changed.

'Is Germany like a colony now?'

'Not exactly. In time, we'll give it back – when we've fixed it.'

'Have we got the best zone?'

'They say that the Americans got the view, the French got the wine and we got the ruins.'

'That doesn't seem fair.'

'Well, we created the ruins.'

'What about the Russians?'

'The Russians? Well, they got the farms. But that's another story. How is your strudel, dear?'

Lewis noticed Rachael quickly wiping a tear from her eye. She forked some strudel to divert attention, but it was too late:

'Mummy's crying again.'

It was as if Edmund had lobbed a distress flare on to the table and lit up the last seventeen months for his father to see. The glow showed Lewis more than he wanted to know or was ready to face. This compact summary of Rachael's recent history was the tip of something he had hoped physicians, time and distance might have healed.

'Don't be silly, Ed,' Rachael said. 'It's just the music. You know sad music always makes me cry.'

When the singer finished to the non-applause of the room, Lewis saw his opportunity to lift the gloom. Even as he stood up to go and make his request, Rachael guessed his intentions: 'Please don't . . .'

'We need something a bit cheerier, don't you think?'

Rachael acquiesced with a disappointed shrug and, after he had left, turned to Edmund:

'Please don't say such things to your father about me. It will only upset him.'

'Sorry,' Edmund said.

As Lewis whispered his request to the singer, Rachael noted her pained, gritted smile; perhaps she was a performer of international standing, the remnant of a decimated orchestra forced to bow to the requirements of philistine customers. As Lewis walked back, the pianist struck the opening bars of 'Run, Rabbit, Run' and the singer switched from the depths of German existential yearning to the shallows of English frivolity without missing a beat.

'That's better,' Lewis said. 'This country needs a new song.'

With the new mood set to a perky melody and with Lewis unable to wait a cigarette longer, he decided to get it over with. He was not a natural salesman, and his attempts usually exposed an over-reliance on the superlatives 'most marvellous' and 'most wonderful' and their emphasizing adverbs 'really' and 'truly'.

'I have news about our new house. It's really a most wonderful place. A lot bigger than Amersham. Even bigger than Auntie Clara's. It's got a billiard room. A grand piano.' A pause here to let Rachael picture it. 'Wonderful views of the River Elbe. The house is full of interesting paintings – by quite famous artists, I think. What else? Yes. It has a dumb waiter.'

'We have a waiter?' Edmund asked.

'We have staff. Three: a maid, a cook and a gardener.'

'But they're dumb?'

It was a relief to laugh. Even Rachael laughed at this.

'You'll soon see . . .'

'Do they speak English?' Rachael asked, engaging with the conversation now.

'Most Germans know a few words. And you'll pick it up.'

Lewis paused. He'd rehearsed this moment several times in his head. Should he appeal to the human element, make them feel sorry, as he had, for the Luberts? Make them see that these were people, like them? Or should he stick with the material facts, namely that this was a house big enough to accommodate twenty people and that it was plain greedy to turf the owners out? Either way, he was trying to wrap a bombshell in cotton wool.

'The owner of this house is a Herr Lubert. He is an architect. Civilized man. His wife died in the war. He has a daughter, not much older than you, Ed. Her name is Frieda, I believe. Anyway, their house is . . . well, it's huge. Big enough for twenty to live in. And it has an entirely separate apartment on the top floor . . .'

Rachael breathed in heavily and shifted her weight.

'The fact is, the house is big enough for all of us. They will live in the top-floor apartment and we can have the rest of the house to ourselves.'

Rachael wasn't sure if she had heard him right.

'We will live with them?' she asked.

'We'll barely notice they're there. There are just two of them. They can use a different entrance, be completely self-contained. They have everything they need up there.'

'We will live with Germans?' Edmund asked.

'Not completely. But, yes. We will share a house. Think of it as a block of flats with them on the top floor.'

Rachael needed to do something, so she poured herself some tea without wanting it or even looking. She knocked the milk jug over and Lewis, glad to have something practical to do, spread a napkin over it and called a waiter.

'But I don't understand,' Rachael said. 'Are other families doing this?'

'None of them has requisitioned a house like this. It's not really the same.'

Rachael had no space for this. It did not matter how grandiose, how replete with rooms, how exquisite the art or the action of the piano; were it a palace with separate wings and outhouses, there still would be no room for a German in it. She looked for a cigarette in her handbag. She was determined not to let Lewis light her, as was his wont; but he had already flipped his American-style lighter and, as she leant forward, he cupped her now-trembling hand with his and lit it for her.

'Wait until you see it. It's a wonderful house.'

Lewis had always had a two-pronged attack in mind. Should the soft approach fail to convince, then he would give them the hard slap of disparity and drive them through the worst Hamburg had to offer. He instructed Schroeder to follow him in the luggage-bearing Austin 16 on a slight detour through the ruins so that 'Frau und Sohn might understand the situation better'.

Lewis steered with exaggerated care around the bomb craters in the road, but for the first few minutes Edmund's excited response to the Mercedes prevented him from delivering his corrective lecture. Sitting between mother and father, son exclaimed breathlessly and enthused unabashed at the supreme feat of engineering this car represented. In the same way that he had been thrown by Bach being a

German, the sheer beauty of this beast undid Edmund's sense of superiority.

'It goes up to two hundred.'

'That's kilometres per hour.'

'Can we try it?'

'I don't think these roads will allow us, Ed.' And, with this, Lewis delivered the first of his killer statistics: 'Do you know that we dropped more bombs on Hamburg in a weekend than the Germans dropped on London in the entire war?' He said it to Edmund, but he wanted Rachael to hear it, wanted her to take in its full force; to eliminate the prejudice and self-pity. Almost on cue, the ruination of Hamburg opened up around them, and if, at first, it looked no different to the mental pictures they had of London, Coventry, Bristol, the scale of it accumulated with every yard. There were no standing structures ahead of them, behind them or on either side, only rubble, and rivers of people moving at the side of the road.

'They started it, though, didn't they, Father?'

Lewis nodded. Of course. They started it. They started it when their grievances were stirred in a pot by a conjurer; they started it with every arm raised and armband worn, with every rally attended and road built, with every utterance applauded; they started it with every shop smashed, every plane launched and bomb dropped. They started it. But where were they? Where was the master race that swallowed continents now? Surely it wasn't these pathetically clad, feeble-limbed troglodytes plodding along at the side of the shattered road?

'They don't look like Germans, Father.'

'No.'

Still no response from Rachael.

'You see those black crosses? They indicate bodies buried

45

in the rubble. There are still over a million German civilians unaccounted for.'

Lewis looked at Rachael to see if any of this was registering, but her face was a determined blank.

Set your face that way then, Lewis thought. You'll see it soon enough.

They passed several families lugging a lifetime's leftovers on the back of a cart.

'Where are all these people going?' Edmund asked.

'They're DPs. Displaced people returning to the city. Or people who have been thrown out of their homes to make way for the likes of us.'

'Mother says they live in billets.'

'They do. But there aren't enough of them. We're building a new camp every month.' He would have to show them what a camp for displaced people looked like at some point.

'Are those like the camps we saw in the *Illustrated News*?'

'No. Not like those.'

'But they deserve it, don't they? For what they did? In those camps?'

Lewis had to check his irritation. Breathe in. He isn't to know.

'Father?'

Outside, the people flowed on either side of the road with faces bent on nothing more than the immediate, the daily bread and that they might be delivered from any more evil, but Lewis could not bend his spine any further back in support of them. He must say something of justice, too . . .

'Some do, Ed. Yes.'

And, with this, Rachael offered her only words of the short journey:

'Of course they do.'

*

46

As the strange convoy – hunched, doughty British Austin trailing sleek, all-conquering German Mercedes – scrunched up the gravel drive, Stefan Lubert checked his watch and walked down the steps to greet the new occupants. He pulled his jacket straight and made an effort to look dignified, humble and grateful all at once – a difficult combination for a man of his temperament. Next to him, Heike and Greta stood in line, ready to offer their services to the family. He could sense their nerves and hear their whispered commentary:

'They're not as ugly as other English.'

'I like their clothes.'

'Poor Master, he is putting on a brave face.'

'The lady is pretty . . .'

'Not as pretty as our mistress.'

Greta was being loyal to the memory of her mistress, of course, but Claudia had not been pretty. Handsome, elegant, graceful, aquiline, but not pretty. Whereas Frau Morgan, as Heike had spontaneously observed, certainly was, and her unsmiling and stonily set face could not quite disguise it. Dark auburn hair; wide almond eyes, small full lips, petite but full figure, olive skin. Where was she from? Not England, surely. She must be Celtic. Spanish even.

'She does not look happy.'

'Perhaps she is used to living in a castle.'

The colonel came and shook Lubert's hand warmly.

'Frieda wanted to greet you, but she is not feeling well,' Lubert said. 'I hope you will forgive her absence.'

'Of course,' Lewis answered, and he beckoned Rachael forward. 'This is my wife – Frau Morgan.'

Lubert put out a hand, but Rachael offered no reciprocal action.

'How do you do?' Lubert said, retracting his hand and

47

converting the gesture into an ushering, introductory sweep. 'My staff. Heike. Greta. Richard, you met at the gate. I commend them to you.'

Heike curtsied emphatically, Greta minimally.

Still no words from Rachael, Lubert noted. Perhaps some catatonia had afflicted her as she drove through the ruins.

'And Edmund,' Lewis said, turning and calling his son over: 'Ed!'

In his excitement, Edmund had wandered off towards the lawn, where he was now running with arms outstretched like a plane, making noises of war. The boy wasn't thinking and, as if to show he didn't mind, Lubert laughed. But Rachael was embarrassed.

'Ed! Stop that! Come and say hello.'

Lubert was surprised to hear her voice. *She speaks!*

Edmund ran over to greet Lubert and the staff. Heike giggled at his antics.

'How do you do?' Edmund said to Lubert.

'Welcome to your new home,' he replied. 'I hope you like it here.'

Lewis had not exaggerated, Rachael thought. The house *was* wonderful. If anything, he had undersold it, probably from an ignorance of what really made it special but also because he was not entirely comfortable with its grandeur. He was free of the social pretension and material aspirations that drove his colleagues, a characteristic the more socially alert Rachael had always loved in him but which now, for some reason, irritated her. As Herr Lubert gave them the guided tour she felt caught between needing to show the German that she recognized excellence and appreciated culture as much as anyone and making her general misgivings known. With every room he explained, Herr Lubert seemed to be compounding her sense of inferiority and dislocation. Whatever he was actually saying, all she was hearing was: 'You are welcome but it is still my house.' By the time they reached the balcony overlooking the river, Rachael had had enough. As Lubert offered to show them his own apartments – at the top of the house – she cut the tour short, saying she was tired from the journey. The shock of facing her new circumstances had, if anything, jolted the fatigue out of her; but she could no longer tolerate the presence of this urbane and – was she imagining it? – slightly impertinent German who spoke English with a perfect cadence and without the silly plums of received pronunciation. Rachael had half hoped the lack of a shared language would keep things simple and separate, but this man's facility was going to complicate things unless boundaries were firmly and clearly laid down.

Later, when Lewis went to tuck Edmund into bed, he found his son lying on the floor. He had pulled the doll's house out into the centre of the room and Lewis could see that he had already re-created the house in a simulacrum of the Villa Lubert, placing furniture up on the roof where the German family now lived, and finger-sized dolls in their respective spaces: two dolls – one male, one female – for Lubert and his daughter; one each for himself, Lewis and Rachael.

'Bedtime, Ed.'

Edmund got up from the floor and climbed into the four-poster.

Lewis had not tucked his son in for a long time and wasn't sure of the routine. Should he read a story? Say a few words? Offer a prayer? Instead, he pulled the blanket up over Edmund's chest and just over his cloth soldier, Cuthbert. Lewis wanted to touch his son's face and caress a lock away from his eyes, but he lacked the confidence so patted the cloth soldier instead.

'How do you like it here?' he asked.

'It's big,' Edmund replied.

'You think you are going to enjoy it?'

Ed nodded. 'Why didn't the girl come and say hello?'

'I think she isn't very well. You'll meet her soon enough. Maybe you can play together.'

'Will that be allowed?'

'Of course. Once we're settled in.'

Edmund paused, as if about to say something else, but his father had already switched off the bedside light.

'Night, Ed.'

'Goodnight, Father.'

And, with that, Lewis left the room, Edmund thinking that perhaps it was best not to mention the encounter he'd had about an hour before, when he had wandered along the landing to the staircase that led to the top floor, where the Luberts' apartments were situated.

He had only wanted to have a look up there, nothing more. He'd climbed the first flight and, when he got to the turn in the staircase, he'd come across the girl, with a blond pigtail, her arms out, a hand pressed against each wall and her legs suspended in mid-air in front of her as though she were performing on a gymnasium horse.

'Hello,' he'd said. He stood there staring at her, intrigued, wondering if this was Frieda. She looked to be perfectly strong and healthy, not sick at all.

'Are you Frieda?' he asked.

But the girl just stared back at him, keeping her legs perfectly horizontal, and then, very slowly, she started to open her legs to reveal her knickers. Edmund was mesmerized, unable to look away. For how long he looked he couldn't tell – it felt like several minutes – but he was rudely startled from his gawping when the girl suddenly hissed at him – hissed just like a cat – and he backed down the stairs, keeping his eyes on her all the time, lest she suddenly pounce.

Lubert woke from a bad dream to find himself in an unfamiliar room and a house that was no longer his. In the first uncertain seconds of waking, he wasn't sure where he was, and his consciousness, scrabbling for sensory clues, cobbled a confusion of memory, location and time that placed him in the single bed at his grandmother's summer house on the island of Sylt, the same bed where he had once made love to Claudia while downstairs, in the kitchen, his sisters prepared lobster and crab for supper. How well the young lovers had used the hammering of shells to disguise the creaking of the headboard and their ecstatic cries.

He opened his eyes, and the light, seeping through the half-open curtain, broke the illusion: he was not in his own bed (another man and another wife lay there now), he was in the bedroom that his old driver, Friedrich, had used before war had forced a shedding of staff, the same room that Claudia had then used as an adjunct to her always overflowing dressing room. He was in his house but he was no longer its master, and the mistress of the house was gone, never to be smelt or caressed again. And yet, he *could* smell her – or a memory of a time with her. The silk eiderdown he now lay beneath once belonged in that summer house on Sylt, before the island's homes had been commandeered by the Luftwaffe for their seaplane base; it had retained a smell of the sea and it was this that had conjured the vivid association.

Lubert pulled the quilt up to his nose, breathed in its scent and was transported again to the day he came down the staircase with his flushed fiancée to eat the feast prepared by his sisters, the herby, salt-fish smell of Claudia on his knuckles mingling with that of the bouillabaisse, and Claudia smiling at him across the table as he surreptitiously sniffed his fingers for proof of her passion. As Lubert gave himself to this memory, the smell of his own arousal wafted up from beneath the quilt, inviting him to re-enact that scene all over again.

Afterwards, he felt no guilt, just a low-grade humiliation that this was all he had now: reminiscences edited and recut for quick, mechanical effect. He sat up and felt the tepid clump of semen on his belly already going cold. Wasted. Neutered of purpose. It was this legacy – more than the ruins, the material destruction or the atrocities – that Lubert thought about most: the truncating and rearranging of relationships that had once seemed unbreakable, a million lovers losing the loves of their lives and having to start again. Of course, for some – the unhappily married, the unevenly yoked – the interruption was an opportunity. According to the banter of the men at the factory, the shortage of German males was a good thing for all of them. There were simply more women to choose from, and more women choosing. It was the 'new' economics of supply and demand. But Lubert did not want to choose or be chosen; the one he had chosen – and who had chosen him – was still, even gone, more present to him than any prospective relationship.

He wiped his hand on his nightshirt and got up from the bed to pull the curtain fully across. The room was still cluttered with belongings hastily transported from the master bedroom and study after the unexpected reprieve granted by the colonel. They were the things Lubert had always imagined he'd grab first in the event of a fire: his architectural worktop and utensils; the pressed flowers from his wedding day; and two of the most valuable and treasured objects in the house: Léger's self-portrait and von Carolsfeld's naked maid. But, rather than feeling the loss of things, Lubert had experienced an unexpected exhilaration in having to pare back his possessions – a sense of being almost bare, light enough to go anywhere.

At the window, he peered out across the lit lawn. The quarter-moon was visible in the cold, clear, purple sky but the light being cast across the garden was emanating from the master bedroom, where, no doubt, the kind, upright British officer and his pretty but simmering wife were reacquainting themselves after a long separation. Lubert tried not to think of it, but not thinking of it only made a scene spring to mind more clearly: they were in his bed; perhaps they kept the light on the better to see what they had been missing; perhaps they talked and talked before making love; or they made love first, talked then made love again. Were they, as he and Claudia had always preferred, lying on the bed without covering, or were they quiet, furtive lovers hiding themselves beneath the linen?

The light from the bedroom below went out, the balcony, garden and trees pooled into blackness and a fuller canopy of stars revealed itself. Presuming that the occupants of his old bed had completed their rituals of reunion, Lubert left the window and got back beneath the salty eiderdown of his single bed.

Rachael sat at her new dressing table in her new bedroom, brushing her hair. Somewhere, directly above her in the top apartments, she imagined Herr Lubert preparing for bed and laughing at *that woman*'s rudeness and her inability to recognize the artist of one of the paintings he'd pointed out in the billiard room – who was it? Léger? She had never heard of him.

She did not want to move from her kidney-shaped dressing stool. If she had the condescension of a man above her, she had the approbation (and expectation) of the man behind her. In the quarter-section of the mirror she could see Lewis in his pyjamas sitting on the high, narrow bed watching her, and she could sense his mixture of annoyance and arousal. Lewis disliked any form of unkindness, and the fact that he hadn't yet said anything to her was perhaps because he was hoping to 'have a moment'. Rachael stopped brushing her hair; she didn't want to send the wrong signals. The expected moment of their physical reunion had arrived, but she was not ready to give herself to it.

'Don't you like the house?' Lewis asked. It was gentle enough, but, by his standards, this was almost a confrontation.

'I'd prefer it if the owner wasn't living in it.'

Rachael watched Lewis reach for his cigarette case, take a cigarette and light up. A combat reflex: ammunition for battle; tricky terrain to cross: light up.

'You might have been a little friendlier towards him,' he said. Again, reasonable – she had been unfriendly; but Rachael needed no red rag to charge him. Her laugh sounded more hysterical than she felt but her choice of words was calculated. An argument would put off the sex for another time.

'What? And pretend we're all jolly friends? All on the same side?'

'We are. On the same side,' Lewis said.

Rachael stood and crossed the floor to that narrow bed, pinching her nightdress away from her breasts. She plumped the pillows up so that she might sit upright. Her book –

Appointment with Death by Agatha Christie – was already on the bedside table: her escape route if he persisted.

Perhaps sensing the chance slipping away, he asked: 'Are we going to . . . have a moment?'

'Do we have to? Now?'

'We don't have to.'

'I mean, it feels a bit strange. With them up there. It's been a long three days.'

'It's fine. You're tired. It's fine.'

Maybe if he had just taken her without saying, surprised her, she might have gone with it; it might have been how it used to be.

She reached for her book.

'Have you really been crying every day?'

Rachael tensed. He wanted to talk.

'Ed's a whatnot for saying that.'

'But . . . have you?'

'Mayfield says my nerves are still fragile.'

'What about Pring? Have you had some chats?'

'I've stopped going to church.'

It felt good – oddly satisfying – to admit this. But she didn't explain herself. For Lewis, who had little angst (the curious new word Mayfield had used), it was a practical question. What he really meant was: have you spent time with people or have you been isolated? He certainly wouldn't infer from her answer that there was no God because He'd let a stray bomb land at precisely the right spot at the exact moment Michael had come down the stairs in answer to her call.

Rachael could feel a pressure at the sluice gates. She'd held it back for several days, but it was coming.

'It's all right for you,' she said. 'You weren't there. You don't seem to feel it the way I do.'

'I've not had much time for feelings,' Lewis said. Honest but inadequate.

'But why don't you feel it?' She saved him from trying to articulate it. 'It's all right. You have your work. You have a country to rebuild . . .' And, with this, the dammed waters began to burst. '. . . The country that killed my . . . beautiful boy!'

This sobbing that came when she remembered Michael was similar to the way she might have cried when she was a girl; it shook her whole diaphragm and forced her to catch her breath in shudders. Lewis put a hand on her back and stroked her, but he could not enter her chamber of pain.

'And now you make me live here with these people.'

'Everyone here – everyone in this house – has experienced loss.'

'I don't care. I don't care if everyone in the world has lost a son. The pain would be the same. I didn't agree to this . . .'

'None of us agreed to this. But we must make the best of things . . .'

'The best of things. Always the best of things! You seem more concerned with the needs of our enemy.'

'Rach. Please. They're not our enemy any more. They've been utterly crushed. Everything must be rebuilt.'

Rachael tapped her breastbone and paused to catch a breath between sobs.

'Can you rebuild this?' she asked him, half wanting him to rise to that challenge while at the same time wishing he would just walk away and leave her to the comfort of her broken-ness.

4

Frieda finished her morning exercises with the medicine ball and started to get dressed for school. She had no uniform (there had been little school since The Catastrophe) and chose to put on her Mädel parade skirt, white blouse and her gymnasium pumps – a minor provocation to the authorities and a red rag to her father, who had told her to put away the clothes of the old regime. Since their humiliating retreat to the top rooms of the house, she had become even more inclined to defy him. He encouraged her to make her new room a little more homely, saying it all looked 'a little spartan', suggesting she hang some pictures and bring up the rocking horse from her old bedroom, but she liked it this way. She fancied herself as a Spartan child, cast out from her family's comforts into the rubble of a ruined land where she must learn to survive. The only decoration she'd permitted herself was a framed sampler her mother had made; it depicted three figures – a man holding an architect's folding ruler, a woman with a bouquet of flowers and a girl holding the woman's hand – standing in front of a house by a river with a red sailboat on the horizon. Her mother had given it to her for her eleventh birthday. It had been July 1942, the day the British had started to bomb Hamburg, and one year before the firestorm.

At least the move upstairs had given her the opportunity to shed the old toys and those English books her father had insisted on reading to her during the raids – *Alice in Wonderland*, *The Happy Prince*, *Robinson Crusoe* – when he was trying to take her mind off the droning of bombers and the *kakakak* of the Heimwehr guns firing back. 'Imagination will be our defence,' he liked to say. But the stories couldn't bring her mother back.

Frieda set the medicine ball in the middle of the exercise hoop and squatted over the chamber pot. When she had finished, she lifted the chamber pot and carried it out on to the landing. She walked downstairs to her old bedroom in the 'British zone', where she found her intended target playing with her doll's house. She watched through the open door as Edmund enacted a scene between a male and female doll in the attic of the house and, although she didn't fully understand the dialogue, it was obvious from the way he'd positioned the dolls who they represented.

'The little boy plays with dollies,' Frieda said in English, and laughed at him.

Edmund looked up to see Frieda standing in the doorway with the chamber pot, and wondered if she wanted to initiate some kind of cultural exchange.

'Hello,' he said, then tried his just-learned greeting: '*Guten Tag*, Fräulein Lubert.'

Frieda held up the chamber pot as if to say 'For you' and placed it on the floor in the middle of the room. She then smiled an odd smile and backed away, closing the door behind her, leaving her hot, golden gift at the feet of this Happy Prince.

On the way to school, Frieda passed several *Trümmerfrauen* in heavy smocks and headscarves heading into the city, where they would work through mountains of debris and pile masonry and brickwork into salvageable heaps for a bowl of soup, a loaf of bread and some food vouchers, if they were lucky. Many of them were carrying shovels, and one or two joked, happy to have the work. Frieda would rather be with them. She'd not been to school regularly since the summer of 1943, when the British bombers had destroyed nearly every school in the city. But now, the British had reopened the old town hall and divided one vast room – using plywood walls – into 'classrooms'. Because the district was overflowing with refugees, there were too many children for the space, which meant many had to squat on the cold floor. Despite these difficulties and a lack of basic supplies – pens, paper and textbooks – the British had made the education of German children a high priority. They were obsessed with it. Having de-loused their heads, they set about rearranging their minds: teaching them that the Führer (whom they disrespectfully called by his first name) and National Socialism were evils that needed to be completely eradicated from the face of the earth. They talked about democracy, asked questions to establish what the children did and didn't know, and were astonished by their ignorance. Although the teacher, Mr Groves, called everyone by their Christian name and tried to be friendly, preferring to sit in the middle of the class rather than stand at the front, Frieda found the lessons humiliating. She had decided not to respond to any of the questions asked, even when she knew the answer.

As she approached the town hall, Frieda saw that the gates were locked and that several children were gathered beneath a notice that had been posted on the brick wall. The notice, in German, said 'School closed by order of CCG.' Some Tommy military police stood around, and three army trucks with canvas covers were parked up along the line of the railings. A captain addressed the children in German:

'Those of you who are under thirteen are free to return home; those over thirteen who are strong enough can assist with the rubble clearance. You will be paid in food vouchers for your work, given a meal, and then be brought back to this point before dark.'

A cheer went up, and every child that was of that age – and many who clearly weren't – started to move towards the ruin-bound trucks. The prospect of a meal today and maybe tomorrow was too much to resist. Although Frieda had eaten a relatively hearty breakfast and would be fed again upon her return, she'd rather be out than at home; she followed the hungry herd and climbed up into the back of one of the trucks. The boy sitting next to her was about fourteen and a veteran of 'the rubble run'. As they jerked and bounced along towards the western suburb of Altona, he boasted of his exploits:

'It's not bad, you know. I found a necklace and traded it for a chicken. And they give you a good meal. On my last shift we got bread and soup with sausage meat.'

'Was it real sausage?' another boy asked. 'Usually, it's dog meat. Or worse.'

'Real sausage!' the boy said. 'Bierwurst, Bratwurst, Rindswurst, Jagdwurst, Knipp, Pinkel, Landjäger . . .' He named each sausage slowly, reverently and longingly, constructing a whole charcuterie in the air before them, and the already distended eyes of the children popped out in anticipation of this banquet.

Twenty minutes later, they jumped out from under the covering to find themselves in the ruins of Altona, some of it so flattened that it was possible to see all the way across St Pauli, to the old, miraculously intact warehouses and canals of Kehrwieder and Wandrahm. An army of women formed a human chain, passing debris along the line, and some of them looked displeased at the sight of the children coming to help: 'Look at these little rats come to steal our rations.'

Frieda took her place in the chain. The person passing her bricks was a young man, maybe seventeen years old, who seemed somehow above the agitation of everyone around him. He had a languid energy and an easy strength and was well turned out in a blue jacket which had all its buttons. As she passed the debris to him she found herself absently singing the tune of an old Mädel song ('We will continue to march, even if everything shatters, because today Germany hears us, and tomorrow, the whole world. And because of the Great War, the world lies in ruins, but devil may care, we build it up again!').

As she got to the third verse, she felt his warm hand on her wrist.

'Careful, young lady!' he interrupted, keeping his eyes on the Tommy guards. 'Some of them might recognize what you are singing.'

'I don't care,' she said. And she felt power and liberation in saying this to the handsome young man with buttons.

He looked at her, assessing her. 'You're not too young to be shot, you know. How old are you?'

'Sixteen,' she lied.

Just a few yards away, two British squaddies shared a joke and smoked, overseeing the work in a cursory manner.

'They're so stupid,' she said. 'The way they act like they own the place.'

He laughed. 'We're the ones doing the work. They're the ones standing around enjoying themselves. That makes us the stupid ones.'

Frieda flushed: he'd caught her callow. She resumed the brick-passing and held her tongue. The proximity of the young man was a pleasant thing. She could smell his bacony sweat and admire his sinewy, glabrous forearms. Each time he passed a brick to her she caught a glimpse of a scar or a birthmark on the underside of his arm. It was in the shape of the number 88. When he noticed her looking at it he stopped to pull his sleeve back down.

'Oi! Blondie!' The sudden yell from one of the squaddies made Frieda jump. 'Keep it moving! *Schnell!*'

The young man buttoned his sleeve and resumed work. After a short while, he caught her eye with a hesitant but enquiring glance.

'My name is Albert,' he said. 'What is yours?'

'Frieda.'

'Frieda,' he repeated.

She had never liked her name or its diminutive, Freedie, but on his lips her name sounded quite new, quite grand.

'I like that name. A good German name,' he went on. His admiration enveloped her like a quilt.

'It means . . . lady,' Frieda said.

And, with that, he took her hand and shook it politely.

'And so you are,' he said. 'A proper German lady.'

A call went up further along the line – 'Body!' – and everyone stopped and looked towards the woman who'd shouted out and was now standing back from what she'd discovered. Other women joined her and started to pull back more bricks, to reveal a skeletal arm protruding from the ruins, hand cocked to one side in an angle of supplication. The women started to pull the bricks away with more urgency, as though in a race against time to save a potential survivor; and a few seconds later they'd managed to expose the rest of the skeleton, and then another, lying on top of it between the legs of the smaller body in a position of coition. The intimate archaeological find had a silencing effect on the staring women.

Frieda broke from her line and went to look more closely. She stared at the dead lovers in their final clutch, feeling a peculiar pull, rather than the revulsion the others showed.

'All right, everyone. Step back. Come on. It's not a bloody cinema!'

Two Tommies came over and shepherded the gawpers away then went to look for themselves. One of them stood astride the little hollow that served as the couple's tomb and looked down.

'Not a bad way to go,' he said to his mate. 'One final fuck before lights out.'

'They look like they're still enjoying themselves,' his mate replied, and they laughed, before realizing there was still an audience looking down at them. 'Come on, you lot. Back to work!'

Frieda couldn't move. Her eyes were fixed on the gold wedding bands on the fingers of the dead couple. At least they had died together, at the same time. Not like her parents. The Tommy with his legs still astride the hole had seen the rings, too. He bent down and removed them, breaking off one of the fingers in his haste; he then held the rings up to check the carats before handing one of them to his colleague. 'Can't take them with you,' he said, before pocketing the ring. 'Bag these bones!' he shouted at the women, in German.

Frieda returned to her place in the chain next to Albert, her eyes glazed with tears. The tears sprang less from a compassion for the dead couple and more from a brimming contempt for the people who had brought about their end; and for the loss of her own mother, whose body had never been found.

'I must have more light in here. I'd like you to move these. Heike? The plants?'

Rachael semaphored to the offending greenery which filled one of the bay windows and, to her eyes, blocked the light she so craved after months of low-ceilinged, indoor dinginess endured back home. Except for conservatories, and the ubiquitous aspidistra, Rachael had never seen so many plants in the main part of a house before. Perhaps, in

Germany, it was the height of good taste to fill a room with shrubs, but she couldn't live with them.

Heike went to the first offending plant, a waxy – almost plastic – green yucca, and bent to lift it. Just before she did, she hesitated and looked at Rachael, pointing a wavering finger towards the door, making doubly sure this was what the mistress wanted.

'Yes. Put them in another room. Thank you.' Rachael compensated for her lack of German by overenunciating, and inadvertently accented the word 'you', and that seemed to make the maid smile. As Heike carried the plant from the room, she giggled then blushed at her own laughter. It was probably nerves more than subversion, but Rachael was irritated by her amusement, as though her request were proof of some foreign peculiarity.

Rachael was making her first territorial statements in her new home, delivering them with a curt clarity of which Prime Minister Attlee would surely have approved. And if a lack of language and an inexperience with staff made her sound sharper than she intended, it was important she assert herself from the start and define the boundaries by which they might live life under the same roof. But no amount of British military-issue crockery and glassware or rearranging of furniture could change the fact that she was living in someone else's property, sleeping in someone else's bed, moving through someone else's space. If anything, the alterations she instigated – the removal of the plants, the nude sculpture in the hall made modest with a drape, the dining-room chairs swapped with the more comfortable kitchen wickers – served only to entrench the house's character further. As she walked through its rooms, Rachael fancied she could hear its mocking condescension whispering from the walls: *You don't belong here and you never will.*

This self-assured quality seemed to seep into the staff, who, for all their outward deference, the mechanical bowing and nodding, regarded her – she was sure of this – as an imposter. She was both ingénue and parvenue – especially to the weary, closed-mouthed Greta, who had served the Lubert family longest and whose loyalties stretched furthest back. The withering, disappointed looks she gave Rachael were like those of a royal servant who'd seen several queens come and go, all of whom had failed to live up to the first. The place, Rachael felt, was still under the aegis, the spell, of its former mistress, whose presence manifested itself most powerfully in the looks and bearing of the staff, whose hesitations and uncertain responses to instruction barely disguised their real attitude: *Our lady would never have done it that way.*

Upon making her first walk through the house, she had found herself in a small battle with it. It wasn't just the plants: the furniture and most of the fittings and fixtures were anathema to her. She knew she was in the presence of a certain kind of excellence, but it was not a style she could love or even aspire to; and while she could appreciate the space and proportion of the rooms, she felt intimidated rather than liberated by the minimal furnishing. She wanted light and space but needed comfort and familiarity. If asked to describe it, she would have used the word 'modern' and meant it pejoratively. The chairs, for instance, seemed to have been stripped to their barest function, having no softness, comfort or charm – no quality that Rachael thought necessary in a chair. And the same went for the sideboards, the lamps, the tables. There was nothing pretty or frivolous or homely about any of it. Everything in the house seemed a bit clever, a bit clinical and soulless. There was too much to offend the eye of a middle-class Welshwoman raised on dark-wooded Victorian furniture, coal fires, upright pianos, sensible, inoffensive prints of castles and botanical drawings. Only the drawing room, with its ebonized Bösendorfer piano and ottoman came remotely close to resembling a room she might actually want to sit in; if she could just get the strange chair in the corner moved – maybe replace it with the simple, if boxy, two-seat sofa from the master bedroom – then she might start to feel more at home.

Rachael stared more closely at the chrome-framed leather recliner. Was it even meant for sitting on? It looked like a chair on which a painful operation might take place. Perhaps it wasn't a chair; perhaps it was an artefact. Perhaps it was both. Perhaps that was the point. Whatever the idea behind it, she did not care for it.

'You should try it.'

She turned to find Herr Lubert, inexplicably dressed in the navy-blue overalls of a car mechanic and holding a great hoop of keys in one hand. He looked ruffled, his hair unkempt and flying up and out to the side as though he'd slept on it when it was damp. Lewis always gelled his hair back and kept it as polished and immaculate as a piece of uniform; Lubert's free-flowing, boyish style seemed like that of a deserter or an artist trying hard not to conform.

'It's a Mies van der Rohe. The House of Construction?'

Rachael was so thrown by his appearance – his get-up, the hair, his ease – that she didn't hear the words at all.

'The chair,' Lubert explained. 'It's worth trying. It's meant to be one of the most comfortable chairs ever invented.'

'It doesn't look it,' Rachael said. 'It looks – quite the opposite.'

Lubert smiled, a little too cockily, a little over-familiar.

'Well. That is an interesting observation. It was designed by someone who was trying to reject "unnecessary adornment"? Is that the phrase?'

Rachael was still wondering how to comport herself in this scene. What was the appropriate mien? What did she think of this answer? Why was he wearing blue overalls? And his English . . . The man's English was so natural she had to remind herself that he was a German and on no account to be fraternized with unless in the communication of essential practicalities. But he was still doing all the talking.

'He was of the Bauhaus school. They wanted to simplify things,' Lubert went on. 'Take them back to the functional. That was the philosophy.'

'Do you need a philosophy to make a chair comfortable?' Rachael said, surprising herself, and feeling that this was curt enough to punctuate this already uncomfortably long conversation with a full stop.

Lubert's face lit up.

'But that is it! Behind every artefact, behind every object, there is a philosophy!'

She had to put an end to this dialogue. It was setting a very poor precedent for future interactions. The careful lines she had planned to lay down – had started to lay down – were already being crossed.

Herr Lubert held out the key ring.

'As lady of the house, you should have these. The keys to every room, with a label indicating which is which.'

Rachael took the keys. 'Lady of the house'. She didn't feel it, or believe she could play this role convincingly.

'I hope that you slept well, Frau Morgan,' he added.

Choosing to hear in this innocent banality an inappropriate familiarity, Rachael decided to assert herself.

'Herr Lubert, I want to be very clear with you from the start. I am not comfortable with the arrangement here – sharing a house with you – and I think it right and proper that we communicate only about what is essential. We must be civil, of course, but it is not appropriate that we . . . pretend to be friendly when that is not . . . not helpful . . . to our situation here. We must have clear lines of demarcation.'

Lubert nodded at her peremptory abbreviation, but he did not seem remotely convinced by it and – astonishingly to her – continued to smile in a most carefree way.

'I will do my best not to be too friendly, Frau Morgan,' he said. And, with this, he bowed and left the room.

'*Guten Morgen, alle.*'

'*Guten Morgen*, Herr Governor. *Guten Morgen*, Herr Oberst.'

'*Es ist . . . kalt.*' Lewis hugged himself and patted his arms with his gloved hands.

Everyone agreed. It was very *kalt.*

Lewis had started to make a point of stopping to say hello to any German who might be at the gates of the headquarters – a commandeered former library – for the district of Pinneberg. Today, there were more people at the gates than usual. The approach of winter could be seen in their vapour breath, and the usually submissive, docile crowd seemed fretful; with the season's change coming, the need to find a bed in one of the camps for the displaced was becoming urgent.

He said his good mornings, bowing to the women, smiling at the children, saluting the men. The children giggled, the women curtsied, while the men returned his salute and waved the papers they hoped would gain passport to bed and roof. Through this engagement, Lewis tried to convey reassurance that all would be well, that a normality was being restored, even though the stench of hungry breath which Major Burnham had so callously identified, and at which Lewis had trained himself not to wince, was a pungent reminder that they were – more than one year into the occupation – still failing to meet the people's most fundamental needs.

Once inside the perimeter, Lewis made a mental note to have the barbed wire that surrounded their offices removed. He wasn't sure who or what it was keeping out, but CCG seemed to think it needed protecting from a panoply of beasts: the Werwolf, fabled militant resistance to the Allied victory; the feral children scavenging in the rubble; predatory and infectious German women prowling for men. Then there was the rumour that animals had escaped from the bombed Tiergarten Hagenbeck and were still at large in the Hamburg suburbs. If anything, the ugly metal in which the authorities had wrapped themselves made the British the zoo animals and the indigenous people the gawping visitors, pulling faces at the nervous, alien creatures behind the wire.

Captain Wilkins was ensconced at his desk, reading a booklet.

'Morning, Wilkins.'

'Morning, sir.'

'What's that you're reading?'

'It's called "The German Character", and it's by Brigadier W. E. van Cutsem. CCG are insisting we reacquaint ourselves with it. They're keen that we get to grips with the dangerous elements in the German personality before we get things up and running. He makes a good point. Here: "There may not be an outward show of hatred, but it's there, simmering just below the surface, ready to be called forward in all its ferocity and bitterness. Be aware: this is a people that don't know when they're defeated."'

Lewis was still standing, putting off what he felt to be the emasculation that occurred when he was seated behind a desk. He looked at his young second with a barely suppressed exasperation.

'Wilkins. How long have you been here?'

'Four months now, sir.'

'And how many Germans have you talked to?'

'We're not really permitted to talk to them, sir –'

'But you must have conversed with some. Observed them. I mean, met some.'

'One or two, sir.'

'And what do you feel when you encounter them?'

'Sir?'

'Are you afraid? Do you feel their hatred? Do you look at them and think these people are a mere pistol shot from insurrection? A people that are just waiting for the signal to overthrow us?'

'Hard to say, sir.'

'But try: try to say. Have you seen the people at the gates? Do you look at those waifs and strays, those skeletal, yellow, stinking, homeless people bowing and fawning and scraping for food and shelter and think: By God, yes, I must remind these people that they have been defeated?'

Wilkins tried to mutter something, but Lewis wasn't waiting for an answer.

'I've not met a German who has difficulty in believing they have been defeated, Wilkins. I think they have, to a man, accepted it, gladly, and with some relief. The real difference between them and us is that they have been comprehensively and categorically fucked, and they know it. It is we who are taking too long to adjust to this fact.'

'Sir.' Wilkins put the offending booklet down and picked up some less controversial paperwork. He looked almost hurt. There was an uncharacteristic sharpness in his boss's tone today.

Lewis immediately lifted a hand in apology. He had meant every word, but they had come out far too emphatically, spiked with the accumulated tetchiness and disappointment he'd been feeling since Rachael's arrival in Hamburg. He'd not slept well at all and although he'd told himself – told Rachael – that it was all down to having to share a bed after months of stretching his feet out into the cool recesses of requisitioned hotel beds, the truth was that their reunion was not the completion he'd hoped for. He'd hoped she'd take to her new surroundings with the same elan she'd shown in their first home, the grim, colourless rented abode in Shrivenham. She'd once been lithe in times of changed circumstance, but here she seemed quite demotivated, found everything rebarbative. Including him. Michael was weighing her down more heavily than he'd anticipated and he had not only misjudged this but made matters worse with the wrong words, then with no words. Here, at work, he had eloquence and emotion and conviction; with Rachael, he experienced a strangled ineptitude. And still, two weeks on, they had not 'had a moment'.

Of course, none of this was Wilkins's fault or concern.

'I suggest you get out more, Wilkins. Meet the people. It's the best antidote to that theoretical claptrap. It doesn't help having our headquarters here, but you need to see the reality of conditions a few miles east. Fraternize. That's an order.'

'Sir –'

There was a knock, and Captain Barker's rotund, cheery head appeared at the door. He surveyed the scene, sensed an atmosphere and opted to keep the rest of himself in the corridor.

'Sir, the women are ready to see you.'

'Right, Barker. Thank you. How many are there?'

'I've whittled them down to a choice of three, sir.'

'How did you manage that?'

'Chose the prettiest ones, sir.'

Lewis permitted himself a smile. The British zone might

have become a Mecca for the maladjusted – redundant colonialists from India, carpetbaggers, failed civil servants and idle policemen – but the odd gem got through. And Barker was a gem, working hard at everything he did while maintaining the lightest of touches; he was neither out for petty gain nor escaping failure in another realm; he said he'd come to Germany to make a difference and seemed free of the presumptions or the unction with which so many of the new young breed of officers arrived. Such probity sparkled in the dung, gave Lewis hope that he had something to work with.

'Do they speak good English?'

Barker glanced back outside to the corridor, signalling that the women were within earshot.

'Each one is fluent,' he said. 'To narrow it down, I asked them to name as many English football teams as possible. One of them named Crewe Alexandra.'

'You think Intelligence uses such sophisticated recruitment methods?'

'Of course not, sir. Intelligence would pick the ugly ones.'

Crewe Alexandra was first. Lewis stood as she entered and ushered her towards the chair opposite his desk. He pushed aside the files that were blocking his view. In her brimmed hat and velvet gown she resembled an aristocratic suffragette, a look somehow accentuated by her outsized army boots. She had a wide, angular face with heavy eyebrows and wolfish, preternatural eyes that looked both at and through Lewis simultaneously. He had the peculiar sensation of having met her before somewhere, and although this was not the case he blushed, as though the thought were proof of some deeper, inappropriate emotion. He composed himself and scanned the hastily typed-up report that Barker had put together.

'Ursula Paulus. Born 12 March 1918. Wismar?'

'Yes. That is correct.'

Since the war, it had been much harder to guess people's ages. Loss, separation, deprivation and an unrelentingly poor diet had aged everyone, the women especially. Facial lines creased into old fat folds and hair greyed and thinned, plucked or shocked out of colour and vigour. Lewis discerned more life lived, more wisdom, more pain in her expression than in that of the average 28-year-old.

'You come from Rügen Island?'

'Yes.'

'How did you get to Hamburg?'

'I walked.' She looked down at her boots. 'I'm sorry. I have not yet managed to find better shoes.'

'I won't be making my decision based on couture, Frau Paulus. Where did you learn your English?'

'I taught it at an elementary school on the island.'

'You didn't want to stay on Rügen?'

She shook her head and Lewis decoded it:

'The Russians.'

'They do not treat German women kindly.'

'That is an understatement.'

'It is a . . . euphemism?' she asked, checking this was the right word.

Lewis nodded. Smart, as the Americans liked to say.

'You speak Russian?'

'A little.'

'It could be helpful. If the Soviets have their way, we could all end up speaking Russian.'

Lewis looked down at Barker's notes again.

'You served at the naval base in Rostock during the war. What did you do?'

'I was . . . you call it a stenographer.'

'What about your husband? Does he have work?'

'He died at the beginning of the war.'

'I'm sorry . . . it says here you're married . . .'

'Well. I am . . . Until I marry again.'

Lewis raised a hand in apology. 'I understand. Your late husband served in the Luftwaffe.'

'Late . . . you mean dead?'

'Yes.'

'Yes. He died in France. In the first weeks of the war.'

'I'm sorry.' Lewis raised one palm and jiggled his leg impatiently. 'So, Frau Paulus. There are hundreds of German women applying for the job of interpreter. Why should I choose you?'

Ursula gave him a curious smile. 'A girl has to keep warm.'

Lewis smiled at her honest answer. He made a cursory move to check something in the files of the other two women, but it was a token gesture. He had made up his mind. He would have to interview the other candidates, but neither of them would overturn the decision he had already made. It was partly the pressing need to get on and his allergic reaction to sitting behind a desk, but Frau Paulus had won him over before he'd even managed to assess the quality of her English or her suitability for the job. He needed to be around people who exuded such uncomplaining grace. And he wanted to know about those boots – their provenance, the roads they'd travelled, the experiences had in them. He saw himself – later, in his car perhaps – asking her about them and her telling him the story of how she had walked from Rügen Island to Hamburg to escape the Russians. He reached over to one of the freshly delivered boxes containing questionnaires, took one and handed it to her.

'It's mandatory that you complete one of these. I apologize for the silliness of some of the questions.' He then took something else from a drawer in his desk: a booklet of

British Armed Forces vouchers. He tore away two and handed them to her.

'Use those to purchase some new shoes.' She took them tentatively, as though unsure of his intentions; perhaps it was a test.

'Please,' Lewis encouraged. 'A governor's interpreter must look the part.'

And, with this, Ursula lost her poise; she sighed as though releasing a long-held breath and then, reaching across the desk, she took Lewis's hand, clasped it in her two and thanked him, spontaneously in German, and then, remembering herself, in English:

'Thank you, Colonel. Thank you.'

'Tommy, Russki, Yankee, French. Tommy, Russki, Yankee, French.
'Every day they take our things,
'And every day we smell the stench
'Of Tommy, Russki, Yankee, French.
'Tommy, Russki, Yankee, French!'

The ferals sang the ditty, beginning softly then building in a crescendo to an almost spat-vomited 'French!' They sang less from defiance than from a need to distract themselves from the creeping cold. This time, the song petered out after two rounds.

Ozi sat on a suitcase and tossed a hymn book on to the bonfire. As it flared from green to blue to orange the ferals shifted closer to the edge of the fire in the crater in order to receive its weak heat. Ozi was thinking about what to say. They were tired of moving, moving, moving, but that was what they were going to have to do.

The abandoned church had been their home since they'd left the Tierpark Hagenbeck, where they'd lived, undiscovered, for three months in the cave beneath the artificial crag of the monkey-rock exhibit. God's broken homes were safe places to hole up, but they had their limitations. The Christuskirche had a hole in the roof where a bomb had entered and a car-sized crater in the chancel. The great pock was a natural place to set a fire and they had been profligate with the hardwood pews and, since the cold snap, had started burning books, beginning with the sacred texts around them. Books made good kindling but poor fuel, flaring up quickly and brightly but giving off a thin heat. Dietmar had come back with *The Complete Works of Walter Scott*, found in the old university library, in a wheelbarrow, but they'd got through them in just a few hours. A million words to keep five children warm for just one night! Now there was nothing left to burn. Ozi watched the last pages of praise flake to black and float up into the vault above and decided to make his move. He clapped his hands.

'Listen. Tomorrow we will go down to the Elbchaussee. There are houses there by the river, where the top-brass Tommies live. Houses with lawns running down to the river; houses with a bathroom for each person. Tommy takes all the nice houses, but he isn't filling every one. Sometimes he puts a sign outside the house saying "Requisition", but it's empty until the Tommy family comes. And sometimes they don't come and the house stays empty and they forget that no one's there. Berti's found a house he says we can move into soon.'

'I like it here, in God's house,' Otto maintained. 'We are safe here. And no one tells us what to do.'

'We can't stay here any more,' Ozi insisted. 'You're keeping me awake with your shivering. We'll go and find ourselves a fat banker's house with chairs and beds and gold taps. We'll each have our own bath. Baths big enough for the water to cover your knees. Not like Hammerbrook, where we used to

76

hear old Langermaid farting in his tub next door. Then, when we've found a house, we will go and swindle all those refugees from Poland and Prussia in the DP camps. Those fuckers are so desperate they will do anything. They are all looking for papers and work and food. We can do a good trade with them. Pretty soon we will be millionaires and buy our own mansion by the river.'

'What if we don't find an empty house?' Otto asked.

'Then we get the scraps from Tommy's top table.' Ozi drew in an impatient breath. 'Ernst? Are you in?'

Ernst nodded.

'Siegfried?'

Siegfried raised his hand.

'Dietmar, are you in?'

Dietmar was not listening. He was running his fingers over the filigree on a collapsed and cracked reredos depicting the sequence of Jesus's life in four scenes: nativity, baptism, crucifixion, resurrection. He stroked the carved white granite, trying to decipher the story being told in the cold stone. He was wearing an inflated life-jacket, with whistle and torch dangling, and he used the torch to examine the work more closely. The piece had become detached from the altar by the blast and had crashed to the floor, splitting right through. Ozi needed Dietmar's approval. Despite being severely 'fire-brained' and given to repetitive, circuitous ramblings, Dietmar was useful. He looked older than the rest of them and knew his way around the city.

'Didi?'

Dietmar was still preoccupied with the religious artefact. 'What is this meant to be?' he asked, tracing his finger over the figure of Jesus.

'That's Jesus the Christ,' Otto said. 'The saviour of the world.'

There was a half-reverential, half-uncertain silence.

Dietmar shone his weak light on the baptism scene. 'Why does he have a bird on his head?' He started to rock on his haunches. 'Why is it there?'

Dietmar had to have an answer and, as his leader, it was important Ozi give him one. Ozi looked at the dove hovering over the semi-submerged saviour. Confused fragments of related stories, planted in his mind by his mother, combined to form an answer.

'Jesus lived in a boat with loads of animals. But he really liked birds. Especially sparrows.'

Dietmar had moved on to Jesus on the cross, and was greatly agitated by it.

'Why are they killing him?' Dietmar asked. 'Why are they killing him?'

'Calm it, Didi! It's not real.'

'Why are they killing him? Why?'

'He was a Jew,' Siegfried said.

'He was a Jew. He was a Jew,' Dietmar repeated, and this seemed to placate him for a moment. 'He was a Jew. He talked to animals. He lived in a boat.'

'My father gave me a German name, not a Christian name,' said Siegfried. 'He said Christians are weak.'

'Is Tommy Christian?' Ernst asked.

'Tommy believes in demockery. And the King of Vindsor,' Ozi said definitively, wanting to move on.

'How can we trust Tommy?' Siegfried objected. 'One minute he's killing us; the next he's handing out choccies.'

'Enough of this bibble-babble!' Ozi said, his voice croaking with frustration. The smoke and dust he'd inhaled during the firestorm had left him with weakened lungs and a strange, husky whisper of a voice. Tommy had razed his home to the ground and incinerated his neighbours, but breathing in the dust of the vaporized dead had left him with an unexpected asset: a rasping growl that seemed to frighten kids into obeying him and to amuse or appal adults into giving him things. He now stood on top of his suitcase. 'I know – better than any of you – what Tommy's Heavy Angels did when they made the great fireball. I saw it, and my eyes nearly boiled in my head with the watching of it. That is a picture in my head that I don't even have to go to the Einplatz to pay for. I can see walls of houses falling with pictures still on them, I can see a piano flying through the air and splitting with a kwangtingle, pages of books. It's all in my head. Sometimes the pictures just come out on top of my day – when I haven't asked them to. But I don't want that picture. There are other pictures now. Like Henry Five and Oz Wizard. And Tommy isn't so bad. I know he drives fat, useless cars. But he has some good things to share. We don't have to pretend to be happy, like before. Stand up, sit down and salute every four seconds. Now you can say what you like, without some crony blowing your head off or reporting you. This is called demockery. And Tommy jokes about anything. Even the Führer's balls.'

Ernst laughed loudly, but the others looked at each other. Even now, this seemed a blasphemy too far.

Ozi jumped off his suitcase and stood upright. 'I'm not hanging around here. Let's go.'

'I don't want to go,' Otto said. 'I like God's house.'

'Look, Otto,' Ozi said. 'You can stay if you want, but we're going to get a mansion with a bloody bath and a bloody bed so soft you'd think you were in heaven anyway. I am done with holes in the ground. I am through with zoos. And churches. Soon we will be living like the Kaiser himself.'

Otto was just about ready to be carried by Ozi's prophecy.

Ozi jumped down on to the last embers of the fire and stamped them dead.

'Who's coming with me?'

Ernst was the first to stand.

Siegfried pulled on his hat and said: 'Let's go and have a bloody bath.'

Dietmar finally looked up from the reredos and completed the new liturgy: 'Let's go and have a bloody bath.'

5

As autumn became winter, Rachael felt the shortening days dragging out. With Lewis hard at work all day and a staff performing chores she'd usually do herself, there was little for her to do and too much time in which to do it. As if anticipating this, Lewis had encouraged her to take up the piano again. 'I miss hearing you play,' he'd said, adding that it would 'do her good'. He'd always shown genuine enthusiasm for her playing and, in a blindly loyal way, thought her better than she was; but she knew that what he really wanted was for her to take her mind off 'unhelpful things'. And so, every morning, while Edmund had his tuition with Herr Koenig, the teacher that Lewis had found at one of the refugee camps, she went and played the mini concert Bösendorfer.

Having such a lovely instrument at her disposal should have been a boon, but it was not as straightforward as that. She had not played any piano since Michael's death. Her elder son had been a very able pupil and she associated the piano with him more than anyone else. He had always been hovering at the old Norbeck upright (bought at a great stretch by Lewis on his measly subaltern's wage), asking her again and again to play and sing Schubert's spooky 'Earl King', with its threatening, insistent note and tragic arc, its story of the sickly boy asking his father to ride faster because he is convinced that the Earl King is coming to claim his life.

She'd started with something light which she knew by heart – 'The Girl with the Flaxen Hair' by Debussy. She managed to get halfway through then stopped. The overtones were too much. She lay her forehead on the rim of the lid and tried to recompose herself. She needed new music. How had Lewis put it that first day, at the Atlantic Hotel? 'This country needs a new song.' She dived into the piano stool for tunes without any associative baggage. The double seat was full of loose-sheet scores: a Bach prelude (too familiar), a deceptively tricky Chopin nocturne (too melancholy) and even her favourite Beethoven sonata – his last (too difficult). The head of every score was inscribed with an inked signature: 'C. Lubert'. If the previous lady of the house had played all she'd inscribed, she must have been more than a parlour-room player, for no one with less than formidable technique would tackle these pieces for amusement. The idea piqued both a curiosity and a competitive response in Rachael; she formed a quick mental picture of Claudia Lubert sitting there at the piano, playing (of course) Beethoven's ethereal and complex 32nd Sonata to a roomful of what Rachael imagined constituted high German society: bohemians, artists, poets and architects, alongside high-booted military. Of course, in this idealized image, the phantom rival was perfect: Claudia Lubert a brilliant and refined player, all balance, passion and restraint. And perfectly modest in the way she received the rapturous applause. The detail of the scene was full in every way, except for the face of its heroine.

Rachael settled on a short composition by Schumann entitled '*Warum?*' She didn't know the piece, but she was a good sight-reader, quick to learn. Her parents' rickety upright had offered free, swift transport to far from parochial worlds. She might have made the piano her vocation, but marriage, children and the war had limited her development to Christmas and birthday singalongs and the odd parlour-room performance at drinks parties. This piece looked interesting. It was slow and airy enough to find an easy way in, and once she'd got beyond simply grasping the tune she encountered a composition with depth in the pauses and a yearning draw in its melody. It was like coming across a small but very deep lake, and she dived into it, playing it over and over, like a keen schoolgirl cramming for an exam, determined to master it and, ultimately, losing herself in it. For the first time in months, she felt the meaning of things coursing through her veins. She'd found unexpected medicine in playing; it hadn't just taken her mind off unhelpful things; she'd managed to forget herself.

One afternoon, in the first week of November, Rachael went to put in an hour's practice before Lewis got home. As she approached the drawing room, she could hear someone playing her 'new tune' – badly. She entered the room and found Herr Lubert, dressed in his blue overalls, hunched over the keys, playing the Schumann piece with the intense concentration of someone whose determination must make up for lack of talent. He played ploddingly, with far too much loud pedal. And his usually handsome face was made gormless by the effort.

'Herr Lubert?'

He was trying so hard not to make a mistake he did not hear her at first.

Rachael moved to the space within the lifted lid where he could not fail to see her, and repeated his name, louder.

'Herr Lubert!'

Lubert jumped with the surprise of it, put up his offending hands by way of apology. He scraped the piano stool on the oak floor as he abruptly stood up, closing the lid over the keys.

'*Bitte verzeihen Sie mir*, Frau Morgan.' It was the first time she had heard him speak German. 'I should have asked. Forgive me, Frau Morgan.'

83

Rachael wasn't sure what to say, and in the second's silence that followed she self-consciously adjusted her hair.

'I always used to do my half-hour practice,' he said. 'It is an old habit . . . hard to die.'

She thought about correcting his mistake but did not want to encourage him. Lubert, however, continued in his familiar way:

'I play very badly. No matter how I practise. Terrible, I know. But it helps me . . . I don't play to get better. Just to . . . remember and forget. I have heard that you play very well. Your son tells me that you are an excellent player.'

Even in their few, terse exchanges, she had sensed Herr Lubert lowering hooks and baiting her with questions and, although she wanted to answer him, she retreated to her original position just behind the lines of their original treaty.

'I thought we had agreed on certain boundaries, Herr Lubert.'

'Yes. I am sorry. I meant to come and ask you first. But I came home from the factory early today. There was a protest. I needed to forget the day but I ended up forgetting myself. I am sorry, Frau Morgan.' And he looked at her with a crinkled brow that moved between impertinent and inquisitive. She could not decide.

Again, he stepped into her uncertain silence.

'"Morgan". I have been wondering if this a common name in England?'

'It's Welsh,' she said, nibbling the bait.

'Wales,' he reflected. 'I've heard that it is a small but beautiful country.'

'It was big enough to get bombed.'

How irksome it was finding herself caught up in playing this role – one of a number of roles she felt herself reluctantly playing with people: the Grieving Mother, the Distant

Wife and now the Curt Occupier. This last role was the one she had to do most to affect, and Lubert didn't seem convinced by it – or even to notice it. He simply brushed off her quip with an understanding nod, leaving her to blush at her own put-down and the good grace with which he took it.

'I will talk to Colonel Morgan about letting you use the piano,' she said, in as conciliatory a tone as she could muster.

'Thank you, Frau Morgan . . . I would be very grateful.' And he smiled with what seemed like sincere gratitude.

'I see that your wife played?' Rachael asked, indicating the signatures on the top music sheets.

'Claudia had many talents . . . She –' Lubert broke off. The mention of his wife stumbled him. His guard dropped and the perky arrogance evaporated. 'She was completely tone-deaf. Her mother was the pianist.'

The news came as a relief to Rachael but, in bursting the illusion of Lubert's perfectly brilliant wife, it further piqued her curiosity. The way he spoke of her and the expression in his eyes when he did, the hesitation between words . . .

'I was wondering what the name of this piece meant? "– *Var-um?*" Is it "Why?"'

The pronunciation as well as the question were a concession. Until now, she had stubbornly refused to convert the native 'W's to sound as 'V's.

'It doesn't translate exactly. It is "why?" But it is more "Why did this happen? For what reason?" Something like this, I think.'

'It's . . . lovely.'

'It is . . . sublime.'

Rachael nodded in agreement. It was heavenly. Somehow, 'utter'. But, like a traveller suddenly realizing they've strayed too far up an unmapped road into unknown territory, Rachael looked to her inner compass and checked her step.

'I will talk to Colonel Morgan,' she said. And, with that, she made a little bow and withdrew from the room.

Edmund ran his hand along the spines of the books in the library, whole worlds at the tips of his fingers. He wasn't looking for a book to read – touching was enough for now – he was just getting the measure of his new playground. With its spacious and arcane rooms, science-fiction furniture and unpredictable encounters, the house provided him with all the stories and incident he needed. Indeed, it was less a home and more a living, organic set for a drama in which he was the lead player; while his mother trod like a nervous stand-in, Edmund, with his sidekick, Cuthbert, went from room to room like the protagonist in a mystery he was destined to solve.

Frieda was the obvious antagonist on this stage, and her actions, rather than repelling him, only added to her allure. The image of that initial encounter on the stairs – the glimpse of something he didn't understand but wanted to see more of – drew him to the foot of the Luberts' staircase in the hope that he might. The gift of her full chamber pot seemed like a warning, but also an invitation. It should have disgusted him, alerted him to a danger (he wondered if he should report her behaviour to his parents), but he knew it was leading him somewhere interesting, like a rickety bridge across a ravine to an exotic, dense jungle full of secret smells and sounds. Even her piss, filling the Delft bowl, had smelt mysterious; it had made an intriguing sound as he poured it down the toilet.

'Is there a particular book you are looking for?'

Herr Lubert had entered the room on his way to the drawing room, still dressed in his blue overalls. If Frieda was Edmund's adversary, then the twinkling Herr Lubert was his surprising ally. He did not seem to possess any of

86

the German characteristics outlined so authoritatively in the guide. He was not haughty or proud, just confident and friendly; he was not serious or saturnine, he had a lightness; and his expression – sparkly eyes, flaring nostrils and upturned mouth – was always on the cusp of laughter. In fact, in the past few weeks, Edmund had found he liked this German; he seemed genuinely interested, wanting to know all about Wales ('What is this country like?'), life during the war ('Was your father away for long?'), even asking if his mother was settling in ('I hope she is able to feel at home here'). And he knew things. The last time he had met him in the hall, Herr Lubert had pointed out that the red-coated tin soldiers he was playing with on the staircase were models of the troops sent by the Anglo-Germanic King George III to fight the rebel Americans.

'I was just looking,' Edmund said. 'Are they all in German?'

'Most. But some are in English. The children's books especially. You are welcome to read any of the books here. And, if you look hard enough, you'll find a secret chamber.' Herr Lubert adopted a conspiratorial air, checked over his shoulders for maid or mother then ran a finger along the second tier of shelving, stopping at a book halfway along. He pulled it out and showed Edmund the cover. It depicted a charcoal sketch of four figures on a rickety wagon escaping some unseen trouble and was called *Vom Winde verweht*.

'*Gone with the Wind*,' he said. 'This was my wife's favourite book.' He paused and became sad and reflective for a moment. It reminded Edmund of his mother drifting away, but Herr Lubert quickly recovered himself and continued.

'We saw this movie in the first years of the war. She did not like it as much as the book. We had an argument about this. But I loved it very much. Clark Gable. "I don't give a damn!"'

87

Edmund didn't know the line, but he liked the fact that Lubert could do an American accent and say 'damn' with so much pleasure and style.

'You have seen this movie?'

'My mother has seen it,' Edmund said. 'She saw it with my aunt.'

'It is a very exciting movie. Your mother reminds me of the actress Vivien Leigh a little. Anyway. Look at the gap there.' He pointed to the space left on the shelf, reached into it and pulled out a colourful box of Cuban cigars. He then pushed it back in and replaced the book.

'Don't tell anyone. Not even my wife knew about this space. Men have to have their secrets.'

Later, Edmund was helping his mother check the crockery, which had finally arrived, a month late, and lay spread across the dining-room table like the model of a futuristic city. He'd just finished counting off the sage-green dinner service, impressing and unsettling his mother by getting all the way to twelve in confident and correct German. She was halfway through counting out the cutlery, relieved that it had come and that she wouldn't have to take up Herr Lubert's offer of using his admittedly fine solid-silver service in the interim.

'Mother. What does Vivien Leigh look like?'

'Vivien Leigh?'

'Is she pretty?'

'Why do you ask that?'

'Because Herr Lubert said that you look like her.'

Edmund shared this in the hope that it would soften his mother towards the former master of the house, but for some reason it made her blush and prickle. Perhaps Vivien Leigh was ugly.

'When were you – or rather – *why* were you talking to Herr Lubert?'

'He was just . . . showing me some things.'

'What things?'

'Some . . . toys and some books.'

'You mustn't encourage him, Edmund. It only makes things awkward if you are too familiar.'

'But he seems very nice . . . He –'

'Just because someone seems nice, it doesn't mean that they are,' Rachael said. 'You must be careful not to talk too much to him, or his daughter. It will create resentment.'

Edmund nodded. He certainly wasn't going to mention his visceral parleys with Frieda. If his mother was unsettled by the affability of Herr Lubert, she would surely explode at the antics of his underwear-flashing, pisspot-proffering daughter.

'Can I go and play in the garden?'

'All right. But don't wander too far. And put your jumper on. It's cold outside.'

On his way out Edmund ran into Heike, who had been trying to flit unnoticed between floors on phantom feet. *'Guten Morgen, kleine Mädchen,'* he said as she bustled by, trying out a combination of just-learned words. He liked these German words: they were honest, precise and, when strung together, they had a percussive music.

Heike curtsied before resuming her passage upstairs, greatly amused by something.

Edmund entered the conservatory and went out through the French windows. He ran across the lawn to the lush, evergreen rhododendron that formed the natural boundary of the grounds. The plant was three times his height and large enough to contain a world within itself, a mature tangle of criss-crossing pathways. Its late flowers were just past their fullness and passing into their annual death, but still showy enough to conjure a credible jungle, and Edmund pushed into its undergrowth like a Pizarro or a Cortés, beating back the branches with imaginary cutlass, losing himself in this fantasy, until he came to a wire-mesh fence – the man-made boundary of the property.

A rough meadow stretched out before him with the river to one side, a reminder both of their seclusion from and proximity to the war's brutal consequences. The field was scarred with stubble and bare patches of earth. Some stables and chicken coops had been converted into shanty homes at its far end. By these shacks he could see figures – they looked like children – standing around a small bonfire. And in the middle of the meadow stood a scrawny, motionless donkey with a distended belly.

Edmund jumped the fence and walked across the field to get a better look at the animal. Even as he got close, it remained dead still, untwitching, tail limp. Its neck was blotched with sores and it barely seemed to have the strength to support its head; its overpronounced bones looked as if they were going to burst through its tired hide. 'Poor donkey,' Edmund said, and his eyes watered at the creature's hopeless state and matching expression. He was surprised at his tears. He had not shed them even for his own brother, and here he was weeping for the least of beasts, and a German one at that – although he wasn't sure if animals had a nationality. He reached into his pocket and pulled out a sugar lump that he'd taken from the kitchen when Greta was somewhere upstairs. He held it under the donkey's mouth, but not even sugar could raise a response.

'*Mein Mittagessen!*'

Edmund turned towards the sound of the shout and was confronted by the mad spectre of a boy wearing a Russian

Cossack hat and a dressing gown marching towards him and speaking German in a croaky, rasping voice. Other children followed a few yards behind him.

'*Finger weg!*' the boy shouted. He had an aggressive tone but Edmund didn't feel threatened; there was something comic and affected about his manner: it was all a bit of an act for his gang. '*Das ist mein Mittagessen!*' he repeated, and Edmund pulled his hand back from beneath the donkey's mouth. The other children came and stood at the shoulder of their mad-hatted leader, who was now circling Edmund, sniffing the air around him. The children were dressed in an array of clothing that looked as though it had been hastily grabbed from the dressing room of a vaudeville troupe. Edmund felt suddenly conspicuous in his perfectly normal clothes – brown Oxfords, woollen knee-socks, grey shorts, Viyella shirt and V-neck jumper – and the gang started to circle and stroke him. One of them, a boy wearing an inflated life-jacket, even bent down and touched Edmund's shining toecap then poked him in the ribs, like the advance party of an ancient civilization sent to make contact with a future being to test that it was real.

'*Englisch?*' the leader asked.

'Yes,' Edmund replied, and they all stopped at the sound of his one-word reply.

'Yes!' the mad-hatted leader repeated, trying to emulate Edmund's clean enunciation.

'Yes!' the feral children repeated.

'Fuck my arse, Captain!' the boy suddenly said.

Edmund was astonished at the boy's brazen use of words he knew to be prohibited. He wanted to laugh, but checked himself.

'Damn bloody hell fuck-bastard and kunts! You are fucking dumb bloody Hun scum fuck!' The boy continued to lob English expletives as if they were grenades. He then pointed

at Edmund to respond to – correct, even – his pronunciation. 'You. Tommy . . .You do "bloody hell!" You.'

'Bloody hell,' Edmund said, delighting in saying it and in
the response it garnered. A chorus of 'bloody hell's came
back from the gang, and there was a concentrated attempt by
their leader to get it exactly right:

'Blood-ee . . . hell! Blood-ee hell. More "blood-ee hell",
bitte!'

'Bloody hell,' Edmund said. 'Bloody hell and . . . piss . . .
and . . . shit and bugger!'

'Piss *und* shit! Piss *und* shit! *Und* bugger!'

Edmund nodded, approving the pronunciation. The cultural exchange seemed to be going well, and everyone relaxed.
The leader beamed, but the boy in the life-jacket wanted
more than swear words and continued to circle Edmund,
stroking the Shetland-wool jumper with a covetous leer and
muttering words Edmund couldn't hear. The leader snapped
at Lifebuoy:

'Didi! *Lass ihn in Ruhe!*' He pointed at him then waved him
away. But Lifebuoy either couldn't stop or didn't hear because
he started to tug at Edmund's jumper, and, although Edmund
tried to bat his hand off, the boy kept his scrawny, desperate grip, stretching the jumper out of shape as Edmund tried
to pull himself away. Then, not quite sure of his move,
Edmund grabbed the boy's shoulders and the back of the
inflated life-jacket and lifted him off the ground with an ease
that both shocked and inspired him. For a few seconds, he
held the boy aloft, turning him in the air, before dropping
him and pushing him away in one movement. The moment
Lifebuoy landed, he launched himself back at Edmund,
making a low, gurgling sound and, curling his fingers into
talons, he started to paw at Edmund's face with his cracked,
dirty nails. The other children formed an amphitheatre

around them and were cheering, shouting and even growling. Lifebuoy grabbed Edmund around his neck and tried to pull his head into a lock, but he had no power, only a quickly dissipating nervous energy, and Edmund easily got on top of him and pinned him to the ground, his knee pressing down on his chest. Lifebuoy twisted and wriggled and spat, but he couldn't get to Edmund. Around them, the jeering escalated into a frenzy with cries of '*Bring ihn um*' And Edmund saw that these children weren't cheering their own, they were cheering him, demanding with their cries and stabbing gestures that he finish him off. Lifebuoy stopped wriggling. Spent or resigned, he lay there ready to accept whatever Edmund dished out. '*Bring ihn um*' the children called, and Edmund knew what this word meant without needing it translated. The leader stepped forward and gave Edmund a stick with which to deal the final blow. Edmund took it out of politeness, but he wasn't going to use it. Instead, he lifted his knee from the stricken boy and stood back as he crawled away to jeers from his supposed friends.

The leader looked at Edmund with amused admiration as he brushed the dust off his shorts. 'Good Tommy,' he said. 'Fucking good Tommy. *Ich heisse Ozi,*' he said.

Edmund put out a hand: 'Edmund.'

Ozi looked at Edmund's hand, but he didn't take it; he simply stared at it and then started to have a conversation with someone else.

'*Mutti. Er ist in Ordnung. Er ist ein guter Tommy. Er wird mir helfen.*'

He seemed then to wait for a response, some sanction from a guiding spirit, cocking his ear for it then, having apparently received it, he nodded. He spoke to Edmund: 'Good Tommy, get ciggies.' And dragged on an imaginary cigarette and pointed at his own chest. 'Ciggies,' he said again, and rubbed his stomach in anticipation, pointing at the stables where the bonfire burnt and more figures milled. 'You bring. *Das ist mein Haus.*' And then, looking across the field towards the hedged boundary of the Villa Lubert, he asked: '*Ist das dein Haus?*'

Edmund, who didn't have the nuance to explain the intricacies of its ownership, nodded and answered in his own Deutschglish:

'*Das ist* my house.'

Lewis was only half listening when Rachael put the issue of Lubert playing the piano to him during dinner.

'Do you think we should let him play? I'm just not sure. I worry that it will complicate things.'

'Why would it do that?' Lewis asked.

'I don't know. It might send the wrong signal. I don't wish to be mean about it. But if we allow one thing, we end up allowing everything. Perhaps it's healthier for all of us to keep to our separate quarters. Everything in its right place. I don't know.'

I don't know. It was suffix and prefix to her every other thought. This indecision was becoming her signature. But Lewis wasn't helping. Was he even listening? She could see he was preoccupied. Preoccupied with the occupied. His mind was divided into two zones, the larger, and by far more interesting, being his zone of work, with its needy subdivisions. He was fine as long as the other zone – the domestic zone inhabited by her and Edmund, the Luberts, the staff – was able to take care of itself with minimal input from him. She ought to ask him about his day, she knew it was more important than this; but just for now she wanted him to engage with her realm, however small.

'Well?'

'It's up to you, dear. I don't see what harm it can do,' he said.

Rachael looked at him. Was he just being his usual accommodating self? Detecting a fob-off, she continued: 'When do you think would be a good time? Mornings, before he goes to work? Or afternoons? The evening is probably not appropriate.'

Lewis put down his knife and fork, to show he was thinking.

'Let him play for half an hour, at a time that suits you.'

Rachael knew what he was doing. He was playing a game of tennis with someone who needed coaching rather than trouncing. He could have blasted a return past her, but he wanted her to stay in the game so he kept hitting nice, clean returns of serve into the right part of the court, leaving her space to hit back. It was his way of not playing the game at all.

Rachael wondered why it was so difficult. She had left Lubert with the impression that she was happy for him to play. She *was* happy for him to play, wasn't she? And she knew perfectly well that Lewis wouldn't mind. She could have agreed to it there and then, at the piano, without even bothering her husband, so why this constipated rigmarole of bothering him? Why expect him to solve trivial disputes over pianos and plants when he was dealing with people who needed food and clothing? She knew it was unreasonable, but she couldn't help herself.

'Very well. I'll inform Herr Lubert that he can play . . . every afternoon then. At four. For half an hour. An hour.' Just saying it felt like a momentous achievement.

'Good,' Lewis said, with some relief. 'That's fixed then.'

The three of them ate on in silence for a while. Lewis finished first, putting his knife and fork together at six o'clock then dabbing his mouth with a damask napkin. He patted the armrest of his chair.

'It's good to see you've been stamping your personality on the place. These chairs are better than those leather thingies.' He made the kitchen wicker squeak and crack, showing his appreciation. In truth, she'd done very little to change anything, but she let it go.

'How are you finding the staff?' he continued, in that too obviously compensatory way.

'They still look at me as though they don't understand a word I'm saying.'

'Why don't you sit in with Ed's tutor? Pick up a few basics?'

'Oh, I think they understand me perfectly well. They're just choosing not to. At times, I feel they're all laughing at me.'

Lewis didn't comment. He turned to Edmund, who was pushing peas around his plate.

'And how are things with Herr Koenig? *Sehr gut?*'

Rachael poured herself a glass of water to quench her annoyance then started to stack the plates, before remembering that this was now someone else's job.

Edmund, who had finished his meal, was enacting battles of his own: the peas were landing on gravy, forming a beachhead there before pushing on to the mash inland.

'*Sehr gut, Vater.*'

Lewis laughed. 'You've been here a month and you've already got better pronunciation than me.'

'Why am I learning German if we're not allowed to speak to them?' asked Edmund.

'You can speak to them, Ed. In fact, I encourage you to. The better we understand each other, the quicker we'll get things fixed here.'

'How long will it take to fix things?'

Lewis looked at Rachael this time. He needed to calibrate his answer carefully.

'The optimists think ten years. The pessimists think fifty.'

'So, no doubt, you think it'll take five,' she said.

Lewis gave a concessionary smile: she knew him too well. 'So, Ed, have you managed to talk to Frieda yet?'

Edmund shook his head. 'She's a bit older than me.'

'Maybe we should all have a game of canasta or cribbage one evening. Or watch a film on the Ace.'

Heike entered the room, carrying a tray on which to stack the plates. The maid moved with her customary skittishness, trying to get in and out as fast as she could, like a swallow stealing seed under the watch of a farmer.

'Delicious, Fräulein Heike,' Lewis said in German.

'You are delicious, Fräulein Heike,' Edmund parroted, also in German, not realizing his mistake.

Heike stifled a giggle, bowed and collected the plates, pausing at Rachael, who had not eaten more than half of what was on hers.

'*Sind Sie fertig,* Frau Morgan?'

Rachael waved at her to take her plate away.

Edmund watched the maid carry the plates to the dumb waiter and put them in the hatch. Heike then gave a tug on the rope and they were pulleyed down to the kitchen by an invisible hand.

Rachael waited for Heike to leave the room before speaking.

'See? She was doing it then. Smirking.'

'She's just nervous. Half-terrified she's going to make a mistake and lose her job. Any German with a job is on tenterhooks.'

'Why do you insist on defending them all the time?'

Lewis shrugged. By his standards, it was almost an expression of despair. He took out his cigarette case, clicked it open and offered one to Rachael.

She wanted one, but she refused.

'I'll have mine afterwards.'

Lewis tapped the end of the cigarette, put it to his lips, lit it and dragged deeply, shooting the smoke from his nostrils in a relaxed snort.

The squeaking pulleys of the dumb waiter announced the arrival at the hatch of pudding.

'Does it go all the way up to the Luberts' floor?' Edmund asked.

'I don't want you playing with it, Ed,' Rachael said. 'It's not a toy.'

He nodded. 'Will we have servants when we go back to England – like Auntie Clara did?' he asked.

'Only the very rich will be able to afford servants now,' Lewis said.

'But Herr Lubert has servants, and he works in a factory.'

'That's just until he's been cleared. Once he's been cleared, he can go back to being an architect.'

'Cleared?' Rachael asked.

'Of . . . having any Nazi affiliations.'

'He hasn't been cleared of that already?'

'I'm sure it's a formality.'

'Well, I thought you'd at least check first. '

'Lubert is clean. Don't worry about it.'

'But you don't know that.'

'Barker did the extra background check. I'd never have let him stay here if there had been the slightest hint of anything nasty. Rachael . . . Please.'

Edmund decided to use this moment to say goodnight. This was one of those conversations where Grown-Ups needed Children out of the way.

'May I get down now?' he asked.

'Yes. Of course,' Rachael answered.

Edmund kissed her; his father ruffled his hair.

'Don't do anything I wouldn't do,' he said.

As Edmund left the room, he could hear his parents picking up on their unresolved conflict, their voices rising and falling with those strained sounds of pleading and justification they sometimes made. A parental argument was perfect cover. He went upstairs to his room to get Cuthbert, found a pencil and paper in his desk then took them to the hatch of the dumb waiter on the first-floor landing, just outside his parents' bedroom. He lifted its sliding door to reveal the single rope dangling in the recess of the shaft that ran between the three levels of the house. He tugged it and, a few moments later, the lift came up from the kitchen. He lay Cuthbert on the platform, scribbled a note and tucked it under the grenadier's bearskin.

'Find all the sugar you can, Captain, and bring it back to base.'

'Are you sure this is allowed, sir?'

'Do as I say, Cuthbert, there's a good fellow. We'll meet at 2000 hours in the basement. Keep an eye out for Grown-Ups along the way.'

'Yes, Colonel.'

Edmund pulled the rope and, after a few seconds, Cuthbert descended. Edmund closed the sliding door and tiptoed downstairs to the kitchen, keeping to the carpet runners to muffle his tread.

In the kitchen, he found Heike rolling dough and singing along to a song playing on the radio; the song was being sung in English by a husky-voiced, foreign-sounding woman and Heike was taking great delight in imitating the singer's low growl.

'*Guten Abend*, Fräulein Heike.'

The maid yelped at Edmund's surprise entrance then acted as though she had been caught listening to enemy transmissions, switching off the radio and wiping her hands on her apron.

'*Guten Abend*, Herr Edmund.'

Edmund went straight to the hatch. He lifted the gate, took the note from under Cuthbert and handed it to Heike. She looked at it and read it aloud: '*Zucker?*'

'*Bitte.*'

Heike made a pretence of disapproval but was happy to play the game. She went to the larder and came back with three sugar lumps. She put them on a plate and, understanding his game, put the plate in the hatch, next to the cloth soldier. Edmund gave Cuthbert his orders:

'Take the supplies back to base, Captain.'

'Yes, Colonel.'

He tugged the rope, closed the hatch, thanked Heike and ran back up the stairs to greet the returning hero. When he arrived at the first-floor hatch he slid the door back, but the platform was not there. He pulled the rope again and waited, but there was no movement. He tugged yet again and waited. Still nothing. He ventured putting his head in the hatch to look down. There was nothing but black below. Twisting his head to look up, he saw that the underside of the lift had stopped at the hatch a floor above, at the Luberts' apartments. Perhaps Herr Lubert had intercepted the transport and thought the sugar was for him. No matter. Edmund was happy for the Luberts to have it. They needed the calories. He retracted his head from the shaft, pulled the rope one more time and this time there was movement: the lift began to descend. The rope vibrated and the platform made a squeaking trundle as it came down. When it came into view and stopped at the hatch, Edmund immediately saw that something was wrong: Cuthbert's head was missing. He took the decapitated torso from the platform and examined it. White wool and yellow stuffing hung out of the gape where the head used to be. His head might have got caught in the lift – it had always been slightly loose – and come off in the shaft, but the physics of this didn't seem right. It was only then that Edmund noticed that the sugar on the plate had gone.

Lewis undressed slowly, waiting for a signal, a sign from Rachael that tonight they might make love. He stood in his walk-in dressing room in his trousers and removed his shirt, button by button, pausing to look at something on his cuff, pretending that there was a thread of loose cotton there, eking out the seconds to allow time for Rachael to call it. There had been a time when this subtle dance wasn't needed, when she instigated as much as he did and asking was easy; but now this whole business suddenly required an ability to interpret and understand the nuances of a dialect Lewis had not spoken for over a year.

He pulled off his shirt and stood there stripped from the waist up. It was rare that they made love once they'd put on their nightclothes. If he rushed too quickly into his pyjamas, she would take this as a cue to shut up shop for the night. The opportunity had to be seized in that moment of undressing, or just before it, when one of them – usually him – would suggest they have a moment. It made making love in winter more of a struggle. Rachael felt the cold easily and, after their first years of marriage, did not usually linger long between day- and nightclothes; although the room was warm – indeed, the whole house was easily kept at a temperature that belied the cold outside – he had to strike before the air between them chilled too much. His defence of the giggling maid and then the issue of Lubert's undecided status had upset her, but he was determined. This drought had to end. He must make his move.

She was at the dressing table and down to her camisole, pulling her hair back with one hand and taking off her make-up with the other. Lewis watched her perform her routine ablutions, her bare arms and straight, petite shoulders tormenting him with their loveliness.

'Are we going to . . .' His voice trailed off.

Rachael had opened one of the small drawers in the dressing table and found a necklace of interlinked garnets which clinked and crackled as she held them up to the bedside light.

'This must have belonged to . . . her.'

She held the cold stones across her throat and then across the span of her hand, feeling the weight of them. 'They're pretty.'

'Darling? Aren't we going to do this . . .?' He said it with more purpose, more force than usual. Had they not once made vows to honour one another's bodies? He was prepared to use this line if she refused him now.

Rachael put the necklace down and dropped a soiled cotton dab into the waste-paper basket. 'Do you have a thingy?' Her expression was neutral, giving a hint neither of desire nor distaste. But it was enough. He immediately felt himself stirring. Faint with the anticipation of it, he rummaged in his kit box for the regulation prophylactics issued along with cigarettes to all servicemen across Germany. A soldier's every appetite and addiction catered for.

Lewis saw Rachael stand and slide under the sheets in her camisole. Still no suggestion of excitement or even anticipation in her movements, but he didn't care. He tore off a contraceptive from the strip of six and walked towards the bed, his erection already pushing at his trousers. He sat on the bed with his back to her, hoping she hadn't noticed, and pulled off his socks, trying to calm himself.

Rachael leant over to his side of the bed and picked up his silver cigarette case.

'Did you think of me when you smoked?' she asked.

'Sixty times a day.'

'You don't have to say that.'

'It's true. I worked it out. We were apart for 32,000 cigarettes,' he said.

'And when you thought of me, what did you think about?'

'Mostly?' He gave her the honest answer. 'This moment now.'

Rachael looked at him with surprise. 'Do you have it ready?'

He bit the metallic wrapping and pulled the condom out, placing it on the pillow while he pulled his trousers and undergarments off. Rachael put the cigarette case back and sat up to pull her camisole over her head and shoulders. Even this half-glimpsed, perfunctory movement was exquisite to him. He slipped under the sheet, still hiding himself, feeling vulnerable and uncertain. She lay on her side facing him, head propped on her elbow. Once they were naked together, all the assuredness and confidence transferred from him to her. It was as if he slipped down the ranks from colonel to private while she rose to field marshal.

Rachael picked up the rubber sheath.

'Shall I put it on for you?'

Lewis couldn't answer. He nodded, but as she reached for him under the sheet he intercepted her hand with his and drew her towards him to kiss her. He wanted to slow things down, needed to slow things down. He was well ahead of himself. They kissed, but her lips remained pursed, unopening. She withdrew to continue with her task, pulling back the sheet to sheathe him. Lewis lay back to let her, trying to focus on the ceiling above with its rippled cornicing, anything to avoid getting there too soon, but even the mechanical movements of her first, cold touch were too much to bear and he ejaculated, emitting a gasp of pleasure, relief and despair all in one go.

'Ah! Arrived too soon. I'm sorry.'

'It's all right,' Rachael said.

'I'm sorry,' he repeated.

'You got off at Fratton.'

'Barely left Waterloo.'

Rachael's apparent lack of disappointment added to Lewis's own. He was annoyed at himself. His innate discipline and patience had deserted him when he had most needed it. And the mention of Fratton (the last station before Portsmouth) only reminded him of a time when their desire had always got the better of their common sense.

He grabbed the hand towel beside him and dried himself.

'It's been too long. I'm not used to –'

'It's all right.' And Rachael touched his face, soothing his brow.

'I –'

'Shhh. It's perfectly understandable.'

'What about you?' he asked.

'I'm fine.'

'Are you sure?'

'Yes. I'm fine. But cold.' And she sat up, extracted her nightie from beneath the pillow and started to pull it on.

Lewis sat up and swung his legs to the floor, his disappointment already fading. Even this truncated satisfaction was better than none. The release had broken up the pent-up, colic irritation he'd felt these last few weeks. By the time he was dressed in his pyjamas and lying under the sheets with the lights out, his mind had already returned to the zone where he felt safest and more effective: to the less complicated needs of a thousand faceless Germans and the rehabilitation of a country.

Long after Lewis had fallen asleep, Rachael lay, as she always did, on her left side, listening to her heartbeat. She stared at the glittering mound of the garnet necklace at her bedside, catching the light from the half-open curtain. She resolved to return it to Lubert as soon as possible, although this had as much to do with curiosity as propriety. The fact was she wanted to know more about the woman who had once worn it. The necklace had triggered a sequence of sparkling scenes in her mind in which Frau Lubert starred. And while this imagined Frau was graceful and elegant in each vignette, her visage remained imprecise and generic, no more than a composite of cosmopolitan elegance. Rachael wanted to put a face to the image. She almost needed to have a picture in her mind in order to dismiss it. Perhaps Lubert would settle the issue by showing her a photograph. Something. Under the guise of being friendly and fair, she would be able to settle a matter that had been nagging at her since her arrival in the house.

'So, where do you live?' Albert asked Frieda.

They were queuing for the truck, having come to the end of a long shift clearing the remains of a demolished school in St Pauli. Frieda had worked hard and kept her head down all day. Thanks to Albert, what had begun to feel humiliating and punitive had become something to look forward to – even enjoyable.

'On the Elbchaussee, near the Jenischpark.'

'One of the big houses?'

She nodded, unsure if this was good or bad.

'So you are from a rich family?'

Frieda shrugged. 'Not any more.'

'But you still live in your house?'

She nodded again, embarrassed at this line of questioning; dreading having to explain her current circumstances.

'I live not far from you,' he said.

'Whereabouts?' she asked, relieved that her social status had not put him off.

'I'll show you if you like.'

The Rubble Runners in the back of the truck were made up of middle-class Hamburgers and the flotsam and jetsam of workers drifting in from the east. The women, their hair tied up in tight turbans and dressed in the outsized overcoats of dead husbands, resembled fishwives from Landungsbrücken. They were just as pungent, too. The men were numerically inconspicuous and, apart from Albert, middle-aged. All of them, whatever their former status, clutched the food vouchers received in payment for their day's work, which had become the sole object of their ambition.

Frieda sat next to Albert, their legs touching, both of them listening to the chorus of complaints around them. Today's moaning was led by an effete-looking man who wanted everyone to know his true profession.

'It is impossible to stay warm doing this work. First we get hot and sweat and then the sweat turns cold and clammy.'

'At least we are getting paid,' one of the women retorted.

'I'm a dentist. I have a profession. I'm not made for this kind of work.'

'What's so special about pulling teeth?' the lady came back at him. 'Magda here is a general's wife. And I was a radio announcer at the concert hall.'

The dentist, whose face was ashen from dust and disappointment, had the will to complain but not to argue. Arguing required energy. 'I'm just saying, that's all,' he muttered, his words tapering off.

Then a big bald man, his hair and stubble interchangeable, reached into his pocket and pulled out a bunch of all-day suckers, the coloured boiled sweets on a stick that had arrived with the British. He held them out like a bunch of stunted tulips. 'Not so good for the dentures, hey, Steytler? But good for your rat's breath and staving off the hunger pangs. You can make one of these last an hour if you try.' He put it in his mouth and made a show of enjoying it.

'So, share them out then,' said the general's wife, speaking with the authority of a woman used to getting her way.

'For a price,' the bragging Prussian replied.

Magda shook her head. 'Have you no shame?'

'I have a family to feed. These vouchers aren't enough. I haven't even got the money for the lighting. Every time I put money in the meter it's money I could be spending on food.'

'Better to be in the dark than hungry,' said the former radio announcer.

'You won't go hungry if you're prepared to steal a little here and there. Even the Bishop of Cologne is saying it is fine to steal coal if you have to stay alive. It's the eleventh commandment.'

'They are forcing us to behave like criminals,' the dentist said.

'They already think we're criminals.'

'I am no criminal. And my conscience is clear,' the dentist continued.

'Well. We're all in it together,' said the Prussian. 'They can't incarcerate us all.'

'Keep your mea-culpaing to yourself,' the dentist came

back. 'I am guilty of nothing more than doing my duty. Teeth and cavities are the same – it doesn't matter whose mouth it is. I have a Hippocratic oath to uphold.'

Everyone laughed at this.

Frieda wanted to put the silly man straight and was about to speak when Albert put his hand on her arm again, the way he had when she had hummed the Mädel song in front of the smoking, joking Tommies. He shot her a conspiratorial look. *They're not worth it*, it seemed to say. And she had the sweet thrill of feeling a little alliance forming between them.

'That mark . . . on your arm. Is it a birthmark?'

'Not here,' he said, flashing her a look of prohibition.

Without warning, he stood up and banged the side of the truck twice with the flat of his hand to request a stop. The driver obliged and Albert and Frieda jumped out, alighting at the village of Blankenese, a few miles on from the Villa Lubert, just where the Elbchaussee cut back inland from the great river. The sun was just going down towards the town of Stade across the water, giving the land a fiery glow.

'Don't walk with me,' Albert said to her, pulling up the lapels of his jacket to hide his face. 'Stay at least twenty paces behind me.'

'How far is it?'

Albert set off without answering; he moved at such a pace that Frieda began to think he was trying to lose her; she kept having to break into a run to keep him in view.

The former fishing village of Blankenese was unique in these flat parts for having a steep hill, around which old cottages and some new villas huddled, in the medieval manner. Frieda used to come here with her mother before the war to watch the ships passing up and down the Elbe from a boathouse tavern that played the national anthems of every international cargo ship that sailed into Hamburg. Today, the river was boatless except for a hulking British Navy cruiser; pregnant grey-black snowclouds loomed, ready to dress the village in fairy-tale clothes.

Albert climbed the hill with Frieda just behind him; she wondered which house was his. Eventually, he turned off the road and entered through the garden gate of a *Strohdachhaus*. Albert walked up the path to the front door of the thatched cottage, looking left and right before cutting off to the side entrance and peering in through the frosted lattice windows. As she walked up the flagstone pathway, Frieda thought of Hänsel and Gretel lost in the woods, stumbling across the house made of candy. Muddling her fairy tales, she cast Albert as the prince who had woken her from a long sleep and rescued her from a father who, happily, turned out not to be her father at all.

'How long have you lived here?' she asked as she followed him inside.

'Not long,' he replied.

The cottage was full of rugs, cushions and throws. Albert moved a heavy kilim on to an armchair and sat down to undo his boots. 'It belongs to a military doctor. Major Scheibli. He's stuck in a displaced persons camp, waiting for his certificate of clearance.'

Frieda saw a photograph of the doctor seated in the side-car of a motorbike somewhere in the desert, dust-grimed goggles over his eyes, red cross on his helmet. At his throat he wore the Iron Cross.

'You know a war hero?' Frieda said, picking up the photograph to look at it.

'I don't know him. I'm just borrowing his property for a short time. If the British can, why can't we?'

'Maybe they will put him in prison. If he is a hero.'

'Once the British find out he fought with Rommel, they will release him. Anyway, I have to keep moving. Already too many people have seen me come and go. I have already found another house. Nearer you. On the Elbchaussee.'

'Then we will be neighbours,' Frieda said.

Albert nodded. 'So . . . what did your family do to be so rich?'

'My father is an architect . . . my mother's family had connections with the shipyards.'

Albert's eyes lit up. 'Blohm and Voss?'

She nodded.

'Don't they mind you wandering around?'

'My mother is dead. And . . . I don't care what my father thinks.'

'He won't be looking for you?'

'He works at the Zeiss plant during the day. I can come and go as I please.'

Albert eased off his first boot then his second. He stood and went through to the kitchen area and started looking for fuel to put in the stove. The hod was empty and there was no wood in the basket. He looked around the room, and his eyes settled on a hand-carved, three-legged stool in the corner. He went to it and broke it to bits with three hard strikes on the stone floor.

'I have been waiting to burn this.'

He pushed the splinters into the stove and lit the fire. He then filled a large saucepan with water and placed it on top to boil.

'So how come you are still living in your house? I thought the Tommies had taken all the best ones.'

Frieda picked at her nails then began to explain, with increasing animation and animosity, how they had come to share their house with the English family; of the colonel's odd decision to let them stay, when he could have – should have – thrown them out; of the colonel's wife, who talked to herself and had a shaking hand; and their boy who played with her doll's house and carried a cloth soldier everywhere. As she described this situation, Frieda could see Albert's body tense and his interest sharpen.

'What does the Tommy colonel do?'

'He is the Governor of Pinneberg. I don't know what he does. He is hardly ever there,' Frieda replied. 'It is shameful. He drives the same kind of car the Führer was driven in.' She added this to impress him, but Albert looked thoughtful, exercised by this piece of information

'He's the governor?' he asked again, moving around the room now.

She nodded, still unable to tell if he was pleased or appalled.

'This is good. This is very good.'

Frieda felt a warm inner glow. The humiliation of the requisition suddenly sounded purposeful. Albert made her feel that she had much to offer him. He turned back to the pan and tested the water with his finger. Then he stripped down to his undershorts. There was nothing extraneous about his movements or his physique. In Frieda's eyes, he was perfect. Even his 88 scar.

'You haven't told me what that is yet,' she said.

He touched it and looked at her.

'It's a mark given to the resistance movement. Those who have not yet accepted defeat. Here.'

He held out his arm to let her touch it. She traced the first eight then the second with her finger, feeling the embossed ridges of the scar tissue. 'How did you get it?'

Albert went over to a dresser and produced a packet of cigarettes from the drawer.

111

'With these.'

He lit one and, after taking a deep drag, he offered it to Frieda. She took the cigarette, placing it gauchely mid-mouth, and inhaled. She immediately spluttered and coughed and Albert laughed an unexpectedly broken, high-pitched laugh – the laugh of a boy rather than a man.

'Too much! Take it slowly. Like this.'

He took the cigarette back and showed her how. 'Just a little,' he said, sucking in a quick drag and handing it back. She took it from him and held it for a moment, looking at it. Instead of taking another pull on it, she held it up like a magi-cian about to perform a trick. Sure that she had his attention, she then turned the cigarette around so that its burning end was pointing towards the palm of her other hand, which she held open, facing the cigarette. She then began to move the cigarette towards her hand as if to stub it out on her palm.

Albert intercepted her attempt and took the cigarette back.

'That's a waste of a good cigarette.'

Frieda felt tears welling. One moment, she was his proper German lady; the next, a stupid little girl.

Albert held up the backs of his hands towards her.

'Do you see these?'

Frieda looked, unsure of his next move.

'What do you see?' He moved towards her so that she could see the skin, his fingers and his fingernails. She kept her silence, fearful of giving a callow answer. If she was going to please him, she'd best stay quiet. Behind closed doors, out of view, Albert changed from a watchful, careful young man into something more forceful. Something of what was pent up and held back in him began to leak out.

'You see the nails?' His fingernails, like hers, were still black with the day's digging. With his thumb he scraped some dust from under his middle fingernail and held it up for her to see: little specks of ash and dust congealed. 'The dust of our city. The ashes of our people. Look. Here.' And he held out some specks. 'The remains of a young German maid. Do you see it?' And he scraped the 'remains of the young German maid' on to the palm of his hand then lifted his palm to his mouth and licked the dust from it, mingling it with his saliva and then swallowing. He picked out some more dust and held out his palm for Frieda to lick. 'The ashes of innocent German children who will never know what we know and see what we see.' Frieda took his hand and licked the 'ashes of innocent German children', taking them into herself. Albert reached out and took Frieda by the wrists. He pulled her hands towards him and opened them out. He ran a finger from her palm across the soft white skin of her inside arm up to the crick of her elbow and back down.

'You can't help Germany if you hurt yourself,' he said. 'Living where you live, you can be very useful – to the cause. We need things we can sell on the black market: cigarettes, medicines, jewellery, clothes. Anything of value that we can sell. Can you help?'

She nodded. 'Who is "we"?'

'The resistance. You'll meet them soon enough.'

'Are there many of you?

He suddenly lifted her chin and kissed her, pushing his tongue into her mouth so that she could taste the acrid debris of their day's work. She had been kissed and touched before – at the fuggy log cabin at summer camp, where Mädel and Hitler Youth were encouraged to share quarters, to explore and seek 'wholesome delight in exist-ence' – but this was different. The youth who'd pushed his fingers into her then was a boy, and several of his friends had insisted on watching while she lay there feeling nothing. Compared to him, Albert was a man.

'You must find out some things for me about the colonel. If he is the governor, he will know things.'

She nodded again.

After that kiss, she would even go to the Russian zone if he asked her to.

He pulled her closer towards him.

'But you must tell no one about me. Do you understand?' His grip was quite painful, and his expression frightened her.

'Yes.'

'I don't exist. Tell me!'

'You don't . . . exist.'

Then he relaxed his grip and smiled. 'Good.' He went to the coat hanging over the back of the chair and took from a pocket what looked like a tube of lozenges. He took one and washed it down with a glass of water. He paced around the room then settled on the edge of the armchair, his legs jiggling with nervous energy. He seemed to have lost all his composure.

'Why are you taking medicine?'

'It helps me stay awake.'

Albert suddenly looked scared and scarred. At first, Frieda didn't want to believe it: it didn't suit her idea of him, it made him seem less of a man; but it also made her feel something else. And she reached out to touch his face and soothe his brow the way her mother used to do to her when she couldn't sleep for the drone of bombers and for fear of dying in a terrible conflagration in her sleep. 'What happens if I am in the middle of a dream when I die?' she would ask. And her mother always said, 'They won't hurt you.' And she found herself repeating the same as she caressed his face.

'They won't hurt you.'

Albert flinched at first, unsure how to receive her gesture, like a creature that had never been touched this way. He let her do it once, then again, then he pulled away, muttering something about washing off the dust. Whatever was disturbing him, it couldn't be tamed by touch.

As the Morgans sat in front of the fireplace in the hall playing cribbage, Herr Lubert appeared on the stairs; a few steps behind him, a sheepish and reluctant Frieda.

'Please excuse this interruption,' Lubert said. His face was stern.

Lewis stood up. 'Herr Lubert. We were just talking . . . we were just saying – weren't we, darling? – that you should join us one evening for a game and perhaps watch a cine film. Is everything all right?'

Lubert nodded and waited for Frieda. She stood one pace behind him, just out of his peripheral vision, forcing him to turn to her.

'We have come . . . Frieda has come . . . to apologize.'

Rachael fixed her eyes on the girl: she had her eyes to the floor, one arm straight down by her side, the other crooked across it, her fingers scratching the skin nervously.

'What for?' Lewis asked.

'This.' Lubert held out Cuthbert's head.

'You've found it!' Edmund said.

'Frieda?' Lubert took a half-step back and gave her the floor.

After a long, excruciating silence, which Rachael wanted to fill by saying that, whatever it was, she was sure it didn't matter, Frieda spoke.

'*Es tut mir leid.*' Frieda's words were barely audible.

'In English!' Lubert snapped at her, his manner still awkward and forced.

'I am sorry,' Frieda said.

The sound of Frieda speaking English – and speaking it well – was a surprise to Rachael.

'Thank you for saying it, Frieda,' Rachael said.

'And to Edmund,' Lubert pressed on.

'I am sorry,' Frieda said, looking at Edmund.

'It's all right,' he said. 'It doesn't really matter.'

'With respect, it does matter, Edmund,' Herr Lubert said. He held out Cuthbert's head. 'This is your property.'

'*Er gehört mir!*' Frieda shouted, and she turned and left the scene, bounding up the stairs three at a time.

Lubert yelled after her – '*Komm sofort zurück!* Frieda!' – and for a moment it looked as if he might give chase.

'Herr Lubert,' Rachael intervened. 'Please. She . . . has done enough. Her apology has been accepted.'

'Ah!' Lubert threw out his arms in a gesture of despair. 'My daughter is . . . full of rage and anger. I . . . apologize . . .'

'Herr Lubert. I . . . we . . . all appreciate and accept Frieda's apology,' Lewis offered. 'It must be harder for her than anyone.'

'All this trouble . . .' Lubert said. 'Perhaps we should go . . . and live with my sister-in-law – in Kiel.'

'That is not necessary,' Rachael said firmly. 'Why don't you give me that?' She put out her palm and Lubert gave her the severed head. 'I can easily mend it.'

Lubert bowed to Rachael. 'Thank you.' He clicked his heels to the colonel, not really meaning to. 'Colonel.' He then turned to Edmund. 'I am sorry for this. I promise nothing like this will happen again.'

6

'Do you like my hair? Be honest.'

'Yes.'

'You don't think I look like a poodle?'

'No, it suits you.'

'Mmm. What does that mean, Rachael Morgan? That sounds like a back-handed compliment. You think I'm a pampered, spoilt cow? No matter. My hairdresser – Renate – said it was the latest look. "Ze Katharine Hepburn." She has terrible teeth, and she sings popular American songs in a ridiculous accent, but she's a complete virtuoso with the pins and curlers. You should give her a go.'

'Do you think?'

Susan Burnham paused and gave Rachael an exaggerated look of exasperation.

'Well, of course I do. Look at you: you're an ill-tended garden. You're not making the best of yourself. And you need to remember that we have competition. German women outnumber the men two to one in this city. We need to protect our hubbies from themselves. Keep their eyes – right!'

And, with that, Mrs Burnham performed a sexy parade-ground salute and Rachael heard the rare sound of her own laughter, the witchy-cackle that didn't sound as though it should come from her and that Lewis had always said was one of the reasons he'd fallen in love with her.

Rachael laughed a great deal more during the twenty-minute car journey to the NAAFI in the centre of Hamburg. They were in the back of Mrs Burnham's bug-eyed, beetle-shaped car, one of the new 'Volkswagens' that everyone seemed to be driving and which were now known as The Wheels of the Occupation. It was as uncomfortable as a chapel pew and as noisy as a biplane, and they had to shout to hear themselves above the engine in the boot, but it made them smile.

The outing was more like an expedition than a shopping trip. Susan Burnham joked about everything, from the car ('A strange little back-to-front thing, looks like a ladybird, but I rather like it') to intimate conjugal details ('We've been like rabbits since I got here'), falling just short of describing the sex act itself. 'I don't know what it is, but there's something in the air here. Don't you feel it? It just feels different; as though we have permission to let our hair down. It's all quite liberating.' Despite Mrs Burnham's obvious vulgarity, Rachael was happy to give her the benefit of the doubt. If she was brazen, she was big-hearted; if she was lewd, she was honest and said only what others were already thinking; and, while she might be intent on climbing the social ladder, she seemed just as ready to kick the ladder away. And she never missed a trick.

'And you two? Have been making up for lost time?'

Rachael glanced at the driver – a young man not much older than Michael, and with the same downy, tapered duck-tail hairline as her late son. His ears must have been burning below the rim of his tram driver's peaked cap.

'Don't worry about Erich. He understands nothing. Isn't that right, Erich?'

'*Bitte*, Frau Burnham?'

'Nothing. Carry on.'

Mrs Burnham started to do her lips in the driver's

rear-view, leaning into the middle, across Rachael, her ample bosom squishing as she contorted to see herself. In the same mirror, Erich looked then looked away, his hands twitching on the steering wheel.

'Well? How has it been?'

'I have nothing to report.'

'Come come, Rachael Morgan. This will not do. Auntie Susan needs to know.'

'Really . . .'

'Nothing?'

'Not really, no. How are you finding the whole staff business?'

'Oh no, no, no, no. You can't duck me that easily. This is not good, Rachael. Have you lost your desire?'

Rachael simply had no precedent for talking about her sex life; not even Dr Mayfield, with his new-fangled ideas about neuroses and manias and libidos, had pursued it; she had always assumed that sex, like religion, should not be discussed with anyone, not even the person with whom one was having it.

'What is the matter exactly?'

Rachael shook her head, trying to visualize what the matter was. All she could picture was the ceiling of their bedroom with its subtle cornicing and the swan-wing lampshades and Lewis biting the strip of the prophylactic wrapper.

'To be honest, we haven't seen that much of each other. He's working –'

'– Hard. Yes, yes. But aren't they all? You have to take control. You cannot simply rely on there being a right time.'

Rachael felt a disturbance at her throat. 'Susan . . . I'd rather not discuss it.'

'Well, of course. It's embarrassing when what should be

natural and good becomes so difficult and awkward. But it's important. As important as any work our hubbies might be doing. And, if anything, it helps them do a better job.'

'It should be a private matter.'

'I disagree. We should talk about it more than we do. A healthy sex life in a marriage affects people more than you'd think. Whole wars might have been averted had people committed as much time and effort to their sex life as they did to trying to take over the world. I'm convinced of it. That grotty little man Hitler should have got himself a proper wife instead of that strumpet secretary. Stalin whored. Mussolini had mistresses galore – but who knows? In the end, the war was won by married men enjoying a regular sex life – I am sure!'

Mrs Burnham's theory made Rachael smile but provoked a sequence of peculiar and unwanted images: Hitler in pyjamas, Stalin in the arms of a fleshy Caucasian wench and Mussolini and maid strung up, bloated and beaten and hanging from a ramp . . .

'You will be blaming me for starting a war next!'

'As long as we are friends, I will continue to ask. And probe and nose around. It is my duty. Keith tells me that they're meeting that ragged socialist next week. Shaw? I assume Lewis is going to be there?'

'He mentioned he had a big few days ahead. But he tells me very little about his work. He prefers to leave it at the gates.'

'Have you vetted his interpreter yet?'

'Should I?'

'I insisted that Keith choose the ugliest he could find, and, by God, she is an utter fright. Make sure you invite Lewis's in for tea soon and have a good look. If she is remotely attractive, have her fired.'

The idea that another woman might pursue Lewis was curiously comforting, for, if Rachael was certain of anything, it was that he would never fall in that way.

'You need to get a firmer grip on things. I'd never let Keith fob me off with some phrase like "I've got a big few days." What's so big about them that you can't tell me? Insist on information. Don't be satisfied until you have some. Oh, yes, I make sure I know what's going on and I get it in the end. Keith learned most of his interrogation techniques from me, you know.'

'Does he like his work?'

'I'm told he's very good at it. He has patience. I think that's important. I'd make a terrible interrogator.'

'Do you tell him everything?'

'Everything he needs to know.' Mrs Burnham winked and closed her lipstick, pursing her lips with a smack and leaning back to her side of the car. 'Don't worry. Your secrets are safe. He is useless when it comes to getting things out of me.'

This was no reassurance. Rachael had shared nothing of consequence and yet she felt she'd given too much of herself – too much of Lewis – and left things wide open to all manner of conjecture.

'We have no secrets. We're fine. We'll be fine.'

And, with that, Susan Burnham looked at Rachael in the way an adult looks at a child who has just announced that they're going to fly to the moon and back.

The British Families Shop – or NAAFI – was housed in a neat, intact two-storey building near the Alster. To get there, the car passed by the opera house, with its bombed auditorium, and the Astra cinema, which was showing Laurence Olivier in *Henry V* in English in the afternoon and Laurence Olivier in *Heinrich V* in German in the evening. There were even two posters side by side to prove it.

'One hour, Erich,' Mrs Burnham said, as they drew up outside the store. '*Zurück in einer Stunde.*'

In the street, a number of German women stood wearing placards around their necks. At first, Rachael thought they were protesters but, as she got closer, she saw that each placard had a photograph of a man – either husband, son or brother – a short biography, an address to contact and a plea for any information concerning the missing person. Rachael was drawn to the face of the man on the first woman's placard. His name was Robert Schloss and he'd been a paymaster. He wore the unthreatening cloth cap of an orderly and had rimmed glasses. Something in the curvature of his chin and his open expression recalled Michael. Rachael suddenly wanted to know all about Herr Schloss. The address to contact was . . .

'*Bitte?*' the woman said, hopeful. '*Haben Sie ihn gesehen?*'

Rachael looked up from the placard into the face of the woman. Her elegant hat was secured to her head with a neck scarf tied under her chin, its brim bent up to form the shape of a bonnet; it made her look like a shepherdess. There was a desperate and ludicrous expectancy about her, as though Rachael could actually have information about her missing husband and had come here especially to tell her the good news.

'*Haben Sie ihn gesehen?*' the woman repeated.

Rachael felt Mrs Burnham's hand at her elbow.

'Of course she hasn't! *Lassen Sie sie in Ruhe!*' Mrs Burnham waved the bereft lady on and muttered to Rachael, 'Remember that they're after our men,' as she steered her past what would normally have been the building's main entrance to an innocuous side-street door. Unless you knew what it was, you'd never think to enter it. The glass front of the shop had been blacked out so that nothing of what was on sale could be seen.

'They don't want the Germans to see what's inside in case it makes them feel more deprived than they already do,' Mrs Burnham explained. 'I actually think it makes matters worse.'

Rachael agreed. If anything, the obfuscation teased the passer-by. The hiding of what was inside became less a sensitive veil than an admission that the goods within were beyond the reach of most people walking past and that there was – despite the efforts of the Control Commission to say otherwise – a dual economy in operation in the zone: one for the natives; one for the occupiers. 'You know what I really think,' Mrs Burnham went on. 'I think CCG want the Germans to think we're richer than we really are. It's a matter of honour that the occupying country is still perceived to be rich and powerful.'

Once inside the store, this cynical view seemed more like a truth. It wasn't British embarrassment at their riches that had led to the blacking out of the windows, it was shame at the lack of them. Had the Germans been able to view the full display of goods on offer, they'd have been surprised to see just how paltry it was, and probably alarmed that the country running theirs could barely rustle up a square meal for itself.

'The only thing that makes shopping here bearable is knowing I've more choice than my sister in East Sheen. They're rationing bread in England now. Would you credit it? Bread! They didn't even do that during the war.'

There was gin, of course. Walls of it: Gordon's, London Dry, Booth's. The familiar brands were reassuringly present and correct, their production seemingly unaffected by the problems besetting the manufacturers of other goods.

Essential commodities may have been scarce, but the tried and tested stimulants and suppressants of Empire continued to flow like oil from a deep reservoir. This was no glitch. Gin, as every commissioner, general and governor knew, could bring sophistication to the bleakest of outposts and lift the spirits of Britain's most downhearted servants. Its manufacture and distribution was a national priority.

It was to the gin wall that Mrs Burnham marched them first.

'Keith complains that without tonic it tastes like paraffin, but beggars can't be choosers. God knows when we'll ever see tonic again. But, as long as we have vermouth, we'll have gin and it. As long as we have Angostura Bitters, we'll have pink gin and, of course, if we have orange squash we have gin and orange: gin, squash and a dash of water! No one ever complains. With these mixers, we'll survive until those lovely tonic chaps resurface. Until that happy day we will be inventive. Look how cheap it is! Four shillings a bottle! They clearly want us all to get drunk and socialize as much as possible. Well, we will oblige them. Besides, I think it's high time the governor's wife held her first social function.' And, with that, Mrs Burnham grabbed four bottles by the neck and dropped them into her bag.

The people who ran the NAAFI made no attempt to display the goods in a better light. All the food and drink was simply plonked in rows and left in boxes, arranged in bulk without any effort to dress it up. Rachael found the lack of pretence oddly calming. She'd never really enjoyed shopping, and she found this a less fraught way of going about it. Having whole aisles selling one product made things simpler. There was something almost futuristic about it. Having to pay for each item with the BAFS vouchers or the fake octagonal 'coins' pressed out of cardboard added to the feeling that it was all make-believe.

Around her, British women – it was almost all women – shopped with a barely disguised hysteria. A number of them were dressed up as though they were going to the theatre. Rachael had herself made an effort for the outing, selecting a slightly smarter woollen twin-set than was necessary, and, to any outside observer, she blended in seamlessly with the press of wool and nylon and the fug of perfume and talcum powder, but she still felt out of place, and it wasn't just the dislocation, or even 'the fragmentation of self' that Dr Mayfield had diagnosed. Shopping always felt so unsatisfactory.

'Ready for the second floor?'

Mrs Burnham pointed Rachael towards the lift that ferried people between Food and Drink on the first floor and Clothes and Toys on the second. It was an open-caged paternoster, allowing people to step on and off. Rachael, who had not seen such a thing before, hesitated as she approached it, afraid she'd get caught in the no-man's-land between the lift going up and the lift going down. She took her place next to a young boy who was beaming with the thrill of shopping with Mother and running the wheels of a Dinky car on the palm of his hand.

'That's a nice car,' she said. 'Where did you get that from?'

'I got it from upstairs. It's a Lagonda Tourer,' the boy said, proudly holding the miniature up for Rachael to see. 'And today I am going to get the Auto Union Grand Prix car. They have all the new ones here.'

Rachael hadn't thought about Edmund once this morning, but she thought of him now, back at the house having lessons with the skeletal and slightly intimidating Herr Koenig, and she scolded herself inwardly. She'd grown negligent and inattentive and, while some self-justifying mechanism tried to convince her that the space and freedom she granted Edmund offset any deficit of affection and attention he might be suffering, she'd let him roam too far, and if she wasn't careful she'd lose him. With sudden urgency, she went to the second floor, bought a Lagonda then almost ran back to the waiting car.

'Mind the ice!' Mrs Burnham warned, before redirecting her from the back of the car to the front. 'Other end! Engine's in the boot.'

Rachael handed Erich the heavy paper bag full of gin and whisky and cigarettes but retained the gift she'd bought for Edmund.

'Do you want to stop off at the Carlisle Club? Have a coffee? Pick up a copy of *Woman's Own*?'

'Actually, Susan, I'd like to get back – home,' Rachael said, surprising herself with her choice of the word.

'Right. Let's see this palace of yours then.'

As they passed Dammtor train station they saw the placarded women again, gathered like a funnel. Hundreds of heavily clad men, arriving from various corners of the country, poured into it. The heads of the women bobbed and craned and peered as they tried to see if their missing man was floating in the river of refugees flowing from the trains. Rachael saw a man run and embrace one of the women. He fell to his knees and kissed the photo of himself hanging around her neck then stood and lifted her into the air by her thighs and hips, twirling her around and around.

'Eyes front!'

But if Mrs Burnham thought she'd caught Rachael being drawn back into unpatriotic sympathy, she was mistaken. This wasn't a trap of compassion; it was envy. Envy for the completed, carouselling couple. If Lewis had gone missing, would she have made a placard and stood outside train stations in the freezing cold waiting for him to show up? She really wasn't sure.

'*Ich heisse Edmund. Ich bin englisch.*'

'*Engländer,*' the Skeleton corrected him, gently.

'*Engländer. Ich heisse Edmund. Ich bin Engländer.*'

'Your accent is excellent.'

The Skeleton shivered and tried to disguise the tremors by rubbing and clasping his hands tightly together in a priestly manner. Edmund wasn't fooled but, out of sympathy and respect, he pretended not to notice, just as he pretended not to notice Herr Koenig's waxy, shellac smell. Despite the room being as warm as any in the house – in Hamburg, in probably the whole of the British zone – Koenig kept his coat on throughout the lesson, as though he were trying to store the heat for later or thaw some deep, glacial ice within himself. He threw a covetous glance at the slice of cake and glass of milk that Heike had brought for him. The maid usually brought it after the lesson but today she'd brought it before and left it there on the pedestal table, and it had been calling to Koenig all morning.

'Would you like your cake now?' Edmund asked. '*Kuchen?*'

Under his breath, Herr Koenig muttered, 'Dear God, yes,' in German. Then, audibly, in English: 'Thank you.'

Edmund got up from the desk and fetched the plate of cake and glass of milk and put them in front of his tutor. Herr Koenig grasped the glass and drained it, fast but carefully. He set it down and licked his milky moustache, his tongue darting discreetly. He then ate the cake, using two hands, like a finicky mouse, then pushed his forefinger into the glass to wet the tip before pressing it into a remnant on

127

the plate, gathering all the crumbs, like iron filings to a magnet, into a last morsel. Afterwards, Koenig's plate looked shiny and clean, as though licked by a dog.

Edmund's father said that Koenig was the former headmaster of a school in Kiel and a man of excellent all-round ability – a real polymath – so Edmund was surprised at his tutor's tatty apparel and reduced physical condition. He looked too old and diminished to be a headmaster; there was little in his appearance that suggested authority or erudition. But after a few hours in his company Edmund began to appreciate his father's commendation. Herr Koenig turned out to be as adept at mathematics as he was knowledgeable in history and English literature. And he was as careful as a creature of the forest, too. Just as there was no fat on his body, there was nothing superfluous in his speech; everything he said seemed filtrated, purged of impurities, before being uttered. This, and the hint of a more respectable past, gave him a modest dignity.

'Let us look at the atlas.'

Looking at the atlas marked the end of the session and allowed Koenig to give Edmund a synthesized history and geography lesson in German. Edmund fetched his old Cassell atlas and opened it to the map of the world. Koenig asked Edmund to name the colour of the countries he pointed to, placing his finger on Canada first.

'*Rosa.*'

The United States of America.

'*Grün.*'

Brazil.

'Er . . . *gelb?*'

'Good.'

On India.

'*Rosa.*'

On Ceylon.

'*Rosa.*'

Australia.

'*Rosa.*'

'*Warum sind sie rosa?*' Koenig asked.

'They are all part of the British Empire?'

'Good. You are quick to learn.'

'My father says that the British Empire will shrink now, because of the war. He says that we don't have any money left and that America and the Soviet Union are now the most powerful.'

'There will be many changes to this atlas. It will not be as pink as this.'

Edmund wondered what Herr Koenig really thought about the British and their Empire. Was he being polite by pointing to its extensive reach and rule? It might have been chance, but Koenig's finger had ignored a brown Japan, a yellow Italy and, most conspicuously, a blue Germany, which, even with its borders cut back and set to the terms of Versailles, sat there centre stage, a potent hub at the heart of Europe. It was surprising that only a handful of the world's countries – Tanganyika, Togo, Namibia – were tinted with the same blue.

'Was Hitler jealous of our Empire?'

The effect of this question on Koenig was instant: he stiffened, straightening his back, and clicked the tensing cartilage in his neck, his mind performing a lightning calculation.

'I am not permitted to talk about these things,' he said.

Edmund half understood.

'It's all right. My mother isn't here.'

Koenig stayed silent, not happy at all.

'Is it because you are waiting to be cleaned?' Edmund asked.

'You mean "cleared",' Koenig corrected. 'Germans do not like to talk about those days.'

'But you were a headmaster. You will be all right, yes? You will be given your white certificate?'

'I hope so.'

'You will have a *Persilschein*?'

'You know this word?'

'I learned it from my friend.'

'German friend?'

Edmund nodded. 'He says all Germans want is to have a *Persilschein*.'

Koenig rubbed his hands again, as though trying to wring something from them.

'Yes. To be like laundry. Without any stains.'

'Some people are buying them on the black market. A certificate costs four hundred cigarettes.'

'You are very well informed about these matters, Edmund.'

'Maybe I could get one for you?'

Herr Koenig put up his hands. '*Nein*. I must go through the right . . . channels, like everyone else.'

Of course. Koenig was a headmaster, and headmasters had to play by the rules.

'Then you will be a headmaster again?'

For the first time, Herr Koenig became wistful. He looked at the atlas, and at the big, *grün* nation across the blue water. 'My brother has invited me to America. He emigrated there after the Great War. He invented a machine for milking cows more quickly than any other machine and now he drives a Buick and lives in a house with a lake. In Wisconsin. Wisconsin is nearly as big as Germany. He tells me everything is bigger in America. The cows. The meals. The cars. His Buick has bullhorns on the bonnet.'

Edmund was ready to make the journey himself. 'Then you will go?'

Herr Koenig stared at the atlas. He touched Wisconsin.

'It's too late for me now.'

'Why?'

'I will be sixty in a few years.'

To Edmund, all grown-ups beyond the age of forty bled indistinguishably into one category. He could not appreciate the subtle difference between the expectations and ambitions of a still-fit 41-year-old and those of a 59-year-old on the cusp of decline, the shifts in vitality and energy levels, the surfacing of ailments that restrict and shape a person's course in life. Koenig had the opportunity to go to America. Why would age be a barrier to such a thing?

'But you will be the same age if you stay in Germany.'

Koenig smiled, keeping his mouth closed but making tiny laughing whistles through his nostrils.

'Is it because it is too expensive?'

'All these questions. This is like a little *Fragebogen*. No. My brother would pay for my passage.'

'So . . . then, you could go?' Edmund was enjoying the vicarious thrill of imagining his tutor America-bound and the idea of playing some part in propelling Koenig across the Atlantic to a new life. But Koenig seemed to have reached the end of comfortable explanation. He changed position in his chair, sitting up and asserting a little more authority.

'It is . . . complicated.' Koenig closed the atlas and, with it, the possibility of further exploration.

Edmund knew his questions would have to stop there. Once a grown-up used this word, there was no going on.

The carriage clock chimed midday and masked the awkward moment.

'It is time,' Herr Koenig said, with relief. 'Tomorrow we will look at population and resources. We can work on your big numbers.'

'Thank you, sir. I would like that.'

Herr Koenig usually left by the side entrance, but the snow had formed a drift there and Richard had not yet got round to digging a clearing. In the absence of any grown-ups, Edmund saw Herr Koenig to the front door, where his tutor spent some time tying his hat to his head with his scarf with the same rodent-like fastidiousness he'd shown with the cake. A gust of cold air rushed in through the open door, scattering powdery snow crystals across the hallway. Koenig instructed Edmund to close the door quickly after him so as to keep the precious heat in; but some instinct made Edmund keep it ajar. The wind was such that he'd have had to slam it at Koenig's back to close it, and he didn't want to do this. Instead, he held it open and, leaning into it to counterbalance the force of the wind, he saw his tutor off. Koenig trod quickly, like a man on ice, trying not to stop lest he slip up: a diminishing grey-black blemish in a snow-white *Persilschein* world.

Edmund ran upstairs to his parents' room to look for cig-arettes. While frisking through his father's jackets, he found his silver cigarette case. It was empty – his father had not yet transferred his supply from carton to case – but Edmund was immediately distracted by the two photographs held behind the elastic. The first was of his mother, sitting on a beach in Pembrokeshire, where he and Michael had tried to hold back the sea with a sand-dam; the second, tucked just behind it, was a dog-eared snapshot of Michael in their gar-den at Amersham. It was a jolt to see his dead brother as alive as this, wearing his cable-knit cricket jumper, making a funny little smirk as though sharing a joke with the picture-taker, who, in this case, must have been their mother. Edmund had a vivid flash of the wake, his mother wiping snot from her cheek in the Narberth garden, his father too concerned about everyone else to tend to his own emotions and already on his way back to war, and himself trying to prevent the tears that welled in his eyes from rolling down his cheeks because he didn't want his cousins to see. Edmund now felt the same emptying-filling sensation inside him, like water being drawn from his belly up through his chest to behind his nose and pushing at his eyes. But it wasn't for Michael. It was for himself. There was no photo of him in his father's cigarette case. *Why* didn't he have one? Maybe there was one in his wallet. Perhaps his father didn't need a picture of him, because he was alive. Or did Edmund need to die a dramatic death to get his picture in that intimate gallery? Edmund imagined himself dying in a medley of heroic and beautiful ways – in a fire, in a war, in a snowstorm – as his mother hammered the staccato notes of 'The Earl King' in the background; then his father looking through a shoebox, selecting a snap to remember poor Edmund by then cutting it down to fit inside the silver cigarette case.

Edmund clicked the case shut and put it back in the pocket of the jacket, breathing in his father's meat-and-moss smell. He loved his father in a simple way; he loved his mother, too, but his feelings for her were like a maze compared to the straight pathway to his affection for his father. It was somehow easier to love a person who wasn't there.

The way the case slid into the lined pocket – the weight of it – was perfect, and he repeated the action several times. Then, resuming his search for tobacco, he rummaged through his father's washbag. It smelt of coal-tar soap and eucalyptus. Inside, there was a tortoiseshell comb, a damp flannel and the Distinguished Service Order medal. Edmund lifted the gold-edged, white-enamelled cross from the bag and examined it. What was it doing in here? It was surely a kind of sacrilege to toss a medal into such an undistinguished receptacle. It should have been in a velvet-lined box or, better still, permanently pinned to the breast of his father's overcoat, the way the Russian soldiers wore theirs – even as they went into battle. The date the medal was awarded – May 1945 – was engraved on the back, and a blob of soap had stuck to and stained the red-and-blue ribbon. Edmund flicked the soap away and held the medal up to his own breast. He was just about to commend himself for his own heroic action when a piercing shout from downstairs had him running for cover.

Mrs Burnham moved through the house like a hot, swarming wind, causing swirls and ripples in the atmosphere, changing its temperature. Rachael, regretting that she'd let such a powerful force loose, followed in her wake, praying that Herr Lubert had not returned home early.

'We'll start here,' she began, requisitioning the place for her own fantasies. 'We'll shake off the snow and warm ourselves by the fire. We'll have a few pink gins. Or maybe hot hock. The Thompsons will be late. They are congenitally late; it's a posh thing. I suggest you give them an earlier start time. We'll chit-chat about nothing much and this and that. Of course, everyone will be making polite noises about the house while desperately trying to hide their envy. Then we will promenade on through to . . .' she said this instinctively knowing where to go next, and letting herself through the double doors '. . . to the – Good Lord. It's a whole billiard room! Look at these pictures. I take it they're not yours. What on earth is it?' She looked at the picture as though it were about to bite her. 'Modern art. I don't understand it. Mind you, Keith has an eye for it. So. Then. On through . . . over here . . .' through the doors to the dining room, which were already open '. . . And into the . . . That's more like it. Although I think I've rather undercooked the guest list. We can get at least – sixteen? – around this table? Perhaps you should have the air marshal and his wife? They have a taste for the grand. So. Dinner will be served. Five courses? Please, no sauerkraut. It tastes of poverty and pubs. Anyway. We'll all get into the inevitable discussion about the state of things back home. Someone will mention the Russians. Blah blah. Someone will mention the lack of fuel. Blah blah. Around about pudding time – I will bring a dessert – we'll all be feeling the effects of the gin, or whatever we're drinking. Keith will be looking a little puce with it. He will have an argument with someone and it'll be time for the men . . . No! Perhaps we will subvert things and let them stay here while we withdraw –' She pushed the arched door open and stepped into the loveliest room in the house, so lovely she couldn't bring herself to compliment it: 'Mmm. Yes. This will do. A piano. Excellent. We'll all be roaring enough to sing some Gilbert and S. We'll let Diana warble away and we'll all pretend she has a stunning voice. You, I suspect, sing? And play? Good. Perhaps a game of charades –' She paused to look out of the main window towards the gates. 'Is that the daughter?'

Frieda was walking purposefully up the drive. In the snow and with her braided hair she looked like a child from a Grimms' tale, vulnerable to witch and wolf.

'She's home early today.'

'She needs to do something about those pigtails. You should set Renate on her.'

As Rachael watched Frieda, she had a pang of remorse for

not seeing the need before. She promised herself to offer Frieda a session with the hairdresser when she next came.

Mrs Burnham screwed her eyes for a final snapshot and then turned back to the room to finish her tour. 'Anyway, I suppose we can have our nightcaps here – or, no . . . Ah. Back through . . .' Back through the second door leading to the fireplace in the entrance hall and completing the circuit with a flourish: 'Ta da! Back where we started. Now *this* is the place to have our tipples. We'll watch the last embers of the fire burn down and then . . . carriages at three. Have I missed anything?'

'You've set the bar quite high, Susan.'

'That was the dress rehearsal. The real thing will be much better.'

'I'm not sure I can deliver something quite so . . . efficient.'

'Nonsense. You're a clever girl. And you have staff.'

Rachael nodded, grateful that they were absent from this whirlwind visit.

'Although you said you were having problems?'

'I'm finding it hard to delegate.'

'You have to be firm. Show them you're used to servants. They'll pick up on it if you're not, and then they'll resent you.'

'I think they already do.'

The door to the kitchens was open, and they could hear the sounds of scuttling below. Rachael closed it. 'Especially the cook, ' she added.

'Much better to show them who is boss. Better for everyone.'

Susan Burnham continued to consume and catalogue the room with her eyes.

'And the family? How is it all working? Where on earth do they eat?'

'They have a kitchen on the top floor. There's a dumb waiter.'

'Is there any mingling?'

'Not really. Ed's broken down a few walls.'

'I'd keep them firmly up if I were you.'

Rachael had already decided not to mention the incident with Cuthbert; Susan Burnham would somehow magnify it into an actual murder; within a week, the whole district would know.

'Ah, look.' Mrs Burnham was drawn to the space above the fireplace. 'I see they've taken him down.'

Rachael looked at the spot Mrs Burnham was looking at: a portrait-shaped rectangle of unfaded wallpaper, the imprint of an absent picture.

'Taken who down?'

'The Führer. That's where they would have hung him. German houses are full of those dark spaces on the wall. It's just that most of them are clever enough to cover them up. Don't look so shocked. They all had them. Keith calls it "the stain that cannot be removed".'

Rachael looked at the stain and imagined it well enough. Why had she not noticed it before?

'I think even Keith would overlook a few traces of grey to live in a place like this.'

'I don't think Herr Lubert had anything to do with the Nazi Party. From what I can gather.'

'Well, of course. They all claim that.' She looked at the house and put out her hands, resting her case. 'You think all this comes without compromise? A rich, powerful German family would have to have had something to do with the regime.'

Rachael had the feeling that these judgements were not

Mrs Burnham's; that she had already discussed the matter with her husband.

'I'm sure they stayed out of it.'

'Oh, come, Rachael. It might be the Christian thing to think the best of people, but we mustn't be naive about these matters.'

Rachael had not suspected Herr Lubert in this way. After all, to have agreed with Mrs Burnham would have made her look stupid, Lewis a reckless fool and their place in the villa untenable.

'They can't all be guilty, Susan,' she said, quoting her husband now. 'I really don't think he was involved.'

'My dear, they were all involved. It's just a matter of determining how much.'

7

'Good Tommy. Good, Christian Tommy. I like English way of life. I like King and Qveen of Vindsor. I like demockery. I learn about Dominion New Zealand. I want live in Dominion. You help me go, Tommy?'

'Scram, you little fucker.'

'Good Tommy. I know London. You have River Ritz. Batter-zee power station!'

'Hark at him! Move. Get! *Schnell!*'

'You *sprechensiedeutsch* good, Tommy.'

'*Schnell!*'

'Not Russkies. Not Stalin. I vont English Vay of Life.'

'You should be in school. *Schule?*'

'No *Schule*. No *Haus*. No *Mutti*. Some ciggies, Tommy. Please. You have for me? My *Mutti ist* dead.'

'Mine too. Now sod off. Stop pestering.'

'Ah . . . *Ich glaube, ich werde . . . ohnmächtig.*'

'Agh! Come off it! Don't do that!'

Ozi dead-drop fainted in front of the guard, his body falling into the cushion of fresh snowfall and making a squeaky crump as he landed. Lying there in his fur coat, he looked like a shot fox. The soldier who was guarding the entrance to British Military HQ stood at his post, trying to look resolute, his eyes straight ahead, ignoring the boy. But a woman wheeling a pramful of potatoes paused right in front of the boy now lying on the pavement before her. She looked at the unmoving guard, indicating towards the boy with a flick of her chin.

'*Schämen Sie sich, Soldat!*' She shot him a withering look.

Other German civilians started rubbernecking. Not wanting to create a spectacle, the guard propped his rifle against his sentry box, leant over Ozi – squatting rather than kneeling so as to keep his knees dry – and pulled him up to a seated position by the scruff of his coat.

'Come on, nipper. Wake up.' He tap-slapped the boy's cheeks with his icy gloves. 'Look at you. What the hell are you wearing? You look like sodding Noël Coward.'

Ozi fake-fluttered his eyelids and spieled his well-practised mock-delirium:

'Mr Attlee. *Danke*. King George. *Danke*. Tommy guard. *Danke*. Ciggies. Ciggies for Ozi. Ciggies for bread. Tommies are Christians. Ciggy-givers.'

The soldier pulled a pack of cigarettes from his breast pocket and made a conspicuous play of tapping some out for the boy.

'Here you go, nipper,' he said, offering him not one, not two, but three cigarettes. Content that he'd done his bit for public relations, the guard stood up, half expecting applause, but when he looked around he saw that there was no one there to witness his gesture.

'Now sod off, you little blighter.'

In exchange for his crazed complimenting of English culture, Ozi received three cigarettes and four new words for his already expletive-heavy English repertoire.

'Sod. Off. Little. Blighter!' He repeated the phrase, brushing himself down and setting off at a sprightly pace along the Ballindamm towards the Alster, clutching his hard-won fruits of charity. By his high standards of begging and stealing, this was a paltry haul. All day, he'd foraged for food and supplies in and around the Tommy-requisitioned shops and hotels that surrounded the lagoons of the Alster, doing his praising-English-culture-fainting routine to no avail. The Tommy women shopping at the NAAFI stores seemed immune to his compliments about their hair and hats, while the usually bountiful bins behind the Atlantic Hotel had been sealed off. When he'd begged for scraps on the stairs of the Victory Club – 'Hey, Yankee, what are you doing here? Take me to America, Yankee' – he had been shooed away by an American: 'Get!'

Ozi wondered if his clothes might be putting Tommy off. Today he was wearing maximum mufti: lined leather flying-hat, high-society woman's fur coat, with silk dressing gown on top, and riding boots three sizes too big for him. He'd picked up the coat at the Salvation Army's weekly hand-out; the boots he'd got from the Red Cross. Perhaps he was too well clad to stir their sympathies, but in this cold he could not afford to wear less with his chest the way it was.

Ozi put the cigarettes in his pencil case. Three cigarettes for a day's work. He might get a loaf of bread for them, but it would not be enough to placate Berti, who was getting more demanding these days; he didn't want just cigarettes or medicine any more, he wanted papers and passes: stuff that was hard to find, and expensive. Ozi would have to find Herr Hokker at the Information Centre and trade his watch to get what Berti wanted.

Most of what Ozi knew about British culture he'd gleaned from his visits to the handsome Information Centre, built right next to the Rathaus in the heart of the city. Earlier that summer, the Bürgermeister had opened it with a big speech about friendship and learning. '*Die Brücke*' – the bridge – was built, the *Bürgermeister* had said, 'to educate German visitors about Britain's leading institutions and achievements'. It had a large reading room, an exhibition gallery, a film screening room and a lending library. The centre was always packed. Germans seemed hungry for any information about the outside world beyond their own experience, and were curious to know about the British way of life. But while it was true that they were happy to learn about British rivers or women's rights, what they really wanted was somewhere warm to sit and a place to scrounge a voucher or two. Any German with sense knew: *die Brücken* were places to exchange goods as much as culture.

Ozi reached into the soft pocket of his fur coat and checked his watch. It was a Holdermann und Sohn, but he would be glad to get rid of it. He'd taken it from the pocket of a dead DP lying in a stairwell in Altona. It didn't seem right that the watch had continued ticking after the man's own ticker had stopped; like fingernails growing long after the soul has flown, it was somehow disloyal. It also gained twenty minutes every hour. The day chronometer was now telling him it was Tuesday, when it was Monday; at this rate, it would be 1950 before the month was out.

The centre was stifling with the heat of compacted bodies. Ozi swooned for a moment, feeling the change in temperature. It was hard to see the display in the exhibition room for the press of people seeking the benefits of free newspapers and warmth. A poster for the newly established Anglo-German *Frauenclub* announced a talk on 'A journey from Cairo to Jerusalem to be delivered by a Mrs T. Harry' and a forthcoming visit from the great English poet T. S. Eliot, 'who would be delivering a lecture in German as well as English on the unity of European culture'. Ozi paused to look at the photograph of the stern-chinned poet, unsure if it was a man or a woman. Next to this, another poster advertised a film called 'Britain Can Make It' and a slide show about the Pathan people of the Anglo-Afghan frontier.

Hokker was sitting at his usual place, reading the English newspapers, which were kept in wallets and on chains to stop people stealing them. Hokker spent most of his days here. He didn't need to go out when the world came to him. He was the channel for more illegal freight than any other black marketeer in Hamburg. All dirty rivulets, streams and brooks flowed to and through Hokker. If you wanted something, Hokker could find it for you – as long as you could pay.

Ozi barged through the crowd to get to him. With his black coat and homburg, Hokker looked like a funeral director. He was head down over a newspaper, his finger following the run of the print. His hat was lying on the desk at his side, a pool of snow melting in its brim.

'Hallo, Herr Hokker! What is happening in Tommyland today?'

Hokker didn't look up. He was quite absorbed, his lips moving as he read, in English, to himself.

'Ozi Leitman. Things are not so good in Tommyland.'

'No? What's up?'

'Tommy doesn't like paying for this occupation. Tommy says why should Germans eat when we have no food ourselves?'

Herr Hokker liked to show off his English as well as his ability to translate it. Before doing a deal, Ozi always tried to get him to read something; it usually knocked a few ciggies off the price of whatever it was he wanted.

'This winter is not helping,' Hokker said.

'Otto says it will last for a thousand years,' Ozi ventured. 'It's punishment for all the things we've done. There will be no cherry blossom in Stade. No apples in the orchard. No sunshine on curtains. No swimming naked in the Alster. Just a thousand years of ice and snow. What do you think, Herr Hokker?'

'It feels that way. Every river in Germany is frozen. Even the Rhine.'

143

Hokker licked his finger rather grandly and turned the pages of the newspaper. 'We are famous. Look here. We are on page seven of the *Daily Mirror* newspaper of England: a picture of Hamburg.'

Ozi was dumbfounded. There, in the middle of the English newspaper, was the razed residential area of Hammerbrook where he had once lived. This was where he had seen windows melt and roads bubble and a woman's clothes ripped from her body by an invisible thermal wind. He could hear the sound of that wind again – like someone playing every note of a church organ at the same time. He could see the red snowflakes of ash falling, the doorways burning like the rings of fire through which circus lions jump. Sorbenstrasse. Mittelkanal. People stuck in the melted asphalt. Mutti's hair on fire! Brains dribbling down noses and from split temples. Bodies like tailor's dummies, shrunk to half his size. '*Bombenbrandschrumpffleisch*' was what they called them. 'Bodiesshrunkbyfire.'

'Mutti . . .'

'Are you all right, boy?'

Ozi shut his eyes and opened them again to make these images disappear. He looked once more at the picture of his old, flattened neighbourhood. Superimposed on it was a drawing of a new accommodation complex.

'They will make it new for us?' he asked.

'This is for Tommy to live in. They are going to move everyone out to build it. The headline says: "£160 Million a Year. To Teach the Germans to Despise Us".'

'What is this?' Ozi asked, pointing to a cartoon. It depicted a British couple standing outside a ruined house with the man saying: 'Let's move to Germany. I hear they have nice big houses there.'

'What does he say?'

'They are making a joke. They are saying that it is better in Germany than in England.'

'Tommy is crazy. He makes jokes about anything.'

'So. What do you want today, Ozi Leitman?'

Ozi placed the watch on the *Daily Mirror* and, like a conjurer, Hokker made it disappear, under his hat.

'What do you want for it?'

'Aren't you going to look?'

'I already did. It's a good watch. A fine German make.'

'I need more medicine and a truck driver's pass.'

Hokker looked at Ozi. 'You ask me for difficult things.' He lifted the hat and looked at the watch. He picked it up and put it to his ear. As long as he didn't listen for a while, he'd know no different.

'It belonged to my father,' Ozi said.

Hokker looked at the boy sceptically. 'No man from Hammerbrook would own a watch like this.'

'Can you get me the pass?'

Hokker picked something from his teeth and examined it. It looked like bacon fat. He absently put the morsel back in his mouth.

'The watch is no good to me. Nobody wants to tell the time these days. Time is irrelevant in this zero hour. Everything has frozen. No time for time.'

'It is worth something.'

Hokker reached inside his coat and placed a strip of three food coupons on to his newspaper.

Ozi shook his head. All day Tommy had denied him, and now Hokker was trying it on.

'Ten.'

Hokker laughed and took his hat off the watch, leaving Ozi free to take it back.

'Three or nothing.'

Ozi looked at the vouchers. One for bread, one for milk and eggs and one for margarine. He would have to deal with Berti, find yet another excuse, but, in his head, he was already cooking the breakfast he would eat tomorrow.

Hokker nudged the three vouchers towards him.

'Take them. You can't eat a watch.'

Lewis stood in front of the mirror shaving, trying not to wake Rachael, using his fingernail to extract the stubble from the blade rather than tapping it out on the sink. All the bathrooms in the house had been fashioned from mustard-and-gold marble slabs, and he couldn't get used to it: every time he shaved he felt like an officer in the Indian Army indulging in the munificence of a nabob. Not even the thought of his own benevolence in allowing the natives to keep their property could avert the feeling that he was just another carpetbagger.

He finished shaving, towelled his face dry and tidied up. The silver strip of standard-issue prophylactics lay behind the beaker, showing one used in three months. It made a dismal calendar. Lewis had left them there in the vague hope that Rachael might see them while doing her own toilet and somehow want to improve the record. This was a ridiculously circuitous approach to lovemaking, as unlikely to effect a change as it was unfair; but he'd lost his confidence, his ability to be direct with her. (Indeed, when trying to recall moments from the past in which he had shown openness in such matters, he could remember only their period of courtship, when he had fearlessly told her that she would be Mrs Morgan before the year's end.) Lewis told himself that her loss of appetite for intimacy was, like her headaches and sleeping in late, just another symptom of her condition, of what he summarized euphemistically as her 'post-war blues', and that, in time, things would improve. At least, he hoped so; he was simply too busy to contemplate any other treatment.

Rachael was asleep, lying on her side, making soft, dry clicking noises with her tongue and lips, her face twitching, perhaps from a dream. Dr Mayfield had suggested that sleep would be both a symptom of and cure for her condition, but Lewis would have preferred her to be more active. If he had a philosophy, it was: stay occupied.

The good news was that she was going out again, having accepted an offer to take another trip into Hamburg with Susan Burnham. Lewis had met the Intelligence officer's wife once, at the mess; despite being a busybody, she had a vivid humour and fingers in all kinds of cultural and social pies, and Lewis was grateful for anything that might get Rachael out of the house.

He opted for his Russian front coat; it was one of the few things that offered protection to his fatless body against the spite of a winter that was already setting records. There had been reports of the North Sea freezing at Cuxhaven and of people walking across the Baltic to escape from the Russian zone. He looked at his cache of cigarettes in the chest of drawers; was he compensating for a lack of physical satisfaction by smoking more? The stack seemed several packs down. He took his usual sixty, reminding himself to reduce his intake to twenty by Christmas – if only to show solidarity with the people out there for whom cigarettes equated to bread. He looked at Rachael again, thought about kissing her on the forehead, but elected not to; instead, he slipped from the room, leaving her to her dreams and permitting himself to wish that he might be featuring in one of them.

Even in the snow, the car was as steady and thoroughgoing as a battle cruiser slicing through the ocean. When

Schroeder retired, owing to a resurgence of an old war wound, Lewis should have found someone to replace him, but he enjoyed driving himself too much. The Mercedes had become an important daily pleasure; a warm, mobile cloister in which he was free to contemplate. As soon as he was behind the wheel, the commotion in his thinking cleared and he felt sure of himself again.

Outside, there was balm in the scene: the skies had cleared of yesterday's slate-grey snowclouds and were as blue and clean as a senior ward sister's tunic. The low-angled sun made everything sparkle, while the thickness of the snow was felty and reassuring and as white and bobbly as hospital linen. It was beautiful, but frustrating. It would give the minister a false impression. On such a day as this, a visitor who had just arrived might be forgiven for thinking that Hamburg was making a startling recovery. The snow disguised the trauma by throwing an equalizing blanket over everything, giving jagged metal and broken brick a new, hopeful covering. It was a bad day to conduct a tour that was meant to show how ugly and grey life was amidst the German ruins.

Lewis entered through the revolving doors of the Atlantic Hotel and passed the reception area, where a painting of the Duke of Wellington had been hung on the wall behind the concierge, transforming the building into a little piece of Whitehall. The minister would hardly know he'd left home.

Ursula was standing in front of the great fireplace, warming herself. She looked both elegant and modest in her knitted woollen blouse, herringbone skirt and black, wedge-heeled court shoes. She'd done her hair in the conventional and appropriate way of the CCG interpreter – back and up behind the ears – but if it was meant to underplay her looks, it served only to enhance them: the wolfish eyebrows, the slender antelope neck. Lewis found himself clumsily complimenting her.

'. . . *Schön*.' It wasn't quite the right word but he'd started speaking before knowing what word he was going to use. '*Lieblich*' was probably better but it was hardly appropriate to ask her to translate and correct her own compliment.

'Thank you.'

'Sorry I'm late . . . *Die Strassen sind eisig*. Is that right? *Eisig*?'

'Yes. Icy.'

Ever since Edmund had asked Lewis a question in clear, precise German, Lewis had insisted on trying to speak the language to Ursula as much as he could. His son's fluency was shaming.

'There were no trams today.'

'*Eine schlechte Reise?*'

'It was fine. I have a warm coat and it was a nice walk. Here – your routine for the day.' Ursula handed Lewis a typed itinerary. He scanned it, seeing Minister Shaw's full title at the top.

'You see a mistake?'

'No . . . *Nein. Ist. Perfekt*. But it's Kensing*ton*. Not Kensingtown.'

'Ah!' Ursula seemed genuinely annoyed at herself. She re-read the word aloud: 'Ken-zing-tonn. I am sorry.'

'It's fine. An easy mistake. No one will mind. *Ist der Minister schon hier?*'

'He is in the salon.'

'Let's hope he's one of ours.'

'One of ours?'

'As opposed to "one of theirs". I mean, let's hope he's on our side. One of the good guys.'

Ursula indicated that he had something on his chin by touching her own.

'You have blood.'

Lewis touched the spot and dotted blood on to his finger.

'That'll teach me for trying to shave without soap. My feeble attempt at saving resources.' He licked his finger and sealed the cut with his spit. 'Still bleeding?'

Ursula took a kerchief from her coat pocket and held it up to dab the cut. She paused, waiting for him to give her permission to proceed. Lewis pushed out his chin, hoping that no general or *Bürgermeister* would be passing by at that precise moment.

'*Bitte.*'

Ursula tended his cut like a mother, and, although she did it with an unfussy matter-of-factness, her attentions made Lewis blush. Her smell close up was like fresh linen.

'There. Now you are ready to meet the minister from Kensing-ton.' She stepped back a pace, sensing his embarrassment.

'Thank you. *Auf in den Kampf!*'

She nodded. '*Auf in den Kampf.*'

And the two of them set off towards the main salon, 'to battle'.

The men were standing in smoky clusters of twos and threes, and the hubbub of their voices was intense. It was quite a turn-out: General Surtees had come, along with other CCG top brass; the rotund Bürgermeister was here, smoking his full-sized Cuban cigar like some German Churchill; and Vaughan Berry, the commissioner, was in attendance, looking strained and dutiful. Shaw was easy to spot; one of only two men not in uniform, he was surrounded by an attentive petitioning cabal, each one keen to get their pennyworth from the MP while they could.

Lewis quickly explained who was who to Ursula. 'The thin man is General Surtees. My ultimate boss. And yours.'

'One of ours?'

Lewis smiled. She was a quick learner. He shook his head.

'The man in the banker's suit?'

'That's the commissioner.'

Vaughan Berry was the only other man in the room not in uniform. Lewis thought highly of Berry. He'd famously refused to wear the navy-blue uniform of the CCG, as it reminded him of an air-raid warden's. 'One of ours,' Lewis said.

'And the man talking to the minister now?'

Lewis felt himself bristle. It was Major Burnham and, from the look of things, he was already in the process of lob-bying the MP into submission. Lewis was annoyed at himself for not getting here before Burnham had the chance to pol-lute the MP's thinking. Shaw looked like a man intently trying to solve a difficult conundrum: hand thoughtfully to chin, head tilted sympathetically as if trying to hear and remember everything that was being said.

'Major Burnham. Intelligence.'

'One of theirs,' Ursula said, without needing to ask.

At breakfast, Lewis found himself sitting opposite Burn-ham and a visiting American, General Ryan Caine, here to see how the Brits were getting on and share something of life in the American zone. Caine had the close-cropped hair that even American three-star generals seemed to prefer; it made him look virile and youthful, while the sunspots blotch-ing his skin suggested exposure to sunnier climes and a life fully lived. He exuded the ease of a man enjoying his time in Germany and the low-grade smugness of a man visiting his poorer, struggling cousins.

'Isn't it time you eased up on the fraternization laws? I hear that just talking to a German woman amounts to solicit-ing in your zone.'

'I think, for now, the Germans prefer a clear separation.'

'You know, in Frankfurt now we already have a special civil service for marriages between American servicemen and German civilians. Now, that's a simple way to integrate with a society.' Caine was all over Ursula with his eyes. 'If you ever want to switch to a friendlier zone, Fräulein . . .'

Ursula, Lewis was pleased to observe, remained gracefully underwhelmed.

'The British zone has many more problems, General.'

'Well, you're right there.'

A waiter brought plates of breakfast: eggs, sausages, rashers, grilled halves of tomato, mushrooms, onion, black pudding, liver.

'You may be broke, but it's good to see you're not cutting back on the hospitality,' said Caine. The American then grew serious. 'Don't you think it's time to give the Germans the steering wheel back? We need to act fast. If we're not careful, they'll start thinking the Soviets are a better prospect. We need to get their businesses going. Give them the capital they need. Then give them their head. Give them the tools . . . There's talk of a plan to give them – and Europe – massive aid. It's being discussed in Washington as we speak. We all need a strong Germany.'

'But first we need a clean Germany, General,' Burnham said.

Caine cut a piece of liver in two and forked some into his mouth.

'Well, of course,' he said. 'Root the fuckers out first. Pardon my language, Fräulein.'

With a light smile, Ursula indicated that she was more amused than offended.

Lewis had eaten half an egg and a rasher of bacon, but the conversation was tightening his stomach, shrinking it. He was desperate to say something. He glanced down the table.

De Billier was in conversation with Marshal Sholto, and well out of earshot. But Shaw, who was sitting the other side of Ursula, was now listening in on the exchange.

'I liked what you said earlier, Major: "You can't build a house on rotten foundations."'

Lewis's heart sank. Lewis had heard these same words from the lips of Wilkins. And now Burnham was keeping the Chinese whisper going, no doubt having planted it during his chat before breakfast. In this way, unfounded prejudice cemented into hard opinion and went on to form policy.

'The Germans have had twelve years of ignorance and illiteracy,' Burnham said, encouraged by the minister. 'It's made people into animals. We can start the process of reconstructing their psyches when we have established the rule of law and rebuilt basic infrastructures, but, until then, we need to be vigilant. Kindness is a luxury we can't afford.'

Burnham's lashes blinked at Lewis.

'You believe there's a threat of insurgency?' Shaw asked, taking things in the direction Lewis didn't want them to go.

'The chaos on the ground and the mass movement of displaced people provide perfect cover for the Nazi to disappear, then reappear, having reinvented himself as an "innocent".'

'You have the questionnaire,' Caine suggested.

'The questionnaire is helpful, but we're having to refine it slightly – we have to probe a little deeper into people's pasts to get to the truth. We need more personnel to deal with the backlog. But we also need better intelligence to find the real criminals. It's not just a case of sheep and goats. It's the goats who are sheep and the sheep who are wolves. Or Werwolf.'

The word hooked everyone.

'You have them here?' Caine asked.

'We had a convoy attacked by two insurgents last week. Turned over a lorry full of gin.'

'They know where to hit you guys hard,' Caine quipped.

'Insurgents?' Lewis asked. 'Or people looking for food?'

'The two we arrested looked fairly well nourished,' Burnham returned. 'They both seemed convinced Hitler was alive and well and would come back to trounce us yet. When I pointed out that the Führer was dead, one asked me to prove it, saying that the Russians had never produced a body.'

'Show me the body!' Caine exclaimed. 'As if the Führer were Jesus Christ himself!'

'The Werwolf's value as propaganda far outweighs its achievements, Minister,' Lewis said, determined to kill this myth and bring the conversation back to what mattered.

But Burnham had everyone where he wanted them.

'They both had the 88 tattoos,' Burnham continued. 'Burnt on the forearms.'

'Eighty-eight?' the minister asked.

'It's code. The eighth letter of the alphabet?'

Shaw counted it out. 'H. HH?'

Burnham nodded. He wanted Shaw to say it.

'*Heil Hitler?*'

Lewis urgently felt the need to step in now.

'Stuff and nonsense. You can see 88s painted on walls and ruins all over the city. It simply shows how bad things are that people are prepared to contemplate going back to that.'

'Maybe some Germans haven't learned their lesson?' Caine suggested.

'Justice must be seen to be done,' Shaw said. 'The people back home demand it.'

'Surely it's better that justice is actually done rather than simply seen to be done.'

'You're not a politician, Colonel. Perception is nine tenths of the truth in my world.'

'Chasing a few fanatics is hardly our priority,' Lewis said, his restraint buckling. He was aware that Ursula had gone quiet, as the men dissected her country.

'So what would you say are our priorities?' Shaw asked.

Lewis straightened his back and spread his hands on the table. 'You can't introduce democracy to a people that's starving and fragmented. If we feed people, house them, reunite separated loved ones, create work, then we have nothing to fear. But, right now, there are millions of able-bodied Germans unable to work because of this "cleaning" process. Families are still living apart. Thousands are still in internment camps.'

'Indeed.' Shaw nodded thoughtfully. But this litany of to-do's wasn't as compelling as the stories about the Werwolf.

'You have real sympathy for the natives, Colonel,' General Caine observed. 'Is this why they call you Lawrence of Hamburg?'

Burnham must have leaked this.

'Perhaps you could tell the minister and the general about the special arrangement in your house, Colonel,' Burnham suggested. He turned to Shaw and Caine. 'Colonel Morgan is pioneering a new approach to Anglo-German relations.'

Lewis had always envied the ability of the Intelligence boys to sit with generals and ministers and speak their minds without recourse to authority, but Burnham was sorely testing Lewis's egalitarian bent. And now Burnham was directing the conversation to his will.

Reluctantly, Lewis found himself explaining to the table how he had come to share a house with a German family. When he'd finished, there was a long, stigmatizing silence. What, before, had seemed a humane act now sounded almost scandalous.

'Now *that's* fraternizing, Colonel,' Caine said.

'I wonder. Doesn't it compound a sense of resentment?' Burnham asked, in a perfectly reasonable tone. 'I mean, wouldn't these Germans rather be with their compatriots? In the camps?'

The table looked to Lewis to answer the question.

'In Nissen huts? Freezing half to death?' He knew he was subverting the official line on this, but Shaw needed to know.

'I've heard they're pretty comfy,' Shaw said. 'They have heat. And food. Which is more than half of England is currently enjoying.'

'I think, given the choice, most of us would stay in our house if offered the chance,' Lewis said.

'Well, let's hope your kindness doesn't come back to bite you, Colonel,' Shaw said.

Lewis had already said too much and he could see that General de Billier was agitated at his criticism of British efforts in front of the minister. He'd leave it to the tour to show the Member of Parliament how things really were in the camps.

Lubert sat in the sour-milk-smelling waiting room of the Direct Interrogation Centre, trying to remember anything – anything other than being German – that might incriminate him in the eyes of British Intelligence.

The centre had been set up in the old art school behind the Binnenalster. The last time Lubert had been here was in 1937, with Claudia, to view works by the artist Böcklin, one of the few decent German artists not defined as degenerate by the regime. Hitler had apparently bought eight of his works. Lubert and Claudia had had a great row about him afterwards: she liked Böcklin's clear moral messages; he said that was precisely the problem with him. She had called

Lubert 'snotty' and unable to see the art for what it was, he had got as far as calling her a populist; but the row was not really about art or taste, it was about the regime.

He told himself that he had nothing to fear. He had performed his act of self-recollection – *Besinnung* – which all Germans had been encouraged to make as part of the process of acknowledging their part in the great crimes their nation had committed. He disliked the idea of collective guilt, but he was not one of those yesterday's men who blamed the Allies for Germany's current woes; nor did he rue the hangings of defendants at Nuremberg one bit. He had filled out his *Fragebogen* – the 133 questions that would determine his professional future – more easily than he had expected. Indeed, it was hard to see how they expected to identify the real culprits through it. It seemed too polite, lacking in trickery or any penetrating interrogation. There were one or two odd questions which had made him laugh, but, by and large, he'd filled it out with confidence and a clear conscience. He'd even enjoyed the exercise of 'remembering who he was'.

Lubert's name was called, and he made his way to the interrogation room. As he approached the door, he breathed in deeply, reminding himself not to be combative, to remain humble, to keep it civil. The rumour was that the British were not finding enough Germans of the 'wrong colour' and were being far more vigorous in their interviewing.

His interrogators were both seated behind an oak desk. One of them was smoking, and gestured for Lubert to take a seat. The other did not look up but instead continued to examine the paperwork before him, paperwork Lubert could see – from the green ink and his own terrible, looping cursive – was his completed questionnaire. The man turned the pages, forward, then back, forward, then back, as though puzzled by a discrepancy. Something didn't add up, or was missing. If his long, theatrical pause was designed to unsettle, it worked. Lubert was riled before they had even started.

'Herr Lubert?' the first man asked.

'Yes.'

'I'm Captain Donnell, and this is Major Burnham, Head of Intelligence. We will conduct this interview in English and German according to our needs. Our understanding is that you are a fluent English speaker.'

'Yes.'

The major still didn't look at Lubert but continued to seem bemused by the questionnaire or, rather, by some of Lubert's answers. When he spoke, his voice was low and soft, his German immaculate.

'You're a lucky man, Herr Lubert.'

Herr Lubert didn't dispute this. He waited, knowing that his 'good fortune' was about to be unpacked and expanded upon by this man with the peculiarly long eyelashes.

'You have survived the war intact. Too young for the first. Too old for the second. You still live in your house. You have your assets. You have a sympathetic landlord.'

Lubert wanted to dispute the part about assets, but he kept his peace.

Burnham raised his head, and Lubert looked at him. The man's eyes really were too pretty to be those of an interrogator. He searched for sympathy in them.

'I am grateful,' he replied, in English, wanting to balance things.

'Really?' Burnham answered. He looked down at the questionnaire and turned it to the page that seemed to be causing offence.

'From some of your answers, I detect a certain ingratitude of tone. Even a disdain.'

It was a valid enough criticism. He had never liked having

to answer questions, especially officious ones. They brought out something stubborn and contrary in him.

'I think there was a question about toy soldiers. It ... didn't seem relevant.'

'Great care and time has gone into compiling these questionnaires.'

'Yes. But ... I couldn't see the relevance of the toy soldiers.'

'Did you ever play with toy soldiers?'

'You will arrest all men who once played with toy soldiers?' Lubert couldn't stop himself.

'Herr Lubert, a dismissive tone might push you into a category you wouldn't want to be in. Did you play with toy soldiers or not?'

'Yes. I was like any normal boy.'

'Good. That's all I needed to know.' Burnham marked the empty box. 'And then there was this ...' Burnham's finger moved to a later question, his face screwing up into an expression of confusion. 'Question R.iii. What did you mean by this answer? If I can call it an answer? This seems ... a facetious way of answering such a serious question.'

Lubert knew that Burnham was an intelligent man. He knew that Burnham knew why he had answered the question the way he had: because it was a ridiculous question. At the time, he had had to read it again, thinking it must have been badly translated or especially inserted just to test him. He'd decided that it was just a thoughtless question composed by an unthinking clerk somewhere in Whitehall or Washington. And that it did not deserve a serious answer.

'Well?'

'Whoever thought that was a good question ... can't have been serious. Or have had any idea of what it was like for –'

'It's a perfectly serious question, Herr Lubert. "Did the bombing affect the health of you and your family?" If you want to return to full, professional employment, we need to be sure that you have no mental-health issues. Answering with exclamation marks is hardly the response of a stable mind.'

'I think the bombing affected the health of my wife, Major. She perished, along with 40,000 other people, in July 1943. The day the British destroyed this city in the firestorm.'

Burnham was unmoved, but he seemed pleased that Lubert had brought the subject up.

'Let us talk about your wife. For a residential architect, you live in some splendour. You have a listed art collection. Including works by Léger, Nolde. I presume she was the money?'

'She was from a wealthy family, yes.'

'And how had they acquired this wealth?'

'Trade.'

'Trading what? And with whom?'

'Everything. They owned a number of the shipping yards.'

'Shipping yards used to transfer Nazi weapons?'

'From 1933, they traded what they were told to.' He could have pointed out how many of those ships had sailed to and from England, but the major must have been perfectly aware of this.

'So this is an art collection paid for by Nazi trade?'

How simple this mathematics was: an equation that always ended 'equals guilty'. The numbers and fractions that got you there were unimportant.

Lubert shook his head. 'Hamburg got on with its own business, it was all commercial. We had no Party affiliations. Only Claudia's brother –'

'Yes.' Burnham looked at the relevant page. 'Martin Fromm.'

Lubert hadn't wanted even to write his brother-in-law's name, or his title: Gauleiter. There wasn't space on the page to get into the nuances of his Party ambitions and the consternation that his joining it had caused the family.

'Let us turn to another question. Question F.iii. "Did you ever hope for a German victory?" You wrote . . . "I wanted the war to end quickly."'

'Of course. Everyone did.'

'You wanted Germany to win?'

'I was – I still am – a nationalist, but that doesn't make me a Nazi.'

'I think that is a sophistry. In 1939, a nationalist was a Nazi.'

'I didn't want a war at all.'

'Tell me about your daughter.'

The man knew how to keep the ground shifting. Lubert felt himself lose his footing.

'What about my daughter?'

'Well, I presume she was affected by the bombings. By the loss of her mother?'

'She's . . . still . . . angry about it.' For the first time, his tone was defensive and unsure. 'And . . . she has found it very difficult to share the house with a British family.'

'Angry? At the occupation?'

'Angry at the loss of her mother.'

'She was a Hitler Mädel.'

Lubert had nearly not written it – but it was a fact. 'It was mandatory – from 1936.'

'You didn't stop her?'

'We . . . my wife and I did . . . have a disagreement about it. I was against her joining . . . but, ultimately, we had no choice. I have a bad conscience about this. But to refuse would have been treason. And that would have been worse for us.'

'But a man of conscience would take prison over evil, would he not?'

'You seem determined to find me guilty of something, Major.'

'Your guilt is just a matter of degree to me, Herr Lubert. My job is to determine its colour, its hue. So tell me . . . I'm intrigued: how can you stomach living with your former enemy?'

'They are civil to us.'

'How does your daughter feel?'

'She is . . . sullen about it.'

'How does this manifest itself?'

'She's . . . well . . . She doesn't appreciate how . . . privileged we are to still be in our house.'

'And why should she?' Burnham said. 'After what happened to her mother. What is she doing now – with the schools closed?'

'She's working on the rubble runs.'

'When you see all this rubble you must wonder if architecture has any point, Herr Lubert. Are you sure you want to go back to this career?'

'I'm not good for much else. I would like to be' – he tried to think of the word – '*involved* in the rebuilding. I make a poor factory worker.'

'You miss the days of building summer houses for Party officials?'

It was true that he had enjoyed an upsurge of commissions for summer villas at that time – including a 'small palace' for Harold Armfeld, the arms manufacturer – but non-military work had been sparse.

'After 1933, there were few opportunities. It didn't help that the Party despised the school of architecture I came from.'

Burnham flicked to another page of the *Fragebogen*. 'You miss the past?'

'All I miss of the past is my wife, Major.'

'You don't miss the good old days?'

'I don't know which days you mean. After 1933, Germany became a prison for most of us.'

Burnham sat back, opened a drawer and pulled out a pile of photographs. He threw them on to the desk and spread them like cards.

'Was it a prison like this?'

He picked up a photograph of a skeletal Jewish prisoner. Then another. And another. All the time searching Lubert's face for his precise reaction. Lubert had seen these pictures in the first months after the war, pinned against walls for all Germans to see. He wearily looked at them now then looked away.

'Whatever inconveniences you might have suffered, Herr Lubert, I'd advise you never to compare your circumstances to this.'

Burnham picked up the questionnaire and turned to the last question, on the last page. Question Y.

'I see you've left "Any further remarks?" blank. Is there anything you'd like to say now?'

Lubert looked at the major in as contrite and courteous a manner as he could manage and said, 'I don't think so, Major.'

'Why did you hang this without asking me?'

'There used to be a picture there. It left a yellow mark. I thought you might like –'

'Well, I don't.'

Rachael was waiting in the hallway, pacing the room. She addressed him with a steady stare and ramrod posture, as though coached by a stern governess in how to deal with a recalcitrant pupil. Lubert had just walked through the door. He was hungry, cold and angry. After his interview, he had gone to work, only to discover that the factory had been closed. The British claimed it was because of the weather, but everyone knew it had been done to keep a lid on the simmering dissent there. His fellow worker Schorsch had been at the gates, handing out leaflets. They were planning a big rally, encouraging all workers in the British zone to picket the factories in protest at them being dismantled. 'Remember whose side you're on, Herr Lubert,' he'd muttered as he handed him the flier. Lubert was fed up with being told what to do.

He looked up at the picture he'd asked Richard to hang that morning. He'd gone to some trouble choosing it, taking the Morgans' provincial sensibilities into account: nothing too outré, nothing too abstruse. He'd initially selected the lovely Liebermann landscape, but it failed to cover the old discolouration left by the portrait. The 'half-nude female' by von Carolsfeld was, he thought, perfect: elegant and understated, it covered the stain and lifted the whole room; it was a rare masterpiece, worthy of any wall in any hall in any land. Only a philistine could object to it; a philistine or, perhaps, a prude.

'He was one of Germany's great nineteenth-century artists.'

'I don't care who he was,' Rachael said, folding her arms, refusing to acknowledge the gentle glory of the maid behind her.

'You don't like it?'

'That isn't the point.'

Was it the nudity? Lubert wondered. The picture was perhaps on the cusp of erotic, but it was too restrained and delicate to be offensive. He was suddenly hit by an unstoppable urge to make this moment as difficult for Rachael as possible, to make her blush and squirm, to put her in her place.

'Perhaps you would prefer depictions of the countryside. A hunting scene? Or perhaps someone with their clothes on?' As he said it, he felt like a contemptuous older brother patronizing an uppity little sister. Thrillingly, he didn't care.

Rachael looked away, feeling herself reddening. Mrs Burnham was right: the Germans were a haughty lot, and she'd allowed this one to get way above his proper altitude.

'Herr Lubert, I really don't like your tone –'

But Lubert couldn't stop himself. 'I would like to know why you don't like it. It is such an honest picture. It isn't – I don't know what the word is in English . . . *unschicklich*: just for the sake of something to shock. I mean, look at her. It is a beautiful piece. I thought you would appreciate it. That you were a woman of taste.' He paused for effect. 'I must have been mistaken.'

This seemed to light the fire.

'What are you implying? Of course I can see that it is a good piece. I object to your insinuation. You know nothing about my taste or my background.'

'This is true,' he said. At the end of a long, frustrating day, this was good sport.

'What could you possibly know about my preferences? Or my taste – what I think is good art. You know nothing about me or where I come from.'

'This is the problem!' he said. A reckless mood was on him. 'How can we begin to understand each other when both of us have pasts neither of us knows anything about?'

'But it's your past that troubles me, Herr Lubert.'

This struck a different note. She looked at the picture – or rather at the space inhabited by the new picture.

'It was a picture of "him", wasn't it?'

Lubert was stunned into silence by the contempt and incredulity this question aroused in him.

She breathed heavily through her nostrils and started to nod.

'It was, wasn't it? A portrait of the Führer,' she said, avoiding the dread name.

Lubert emitted a laugh which sounded more frivolous than he felt.

'Well?' she asked, backing him on to the ropes, sure she had him. 'Was it a portrait of the Führer or not? I know that most of you had them. I just would like to know.'

He didn't quite believe her suspicion. It seemed borrowed. By rote.

She couldn't resist one final swipe: 'I'm disappointed in you, Herr Lubert. I thought you, of all people, would have had better taste.'

The contrarian in him wanted to say nothing. But her ignorance was too provocative for him to resist.

'Take a look around, Frau Morgan. Take a look at the furniture. The books. Take a look . . . at the music sheets in the piano stool. Music by Mendelssohn and Chopin – two composers banned by the Party; browse the library. You will find works by Hesse, by Marx, by Fallada – books that should have been burnt. And look at the art. I would show you around if I thought you were interested – artworks banished thirteen years ago. Degenerate art. Even this woodcut by Nolde.' He pointed to the simple cut of a trawler on the wall of the first staircase. 'All of it unGerman. Jewish Bolshevist. Artists unable to work or sell, because they were not to the Führer's taste.'

Lubert started to circle the hall, declaiming to the fittings and fixtures.

'I know someone has to be blamed. And it must be helpful to have someone to blame. I am sure it is convenient for you – to give it a face. But do you think that I would give pride of place to that man . . . whose stupid thinking led to these things being banned and burnt? He was a vandal. His only . . . creed was to destroy – not just art, but lives, families, peoples. Cities, countries – even God himself! His only legacy is death and ruins.' Lubert stopped circling and paused for breath.

Rachael needed to move. She looked away from the offending portrait and down at the fireplace. She started to fuss at the grille with the poker; her hand was trembling.

'I think you've said enough, Herr Lubert.'

'No. I haven't.' If anything, he was just finding his theme. 'You are right. We know nothing about each other. You know nothing about me. My past. My present. My future. Yes, that's right. I have future hopes. Yes, even I: a German!'

Rachael set the poker back on the hod. She folded her arms to hide her shaking hand.

'You say you are troubled by my past, but really I think you are troubled by your own. I know little about it. Apart from what Edmund has told me. But at least I have tried to imagine it. To see beneath the surface of things.'

'What has Edmund told you?'

'He's told me about your son, Michael. About your . . . grief. He says you used to be happier. Apparently, you told lots of jokes and sang. He says I would have liked you more if I'd known you then. That you are not quite your old self.'

Lubert could see – from her deep breaths – that this hurt her.

'And I feel sympathy: for your own loss, for your dislocation, for the difficulty of living here with your former enemy and a husband you hardly ever see. It makes it easier to believe that you are more than just a bitter woman who is full of prejudice. You have your own pain. I have seen it in your eyes and heard it when you play. But there are others like you. Wake up! You are not the only one.'

He was standing right in front of her, square on now.

'You have said enough, Herr Lubert. You must stop.'

'What will you do? Have me thrown out? Isn't that what you would like? Well. Here. Let me make it easier for you.'

Lubert suddenly took her by the shoulders and kissed her. He slightly missed her mouth, and it was rough and quick. He stood back, waiting for the backlash, his face craned a little forward, offering a target.

'There. I have done it,' he said, not entirely sure what he had done.

The expected slap didn't come. Rachael turned away, touching the side of her upper lip.

He was not thinking straight. His adrenalin was pumping too fast. He had to leave before he did something worse. He put up his hands and backed away.

'I will go,' he said. 'I will go and pack our bags. I'm sure this is what you want.' He turned and started towards the staircase.

'No, Herr Lubert,' she said, with unexpected calm. 'That really won't be necessary.'

Lubert had one hand on the banister and one foot on the stair. 'I . . . should not have made the accusation I made. I provoked you. It was a misunderstanding. Let us leave it at that.'

He didn't look at her but, instead, after a long pause, patted the newel post to acknowledge her truce and continued on upstairs to his rooms.

Edmund drove his new Dinky along the road of the landing runner, between the doll's house and the source of his cigarette supply, and back again. He caught the sounds of words rising up from below – 'forget', 'past', 'picture' – half aware of the dicey tone being used, but too focused on his mission to make sense of what was being said. To a passing maid or mother he was doing what any normal, healthy boy would do with their new toy car; but for Edmund it was all a ruse masking the much bigger game he was playing.

He could still smell his mother's perfume on the car as he turned it into his bedroom. She'd made quite a palaver of giving it to him: bidding him come sit on her knee, taking his face in both her hands and planting a kiss on his forehead before handing him the present. She said it was an early Christmas gift and added that it wouldn't count against whatever else Father Christmas might bring home. She seemed very keen to please him, and this made him a little uneasy.

'I know I haven't shown it much, but I just want you to know . . . that I love you,' she'd said.

To have it expressed this way seemed to throw it into doubt rather than prove it. Like gravity or oxygen, Edmund had always taken this for granted.

But he was pleased with the car. Although the model and scale were wrong, the Lagonda was now the stand-out prop in his attempt to replicate the Villa Lubert. If those manufacturers of Dinky cars could bring themselves to make a Mercedes 540K, the replication would be complete. He even had a Richard the gardener doll, distinguished by a home-made cardboard shovel. As Edmund parked the car outside the doll's house, he made the Richard doll collect the shopping supplies, while the Edmund doll collected the real cigarettes. Checking to see that the Mother doll was in the front parlour playing the piano, the Lubert doll watching her, the Greta and Heike dolls in the kitchen, the Frieda doll in the attic and the Father doll across the carpet lawn, saving Germany, the Edmund doll ran with the two giant packets to the large central bedroom. Edmund looked back to the door, listening for sounds of approach. Sure that no one was coming, he moved the furniture to the sides of the main bedroom and lifted the miniature Persian rug. There were eight packets underneath it; with the two new ones, he now had the two hundred cigarettes Ozi had asked for: a soldier's monthly ration; an orphan's fortune. It was time to airlift this haul across the snow-covered tundra of the meadow to the Boys Without Mothers.

The snow in the meadow was virgin, and Edmund took delight in making the first prints in it, relishing the sound of his sinking boots and the fact that his wellingtons were just tall enough to keep the snow out. Ahead, he could see a bonfire burning, its black smoke marking the point where the sky touched the earth, the grey cloud so low it bled into the ground and killed the horizon. A black remnant of river broke the ubiquity of white, but the all-consuming force of the cold had decimated its width by freezing it from the banks inwards by hundreds of feet, leaving brook-sized rivulets here and there in the ice archipelagos. In an ox-bowed section, now completely iced over, a sailboat had been caught in the freeze, its prow thrust up, its stern held back, caught in a dead, cold ripple. The force of the still-flowing river had pushed up chunks of ice that jagged this way and that: they reminded Edmund of the photos of the alien ice-fields that Scott had crossed on his fatal trek. In the middle of the river, where the water was still moving, barges of ice floated hearse-like downstream. On one of these sat a murder of crows. Nature didn't intend one to feel sorry for a crow, but the sight of these birds moved Edmund. Too cold to fly, and fat from puffing out their feathers, they looked as though they had surrendered their carrion calling and resigned themselves to riding their ice-boat to the sea.

Edmund approached the camp, the brown NAAFI paper

bag tucked under his arm, sure that his largesse would bring him respect and promotion in the hearts of the ferals. Ozi and company were gathered around a bonfire, closer to the flames than looked humanly possible. One of the boys was fuelling the roar with bits of broken-up chicken coop. There were fewer outhouses than before: the wood shed was gone, as was the stable; it looked as if the ferals had burnt half their accommodation. Ozi was sitting on his suitcase like an old man waiting for a long-delayed train; he was so still he looked as though he had frozen on his perch. One of the boys nudged him to life.

'Good Tommy.'

Ozi jumped up, saluted someone in the fire then turned towards the approaching Edmund, walking around the bonfire but remaining within the circumference of its heat, his face cracking into a wild, half-demented, half-ecstatic smile. 'Ed-mund,' he said, delighting in the way he said it. 'Vot you got?'

Edmund reached the edge of the bonfire's muddy hearth. The heat had driven back the snow and made a circle of brown mulch in a three-foot radius around the fire, in which the ferals stood unflinching, as if adapted to withstand the intense heat.

'Vot you got?' Ozi asked again. 'Vot you got? Vot you got?' he repeated, his teeth chattering after every 'got'.

'Ciggies.'

Edmund handed Ozi the bag, having to turn away and shield one side of his face from the heat. The sight of the contraband turned Ozi from expectant child to forensic professional. He dipped into the bag and produced a packet of Player's, sniffed it then checked to see if the seal was broken. Good. They were as fresh as morning eggs. An unbroken seal would give him more bartering power. Ozi held the packet up and announced: 'Player's. Fa-mous cigarettes.' The cellophane started to brown and blister from the heat.

'*Gut* ciggies,' Edmund said. 'Player's.'

'Good fucking Tommy ciggies,' Ozi said.

A round of appreciative expletives seconded this as he passed the pack around. The boy whom Edmund had so easily wrestled to the ground was standing a little further back, looking on indifferently. Edmund used this moment of maximum favour to show that he had no hard feelings. He took a packet from the bag in Ozi's arms and held one out for his former adversary to take. The boy resisted for a second before stepping over and taking it from Edmund, his need trumping his pride.

There was the smell of something other than burning wood coming from the fire. Something was cooking. An animal was being roasted on a spit. It was hard to see exactly what it was: its head and feet had been removed; it looked bigger than a pig but smaller and skinnier than a cow. Whatever it was, it smelt good. Ozi took Edmund by the arm and led him round to the sizzling thing. He cut a strip from the lean haunch of the roasting beast and handed it to him. The meat was blackened and crisp.

'*Was ist los?*'

There were titters, which Edmund interpreted as a reaction to his poor German.

'*Esel,*' Ozi said.

Edmund knew the German for pig, dog, cow and lion, but he didn't recognize this word. Maybe it was another word for beef. Not wanting to offend his host, he put the piece in his mouth and chewed.

'Tommy like?' Ozi asked.

Edmund chewed on, with all eyes on his response. The meat was tough, with a flavour of something he couldn't place. It was like beef, only sweeter. But it had been so over-done it could have been anything.

'*Ich liebe*,' he said, finally, unsure if this is what he meant, but it seemed to be the right answer.

'*Tommy liebt Esel!*' Ozi said, and everyone laughed and cheered and made gestures of approval and, for some reason, donkey brays. Edmund felt he had passed an initiation of some kind. Then he remembered that he had more to share. He reached into his coat pocket and produced a handkerchief tied into a pouch. Edmund looked for somewhere to set it down. Ozi directed him to his suitcase, turning it flat to make a table.

'*Muttis Haus*,' he said.

Edmund lay the kerchief on the suitcase as the boys jostled themselves into a ring around him. He untied the knot and opened it out to reveal a sparkling mountain of sugar cubes. The sight drew an immediate and collective intake of breath, as though a magic trick had been performed. Unsure that they even knew what sugar was, Edmund took a cube from the summit and held it up to the light. Its granules sparkled.

'Sugar,' he said. He handed the cube to Ozi, who put it straight into his mouth.

Ozi held it there, without moving his mouth, before crunching into it with his back teeth. Then he winced. A red mulch of spittle dribbled out of one side of his mouth. He reached inside to his lower jaw, felt for something and pulled out the bloody triangle of a rotten yellow tooth. He grimaced for everyone to see then looked back down at the tooth drizzled in blood sitting in his pink-black paw. His hand closed on it and he pocketed it. Edmund wondered what he could possibly do with it. It was beyond repair, and no tooth fairy would visit Ozi's stinking manger. If indeed she visited any

German kid any more: they had surely fallen a long way down her list of deserving recipients – below the Italians and the Japanese, at the very back of the queue.

Ozi bent down, scooped up some snow and pressed it against his still-bleeding gum. Someone shouted: '*Mann auf dem Fluss!*'

Everyone turned to look, and there, approaching them across the oxbow, was a man, ageless at this distance but springy and lithe and definitely coming towards them, walking on the frozen water of the Elbe with intent, an intent which seemed to telegraph itself to them and change the gathering into a twitchy herd. If they weren't sure who it was, they all seemed to know who they didn't want it to be.

'*Tsss. Ist er es?*'

'*Nein.*'

'*Ich kann ihn nicht erkennen.*'

The ice walker continued on and, for a moment, the air-bending heat of the fire made it appear that he walked on water.

Only Ozi remained unimpressed. 'It's Berti, you chumps.'

Siegfried said, 'He won't be happy. We hardly snitched anything.'

The figure reached the bank and stepped up, his gait more upright and his stride lengthening as he stepped from ice to snow; and as he came across the meadow, all black and grey, a single orange glow of a dragged cigarette flared in the colourless wash of the winter air.

'It's only Berti,' Ozi repeated. 'I have what he wants.' But it was clear that, beneath his bravado, he was steeling himself for something.

Edmund felt nauseous with apprehension. He wanted to fly back across the meadow to the safety of home, but it was too late.

'Ed-mund!'

Ozi had his head in his suitcase. He barely lifted the lid, shielding its contents. He produced a Russian Cossack hat and tossed it to Edmund, pointing at his head.

'No speak.'

Edmund pulled the hat on and took up a position at the back of the pack; his feet felt thick and numb in his welling-ton boots; the Cossack hat smelt of diesel and was frozen hard as a helmet.

Close up, this Berti didn't look much to be afraid of – he was not much older than the rest of the boys; not much taller, his stature belittled by his outsized coat – but by the time he was within the orbit of the fire the boys had clus-tered into a trembling, mute huddle. Edmund felt himself being pushed back into the fire as the pack unwittingly backed away. Only Ozi, keeping up his faux indifference, remained apart. And it was to Ozi that Berti went, barely noticing the presence of anyone else. He asked Ozi some-thing quietly, not wanting anyone else to hear. Ozi handed him a piece of paper and chuntered and chirped as it was inspected. The young man looked neither pleased nor displeased. He folded the paper carefully and put it inside his coat.

'*Was hast du für mich?*'

This question sent Ozi into a full repertoire of shrugs, beseeching hands and head-shaking, then he pointed his thumb over his shoulder to some imaginary accomplice who'd let him down. Halfway through his unconvincing riff – even Edmund thought Ozi resembled a squirming, shifty little worm – Berti silenced him by grabbing his face in the pincer of one hand. The movement, its violence and proximity, pumped adrenalin and dread into Edmund's sys-tem. He felt he was going to vomit.

Released from his grip and seeming immediately to forget the abuse, Ozi became a maître d', pointing Berti towards the spit as though to a table in the best spot in a restaurant. Berti approached the animal. He studied it for a moment then turned to Ozi and the rest of them. He looked even angrier.

'*Wir essen Esel, während die Engländer Kuchen essen!*'

There was that word again. *Esel.* And something about the British eating cake.

Ozi tried to distract Berti with his next trick, waving what looked like a tube of medicine. He was like a lion tamer whip-cracking his beast from chair to flaming hoop to stair, permitting the lion no time to remember its essential 'lionness'.

'Berti, *schau mal, was wir für dich haben! Pervitin!*'

Berti snatched the tube and took two tablets straight away. Ozi then clapped at the others to give up what was in their pockets. Otto produced a church collection tray and laid it on the ground. The ferals tossed whatever they had into it, a measly but eclectic offering: some medicine for venereal disease, prophylactics, sugar cubes. Reluctantly, Ozi added most of Edmund's contribution.

This last caught Berti's eye.

'*Wo hast du den Zucker gefunden?*'

No one answered.

Ozi said something about hotels, but Berti didn't like it. He grabbed Dietmar and held him in a headlock and drew the orange tip of his cigarette to within an inch of his eyelid. Dietmar moaned as the cigarette singed his lashes.

Edmund swallowed the acid rising in his gullet. Hot urine burnt into his thigh. He wanted to tell Berti to stop, but he was too afraid to speak, even though he knew that in some way he was responsible for the torture being dispensed. What would his father do?

'Stop! Please . . . Stop it.'

The English words disarmed the assault immediately. Berti released Dietmar, and the huddle cleaved to leave a channel from Berti to Edmund.

'He's all right, Berti,' Ozi said. 'He brings us ciggies . . . and he brought the sugar. He is a good Tommy.'

A full flow of hot piss flooded Edmund's pants and trickled down inside his trousers, all the way to his wellingtons. The heat was momentarily comforting, but his legs felt rubbery and weak: he couldn't have run even if he'd wanted to. He thought of his father again. This was not the heroic death he'd envisaged. If they found him, they'd see the yellow stain in the snow. Medal winners didn't piss their pants. Edmund Morgan: Rest In Piss.

But, for some reason, Berti didn't move. He remained where he was, calculating something. He conferred quietly with Ozi, glancing occasionally at Edmund. Eventually, he turned to him, wary. He looked down at the tray and gathered up a packet of Player's.

'Bring ciggies,' he said in English. 'Here. Every week.'

'Yes . . .'

'Or I will do this.' He held up the cigarette to his eye. 'To you.'

Ozi turned to Edmund. 'Good Tommy. You bring ciggies . . . here . . . tomorrow *und*' – he made a forward arch with his hand to indicate the leap of a week – '*und* next.'

Edmund nodded furiously.

Berti then threw his sugar cubes into the fire. They landed on the wire mesh of the chicken coop that was burning and Ozi made a squawking noise and leapt right on to it to get them; but the heat was too fierce and, almost in the same motion, he sprang back and out like a frog, landing on the ground, his coat-tails alight. The others laughed at him as he rolled in the snow to dampen the flames.

Berti picked up the rest of the ferals' offering and pointed at Edmund then back towards the Villa Lubert. Edmund didn't need to understand exactly, he could feel the intention and he started to obey, backing away from the ferocious weight of the man's stare, his scared legs buckling and stumbling as he broke into a run.

The Nissen huts of Hammerbrook were banked up to the eaves with snow and the golden glow of kerosene lights at their windows gave the impression of a cosy, contented village hunkering down.

'Oh come, oh come, Emmanuel,' Minister Shaw said, recognizing the tune, as Lewis led him up the snow-swept path between the huts towards the people at the hand-out point.

As Lewis had predicted, the steady snowfall of the last two days had cleaned up any signs of discord, driving people indoors and protesters off the streets. So far, everything the minister had seen on his tour had given the impression of a difficult situation being brilliantly managed: even the factory protesters had put down their placards, while, here at the camp, where Lewis had hoped to present Shaw (and the accompanying photographer from *Die Welt* newspaper) with some irrefutable images of hardship, charity was out in force. The Red Cross, the Quaker Society and the Salvation Army were present, its brass band playing carols while their colleagues dispensed soup and food parcels to queues of DPs.

'It's good to see that you're getting them fed, Colonel.'

'Twenty people have died of starvation this month, Minister. It's only going to get worse. Without the food parcels, these people would starve. Germany can't feed itself.'

'But there is rich farmland all around.'

The photographer was trying to manoeuvre Shaw into position for the next shot.

'The Russians have the breadbasket, but they're not sharing,' Lewis replied, knowing Shaw was only half listening. 'The city's supplies usually come from farmland that's now in the Russian zone, but the Russians won't give us grain until we dismantle more factories. As a result, 90 per cent of the food in the British zone is imported. That's 2 million tons of food a day, Minister. And already the ships can't get through the ice. If we dismantle the factories, the Germans won't have work. Meanwhile, many of them can't work anyway, until they've been cleared through the de-Nazification process. It's a vicious cycle.'

Shaw nodded thoughtfully, but Lewis felt he'd given him too much: a scattershot rather than a bullseye. And now the photographer was moving in.

'Minister. If I could get you to take a position behind the trestle. I would like to get a shot of you handing over a parcel.'

For Leyland, the overseeing officer from *Die Welt*, the brief was simple: show the British in a good light to the German public, standing side by side with Germans in their hardship. He already had a few reputation-saving pictures in the can: Shaw perched on a child's school chair, next to three smiling German girls as they studiously examined a history book depicting the Houses of Parliament ('German children learn rudiments of democracy'); Shaw standing over a printer's block at *Die Welt* ('Germans enjoy the benefits of a free press once more'). But 'Minister hands out food parcels to grateful Germans' was surely going to be the shot of the day, providing the syncretism everyone needed: it would show Germans that the British were compassionate and competent; it would allay the criticisms being levied at the Control Commission; and leave Shaw looking like a man of action. Shaw knew the drill: ask a question, shake a hand, look concerned.

Shaw said hello in German to an elderly woman and stooped magnanimously to present the gift. The woman took it with a grimace and left without saying a word, unmoved by the minister's studied compassion. The photographer snapped, but where was the gratitude? He needed to capture the gratitude. A mother with a toddler riding her hip came to the table next. The photographer closed in. Shaw instinctively blessed the little girl with his gloved hand and handed the food parcel to her like some plain-clothes St Nicholas. The photographer crouched, aimed and got the shot.

A scruffy young man, who had been following them ever since they'd arrived, called out to Shaw:

'*Tommy, gibt uns mehr zu essen, sonst werden wir Hitler nicht vergessen!*'

These words had been shouted at Lewis before: once by a woman stealing coal at Dammtor station and once by a young boy at the Goosemarket.

Leyland told the man to move on, apologizing to Shaw for the man's rudeness.

'But what was he saying?' Shaw asked, looking at Ursula.

'He said: "Tommy, give us more to eat or we won't forget Hitler."'

Shaw seemed pleased at this rather than offended. The challenge gave him the opportunity to demonstrate something.

'Ask him if he really means that?' he asked her.

Ursula relayed Shaw's question to the man, whose response came back firmly and with a bold contempt.

'He says: "We were better off then than we are now. Things were never this bad – not even in the last days of the war."'

The photographer, a man no doubt fearful for his prized job, told the troublemaker to keep it down. But Shaw seemed genuinely interested. He turned again to Ursula.

'Ask him if he is grateful to have his freedom.'

In answer, the man pointed to the hut. Ursula translated again:

'"Does this look like freedom? I have been in three camps since the end of the war. In Belgium, in Cologne, and now here. I haven't seen my wife for nine months. Why? Because I fought for my country?"'

'What would make it better?' Shaw asked.

The man muttered his reply sotto voce.

Ursula suppressed a smile and looked at the backs of her hands.

'What did he say?'

'He . . . is just angry,' Ursula replied, trying to protect the man from himself rather than Shaw from the insults. 'It is the stomach talking.'

Shaw wanted to show that he was a hard man of the hustings. 'He's free to speak. I don't mind. Come on. What was it?'

Ursula hesitated and looked at Lewis for permission.

'I think it's important the minister hears what he said,' Lewis said.

'He said, "Stop treating us all like criminals." And then . . . "Go back to England."'

'I suspect it was stronger than that . . .'

Lewis tried not to smile and nodded at Ursula to translate fully.

'It roughly translates as "Fuck off back to England."'

Lewis drove Ursula home, paying scant attention to the road, his head full of the things he'd meant to say to Shaw.

'Thank you,' she said.

'For what?'

'For trying to say the difficult thing.'

'I didn't say nearly enough. Didn't make myself clear at all.

I had an opportunity to make a difference. Now he'll go back to London and no one will know how extremely grave the situation here is.'

'You are being hard on yourself.'

'I am a chump. I blew my chance.'

'You can't do everything.'

This sounded like a reprimand. Up ahead, an abandoned lorry lay jackknifed across the road, its front mounting the pavement, the tracks of the accident already covered in fresh snowfall. As they passed, Lewis saw a figure scurry from the cabin clutching something. He pretended not to see it.

'You don't have to drive me all the way.'

'I'm not having you walk in this.'

'But this is the wrong direction for you.'

'I insist.'

The car's powerful heater pushed hot air out over Lewis's legs, and the warmth started to rise up and envelop his chest; his fingertips became tingly as the circulation returned. As the temperature rose, the smells of wet wool, tobacco and Ursula's linen scent mingled inside the cabin.

'What was this name they called you? Lawrence of Hamburg? Is this a good name or a bad name?'

'It depends who says it.'

It was Barker who'd christened him with that nickname and, at the time, Lewis hadn't objected: it played to a secret vanity. 'He's referring to T. E. Lawrence. Lawrence of Arabia?'

Ursula hadn't heard of him.

'He was a misfit British lieutenant. Stationed in Egypt during the First World War. He had a great knowledge and understanding of the natives – the Bedouins. He wrote a book called *The Seven Pillars of Wisdom*. It's a kind of bible to me. I carry it everywhere. Barker calls me Lawrence sometimes. Someone in the office must have overheard him.'

'I am interested to know this character.'

'He was always upsetting the authorities. Sticking up for the locals. The army considered him insolent. They hated him for preferring the natives to his own kind. I will lend you my copy. It's signed. I met Lawrence briefly once. At a Forces do.'

'What was he like?'

'He looked as though he wanted to be somewhere else.'

'So do you prefer the natives?'

'It's a common enough criticism. Even my wife says as much.'

The noise the car made on the road changed from a sloshing to a blanketed scrunch, and Lewis felt the difference in the softened vibrations of the steering wheel. The mention of Rachael made him grip the wheel tighter.

'I think this is very brave of her to share the house – with the German family. Not many people would be able to do this.'

Lewis knew this to be true, but he'd not thought of Rachael as being brave.

'Is she . . . settled in?'

Settled. Now there was a word.

'I think she . . . is getting there. She wasn't . . . she hasn't . . . been well. It's taken her a long time to get over the loss of our elder son.'

Lewis had given Ursula the bare fact of Michael's death after he had discovered her own bereavement. It felt like a fair exchange – a dead husband for a dead son – but he'd not elaborated. Nor did he intend to.

'I think I would find this very difficult. Living with my old enemy. When I blamed them for the death of my son. And then to have a husband who now cares about the enemy. This is difficult.'

She'd garnered this from very little information. How had she got there so quickly?

'Yes. But . . . she has to . . .' Lewis stopped himself. He was giving too much away.

'Has to?'

'She . . . I had hoped that with time . . . she might move on.'

'Why? Time does nothing.'

Lewis had no answer for this.

'The death of a son does not heal,' Ursula said.

Lewis exhaled, long and hard enough to steam up the inside of the windscreen. He reached forward to wipe it with his glove.

'This weather is quite something,' he said.

Ursula understood the code. 'I'm sorry. It's not my business.'

'No, no. It's fine.'

There was a pause.

'You have another son, yes?'

'Yes.'

'What is he like?'

Thinking of Edmund made Lewis smile. He enjoyed him, wanted to know him better; but the lack of knowing him niggled and stymied his ability to say so.

'He's . . . a good boy . . .'

The steering wheel was suddenly yanked from his hands, jerking clockwise then anti-clockwise as though being turned by a drunk ghost-chauffeur. By the time Lewis regained the wheel the car was already sliding sideways, entering into a deceptively calm and elegant spin; rather than struggle against it he let it float across the road and land where it would. Somewhere, he heard himself say, 'Brace!' and he reached a stiff right arm across Ursula's midriff, locking her there until the car landed soft and soundless in a deep drift. Even though the car had come to rest, he left his arm across her and, in the split within the second, he overrode his instinct to retract it.

'I don't know what happened there,' he said. 'It just . . . the wheel just . . .'

Still his arm lay like a barrier, no longer offering protection. He stared at it, waiting to see what she would do. She put her left hand on his forearm and lifted it away.

'I'm sorry. That was . . .'

'It's fine, Colonel. It was an easy mistake.'

The car was firmly lodged in the drift. Lewis decided that he would see Ursula home and then get himself to the Officers' Club on the Jungfernstieg, find transport home and get REME to dig the car out when they could. He was desperate for a cigarette. Even the car's armrest stash was empty.

'I will walk you to your house.'

'You don't have to, Colonel.'

'It's fine.'

They walked up the deserted Neuer Steinweg in the old, intact part of the city, the embarrassment Lewis felt over his indiscretion making him walk slightly too fast.

Rachael had always teased him for his guilelessness when it came to the opposite sex. It was his best defence when away from home: his simple fidelity had always allowed him to survive situations others found too tempting. Sexual shenanigans among his fellow servicemen were common enough, and blind eyes were often turned on their frequent affairs. But he'd never been beset by the temptation that often consumed and sometimes destroyed perfectly rational men. He'd once wondered if there was something wrong with him in this regard. There had been that night in Bremen when his then second-in-command, Blackmore, accused him of being a 'spunkless monk'. It was in the first weeks of peace, and the celebrations had turned orgiastic, with whole platoons of men pairing off with local German girls. He'd had to rescue the just-married captain from giving it all up for a barmaid. 'You are a fucking spunkless monk, Morgan. A spunkless monk,' he'd taunted as Lewis stood in the doorway waiting for his second-in-command to get dressed. 'I mean, look at her! How can you resist? Don't you want to?' The girl lay with one leg straddling the bedsheet, spent and in a deep sleep. She was milky and soft and inviting, but no, he hadn't wanted to. And it wasn't, as Blackmore had accused him, due to a lack of red blood cells or an excess of self-control. He really only had those kind of eyes for his wife. But, now, watching Ursula make antelope skips as she tried to avoid sinking into the deeper patches of snow, he wondered if he could rely on that protection. He'd noticed things about her – little movements, little looks – that he'd never thought to notice in anyone other than Rachael; clear, keen, minute observations. It was like being given a pair of glasses that exposed a long-lived-with myopia. What would Rachael see now if she were watching from an alcove? Would she see a British officer doing the decent thing, or a husband taking the first tentative steps towards an affair? He knew what Blackmore would think – indeed, half the men at HQ – but what was *he* thinking? Was he really just walking his interpreter home, or was his gallant insistence a cover for ungentlemanly intentions? This cold was making a monkey of his mind and a brute of his senses.

They came to a six-storey town house opposite an old merchant's house. Ursula began to look for her keys in her handbag.

'This is my aunt's apartment.'

Of course. She lived with her aunt. It was why she'd tried to get to Hamburg after fleeing the Russians.

'I would invite you for a coffee, but my aunt is a gossip.'

186

'That's . . . perfectly fine. I wouldn't expect it.'

'Thank you for walking me home. I will see you tomorrow at the office. Weather permitting.'

'Yes. Weather permitting.'

Rachael lay in bed, replaying her spat with Lubert over and over again, word for keenly remembered word, right up until the moment he'd kissed her. Despite the shock of the kiss, she did not feel affronted by it. There had been something almost endearing in it: the way he'd slightly missed her lips, his boyish expectation of the slapped cheek. She'd surprised herself how quickly she'd called a truce, but she'd certainly had no peace since. She wanted to ask him why he'd said certain things about her: her past, her loss, her marriage. He'd described her condition with some precision, and it had unnerved her: it was the feeling, one she had not recognized at first, of being understood.

'I would have liked you more if I'd known you then . . . you are not quite your old self.' 'Not quite your old self'. Lewis had said it to her a number of times since Michael's death, and Edmund must have heard it from his father. Lewis didn't mean it as a criticism – if anything, he was try-ing to encourage her – but implicit in it there was a desire, a hope, that she would just go back to being the person he used to find easier to love. To be the person she'd been before the bomb, the 'old self' who didn't think about whether she was truly 'herself', happy, or about whether she wanted to make love. But she couldn't go back. That inno-cence was lost. The bomb had undone her and she could not see how she would ever return to being that person. And if Lewis couldn't see this, then he could never help her. When she had asked him, 'What was it you loved about me before, Lew?', he had simply said: 'I just do, Rach. I can't explain it.' If she was ever going to heal, she needed some-one to explain it.

She pushed her arm into the expanse beside her. It was cool and empty and, although she'd grown used to having the bed to herself, Lewis's warm body should have been there. Instead, her groping hand found his folded pyjamas underneath his pillow, confirming his absence. She felt the Viyella and the rope-cord tie. For the whole first year of their marriage they'd gone to bed naked, even in winter. There were no barriers between them, then, and no shame. Of course, they'd had the energy of youth and the confi-dence and freedom of unsullied pasts, but over the years there had been a steady covering up and putting on of lay-ers. And, since putting on the hard, mourning clothes of Michael's death, she wondered if she would ever be able to shed them.

She sat up. There was a light on somewhere in the house, illuminating a strip of the floor through the chink in the cur-tain. She turned on the bedside light. She had a strong urge to make herself some hot milk: a habit she'd developed dur-ing the war when Lewis had been away.

She listened to the night. It was silent, except for the radi-ators, which clicked and clanked. She eventually got out of bed and went and peered through the curtain. It was down-stairs that a light was on. Perhaps Lewis had got back and was fixing himself a late snifter. She swung her feet into slip-pers, pulled on her dressing gown and went to see.

A single orange ember was glowing in the grate of the hall fireplace. She looked up at the disputed picture of the naked maid, and felt galled at allowing herself to be ven-triloquized by the controlling spirit of Mrs Burnham. In her own way, Rachael appreciated the painting: it was exquisite – beautiful and inoffensive and all done with the lightest of touches. Perhaps she would make a point of asking Herr Lubert about its back story. And then, she would ask about *his* back story.

The drawing-room light was on, and she entered the room expecting to find Lewis nursing a whisky and reclining on the Mies van der Rohe. But the room was empty.

She went to the bay window overlooking the back lawn, which angled gently down to the river. A few lights across the river twinkled and the snow was still falling steadily. Rachael stared towards the Elbe, which she couldn't see but knew was down there, flowing towards an England she found increasingly hard to imagine.

Something then moved across the lawn. It was the size of a deer or a very large dog but too low slung to be either, and it had a thick, curled tail as long as an arm. She switched off the light to see better, and there, striding indifferently across the snow-carpeted lawn, was a great, dark cat – not a dog or a deer but a cat – bulky enough to be a leopard or even a small lioness, languid and unconcerned. It shouldn't have been there but there it was and it looked quite at home, quite in its natural habitat.

'Wait,' Rachael said. 'Come back.' She wanted the cat to stop – to be sure it was the thing she thought she was seeing. She wanted it to pause and acknowledge her watching; to turn and lock eyes with hers, give her some complicit, meaningful look, a sign; but the animal passed on without a backwards glance and deliquesced into the night.

8

Lubert and Frieda ate a supper of boiled eggs and black bread spread with Petersen and Johannsen margarine. Lubert marvelled at man's capacity – indeed, his own – to adapt to diminished conditions and recalibrate expectations accordingly. Even in the last, desperate year of the war, a meal such as this would have been considered paltry; now, he savoured every morsel. Even Petersen's slimy margarine tasted good.

'Frieda? Would you pass the margarine?'

Frieda slid the porcelain tub across the table and continued to dip her bread into the thin end of her boiled egg, sitting hunched, her forehead oily and one or two spots breaking out, her braided hair and hands still dirty from rubble dust. Her mealtime silences had become so normal that Lubert had taken to reading – something Claudia would have deplored and another sign that his late wife's influence was waning. 'Stefan. Are you going to join us?' she would ask halfway through a meal at which he had been present only in body because he'd been absorbed in the newspaper. 'Is the world of squabbling men really more interesting than me?'

Die Welt now lay spread beneath his meal, open at a report about the number of Germans living in camps in the British zone. Since his reckless kissing of Frau Morgan, he'd been half waiting for the eviction notice. Although she'd been quick to forgive, he could feel ramifications brewing in the rooms below. Perhaps he was more like his daughter than he cared to admit. They were both headstrong and a little rash. And, like her, he felt little remorse for his actions.

'I saw someone trying to break into Petersen's house the other night,' Lubert said to Frieda, thoughts of Claudia prompting him to make an effort with his daughter. 'I was going to stop him, and then I thought, no, they might as well use it. It's a scandal having all these houses sitting empty. It doesn't make sense.'

Frieda continued to eat, without looking at him.

'Poor Petersen,' he said. He spread some more black bread with the margarine. If having to eat in Greta's old kitchenette was a demotion, thinking of his neighbour stuck in some Nissen hut put things in perspective. The margarine magnate had once owned a Rolls-Royce, a racehorse and a huge sailboat which he used to sail up and down the Elbe like an ersatz von Spee. His mansion had been the first house on the Elbchaussee to be requisitioned, along with his boat, cars, horse and pride; not only had he suffered the humiliation of being rehoused in the Nissen huts in Hamm, but, nine months after being requisitioned, his property remained empty, the British having either failed or forgotten to fill it.

'How are things on the rubble runs?'

'It's hard work.'

'Your mother would be proud of you.'

'Have you forgotten? She's dead.'

'I haven't forgotten this, Freedie. How could I forget? I know that I looked for her all those months when I didn't want to accept it. I have accepted it now.'

He could only get so far in his attempts to reach his daughter before he hit rock. And this was the seam through which he could not drill, the hard foundation of all her anger. A knock at the door saved further pointless excavation.

'Come in,' Lubert said, expecting Heike.

It was Rachael. Lubert stood up, more from sudden nerves than politeness. This was surely going to be it. As far as he knew, it was the first time Rachael had been up to their quarters. Perhaps the colonel was waiting downstairs to speak to him. They would chat about the weather and then he would challenge Lubert to a duel.

'Frau Morgan.'

Rachael quickly – respectfully – took in their surroundings, the humble kitchenette, calculating the square footage relative to her own.

'I found this – in a drawer,' she said. 'I thought I should return it.' She held out Claudia's garnet necklace.

Lubert took it and, as he felt the weight of the necklace and heard the crystal clink, he had a flash of remembrance. He had purchased it for Claudia when they were courting and he'd been nervous that it would be no match for her own, inherited finery. Her evident delight when she saw it quelled his panic and confirmed what he'd hoped, namely that she didn't really care for riches.

'Thank you, Frau Morgan. Frieda, you should have this.' He passed the necklace to his daughter. Frieda took it, squirrelling it away in her smock pocket without a word.

Rachael addressed Frieda directly now. 'I also wondered if you, Frieda, would like to have your hair done. We have . . . I have a hairdresser coming to the house tomorrow.'

Rachael looked to Lubert for the translation.

'Freedie,' he said in German. 'Frau Morgan is very kindly offering to let you have your hair done. Would you like this?'

'What's wrong with my hair?'

'Nothing. But . . . think this would be a good thing . . . for a young lady. This is . . . a kind offer.'

Rachael seemed aware of Frieda's discomfort. 'Only if you want to . . .' She turned to Lubert. 'She doesn't have to give me an answer now. Renate is coming tomorrow. If she would like to come, then she will be here in the afternoon.'

Rachael looked quite different today, Lubert thought. Her hard carapace had fallen away.

'Thank you. Frieda?'

'*Danke.*'

It was mumbled, but it was thanks nonetheless.

The Skeleton was late. It might have been the weather, but this had never stopped Herr Koenig before. It could have been his weak chest – the pulmonary susceptibility he said had kept him from having to join the Wehrmacht – although in recent weeks he'd looked well: less cadaverous than usual and with some pink to his complexion; no longer the senescent man Edmund had first encountered. The cake and milk that Heike brought and the chocolate bars that Edmund slipped his way had plumped him out. He'd started taking his coat off for the lessons. He'd even talked about his hopes.

Edmund watched the entrance as keenly as a sentinel, waiting for a dark figure to break the white scene. He was impatient for his tutor to come. Today was their last lesson before Christmas and he was going to give Koenig a surprise early present: the four hundred cigarettes that would enable him to get a *Persilschein* and thus free him to start that new life in Wisconsin with the brother with the bullhorned Buick. After initially declining Edmund's offer of help, Herr Koenig had changed his mind, saying that if 'Hamburg's Robin Hood' could help him get to America he would be very grateful (just as long as he said nothing about it to anyone). The flattery of being compared to England's greatest hero-thief stirred Edmund to be a little bolder with his filching: taking cigarettes for the ferals had proved easy enough; and it had taken him only two missions to take what he needed for his tutor. The full four hundred – smuggled downstairs in the doctor's bag he used for his toys – now sat at the foot of Koenig's empty chair.

Heike entered with a slice of cake and glass of milk – and Herr Koenig had still not arrived.

'Hello, Edmund.'

'Hello, Heike.'

As Edmund's German had improved, the two of them had begun to speak to each other with a flirty confidence, adopting a greeting built on Edmund's original linguistic faux pas.

'How are you today?'

'Today I am very well.'

'You are a delicious girl.'

'And you are a delicious boy.'

She set the tray down on the coffee table.

'Where is Herr Koenig?'

Edmund shrugged.

Heike went to the curtain to look out of the window, her feet passing perilously close to Edmund's life-changing gift. She did a little Koenig impersonation, lifting her hands into paws and screwing her mouth and nose to rodent effect. 'Perhaps . . . he is still underground!' The maid was a comic in any language, and Edmund giggled, despite feeling faintly disloyal to his tutor. Heike nosed around the room, her gaze landing on Edmund's book. 'What is this?'

Edmund looked down at the illustrated German translation of *Gulliver's Travels* that Lubert had lent him and which Herr Koenig had got him to read out loud. He showed her his favourite colour plate: Gulliver pinned down by the Lilliputians.

Heike looked at it in astonishment. 'Read some to me . . .' she ordered.

Edmund opened the book at no page in particular and

read in a confident and fluid German: 'This made me reflect upon the fair skins of our English ladies, who appear so beautiful to us, only because they are of our own size, and their defects are not to be seen through a magnifying glass where we find by experiment that the smoothest and whitest skins look rough and coarse, and ill-coloured.'

'English ladies have the best skin,' Heike said. 'Look at your mother. She has beautiful skin.'

Edmund nodded, although he had never had cause to think his mother's skin beautiful or made enough comparison between English and German women to know.

Heike started looking at her own skin in the mirror over the mantelpiece, turning her jaw this way and that, pinking her cheeks with little smacks, looking for blemishes. 'I get many compliments from gentlemen about my skin. Some say it is like a peach. Do you think it is like a peach, Edmund?'

Edmund wasn't sure of this word 'peach' but he understood it well enough when Heike mimed eating a piece of fruit.

'Do you like my skin?'

Edmund shrugged.

'Rude English boy,' she said. 'You don't think I have admirers?'

Edmund couldn't make out this word either: 'admirers'. But Heike continued, sharing more intimate confidences.

'My Josef went to the Eastern Front. He never came back. Perhaps I will have to find an Englishman. Do you think I should marry an Englishman? What do you think, Edmund?'

Was she asking him to marry her? He shrugged again.

Heike lifted a mock-warning finger: 'Don't touch Herr Koenig's cake!' She made another rodent face and left the room.

Edmund stared at the slice of cake and the glass of milk, but they did not induce desire. They just made him feel sad. Whenever the time came for Herr Koenig to drink his milk and eat his cake, Edmund made a point of looking away or reading his book. It was partly out of respect – it felt like a private moment that shouldn't be observed at all – but also because he found his tutor's routine, with its noises of mastication, the little squelching sounds, the collecting of the crumbs, the licking of the milky lips as abhorrent as rubbing a rough woollen jumper against a painted wall.

The clock tick-tocked, and the tick-tocking amplified to a nagging 'Koe-nig, Koe-nig, Koe-nig'. After a few minutes, Edmund put his book down and went to the window.

'Koen-ig, Koen-ig, Koen-ig – where are you?'

Still no sign of him, but as Edmund watched the gates his father's Mercedes appeared, coming up the drive like a black ship dividing the ice floes of an Antarctic sea. His father was never home during daylight; indeed, being gone before breakfast and back after sundown, he might easily have been nocturnal. What was he doing home this early? Perhaps he had picked Herr Koenig up along the road?

But it was only his father who emerged from the car, bending over and leaning back inside to fetch his briefcase and a file. He then did something slightly odd: instead of walking straight up the steps to the door, he stood there looking at the house, as if weighing some important matter. He then took in a very deep breath, the magnitude of the following sigh apparent from the volume of vapour. He came up the steps slowly and entered through the front door, his steel-clipped heels sounding louder and louder as he approached the study. Edmund looked at the bag of booty, but it was too late to hide it. His father was already standing in the doorway.

'Hello, Ed.'

'Hello, Father.'

His father raised a smile that didn't quite make it as far as his eyes. He closed the door behind him and went and sat in Herr Koenig's chair. He leant forward towards his son, lit a cigarette and sighed out the smoke. His movements were precise and particular but so practised they seemed effortless. Edmund noted it all: the way he bit his top lip the moment after exhaling and scratched the back of the hand, not holding the cigarette with his thumb. His father was an agreeable animal to watch and easier to emulate than his mother, who was more complex and chameleon-like. But today his father seemed more serious than usual. Did he suspect something? His father had rarely shown anger towards him; his long absences and the fact that almost all the disciplining in Edmund's life had been done by his mother meant that Edmund couldn't think of a single instance of his father reprimanding him. Despite this, he was sure that admonishment was coming his way.

'Are you all right?' his father asked.

Edmund nodded.

'Good. That's good.'

His father didn't look cross; but he did have the look of someone who had something very difficult to say. Edmund was suddenly reminded of the time he had sat him down for 'a little chat' after Michael's death. An exchange that went something like:

'Are you all right?'

Nod.

'Good. That's good. Well. If you want . . . if you need to talk about . . . anything . . . let me know.'

A shrug. A nod. And that was all.

His father now looked at him in almost the same way.

'I'm afraid Herr Koenig won't be coming today,' Lewis said. 'He won't be coming back at all. He's in trouble.'

'It was my fault . . .' Edmund blurted.

'What was?'

'I told him to go to America.'

His father looked puzzled.

'I . . . was trying to help him. To start a new life.'

The four hundred cigarettes were creating a Brobdingnagian-sized parcel of guilt that was either going to burn its way through the bag or render it transparent. His father traced Edmund's eyes.

'There's something in the bag? For Herr Koenig?'

Edmund nodded.

Lewis leant forward, cigarette in the middle of his mouth, eyes screwing up from the smoke, and opened it.

'Mother said you were trying to smoke less. I didn't think you'd need them all.'

Lewis studied the loot. 'I was wondering where they'd all gone.'

'He needed four hundred to get a *Persilschein*.'

'Four hundred?'

'It's four hundred for a *Persilschein*. Two hundred for a travel pass. Five hundred for a bicycle.'

'How do you know all this, Ed?' His father seemed amused – almost impressed.

'From . . . my friends. The ones across the meadow. The Boys Without Mothers.'

'Have you been – "helping" them, too?'

The shame bowed Edmund down and lowered his voice. His 'yes' was almost imperceptible. Through his regular stipend to Ozi, he must have already passed on dozens of packs in the last two months.

'I was only doing what you have been doing.'

Lewis stubbed his cigarette out in the onyx ashtray on the desk. 'Giving is good. But stealing isn't, Ed. Even if you're trying to help people, it's not the best way. You should have asked me.'

Edmund nodded. He felt the sad weight of his father's disappointment. He ran one thumbnail up and down the back of the other, keeping his emotions at bay. He couldn't look at his father in case he cried. He must not cry.

'Anyway, it's just as well you didn't give them to Herr Koenig. He was not what he seemed. Not a headmaster. He worked for the Nazi Special Police.'

'But he couldn't fight. He had a weak chest. I could hear him wheezing. All through the lessons. He didn't like Hitler. He wouldn't even talk about him.'

'No.'

'But . . . I don't understand. Are you sure? He didn't seem a bad person.'

'You can't always judge a book by its cover, Ed. Sometimes . . . the bad in someone . . . is buried quite deep.'

Edmund felt a looping in his chest. Whatever heinous crimes his tutor had committed, he was sad at the idea of not seeing him again, of him never making that new life in Wisconsin. This was even worse than having been deceived.

'What will happen to him?'

His father scratched the dark hairs on the back of his hand. 'He will probably go to prison.'

The cake and the milk looked bereft. Koenig would never drink that milk or eat that cake. Edmund started to worry at the cover of *Gulliver's Travels* with his fingernail.

'So are you a Big Ender or a Little Ender?' his father asked.

Edmund shrugged. He knew that his father was referring to the war in the book waged between people who ate their boiled eggs from the fat end and those who ate them from the thin, but he couldn't respond with lightness.

'I was thinking we might get Herr Lubert to help out

199

with your lessons – at least until we find a replacement tutor.'

Edmund was trying to recall every moment he'd spent with Koenig, trying to find the clues he'd missed so that he might reassess him in the light of this awful revelation. 'He just didn't seem a bad person,' he repeated.

'I thought he was a good man, too. I took him at his word. I was wrong. But that doesn't mean you shouldn't trust people. Sometimes you have to trust bad people in order to help them. Even if they betray that trust.'

'I'm sorry I took the cigarettes.'

His father nodded.

'What are you going to do with them?' Edmund asked.

'Well, I might smoke them.'

Edmund stared hard at the bag. 'Can I give them . . . to my friends? They need them to trade for food.'

'They should get food from the camp. Where are your friends living?'

'I'm not sure. They seem to move around.'

'Orphans?'

Edmund nodded.

'How many of them are there?' His father seemed more curious than cross.

'Six or seven, I think.'

His father looked at the bag for an age. He joggled his leg again, the way he did when he was thinking about something, then pushed it across the floor towards Edmund.

'Make sure they don't spend them all at once.'

Rachael was inking the last place card as Lewis entered the dining room. She wrote the name – Major Burnham – in her flowing cursive then folded the card and placed it on the seat next to hers.

'What do you think?' she asked him.

'Lovely,' Lewis said. 'It suits you like that.'

'I meant the table – but thank you.' She touched her curls. 'I had Renate do a job lot. After she did me, I got her to do Heike. And then she did Frieda. Although Frieda took a bit of persuading.'

'Herr Lubert must have been grateful.'

'Yes.'

'These things all help. I'm sure Frieda will remember it.'

Rachael had been moved to see Renate set her hands on Frieda's shoulders, using gentle words to distract her, before undoing the tightly wound plaits and stroking out her hair, combing it down to the small of Frieda's back. 'My, my. What do we have here? Like Veronica Lake,' she'd said.

'There,' Rachael said, stepping back from the table.

Lewis took it in. The table was set for eight and freighted with the full works: the sage-green Wedgwood dinner service courtesy of His Majesty's Forces; the silver candelabra that had belonged to his own mother (the only family silver they possessed); place mats depicting famous landmarks of London; and Lubert's lead crystal effortlessly gilding the whole parade. What toasts had been made with these goblets? What hopeful faces refracted in their surfaces? It was heartening that Rachael had revived her old practice of making individual place-names from white card, drawing a different flower motif beneath the name of each female guest and crossed swords or rifles for the men.

'It looks splendid,' he said, suppressing the thought that there were people on the verge of starvation just a few miles away. Besides, this dinner party was partly his idea; it was his challenge to Rachael, and she'd risen to it. With a task to implement, she had come alive, and Lewis felt an old excitement watching her.

'Susan insists on sitting next to you, so, for symmetry, I will sit next to Major Burnham. I'll put Mrs Eliot in the middle next to your Captain Thompson, the other side of the major. Do you think they'll get on?'

'Like houses on fire.'

'You're not going to start an argument with him, Lewis? Susan said you didn't quite see eye to eye.'

'I'll be on my best behaviour.'

'You can talk about anything: cricket, the weather, even politics. Just not work. See no ships. Please, Lew? For me?'

There was something new in her: since that snowstorm, she'd stepped up to her role as lady of the house. The staff were in obeisance, and all the better for it. She'd gone to a coffee morning with 'The Crew', as the ladies who'd met on the SS *Empire Halladale* called themselves. And terms of endearment were back in fashion.

'Is that right? It doesn't look right.'

Rachael had started to place the name cards on side plates but stopped halfway round the table. 'Names on side plates or place mats?'

'No one's going to mind.'

'These are precisely the sort of things the governor's wife should know. Celia will have something to say. What was it she picked me up on . . . at the coffee morning? Oh yes: I said, "Pardon?" She said, "It's 'What?' Not 'Pardon'."' Rachael mimicked Mrs Thompson's stentorian snort. 'And then something about serving greens for dinner. "It's not greens," she said. "It's vegetables, my dear."'

Rachael retraced her steps, moving each name card from side plate to place mat. Lewis moved his own name card from plate to mat, noting that she'd given him his favourite, the one depicting the troops on the Mall. He looked at his handmade card with its lovingly drawn criss-crossed rifles.

'You've given me guns.'

'Would you prefer a flower?'

Her teasing question and its accompanying three-quarter look were unexpectedly flirty.

'There. Now. What do you think? Really?'

'I think' – he searched for a better word than 'splendid' this time – 'it looks gorgeous.'

He touched her shoulder and was surprised to have his hand met with a clasp. He could never fully decipher a woman like Rachael, but he needed no Bletchley Park boffin to break this code.

'Shall we?'

'We'll have to be quick.'

'What about Ed?'

'I've sent him to Coventry.'

'For what?'

'He's been staying out late, playing with some local boys. It's all right. We've had a little talk. Early nights for a week.'

Heike entered the room and curtsied, looking down at the floor, conscious of interrupting an intimacy.

'*Bitte*. Telephone, Herr Morgan.'

'Thank you, Heike.' Lewis waited for the maid to leave.

'Who would that be?' Rachael said.

Lewis sighed. He knew that the telephone, set up with an extension on the military exchange, took calls only from one place: his HQ. And one kind of call: urgent.

'Aren't you going to take it?'

It was like being pulled apart by horses: the solid work-horse of duty and the skittish Arab of desire.

'You go on. I'll be up in a jiffy.'

Minutes later, he found Rachael standing at the bathroom mirror in just her knickers, testing a necklace against her naked breasts. 'You'd better lock the door,' she said.

He closed the door, but didn't lock it.

'Something bad?' she asked, looking at him now.

'There's been a riot at the factory.'

'Oh.'

'Some people have been shot.'

'But . . . Lewis, you can't leave now. The guests will be here in just over an hour.'

'Darling, I'm sorry. I'll try to get back before . . . the end of the evening.'

She dropped the heavy necklace on the sink and covered her breasts with her right arm.

'Go on then. Go and save Germany.' She said it with an old weariness, more in resignation than anger. And then, with her right arm still covering her breasts, she dismissed him with an indifferent wave and turned away.

Rachael answered the front door wearing the peacock-blue, low-cut, sequinned evening dress that had never been bested at any of her ladies' guest nights before the war. Her hair was up to show off her neck and jawline; her lapis necklace drew the eye to her other strengths. She'd dressed to kill the voices in her head and show the guests that she was fully alive and perfectly able to function without her husband at her side. She was thirty-nine years old. She was not done yet.

Susan Burnham conceded defeat before she'd even taken off her coat:

'Rachael Morgan, you have quite done for us all!' She handed over a trifle in a heavy cut-glass bowl. 'There's enough sherry in that for a separate drinks party. And don't let me forget the bowl afterwards.'

'You look . . . Tolstoyan,' Mrs Eliot said.

'I'll take the best of that, Pamela. You look lovely, too. Both of you.'

As the guests handed their coats to Richard, she breezily announced: 'There's been some crisis. Lewis sends his apologies to you all and hopes to be back in time for dessert. Or does one say "pudding", Celia?'

'Always "pudding". "Dessert" is for other ranks.' Mrs Thompson was so sure of her role as Minister for Etiquette that she missed the tease.

Rachael was determined that Lewis's absence would not be dwelt on for longer than was necessary. She allowed them a single round of reaction – 'What a shame!'; 'How disappointing'; 'Poor chap' – and then waved them to the fireplace, where Heike was waiting with their drinks. By the time the Eliots, Thompsons and Burnhams were sipping their pink gins and toasting the reunion of 'The Halladale Crew', Lewis had been all but forgotten.

'Well, here we all are again,' Rachael said, raising her glass. 'To the Crew.'

'The Crew,' the women agreed.

'Funny how fondly I think of it now,' Mrs Eliot said. 'At the time, I felt quite sick.'

'It's a good job you're not on that ship now,' Captain Eliot said. 'The sea has frozen.'

'Officially the coldest December on record,' Captain Thompson declared. 'Everyone in Camberley is saying they can't remember one like it. Ten-foot drifts in Kent. Minus twenty in Devon.'

'At least they have heating. And food.' Ever the Crew's nagging conscience, Mrs Eliot could be counted on to bring them back across the North Sea to the hard, hoary ground of Hamburg. 'We found ink frozen in the inkwells at the schoolhouse we're using. And yesterday I saw a boy going through our bins and trying to lick an empty rice-pudding tin. He was wearing a dressing gown and had paper bags on his feet. It was pitiful.'

Mrs Burnham sighed. 'Pamela, can we have one evening without having to think about the suffering of the world?'

'I'm sure you'll manage that, Susan,' Rachael said, throwing her a look that said *I'm going to set the tone tonight* before seamlessly encouraging Mrs Eliot to continue: 'How is that group of yours going, Pamela? The discussion group?'

Mrs Eliot had found a natural outlet for her busy concern in one of the many women's groups which Rachael had scrupulously avoided joining: an Anglo-German group started by the district chaplain, Colonel Hutton, in an attempt to encourage Germans in free debate.

'It's become very popular. Although I suspect most come for the free biscuits and a warm room. They sit around, rather stiffly at first, but with the aid of the tea they soon thaw out. We've had some wonderful discussions – arguments even. We had a fascinating one about the differences between the English and German character. And last week we debated: "Should a woman's place be in the home?"'

'Depends on the home,' Susan cut in, making no attempt to disguise her evident impatience with all this 'humanitarian indulgence'.

But Rachael was interested. Mrs Eliot had found something practical to do with her nervy earnestness and she looked invigorated by it. 'Go on.'

'They're not used to debate at all – or to disagreeing publicly with the majority. But they're getting the hang of it. It's harder for the younger ones. They're fine with the games. But the discussions are a challenge. Most of them are disillusioned and suspicious and seem to have no hope.' Rachael thought of Frieda. 'Colonel Hutton is trying to show them that they have a future. That there is some meaning and purpose to life.'

'Like eating and drinking and not banging on about life's

meaning!' Susan said. She really was in combative mood tonight.

'Ignore her, Pamela,' Rachael said, before taking the jug of gin from Heike and turning to the men. 'More gin, gentlemen?'

Lewis was almost clairvoyant at anticipating when to charge someone's drink, and Rachael had made a special note to self to keep everyone's glass replete at all times. The captains were fine, lost in discussing the Edrich–Compton run-feast of the cricket season just gone. The major, however, was standing slightly apart, rotating his glass, which was already almost empty. Rachael went and filled it without asking.

'It's nice finally to meet you, Major. Susan talks about you a great deal.'

In truth, he was not the man Rachael had imagined: her composite picture of him, constructed from Lewis's reports and Mrs Burnham's anecdotes, sketched a cold, ambitious ideologue whose ruthless determination to rid the zone of the Nazi virus had rendered him a humourless bore; she wasn't expecting this shy, almost diffident, man with dark, Levantine looks. His outward modesty – it might have been a studied self-deprecation – undermined his stern reputation. Perhaps Lewis had got him wrong.

'I see you've covered the stain.' Susan Burnham's eyes had landed, as they were bound to, on the new picture above the fireplace.

'Yes.'

'It must be an improvement on what was there before.'

'It wasn't . . . what we thought.'

'You asked him?'

'He was quite . . . affronted.'

'And you believed him?'

'I did.'

Rachael didn't want to loiter here; she clapped her hands to get her guests' attention. 'Shall we go through?'

Mrs Burnham screwed up her eyes. 'Mrs Morgan, you are showing something quite new tonight.'

Heike served the first course, a clear onion soup with a kick that had everyone commending the cook after the third spoonful. The conversation stayed shallow and cross-table until the main course arrived and Rachael decided to commit to Major Burnham, whom she'd sat beside her. If he'd been quiet and vague during the group banter, one on one he was acutely focused.

'Must be serious. If Lewis couldn't leave it until the morning.'

Rachael wasn't sure what she was meant to know or say about it. Like most military wives, she was so used to not discussing manoeuvres and missions, it was quite natural to keep information vague. 'He's conscientious about every-thing that happens in his district,' she responded.

'For our tomorrow he gives his today?' Burnham said.

It was the subtlest of digs, but it teased out one of her own: 'He's certainly fighting the peace as hard as he fought the war.'

'In some ways, peace is harder. The enemy is more diffi-cult to spot.'

'Lewis doesn't like the word "enemy". He's banned it. But he's quicker to forgive than I am.'

'Maybe he has less to forgive than you.'

Lewis had once said that forgiveness was the most power-ful weapon in their armoury. And although Rachael thought this true in some abstract way, Burnham articulated what she believed but couldn't say: that it was easier for Lewis to for-give because he had not experienced the loss the way she had. It had all been at a distance for him; she had been there. She quoted herself: 'I'm not sure you can measure it.' But this was taking her in the very direction she wanted to avoid.

'Susan warned me that you are a good interrogator. How is the whole questionnaire process? Are you rooting out the criminals?'

'It's too easy to obfuscate. It's why I make a point of interviewing as many people as we can. In the end, there's no substitute for looking them in the eye.'

'Can you tell? By looking them in the eye?'

Burnham looked Rachael in the eye. His own eyes – the long lashes and tiger-yellow irises – were disarmingly pretty.

'The ones you think might be guilty, from their demeanour or history, often aren't. I questioned an ex-colonel this week who was trying to get into business. In person, he was classic Prussian: authoritarian, belligerent, unrepentant. Hated the Southerner. Used to having his way. But he utterly despised Hitler and the Party. As many Prussian military did. He was clean. The people I really want to interview – need to interview – avoid the process of filling out the forms altogether. The big fish tend to have the contacts – or the resources – not to have to work, so they don't bother with the forms.'

'Have you caught many?'

'Not enough. We've imprisoned about three thousand.'

'That seems a lot.'

'Not when you consider that a million questionnaires have been filled out.'

'How many will you be satisfied with?'

Burnham lined his crystal goblet before the flame of the candle, refracting the light. 'It's not about numbers, Mrs Morgan.'

Rachael felt for a moment what someone being questioned

must feel under his scrutiny. Whatever it was that motivated Burnham, it seemed to go deeper than just doing his job. Despite the self-control, the separation of emotion and intellect, there was something overly managed about him. She suspected that his motivation was not as rational as he liked to project.

'What made you choose interrogation?'

Burnham set his knife and fork down and dabbed his mouth with his napkin.

'Now you're interrogating me, Mrs Morgan.'

Rachael laughed. 'I'm sorry. I'm just . . . intrigued as to what made you choose your line of work.'

Burnham poured himself a glass of wine. It was the reflex of a man used to controlling the rhythm and direction of a conversation, and he was signalling the end of this one.

'This is a good hock,' he said.

Rachael left it there and, over the rest of the main course, they talked about the merits of German food compared to English, a subject quickly hijacked by Mrs Thompson. As the plates were being cleared away by Heike, Mrs Eliot pointed out that Lewis had not yet appeared. She expressed a hope that he was all right and proposed a toast: 'To the Governor of Pinneberg.'

Rachael had forgotten she had given a time that Lewis would be back. She'd mentioned it to protect him and to keep the guests happy, but she hadn't for a moment believed he'd actually appear. In fact, she now realized that the evening had passed without her once thinking of him. She'd felt a certain liberation in having to conduct things herself, and had even entertained the thought that her good form could be attributed to his absence. Was she better off without him? When she raised her glass, she felt she was toasting not her husband but some faceless official she'd never met.

'And a toast to the hostess,' Captain Eliot added. 'I'd say that was a first-rate meal, Mrs Morgan. To Rachael.'

'To Rachael.'

'It was all the cook, Greta's, work. Not mine.'

'My compliments to her, too, then.'

'I will make sure she gets them – although whether she "receives" them or not is another matter. She's very resistant to my attempts at being civil.'

'Our cook is frightful,' Mrs Burnham said. 'All kinds of airs and graces: "Mina Farter waz unt Nopleman!" But then it turns out that she isn't making it up. I didn't believe a word of it until she showed me her jewellery. My God.' Mrs Burnham pulled back her shawl to show the brooch at her breast. It had a topaz the size of a walnut. 'Three hundred cigarettes and a bottle of Gilbey's.'

Mrs Thompson gasped her approval. 'Good Lord. It's exquisite.'

'Well, Keith has given up smoking. We have extra to spend. And we must do what we can to help. I think she was delighted.'

Rachael recoiled at the sight of the pawned semi-precious gem and the thought of the cook having to sell an heirloom. There was something too brash about Susan Burnham tonight. She seemed irritated by something: was it that she wasn't quite the sun at the centre of this little solar system?

'"Nobleman" is usually code for arms manufacturer, isn't it?' Captain Eliot asked, looking to the de-Nazification officer for verification.

Burnham swilled his wine. 'If it were that simple, we'd round up all the vons in Germany.'

'How is your "Nopleman", Rachael?' Susan asked. 'Is he behaving himself?'

She asked the question loud enough for everyone to hear, and for Rachael to have to answer.

'It has its awkward moments, but I think it's working as well as can be expected.'

'Do tell us about the awkward moments.'

'They're trivial things, really,' Rachael dead-batted. 'What plates we share. Who uses the side door. That sort of thing.'

'I can't imagine what it must be like living under the same roof,' Mrs Thompson said. 'How do you do it?' She asked this as she might ask after a patient who had a terminal disease. 'I would find it quite unsettling.'

'We manage. As you said, Pamela: we are the lucky ones.' With a waft of her napkin, Rachael announced the next phase of the evening.

'I think it's time we had a sing-song.'

The party gathered around the piano. The book of carols was already on the stand and, taking her place, Rachael launched into a rambunctious rendition of 'I Saw Three Ships', before stomping though 'God Rest Ye Merry, Gentlemen'. During each chorus, Major Burnham began smacking out the tidings of great joy on the side of the Bösendorfer with his open palms, drumming with an unco-ordinated rhythm, shout-singing off the beat. His inebriation was probably not that apparent in this relatively intoxicated company, but Rachael was unnerved by it: it had come on him quickly; the urbane, subtle man she'd discussed things with at dinner had turned brutish. She steadied the ship with 'In the Bleak Midwinter' and tried to calm things with 'Silent Night', which Burnham insisted they sang in German and spoilt by cynically over-pronouncing the words to sarcastic effect.

'How about some Gilbert and Sullivan?' Captain Thompson

asked. He'd found the complete leather-bound editions on the back of the piano and opened a volume to *The Pirates of Penzance*. 'Here's one for you, Major.'

Burnham put his glass down and straightened himself. Rachael could smell his hocky breath and feel that suppressed anger bubbling up. He sang in tune, aggressively and without inhibition:

'I am the very model of a modern major general.
'I've information vegetable, animal and mineral.
'I know the kings of England and I quote the fights historical.
'From Marathon to Waterloo, in order categorical . . .'

Rachael slowed the tempo to allow him to keep up, but the witty gallop of the lyrics was too much for him. After getting through the first line of each stanza, he la-la-la'd his way through the rest, while banging his hands more and more violently on the piano top. Halfway through the last stanza the vase on the back of the piano was sent crashing to the floor by the vibrations.

'Oops!' Burnham said.

Rachael stopped playing and stood to inspect the damage: the vase had broken cleanly into four sections.

'Keith!' exclaimed Susan.

'My apologies,' Burnham said. 'I'm sure it can be fixed.'

'It's not my vase, Major. It belongs to the house.'

'Oh. Oh well. That's all right then!' And he laughed, and, to Rachael's alarm, the others laughed, too. As she was picking up the broken pieces, the door opened. For a moment she thought it was Lewis come back, but it was Herr Lubert.

Lubert looked as though he had done, or was about to do, something appalling: his forehead was badly cut just above one eyebrow, the blood still glistening, and his whole frame was heaving from him breathing hard. He stood there staring at them all like some prophet stumbling upon an orgy.

'Herr Lubert?' Rachael said, half clarifying his identify for the guests; half checking his next move. 'Are you all right? You're bleeding.'

Lubert looked at the vase, and then at Burnham. His nostrils were flaring; the rise and fall of his chest and shoulders made him look as though he were steeling himself to lift the piano and crush the major beneath it.

'Sorry about the vase, old chap,' Burnham said. 'I'm sure that with the help of . . . all the king's horses . . . Frau Morgan can put it back together again . . .'

Rachael glanced at Susan Burnham, ordering a swift intervention with her eyes.

'Come along, Keith,' Susan finally said. 'I think you've had enough.'

'What? Let's have another song. Perhaps Herr Lubert can join us?' And he began smacking out the beats to the galloping tune still playing in his head.

'I'd ask you not to hit the piano like that,' Lubert said. He was now staring at Burnham with undisguised threat, his hands clenched into hammers. He had not stopped looking at him since he'd entered. Burnham was sober enough to be riled and hit the piano harder, making the strings thrum.

'I think you'll find this piano is requisitioned, Herr Lubert. Which means it's the property of the Control Commission. Which means – in effect – that it's mine.'

Sure that Lubert was going to strike the major, Rachael stood up, placed the pieces of vase on the piano, and placed herself between the two men. She spoke to Lubert directly and softly: 'We've all had a little too much.'

Lubert looked at her and unclenched his fists. He looked

at Burnham one more time then turned and walked from the room, muttering, '*Sie ekeln mich an!*'

'Ha!' Burnham cried. 'Did you hear that? "You disgust me"! He said we disgust him. *We* disgust *him!*' He turned to Rachael, demanding she instantly extract an apology and mete out some sort of punishment.

'I think he meant you, Keith,' Mrs Burnham said, and this time she took her husband by the arm and steered him towards the exit before more damage was done. 'Time for bed.'

'"But I am the very model of a modern major general . . ."' he protested.

The evening was over. It was not the ending Rachael had planned – they would skip cards and charades around the fireplace – but she wanted everyone to leave as quickly as possible. Her only thought now was to find Lubert. The guests politely withdrew with mingled compliments, thanks and apologies. Ten minutes later, she closed the door on a distraught Mrs Eliot, who hoped that everything would be all right and that Rachael might attend the Anglo-German group and perhaps bring Herr Lubert, too.

Rachael was just about to head upstairs to the top apartment when she heard a groan. There, seated in the armchair in front of the fire, leaning forward with his head in his hands, his hands over his eyes, was Herr Lubert, breathing heavily through his teeth, making a sound like the tide on a pebble beach.

'Stefan?'

Lubert opened his good eye – the other had now closed over – and looked through the lattice of his fingers. He could see the cello of Rachael's hips and the sequins of her dress sparkling in the firelight.

'Are you all right?' she asked.

He felt her hand on his shoulder and dropped his own to reveal his injury, looking up so that she could inspect it more closely. She winced at the gape.

'How did this happen?'

He thought: I was nearly killed by a sign that said 'Let Germany live!', but he couldn't think how to say it, and speaking hurt anyway, so he just groaned.

'Let me get something for that,' she said. 'I won't be a tick.' Rachael went upstairs to fetch treatment, her sequinned dress making a chinkly ruffle as she went.

Lubert rested his elbows on his thighs and his head in his hands again, smelling his wound on his palms and tasting the metal of his blood. The evening's events replayed in a vivid, dizzy spin. He could remember the signs of protest: 'We want to work!' 'Bevin, stop the demontage!' 'Let Germany live!' He'd been a reluctant protester, bullied by his work colleagues into joining. He was afraid of jeopardizing his clearance; but he also hated crowds. With their capacity for brutality, for unthinking, they made him nervous and misanthropic. But this crowd had been reassuringly shabby and serried and he had had a sudden conviction that it was better to be with his brothers and sisters in the cold than in the cosy compromise of his own house. They had listened to Schorsch's clever speech appealing to the British sense of fair play while calling them on their sense of humour, showing Germans that it was fine to laugh and possible to cock a snook at authority – something they'd not done with confidence for years. They'd even sung the German anthem, stoic rather than defiant, and without the demented zeal of recent years. It was the sound of a people finding their voice. And then, suddenly, a honking horn and a revving engine created a dissonance, as a British staff car tried to get to the factory gates. The people tried to move aside. One or two started to bang the roof of the car to register their frustration. Then one of them leant both his hands against its side and pushed it, making it rock. Others joined him, thinking it good sport. They rocked the car so hard, its wheels left the ground. Lubert could see the officer inside, his expression passing from anger to fear. Then, as though they didn't realize their own strength, the young men tipped the car right over, on to its side, sending the officer sprawling sideways against the roof, leaving him with his face pressed against the glass like a gulping goldfish. It was almost comic, but Lubert had sensed that something terrible was about to happen. And then rifle shots sounded. The first froze everyone into a flinch. The second sent them into a swirling stampede like sheep changing direction en bloc, shepherded by invisible bullets. Lubert went with the herd, feeling himself being carried; something had struck him on the brow, but he kept going; for a few yards he moved without using his legs. And then he saw sparks and felt a ringing as a knee struck his temple. He was on his hands and knees, and it took a while to realize that the red dots on the white were his own blood spotting the snow.

Rachael returned to the hall with lint, bandage and iodine. 'Let me see.'

She stood over Lubert and lifted his chin gently with her finger to get to the cut. 'You might have got grit in it.' She pulled up the footstool and sat in front of him. She soaked the lint in iodine, the white material yellowing out. 'This will hurt,' she said.

Lubert winced and shivered with the sting.

'What happened?'

Lubert could picture it, but not explain it. His head throbbed so much.

'They . . . agh!'

'It's all right.'

Rachael held the lint there, with her hand over it, leaning her weight forward to make it easier. Lubert moaned with the deep, cleansing pain of it and reached for her arm for solace. They stayed in this position for a while and, despite the pain – or because of it – he held her arm for as long as possible, and she didn't mind. After a while, she pulled the pad away to look at the cut.

'That looks clean. Right. Let me put this on . . .'

She unfurled the bandage and wrapped it around a fresh lint, soaked in more iodine, moving around him to get to the back of his head, her belly passing inches from his nose; she completed the circuit and fastened the bandage with a safety pin.

'There. That's Girl Guides for you. How does that feel?'

'It stings. But thank you.'

'I'm sorry about the major. He was drunk.'

'Thank you for intervening. This would have been an international incident, I think.'

His face was inches from hers. Rachael noticed the lines around his eyes and saw a sadness she'd not seen in their previous encounters. She imagined kissing him and, in that instant, she knew that she wanted to and that she could. As she held the patch with one hand, she feathered his cheek with her other, then she kissed him gently on the lips, the action overlaying the intent like a palimpsest. She held her lips there long enough for their breath to mingle. She waited for the tripwires and electric fences to kick in, the alarm bells and searchlights, but the restraints did not come. She entered the new territory without anyone stopping her. It was that easy.

'I prefer this kiss to the other,' Lubert said.

Rachael looked down, aware of where she was again.

'Is this . . . part of a plan to get me thrown out of the house?' he asked.

'It's . . . a thank-you,' she said.

'For what?'

'For waking me up.'

9

The factory floodlights illumined a churned-up snowfield where dropped placards lay all around like dead storks. The upended staff car had been cordoned off with tape as the epicentre of the crime scene. A few German policemen stood around in the dark, looking unsure of their place in it all. Surveying the detritus of the riot, Lewis felt overwhelmed by a sense of losing what slippery grip he had on matters.

The military policeman who'd given the order to fire – a Major Montagu – talked him through what had happened, but the how and why couldn't change the what. A monumental fuck-up had occurred – and on his watch.

'The officer was trying to drive to the gates when he was surrounded by an angry mob. They started to attack the car. We fired warning shots, but they continued to rock the car until it was tipped over. Luckily, they couldn't get to him with the car on its side.'

Montagu described the incident with mechanical detachment. Lewis waited for him to complete his report, but Montagu stopped there.

'Then you opened fire on unarmed civilians,' Lewis said.

'We had no choice, sir.'

'It's the dead who don't have a choice, Major. Three of them, damn it!'

Lewis walked around the car to where there was blood on the snow. On its side, the Volkswagen looked even more like an insect.

'They would have lynched him if we'd left them to it.'

'You know that for a fact?'

'Without doubt, sir. They had become . . . a senseless mob by then. We believe there were subversive elements in the crowd,' he went on. 'People who just came to stir up trouble. Possibly Werwolf, sir.'

'Oh, for Christ's sake. Have you arrested any of them?'

Montagu puffed himself up and muttered his answer curtly: 'We are holding half a dozen for questioning.'

'Children, are they?'

The military police had recently been heavily criticized for arresting over a hundred children caught stealing coal. The press had got hold of the story, but the facts – the age of the children – had been changed.

Lewis picked up one of the placards. It read: 'Give us the tools and we'll finish the job!' He held it up for Montagu to read. 'You know who they're quoting?'

Montagu was beginning to chafe at the barrage of questions. 'You would have done the same – had you been here.'

Lewis hurled the placard away. 'We offer them democracy and then punish them for exercising it.'

Barker drove Lewis to an emergency meeting with his boss, General de Billier.

'The major was right,' Lewis said. 'I should have been there. Or at least I should have sent a bigger detachment to support them.'

'It was meant to be a peaceful demonstration, sir. The union assured us of that. The rock apes panicked. That was not your fault,' Barker replied.

'I feel a sacking coming on.'

'I doubt that, sir.'

'Why else would I be called to a midnight meeting with de Billier?'

'He's probably got a new single malt he wants your opinion on, sir.'

Lewis managed a smile. The general was a big whisky man, known for picking men on the basis of their ability to distinguish between a blend and a single malt.

'They can't sack you,' Barker continued. 'You're one of the few people who understand what they're doing here. My guess is they have something else in mind.'

'I'm far from being the indispensable man you think, Barker.'

If, outwardly, Lewis brushed off the compliment, inwardly, he received it, storing it as antidote to his creeping self-doubt. In the army, the straightforward 'Well done' was rare. Praise, when it was given, was usually counterbalanced with insult. This reticence to encourage or compliment wasn't just a military affliction, there was something very English about it, he felt. It sprang from a combination of reserve and realism which Lewis recognized in himself, as well as a fear of letting someone get too big for their boots: one reason why – the English liked to say – they would never suffer dictators as readily as their continental neighbours.

'I've almost got that register done, sir,' Barker went on.

'Register?'

'The missing-persons register. The one you asked for?'

Lewis could hear the sound of crashing crockery: how many other plates had he set spinning and forgotten about? His idea of compiling a list of 'the missing dead' – the unaccounted for from the bombing – and checking it against the names of everyone still in a hospital, infirmary, convent or convalescent home in the region was one of several things he'd instigated but had fallen by the wayside as more urgent matters pressed in.

'I'd clean forgotten. Hope you haven't wasted hours over it.'

'Oh, it's completely taken over my life, sir. But I'll be able to start matching names against the register of patients soon. Give me a few more weeks.'

'How is the other – the valuables report?'

'It's ruffling a few pips and crowns. They don't like it. I'm not going to be promoted just yet.'

'Good.'

Lewis meant it. For one thing, he needed Barker. But he genuinely believed that many people who got to the top lost the motivation that had got them there in the first place, finding themselves in roles unsuited to their skills, leaving their talents to atrophy. Better to stay 'the wrong side of the desk' had always been his motto.

De Billier was leaning on rather than sitting behind his desk when Lewis entered his office. The general was quick to offer him a seat, a whisky and a cigarette – hardly the preamble to a dressing-down. The presence of Commissioner Berry suggested that Barker might be right: they had something other than sacking in mind for him.

'You've met the commissioner?'

'Yes, sir. We met briefly – for the minister's visit.' Lewis liked Berry: he had an impossible and unpopular job and carried it out with grace and dignity.

Berry shook Lewis's hand warmly. 'Hello again, Colonel. The man who shares his house.'

'Not my house, sir, but, yes.'

'The German councillors speak highly of you.'

'Which is precisely why' – de Billier paused to light Lewis's cigarette – 'you are here this evening. Your ability to see the other side.'

Lewis took his seat, remembering that even prisoners were offered a smoke before being shot. With this much butter, they clearly had some shit-awful task in mind for him. From his chair, Lewis could see the full moon through the window behind the general, clearly enough to discern its pocked surface. Perhaps they were going to send him there.

'Any goodwill I might have had in the bank is back there at the Zeiss factory, sir.'

'What happened this evening was unfortunate,' de Billier began, 'but it's part of a much bigger problem. The demontage is causing us real concern throughout the zone. There've been protests in Cologne. Hanover. Bremen. In the Ruhr. It's fomenting huge tension – which the weather and lack of food is exacerbating. The Germans are beginning to hate us. They still think we want to turn the country into a giant farm and that we destroyed their shipping industry to give Belfast and Clyde a lead.'

'We did blow up a fully functioning, world-class shipping yard.'

'Blohm and Voss was an error. We know this now. But aims and goals are changing fast. Almost every month. A year ago, it was our intention to demilitarize. Then it was to de-Nazify. Then to reduce industrial capacity. Then it was just getting these bloody people fed. Now it's clear to everyone – except the French and the Russians – that we need a strong Germany. The merging of our zone with the Americans' has been agreed. We will become the Bizonia in the New Year. And, perhaps, when the French get a better perspective on their place in the universe, the Trizonia. What is becoming clear is that the Russians are looking less and less likely to give their zone back. And the longer we take with the dismantling of Germany's heavy industry, the less likely it looks.'

The general had barely mentioned the evening's tragic events, and it was clear he wasn't going to. As far as he was concerned, it was a local tremor compared to the tectonic shifts taking place between nations. Lewis was almost disappointed. The prospect of being fired which he'd indulged on the way here hadn't been so unwelcome.

'We still have a chance to avoid a total collapse of relations with Russia. Step one in avoiding that is our honouring of the Potsdam Agreement on reparations. Unless this happens, they'll withhold the bread. The Inter-Allied Reparations Agency will impose sanctions we can't afford unless we carry out immediate dismantling. The Americans will have to pay to feed millions of people, and this Iron Curtain that Churchill has been banging on about will become a reality.'

De Billier handed Lewis a file. It was headed: 'Demontage listings. Category 1 sites. Confidential.'

'There are four category-one sites in this region. The Russians are sending a team with the IARA to make sure they are dismantled. We need you to be our point man. And we need you to start immediately.'

Lewis looked at the document and flicked through the sites.

'Heligoland?'

It might just as well have been the moon.

'They're going to put all the munitions in one place and blow it up. We need someone the Germans like and who can communicate these imperatives, someone whose natural sympathies translate. You have a reputation for this, Colonel. The mayor speaks very highly of you.'

To an outsider, this might have sounded like praise, but Lewis knew that this was how they went about getting someone out of the way without causing a stink. They didn't want him sounding off to ministers and the press. He'd criticized their efforts on the ground in front of Shaw. He needed to be disciplined – in a constructive way.

'This is not my . . . area of expertise.'

'It's about people, Colonel,' de Billier said. 'You are our people man.'

'You mean you want someone who can blow things up in a sensitive way.'

De Billier cleared his throat with an impatient growl. He'd used up his selling skills; he wasn't going to package it any better for Lewis.

'Colonel, I despise the Russians and I detest these reparations. But if we want to avoid another war we must get this done. Before the winter's over.'

The sounding-out became an order. 'You'll accompany Kutov and his observers. There will be a French and an American observer travelling with you at all times. I understand your interpreter speaks Russian. If all goes well, you'll be away for no more than a few weeks. Your man can cover things in your district until you're back.'

All through this conversation, Lewis was imagining Rachael in the room with him. How would she take this latest posting? Would this be the very last straw?

'Do I wait till after Christmas?'

'The Russians don't celebrate Christmas any more, Colonel. Besides, it'll be a perfect time to do the deed,' de Billier batted back. 'While we're all singing carols, you can blow stuff up without being overheard.'

The general hadn't got the other side of that desk by being sentimental. And even when Michael had been killed Lewis hadn't been offered – and neither did he ask for – the extra days' compassionate leave after the funeral.

'Sir, I have only had a few months with my family – and

even then I've hardly spent any time with them. This will put huge strain on us . . .'

'Colonel, I'm running a country, not a marriage bureau.'

'Herr Morgan has asked to see you in the drawing room, sir.'

'Did he seem . . . angry?'

Heike had to think. 'No. I don't think so, sir.'

No. Of course not. The colonel was never angry. Even if he'd discovered that his wife had kissed another man, he'd probably talk about the weather then offer him his car.

'Thank you, Heike. I will be down.'

Lubert put down his drawing pen and sealed off the ink-well. He tidied his hair with his hand, thought better of it and ruffled it back to its natural state.

He found Lewis standing at the piano, thinking and looking out across the river. He was in full uniform, gloves and coat on, on his way somewhere – again. Lewis lifted half his mouth into an almost-smile.

'Herr Lubert. Come in. Please. Sit down.'

Lubert went and sat in the window seat.

'How is the head?' Lewis asked, touching his own temple.

Lubert's broken brow was an ugly tortoiseshell of colours, but it was on the mend. 'I am a quick healer.'

'It sounds like quite an evening the other night.'

Lubert waited for Lewis to come out with it, then wondered if the colonel was waiting for him to say something first. These English were meant to suffer from a kind of emotional constipation. Perhaps Lubert should make it easier by offering the laxative of an apology. Tell him that it was not Frau Morgan's fault but his; he'd taken a blow to the head and was not himself and one thing led to another.

'I'm sorry about the incident.'

Lewis looked at him quizzically, and raised halting hands.

'It's not for you to apologize, Herr Lubert. I'm embarrassed on your behalf. For the vase. For any damage done to the property. And the behaviour of a certain guest that night.'

Lewis stroked the back of the Bösendorfer, a corrective touch to the truculent slams it had received at the hands of Burnham. 'Rachael tells me that you handled yourself with admirable restraint. Considering the circumstances.'

Lubert started to stammer a retreat from his headlong confession:

'Well . . . that's . . . I don't blame anyone. It was just high spirits. The vase. It doesn't matter. I did not even care for it.'

'No, but that doesn't excuse what happened. As you said yourself, Herr Lubert, this is your property.'

'Yes.' The colonel was once again throwing a blanket over everything.

'And I'm sorry, too, you had to get caught up in the business at Zeiss.'

'I don't remember much about it. I was listening to a speech. And then the shooting started.'

Lewis's face sank. 'What happened at the factory was indefensible. Just when we think we're making some headway, something like this happens. Someone loses their nerve or panics then everything unravels. We're at a very delicate stage of the whole business. It all hangs by a very thin thread. Anyway, I'm glad that you are all right.'

'You have a very difficult job, Colonel. I don't envy you.'

'You shouldn't. Anyway, the reason I really wanted to speak to you – apart from apologizing for the other night – is to ask a favour. We need to find Edmund a new tutor. I know that you can't work at the factory at the moment. So I wondered if you'd be willing to tutor Edmund, and Rachael . . .

teach them some German. I won't be able to find another replacement while I am away. And it'll be a good chance for Rachael to get to grips with the language. I know that she's been frustrated by her lack of it – especially with the staff.'

'Of course,' Lubert said. 'You are going away?'

'For a few weeks. To Heligoland.'

'So . . .You will not be here for Christmas?'

'Sadly, the military operates to its own liturgy, Herr Lubert. I'd appreciate it if you'd hold the fort for me. I'd encourage you to feel more at home than perhaps you have. I know that . . . things were not easy at first. As you may have guessed, Rachael . . . was not herself when she arrived . . . but I see signs of the old Rachael returning. I think she wants to socialize more, perhaps take Frieda shopping. Company is good for her. It's not good for her to be alone. Especially given the time of year. And, as I keep saying, if things are ever going to work here, our people need to start fraternizing, getting to know one another. I think, what I'm trying to say, Herr Lubert, is: don't keep yourself to yourself. Please feel free to be more at home.'

'Thank you, Colonel.'

Lubert liked Lewis. He respected his generosity. He was grateful for it. And he admired his lack of lofty airs. But he found it hard to listen to this without thinking him blind. Either he was entirely guileless, or his mind was simply elsewhere. Whichever it was, the man's priorities were all wrong.

'I've got rotten news, Rach.'

Rachael was reading her next Agatha Christie and was quite caught up in its delicious web and weave, at a key moment of revelation in the story. When she set the book down, two competing and inappropriate thoughts vied: I wonder who the murderer is; and I hope Lewis isn't now going to tell me that Stefan is 'unclean', like Herr Koenig.

'What is it?' she asked.

Lewis had his posting face on. She'd seen it before – most memorably after announcing that he'd be going straight back to base having just got home for Michael's funeral.

'I've been asked to oversee the demontage. They want me to start tomorrow. It means I'll be away for a few weeks.'

'Oh,' she said.

'I know. It's the last straw,' he said, misreading her and looking for his suitcase in his dressing room.

Somewhere in her were the platitudes of the dutiful spouse; those phrases that army wives had to have ready whenever leave was foreshortened or cut altogether. But her heart wasn't in it. And Lewis, she sensed, wasn't expecting her to wheel them out. 'This is the army, Mrs Jones,' she offered. And Lewis looked at her and nodded.

'I'm sorry, Rach.'

As he started to rummage for kit, she looked back at her book. She really did not want to help Lewis pack. Not this time. It might have been her duty, but she was done with duty. She just wanted to finish this damn paragraph and find out who the killer was. But the sight of Lewis's ineptitude was too much. She set the book down and helped him look for socks in the basket of fresh laundry that Heike had delivered that morning.

'How many?'

'Five or six should do it.'

She threw the sock balls to him one by one, and he scooped his hands together like a wicket keeper and passed each into his bag in one continuous motion. Seeing his pell-mell packing, she started to reorganize his bag for him.

'Is this some kind of promotion?' she asked.

'I think it's punishment for not toeing the line with the minister. Apparently, I said too much.'

'That doesn't sound like you. Who will run the district?'

'Barker. I've told him to check in. Bring the mail. Will you and Ed manage?'

'What do you think?'

He nodded. Silly question.

'When I'm back, I thought . . . Perhaps . . . we might go away. The two of us. When things get a little warmer. Go to Travemünde. Or one of these grand resorts on the Baltic.'

'Yes, that would be nice.'

'But . . . it won't be for some time.'

'No . . .'

Lewis was lost for words; but she wasn't going to supply them for him.

'Well, I'd best be going,' he said. He shut his case and turned to her to say goodbye. Wanting to avoid any heaviness, she kissed him goodbye, on the cheek, as though kissing a departing visitor or passing acquaintance.

10

The manila file, held against her belly by the elastic of her tights, dug into Frieda's ribcage as she walked. She wasn't exactly sure what it contained – the contents were in English – but the word 'Restricted', the red trim and the photographs of various industrial and military sites reassured her that what she'd taken from the colonel's briefcase was something that would impress Albert. The thought of giving it to him made her giddy with pride.

The black-ringed 'R' of the requisition order was hanging loosely on the margarine magnate's railings. Frieda looked right and left, checking for vehicles, and, once absolutely sure the coast was clear, she climbed the low wall at the point where Albert had laid a wooden sledge across the broken glass Petersen had put there to deter thieves. Even with the snowfall, jagged fins poked through the white topping. Before the war, Petersen's security arrangements had caused consternation among his neighbours. Frieda's mother, who had considered Petersen a common social climber, said that no self-respecting thief would steal anything from that upstart's house: his family had made their money fast and loose – first from sisal in the East African colonies, and then from the fake butter – and 'the faster the money is made the more quickly it goes.' Frieda had been too young then to appreciate the subtle hierarchies of old money versus new, but now, as she walked towards the largest house on the Elbchaussee, she saw that her mother's prophecy had come to pass: Petersen's vast, cube-shaped mansion stood sad, silent and empty.

She entered the house through the lower kitchen window, just as Albert had instructed. As she mounted the back stairs to the ground floor she could smell burning wood and candlewax and hear the unbroken voices of young boys. She followed the voices to the drawing room at the back of the house, where she was confronted by a lunatic scene: a room lit by candles and decorated with African artefacts – shields, spears, animal skins and masks. Four boys sat around listening to a kid who was standing on top of a billiard table holding a box full of what looked like sugar tongs; he was wearing a pith helmet, and a zebra skin around his shoulders, and calling out like a St Pauli fishmonger.

'Fresh in from Dammtor!' the boy cried. He shook the box and picked out a pair of tongs, snapping their mandibles together. The candlelight cast a grotesque shadow on the wall behind him, making a giant dwarf of him and turning the tongs into a metallic langoustine.

'What use are they? We don't even have sugar,' one of the boys piped.

'Look and learn, Otto. They may be sugar tongs to you, but to a beautiful lady who needs to keep it that way . . .' The boy set the box down and, holding up a pair of tongs, he started to demonstrate, snapping them like tweezers, plucking at his eyebrow.

'Or . . .' He opened his mouth and pretended to make an extraction, using the tongs as dental pliers.

'Or . . .' He used the tongs to peg his nose and mimicked a flatulent.

'Or . . .' He bent down and pretended to pick something off the ground.

'Or ...' He reached into his pocket and produced a cigarette. He gripped one end with the tongs, brought it to his mouth and puffed like a dandy. 'The ladies will go crazy for them.'

The ferals seemed unimpressed; a boy with a spear led the chorus of criticism:

'People don't want sugar tongs. People want potatoes.'

'This was a waste of ciggies, Ozi.'

'You are getting us some bad deals.'

The boy put up his hands. 'Keep your hats on. I have got something very special. Thanks to the Tommy boy. Something very special.' He reached under his zebra skin and produced a cigar-shaped tube. Frieda recognized it as the medicine that Albert took: Pervitin, the drug that young soldiers had been given to keep them 'up' in the last, bitter days of the war.

'One of these makes you strong. It keeps you warm. And you are never hungry. Berti's got the box. But I got a tube for each of us.' The boy stopped and looked towards the door. 'Eh up. Look who it is.'

'Those aren't for kids,' Frieda said, keeping one hand on the door in case she needed to run.

The feral with the spear raised it to his shoulder, its thin shaft wobbling. 'Who are you, missy?'

The kid in the pith helmet jumped down from the billiard table. 'It's all right – she's Berti's girl.'

His friend lowered the spear.

'How do you know who I am?' Frieda asked the kid.

'I saw you.'

'Saw me where?'

'I saw you ...' The kid pushed his right forefinger through the ring of his curled left forefinger and thumb. In, out; in, out. His friends sniggered.

She ought to strike him for his impertinence. How had he seen them? Was it at the house in Blankenese? Or here?

'Where is he?'

'He's upstairs with his friend.'

'What friend?'

The boy held up a tube of Pervitin.

Albert was in the master bedroom, but he wasn't in bed; he was dancing to a record playing on a portable phonograph; it was one of those rude American tunes that Heike listened to on Radio Hamburg: all jungle drums and squawking brass instruments and disorder. To see Albert dancing to it unnerved her. He was stripped to the waist and moving in a loose-limbed way like a puppet being handled by a drunken puppeteer, placing his feet in random fashion as though crushing ants on the carpet. He was so lost in the dance that he didn't notice her entering. She felt embarrassed watching him; this skipping, hopping, bobbing young man was not the sleek, cool, controlled Albert she knew: he seemed temporarily possessed.

'Albert? What are you doing?'

He turned but didn't seem startled. He continued to dance to the music. 'My proper German lady ...' He stepped towards her with an exaggerated prowling motion, creeping, creeping up on her to the beats of the music, putting out a hand for her to join him. His skin shone and his eyes were slightly too wide and bulging to be trusted.

She tugged the stolen file from her skirts and held it out to him.

'I have something important.'

'Benny Goodman,' he said, still dancing. 'Benny Goodman. Dance!' He held out his hand to her. Insisting. It was radiant and clammy. The 88 scar on his bicep was twitching. She wanted to please him, but she couldn't dance.

'I can't,' she said.

'You can . . . my proper German lady.'

He placed the hand on her hip and led her with his other. Frieda pressed the file against her chest and moved her feet from side to side in a perfunctory manner, but she couldn't let herself go. This modulated music was too anarchic, too hard to grasp. And she needed Albert to be . . . well . . . not this! With every jig and jerk of his body, he seemed stranger to her.

'I can't!'

Albert backed away, still dancing, towards the phonograph. He lifted the needle from the record.

'So. So. So. The girl will not dance. A soldier should know when to enjoy himself. Come on then, my keen friend. Show me what you have.'

She handed him the file. He had stopped the music, but he continued to dance to the tune in his head. Albert took the file then stroked it. '"Restricted" . . .' he read. 'This is good.' He flipped the elastic back and opened the file. He took his time reading the text, his lips moving as he translated it. After a few seconds, he began to nod appreciatively.

'Where did you get this?'

'From the colonel.'

Albert read on, making satisfied humming noises.

'It is good?' she asked.

He put the file down and looked at her, voraciously now. He placed his hot hands on her biceps. She could make out the pulse at his neck, hard and fast, and feel his erection pressing against her. Remembering the power she'd had over him before, she started to undo his belt. He made the humming sound again and pushed himself against her. He lifted her skirt and she pulled her undergarments down. She leant back against the end of the bed frame. He made noises of pleasure as he pushed into her, and this made her feel proud and powerful again. She began to reciprocate the noises to please him, then she found herself making them involuntarily, for herself as well as for him. He took much longer to reach the end this time, and this allowed her time to feel new pleasures. When he was done he stayed against her, slumped and floppy. And then he stepped away, doing up his trousers. She felt as though she could hear and see everything in the room, and everything outside the house.

'Will you mark me?'

He laughed, popping another Pervitin.

'Fine.'

He took a cigarette from the packet on the bedside table. He lit it, took a drag, and then came towards her.

'It will hurt.'

'I don't care.'

'Where do you want it?'

'Here.' She held out her lily-white forearm and circled the soft part of the skin.

'You can take one of the tablets – you won't feel it.'

She shook her head. 'I want to feel it.'

He gripped her wrist hard and jammed the cigarette into her arm, holding it there until it was extinguished. She tried not to cry out, making a moan through gritted teeth. He re-lit the cigarette and made another 'O' above the burn to complete the 8. She looked at the new scar, already red and raw. The smell of burning skin was extraordinary. She imagined her mother briefly, on fire, her whole body being branded, then she nodded for Albert to continue. He tried to re-light the cigarette but he'd been pressing so hard it had concertinaed and wouldn't take. He lit another and made the next

'O', the stings of the first 8 countering the laying of the second. And for the last 'O' she found herself emitting a noise of pleasure not unlike the noises she had been making minutes before. When it was done she took Albert's face in her hands in a manner she imagined adult – for that is what she now surely was – and looked into his eyes. The drugs were making them twitch and flicker, and she wanted them focused on her. She cupped his face again and made blinkers of her hands.

'Why do you take these drugs?'

'I have to be alert. There are many things to think about. They help me with my missions.'

'You don't tell me about your missions. Or your plans.'

'All in good time . . .'

'You keep saying that. Don't you trust me?'

'Of course. But . . . it is better that you don't know. You have been . . . useful.'

She wanted to be more than this.

'You talk about being a soldier. But . . . I don't see you fighting. I see you dancing. And taking these drugs. You aren't doing anything.'

Albert stiffened, his head pulling away from her.

'Don't worry, my German lady. I know what I'm doing.' He smiled at her patronizingly.

'Do you? You talk about an army. But where are they? All I see is those *Trümmerkinder*.'

Albert looked at her, trying to focus.

'My proper German lady . . . you are like a wave of Tommy bombers. Like the *wham wham wham* of ack-ack. Don't worry. I know what I have to do. I have seen it already. I have seen it all.' He tapped his head to show where he had seen it. 'And it will be big.'

*

Mickey Mouse stood at the crossroads with only an umbrella for cover. In need of shelter, he went and knocked on the door of the house, only for the porch to collapse and reveal another door that was open. The wind was blowing the house left and right and almost off its foundations. As Mickey entered the house, the door slammed shut behind him, padlocking itself. Bats filled the room and a terrified Mickey jumped into a pot before running from the room, crying, 'Mummy!'

Everyone in the house, except for Greta, who had declined Rachael's invitation, was gathered around the Ace Pathescope watching the final film of the evening: *Mickey Mouse's Haunted House*. The projector had been Rachael's tenth-wedding-anniversary gift to Lewis (tin and aluminium), but she might as well have given it to Edmund, for it was he who got the most pleasure and use out of it. And he was in his element now: projectionist, sweet seller, diplomat, interpreter, passing round the all-day suckers and the bas-relief ginger and cinnamon Spekulatius biscuits, anticipating every conceivable funny point in the film ('This bit is good; you will like this bit'), laughing then checking to make sure the others were laughing, too. Under the mesmerizing glow of these silly little films, the household had reached a happy unity: Heike was tentative, before collapsing into giggles; Richard was distracted by the mechanics of it all but then started to cackle at Popeye flexing his muscles; Frieda's adamantine face broke into surprising crinkles at Buster Keaton's death-defying stunts, and her laugh, when it finally came, was a fledgling version of her father's.

Lubert guffawed with abandon, a sophisticate enjoying simple pleasures. Rachael wondered if he was genuinely lost in the films or putting on an exaggerated act of appreciation for the benefit of the others. Was he feeling – as she was –

that this was all a prelude to something more interesting? As the picture broke up into dots and scratches, their eyes met, and she fancied she could detect the same anticipation in him.

'The end!' Herr Lubert said with a flourish, clapping vigorously.

Edmund flipped the main light back on and everyone blinked in the sudden brightness.

'Thank you, Edmund. This is a future for you. You will make movies one day, I think. Frau Morgan, what do you think?'

Edmund, who had only ever thought of being a soldier like his father, looked to his mother to see if she would agree to such an outlandish career choice.

'I think he will,' Rachael said, and Edmund swelled with the double endorsement.

Richard thanked Edmund for the show. 'Popeye sailor man,' he said, and he flexed his biceps, chuckling to himself. Heike was speechless with it all, touching her breast to indicate her gratitude while making little curtsies. Rachael was sure she heard her say 'Delicious' to Edmund.

Frieda, whose hair was back in its binding – albeit a single plait now – remained silent.

'Say thank you to Edmund and Frau Morgan, Frieda.'

'Thank you,' she said. She looked at Rachael and tried a smile. 'I would like to go bed now,' she said, in English.

'Of course, Frieda,' Rachael said. '*Frohe Weihnachten.*'

'Can we watch Mickey one more time, Mother? Please?' Edmund was already re-spooling the negative.

'I think that's enough for now, Ed. The quicker you get to bed, the quicker you'll be able to open your presents.'

'Aren't we going to open them now? The way they do in Germany?'

'I thought we were doing things the English way,' Lubert said, winking at him.

Edmund wrestled briefly with the idea of postponing such gratification for future reward, but he accepted it from Lubert. 'All right then,' he said. He then kissed his mother. 'Good night, Mother.'

'Good night, darling.'

Heike had started to clear the plates away.

'You can leave them, Heike,' Rachael said. 'Really. I will do this.'

Heike hesitated, looking to Lubert for guidance.

'Take the night off, Heike,' Lubert said, effortlessly assuming his old role of master of the house.

'Good night then,' she said, bowing and blushing and backing away.

Rachael and Lubert waited for everyone to disappear upstairs to their rooms. Lubert pretended to inspect the lens of the Ace while Rachael stacked the plates. At last, the creaking of floorboards ceased and the crackling of the fire became the only sound in the house.

'Well. That was most enjoyable,' Rachael said. 'It was really lovely to see everyone laughing like that.'

'This is the miracle of Mickey Mouse,' Lubert said. 'Perhaps he can bring world peace to us all.'

'Would you like a nightcap?'

Lubert wasn't sure what this meant.

'It's what we call a last drink before bed,' she explained. 'To help you sleep.'

'A drink is never just a drink with the British.'

'Well?'

'*Bitte.*'

Rachael poured two military-strength whiskies, adding a dash of water to each. She handed one to Herr Lubert and pulled up a footstool to sit in front of the fire, inviting him to do the same. They watched the flames in silence, side by side, inches apart. A fire was a theatre in its own right and this one was loud and lively, full of intriguing plots and sub-plots. Rachael fixed her eyes on the top coal, which was just turning orange.

'I like the way that you make more of Christmas Eve here,' she said. 'I've always preferred Advent to Christmas.'

'Are you a religious woman?'

Rachael shook her head slowly rather than definitively.

'I've always enjoyed the trappings.'

'But the thing itself? When it is all stripped away?'

'I think my faith — such as it was — was blown out of me.'

'Perhaps we should not talk about such things.'

'No. We should,' Rachael said, feeling the need to express a deeper conviction. 'We rarely talk about the things that matter. We sort of crab our way around them. I think it's the spirit of the age. A hangover from the Victorians. Or too many wars. I don't know. If the future can be anything, I would like it to be one where people feel able to talk about what matters.'

The clock in the study chimed midnight.

'Happy Christmas,' she said.

'*Prost*,' Lubert said, raising his glass to chink hers.

'*Prost.*'

'To a new era of talking about what matters,' Lubert suggested.

But the thing that mattered was still unsaid.

'What about you?' she asked, not quite ready for it to be named. 'Do you believe?'

Lubert held the glass to the light of the fire, making the whisky flame and flare.

'In a god who becomes an infant? This is hard.' He tilted

the liquid in his glass; the crystal refracting the gold. 'It's eas-ier to believe in a strong man than a weak God.'

The conversation was still a dance, with neither quite tak-ing the lead. Rachael could see that the cut over Lubert's brow had healed quickly.

'The colonel said he was going to Heligoland,' Lubert said. 'The Holy Island. This is where the saints used to go.'

'He will feel at home there then.' It was out before she could edit herself. She looked down at the flames again. The single coal she had fixed her eyes on had set the adjacent coals glowing.

'When the colonel told me that he was going away, I was . . . pleased,' Lubert said.

Rachael roiled the whisky and water in the tumbler. She could feel the subtle and devious manoeuvrings of her heart. 'So was I.'

Lines. Boundaries. Borders. She had already crossed a few, but these three words felt like the largest leap yet.

Lubert took her hand, his much warmer than hers, and kissed it tenderly. Rachael squeezed and pulled his hand, leading his mouth to hers, angling her head to kiss him. He responded immediately and kissed her deeply. Rachael was astonished again by the quick and easy intimacy. When they broke apart, Lubert tried to say something, but she stopped his words with another kiss. If they discussed what was hap-pening, if she was forced to think about it, she might stop. When they broke off a second time she made to kiss him again, but this time he resisted, pulling back his head like a bird, leaving her kissing air.

'. . . I will go to my room,' he said. 'Wait until my light is on – you will see it through the main window. I will leave the door open.'

The instruction was so precise, he must have thought it

through. He stood up, letting go of her hand but keeping his eyes on her, raising a finger to his lips then holding it aloft to indicate where he was going and how brief a pause this would be.

Rachael counted to sixty, like a girl playing hide and seek, closing her eyes and listening to the creaking floorboards. She waited for the voices – of reason, sense, conscience – to tell her not to go to him. But no such voice surfaced; all she could hear was the thrum of her desire. It would take something exceptional to stop her now – cosmic intervention, an earthquake, something as singular as a great cat walking across the lawn.

At the count of sixty she opened her eyes and saw the light being cast from Lubert's room through the main window. She set off, climbing the stairs carefully, keeping her feet on the carpet and avoiding the exposed and noisy wooden edges, mindful of the creak, the spying maid, the unsleeping child. As well as cunning and stealth, an adultery seemed to require all the innocent daring and invention of a child. Was that what this now was? Adultery? It didn't feel as though it was. But did any adulterer feel that? What defined it? Was a mere thought enough? A kiss? Or would she officially become an adulterer when she gave the rest of herself to Lubert?

She passed the open door of her own bedroom. At the foot of the second staircase, she glanced at Edmund's room. She stepped on to the first step, listening out for the slightest sound. Everything was heightened, and slowing. She was noticing new detail: the embossed heads of stair-rods; a high-pitched ringing in her ears; the warmer air at the top of the house. The door to Lubert's bedroom was a fraction ajar, emitting an isosceles of light. She put one foot in it. She saw her shoe, the same shoe that had walked her, guilt-free, to all manner of rooms to perform perfunctory domestic actions; it did not look like the shoe of an adulterer. She pushed his mercifully uncreaking door open and stepped into the new country.

Lubert was standing at the window with his back to her. She closed the door and leant back against it, keeping her hands on the handle and the questions shut out behind her. The handle pressed into the small of her back. Lubert turned, the anticipation of pleasure – or was it perhaps trepidation? – distorting his features; for a moment it looked as if he wasn't sure, as if he might call it all off. Then he took a single stride towards her and kissed her, and as they kissed they started to undress. No sensible removing of clothes; they came off in a farcical ballet. She had to reach back to unzip herself; he tore his shirt when he pulled it off inside out and it became caught at the cuffs. When they were naked he seemed to want to stop to take her in, but she led him to the bed.

At first, she barely noticed him, his smell, his taste, the difference of him; she did not want his particularity, and she avoided looking into his eyes, or opening her own. She did not want tenderness. She did not want kindness. At the peak of it she cried out louder than she knew, loud enough to obliterate his ecstasies. Loud enough for him to put a silencing hand over her mouth.

'They'll hear us.'

She didn't care.

She lay there, inhaling the smell of the act, feeling its evidence inside her, spreading out from her middle and radiating to her extremities.

'Are you all right?' he asked.

'Yes,' she said.

'I imagined you this way. So . . . fierce.'

She didn't answer. She lay there with her eyes open now. They held hands, their forearms and thighs sticking to each other. She felt highly receptive to the detail of the moment, to him and to the room: a birthmark the size of a sixpence on his side, her pulse visible in the rising and falling of her stomach, the boniness of his hips, the tiny blue veins around his chest. Naked, Lubert seemed longer and slimmer, and his skin was pale white, several tones lighter than hers.

The plain facts of the makeshift room began to develop. She took in the furnishings, hastily removed from the rooms below and stored here to accommodate her: his architect's desk and drawing utensils; books stacked on the floor. And, leaning against the wall, unhung and facing away, a large painting. Its dimensions were the same as the stain in the hall.

Lubert started to caress her shoulder.

'Is that the picture?' she asked.

Lubert didn't answer.

'Stefan?'

'Yes.'

'Am I allowed to see it now?'

His reticence only made her want to see it more.

'Go on,' he said, eventually.

Rachael swung her legs to the floor, pulling off the counterpane and wrapping it around herself, more for warmth than modesty. She knelt on the floor and turned the painting around. She knew, without asking, who it was. Her own speculative picture was not so far off, and the familial similarities too pronounced for it not to be.

'Claudia.'

Lubert nodded.

'She is striking. I see Frieda in her. Why did you take her down?'

'I didn't want her watching me any more. Rachael. Come back.' He patted the bed, not wanting to dwell on this subject.

Her curiosity overrode his discomfort. 'Why didn't you tell me – when I accused you? That it was her?'

Lubert looked conflicted. 'Because . . . I have been trying to forget. And because, if I had told you, I might not have kissed you. And then you would feel sorry for me. And think that I was still in love with my wife.'

'Are you?'

'Please. Turn it around.'

'But are you?'

'I can't be in love with a memory. I want more than this.'

Rachael looked at the portrait one more time then turned it back to face the wall and returned to Lubert's bed.

Lewis was hunkered down behind the protective blast-wall with Ursula and the three delegates from the Inter-Allied Reparations Agency, awaiting the first controlled explosion of their dismantling tour. The Russian delegate, Colonel Kutov, was yelling something, but Lewis couldn't hear a word. He removed his ear mufflers and turned to Ursula.

'What did he say?'

'Something about sending the wheat to your zone.'

Lewis put his mufflers back on. 'The bastard's enjoying it.'

He reflected on the absurd logic of the equation: they blow up a soap factory which employed two thousand Germans, made something everyone needed and had no military value whatsoever and, in return, the Russians sent the Germans bread. It was like balancing Hell's ledger.

The handful of protesters gathered at the gates of the Henkel Soap plant were easily being contained by a dozen black-caped German police. The general was right: Christmas was an ideal time for demolition work.

The agency had calculated that the explosion would be heard thirty to fifty miles away. The detonation, when it came, was unviolent and oddly beautiful: the smoke billowed symmetrically either side of the building and then, like a man collapsing to his knees but trying to maintain his dignity by keeping his back upright, the whole structure crumpled to the ground and disappeared in a nimbus of rubble smoke that flowed out in a radiating cauliflower of dust, almost reaching the blast-shield and enveloping the delegates. The *wump* of falling masonry would be felt far away, mistaken for massive stacked thunder or the nearby passing of a great train. Perhaps some would think it the final ghost-wave of lost squadrons coming to finish what they had started.

The collapsing of a tall chimney provided the *coup de grâce*, after which Kutov stood and applauded the razing as though he were at a private fireworks display. He was right to be impressed, it had been technically superb: the Royal Engineers were getting very good at these controlled explosions. Jean Bolon, the French member of the delegation, and Lieutenant Colonel Ziegel, the American, stood up and clapped, too.

As Lewis watched the dust disperse, revealing the pile of masonry and rubble beneath, he suddenly saw Michael, trapped beneath the beams, mud and clay of the Narberth house. Even though Rachael had described the scene to him, he'd never permitted himself to visualize it fully, constructing instead a picture he could live with – one that consisted only of a neat pile of masonry, not unlike the one that lay before him at this moment, and never included his son's body.

Kutov started yelling something else at the delegates, repeating it over and over and pointing to his watch.

'What is he saying now?' Lewis asked.

'It's midnight,' Ursula said. 'He says "Happy Christmas" – in Russian.'

The delegation was billeted at a small hotel on the road to Cuxhaven. It was one in the morning by the time they arrived, but Kutov was treating this trip as a holiday and he was not going to allow them to get to bed lightly. The five of them went to the bar to toast the day's successfully completed operation and the saviour of mankind. The general produced a bottle of vodka.

'The drink that won the war,' Kutov said, raising the pure spirit. 'You English have your gin,' Kutov said, turning to Lewis.

'The drink that helped us forget the war,' Lewis said.

'And you, Monsieur?'

'Pastis,' Bolon offered. 'The drink for those avoiding the war.'

'But we have the drink that will win the peace,' Ziegel suggested. 'Martini: the greatest of all American inventions. Don't underestimate it. I can handle two,' he said. 'Three, and I'm under the table. Four, I'm under the hostess. This stuff, though – well.' He held the shot glass of vodka. 'I don't seem to notice it.'

'What about you, Frau Paulus?' asked Kutov. 'What drink can your country offer?'

Ursula had been quietly observing things, and Lewis sensed she was having some kind of allergic reaction to the Russian.

'I would say beer, Colonel. But you have taken our hops and wheat.'

Ursula stared at Kutov, giving no indication that this had been intended as a joke. Kutov stared back, his eyes beady and threatening. Ursula held his gaze, staring him down. And then Kutov slammed his hand on the table and laughed like a man utterly incapable of being offended. He was thick-set, without a neck, and strong. The whole table shook when he struck it.

'You have humour, Frau Paulus. I like this. And you have reminded me of a drinking game we used to play in the Red Army.'

The game involved trying not to blink for as long as possible while someone clapped their hands in front of your eyes. Kutov played chief clapper, eliminating Bolon after ten seconds, Ziegel after thirty. Lewis almost survived the minute, but this was more from fatigue than skill; the game was easily won by Ursula, who blinked only after three minutes, when Kutov resorted suddenly to yelling 'Ha!' at her.

Kutov then sang a plaintive Russian folk song, and Lewis was unable to decide whether he was a sensitive soul or an ugly sentimentalist. Lewis was all ready to turn in when Ziegel suggested another game.

'When we were killing time before the landings we used to play this game called But for the War. It helped us get to know the new recruits. You know this game? It's easy. You just have to say what you would be doing now if there had been no war. Good things, bad things, it doesn't matter. But it needs to be true. The others can interrupt you and challenge you if they don't believe you or want to know more.'

Kutov hammered the table in approval. 'Excellent!' he said. 'I do not know this game but I like it already very much!'

Lewis caught Ursula's eye. He widened his in mock-alarm. He was ready to retire, but a sense of obligation and a certain curiosity kept him in his chair.

Ziegel continued: 'I have the bottle in front of me to indicate that I am speaking. We pass to my left. I'll start. Nice and easy. Okay. But for the war, I . . . would still be selling life insurance in Philadelphia. But for the war, I would never have seen the Eiffel Tower. But for the war, I would probably have four kids instead of two by now. But for the war, I'd be a few pounds heavier than I am. There. That'll do for now. You can pass the bottle whenever you want. Keep your powder dry.'

He passed the bottle to Kutov.

Kutov took it in his hand. The Russian's fingers were thick and covered in cuts. He stroked the bottle with his other hand and solemnity came upon the room. 'If not war,' he said in a mournful voice, then he paused for several seconds. The others braced themselves for an atrocity-laden tale; for reminders of how Russians bore the greatest human cost of the war. 'If not war, then this night I would be in Leningrad with my wife.' Another silence. No one was sure what to make of this. He looked forlorn, almost broken; he breathed in histrionically through his flaring nostrils.

'I'm sorry, Vasily,' Ziegel said, and he reached to touch the brute hands.

Kutov suddenly beamed. A broad, conniving grin cracked his egghead. 'And every day I thank the stars I am not with that bitch!'

Relief made the laughter louder.

'So. If not war' – Kutov thought some more – 'if not war, I still be with wife, and three children: my Masha, my Sonya and my Piotr. I would be a bad father shouting. I would be working at the Bureau for Communications. I would be fishing in the ice holes on weekends. And, if not war, I would have no excuse.' He paused again.

'Excuse?' Bolon asked.

Kutov shot another vodka and refilled his glass. He then stood up abruptly. 'If not war . . .' He lifted his shirt to reveal a barrel chest; his belly was pocked with black scars.

'This for stealing cow. A farmer in Polzin.'

'And where is this farmer now?' Bolon asked.

Kutov pointed to the ground.

'Moo!' Ziegel said. 'Good share, Colonel! Good share.'

Kutov then passed the bottle to Bolon.

Lewis could not place the Frenchman at all. He was certainly no soldier. A civil servant? An academic perhaps?

'But for the war . . . I would not be enjoying this international experience of comradeship . . .' he began.

Kutov approved of this choice of word, and he demanded four chinks and cheers from each delegate. 'Comrades!'

'But for the war . . .' Bolon continued, 'I would not be here, of course, but working still in Beaune. But for the war, I would have gone on to finish my doctorate. But for the war, I would . . . still be with Angèle. But for the war, I would never have met my wife.'

'The Lord gives and the Lord takes away,' Ziegel said.

'What about this girl, Angèle?' Kutov asked.

'I was in Paris when the Germans invaded. I could not get back to Beaune. Angèle was a secretary at the department. She had nowhere to stay . . .'

'We get the picture, Jean . . . we get the picture,' Ziegel said.

Ziegel was by far the most obviously drunk, but Lewis was himself feeling it; sure that if he moved he would fall over. Despite this, he accepted another shot from the Russian. It was proving effective at keeping the tide at bay.

'And where is this Angèle now?' Kutov wanted to know.

'She was arrested. My professor denounced her to the German authorities. She was Jewish. I left the university after that. But . . . I met my wife, Juliette. And so. *Comme ça* . . . enough for now.'

Bolon passed the bottle to Lewis. 'Colonel Morgan. I see stories in you.'

Oh yes. Lewis was full of stories – his life as coloured by

war's consequences as any – but he was not ready to tell them. Not at this or any table. He had no stomach for comparing scars. For the last hour, he had been smoking practically in a fugue, trying to hide himself behind a smokescreen fog.

'Colonel?'

He passed the bottle to Ursula. 'Sorry. I'm drawing a blank. You have a go, Fräulein.'

'You must say one thing, Colonel. Anything.'

'Come back to me,' he said. 'You go.'

Ursula put a hand around the bottle.

'But for the war . . . I would still be married,' she said. 'I might have had children. And I would have liked to have four. I would still be teaching in Rügen. I would not have lost a brother to . . . the regime. But for the war, I would never have walked across a frozen sea.'

'You were escaping from us?' Kutov cut in.

Ursula nodded.

He laughed. 'You thought these English would treat you better!'

Ursula looked at the Russian. 'Yes.'

'They did not have to face what we faced,' he replied. It had taken until now, but the pride of one who had suffered more was finally surfacing.

'There are some things war cannot excuse, Colonel. Whatever you've faced.'

'Continue, Miss Paulus,' Ziegel said.

'But for the war . . . I would not have walked from Rügen to Hamburg. And seen . . . along the way how cruel man can be. And how . . . kind.'

'Detail, Fräulein! Detail!' Kutov demanded.

Ursula stared hard at the Russian. He had tested her all day and night. He seemed almost proud of winning her indignation.

'But for the war, I would not have seen the cruelty of Russian soldiers raping an old lady then beating her to death. But for the war, I would not have seen the kindness of their leader, persuading his men to spare me and let me go.'

Kutov immediately waved this off. 'Count yourself lucky.'

There was another staring competition between Ursula and Kutov, which Kutov won by smiling at her then laughing heartily. But this time the others didn't laugh with him. Lewis was glad he'd recommended Ursula for a London posting and that she had accepted. If she and Kutov were in such close proximity for a month together, there would surely be an international incident.

Ziegel tried to move things on. 'So, Colonel, you have an unfair advantage over all of us now. We know nothing about you.'

Lewis tapped out a drum roll on the table with his fingers. 'I'd like to turn in. We have an early start.'

'Come on. How bad can it be, Colonel?' Ziegel coaxed.

'This isn't my kind of game, gentlemen.'

Ursula was agitated by her exchange with Kutov, and that agitation was now trained on Lewis. 'You've listened to everyone else. It's only fair that you share something.'

'Right,' Ziegel agreed, slapping the table. 'You gotta bring something to the table, Colonel. We've all bared our souls. Fair play and cricket and all that.'

Ursula reached for the bottle and put it in front of Lewis. He looked at it, but he wouldn't take it. Ursula impatiently snatched it back and held it in front of her.

'Very well. As your interpreter, I will interpret for you. I think I know what the colonel is saying.'

Ursula looked at Lewis and he suddenly wanted to take the bottle from her hands.

'But for the war, Colonel Morgan would not have been

here to offer me a job. I would not be going to London. So thank you for this. But for the war, Colonel Morgan might be living a nice life somewhere in England or Wales. I don't know. But for the war, Colonel Morgan might have spent more time with his family. But for the war, he would not have lost a son and then tried to stay so busy and work so hard that he didn't have to face thinking about it. Even though it is there. In his heart.'

And, with that, Ursula moved the bottle from in front of Lewis to the centre of the table.

Kutov clapped. Ziegel nodded his approval.

Lewis could feel something swelling inside him, at his sinuses and in his chest. He had worked hard to keep this ghost at bay, but now it was pressing in, coming to claim its dues. The tears were coming, and he had to swallow to hold them. He stood up. The syrupy numbing of the vodka seemed to have concentrated at the backs of his thighs, and he steadied himself. He put his hand over Ursula's – very lightly – and tapped it. 'Good translation.' He bowed to the men. 'I'm going to turn in. Gentlemen. Frau Paulus. Good-night. *Spokoynoy nochi. Bonne nuit. Gute Nacht.*'

11

Richard slowed to drop Rachael off outside the gates of the Burnhams'. As he did so, he stalled the Austin, its judder forcing her to place a hand on the dashboard.

'*Dieses englische Auto ist Scheiße!*' he muttered, then became acutely embarrassed at his outburst. '*Entschuldigung.*'

Even without her daily lessons, she'd have understood these words well enough.

'Don't worry, Richard. It's just the cold. I agree, it isn't the best car in the world. Thank you for driving me. It was actually much nearer than I thought.' She said all this accompanied by compensatory hand gestures: walking fingers, hand indicating small distance, and then a light, reassuring touch of his arm.

'You are good lady,' he said, in English.

As she walked up the Burnhams' drive, Rachael felt both flattered and uneasy at Richard's compliment. She didn't feel like a 'good lady'. The illicit events of the last few weeks had surely disqualified her from receiving that accolade.

If anyone could see through such a claim, it would be Susan Burnham. This invitation to tea now felt like a potential ambush. Rachael's raw feelings, her situation, were exactly the kind of meat on which Susan loved to feed. As they took tea in Susan Burnham's impressive front parlour, Rachael decided to offer a diversion.

'I presume you've heard about Herr Koenig? Edmund's tutor?'

'Yes. Keith said. Secret Police. I expect he'll be shot.'

Rachael nodded.

'Didn't you check his story?'

'Yes. But it was obviously not the one he told us,' Rachael said. 'He filled out his form like everyone else. He just avoided the incriminating categories. He said he had been a head-master in Kiel. Lewis thought him sound.'

'How did they get him?'

'Someone who knew him reported him.'

'Well. Your husband's screening process leaves much to be desired.'

Instead of defending Lewis, Rachael lifted her teacup to her lips and burnt herself. She blew on the surface of the tea, causing little ripples across the surface, and studied the cup. Rachael had a soft spot for crockery. She knew her china, and this was a stunning set decorated in the exquisite Blue Onion pattern. She lifted the cup and looked under-neath for the maker's mark, and there was the blue crossed-swords emblem signifying the town on the Elbe near Dresden which made the best china in the world. How curious that this cup had been made in a town that stood by the same river that flowed just a few hundred yards away. It was her and Lewis's twentieth-wedding anniversary in April, and she had always given him a gift in the appropriate mater-ial. Twenty years was china.

'Meissen,' she said.

'Comes with the house. The place is heaving with the stuff.'

The Burnhams' house was grander than Susan had let on. She had so overplayed the magnificence of the Villa Lubert that Rachael had imagined her living in far less salubrious circumstances than these. While lacking the dimensions of Lubert's house, this was perfectly grand in its own way, and perhaps also a little too refined, a little too cultured for the likes of Susan Burnham. Not that Rachael would say this. They were both uncultured cuckoos in the fancy nests of other birds.

'I would have invited you for Christmas, but we don't celebrate it with much gusto – Keith can't bear it. '

'It's kind of you to say that. We've had a perfectly fine one.'

'Your hubby is quite the absentee. I think I've only met him once in our time here.'

'I think a part of him is glad to get away.'

This was not what Rachael had intended to say, and Susan Burnham scented blood. 'Did he take his translator with him?'

'He didn't say. I imagine so.'

'Keith said he saw her the other day, at the lunch. Said that Lewis has "an absolute goddess of an interpreter". My hubby is usually quite blind to such things, so she must be. You didn't check, did you?'

'No.'

'Doesn't it make you . . . just a teensy-weensy bit suspicious? You've heard about Captain Jackson?'

Rachael hadn't heard – nor did she want to hear – about Captain Jackson, but Susan was going tell her.

'He eloped to Sweden with his translator. Left three children. Didn't even leave a note.'

'Why are you telling me this, Susan?'

'Because I look at the two of you and wonder how you manage. I worry about you.'

Rachael wasn't sure she believed this. Was it concern or prurience that drove her friend?

'What about you? How is Keith? I have not seen him since . . . that evening.'

'God. I don't think he'd even remember it.' She laughed. But the mention of it caused her to pause. 'He's beastly when he's drunk. I worry that it's got worse since we've got here.'

'He seemed very angry.'

'It's his work. Keith's on a mission. He doesn't want them to get away with it.'

'Them?'

'The Nazis.'

'No. None of us do.'

'Well. He was deeply affected by the pictures of the camps. He asked to be transferred to the de-Nazification programme the week the pictures were released. He felt called to root out that evil.'

Rachael's gaze focused on a row of tea chests by the wall. She assumed that they had just arrived from England.

'You're still unpacking?'

'We're sending stuff back.'

'But you have room enough . . .'

'We're . . . you know . . . shipping some bits and pieces.'

'Bits and pieces?'

'Oh, come on, Rachael. Spoils of war. It's all stolen goods anyway. Those paintings in your house – you think Herr Lubert has no blood on his hands?'

How stupid I've been, Rachael thought.

'I wouldn't . . . dream of it.'

'It's all right for you.'

'Why?'

'You come from good homes. You have heirlooms and fine antiques. We've come from nothing.'

'That's not true. Neither Lewis nor I come from privilege.'

A maid entered with a plate of mince pies.

'*Nein!* Goodness me!' Susan Burnham said as she redirected her to the sideboard. She was suddenly quite unhinged.

Rachael started to dab her mouth with her napkin. She wanted to get out of this house.

'He's won you over, hasn't he?' Susan said.

'Who?

'Your handsome architect.'

Rachael couldn't stop the mechanism that connected her conscience and the flow of blood to her cheeks. 'What do you . . . mean?'

'I saw how you leapt to his defence when the vase broke.'

'It was his house, Susan. We were breaking his things – *his* things!'

'You know what I mean.'

'No. I don't know what you mean.'

'When you went towards him – to stop him hitting Keith – the way you looked at each other –'

'Susan! Please.'

'Well, be careful. They're not like us. They're different. Quite different. Not that I'd blame him.'

'For what?

'For wanting to take advantage.'

'Please, Susan.'

'You're an attractive lady. And virtually unattended. I'm only saying this because I envy you.'

'Me?'

'It's all more complicated,' she said. Her skin was suddenly blotching now, around her eyes and nose, stalk marks of emotion flaring. 'I hate being here.'

'I thought you liked it.'

'I put on a brave show. You get good at it when you're married to a drunk.' She gave a frivolous, nervous laugh to try to play this down, but the word was out.

The military was full of secret inebriates, but Rachael had not numbered Major Burnham as one of them. 'I didn't realize it was that bad.'

Susan Burnham suddenly put a hand over Rachael's. 'You won't tell anyone? Please don't tell anyone.'

'No.'

'And about the other.'

'What other?'

Susan Burnham looked to the crammed tea chests awaiting shipping.

'About the china and things.'

Edmund spread a deck of cards face down across the expanse of his bedroom while Frieda lay on her side, her body stretched out across the carpet, her skirt hitched up to her thighs. She was examining the stitches on Cuthbert's neck. Since the Christmas screening, Frieda had started being friendlier towards him, and Edmund had tried to dissociate himself from his cloth soldier and any other form of play she might consider juvenile. No more running Dinky cars along the landing or hunting imaginary beasts in the garden. It was all films and cards now.

'The English soldier is better,' Frieda said, in an English far better than Edmund had thought she possessed. 'He is a king's soldier?'

'He's a Grenadier Guard.'

Edmund wanted to get on with the game of Pelmanism, but Frieda ran a finger along Cuthbert's stitches, up and over his bearskin, smiling to herself. Perhaps she was going to give him a full confession.

'Your mother make him better. From the *stummer Diener*.'

Edmund shrugged nonchalantly to show that he had moved on from soldiers and dumb waiters. He was looking at her bare legs now, and had positioned himself to see them more easily. He was drawn to Frieda in a way that defied

261

sense or his full understanding. At night, when he found it hard to sleep, his mind kept returning to her athletic display, to her white knickers deep in the recess of her thighs, and to the ammonia citrus tang of her piss in the chamber pot. From these moments, he was able to grow a whole sequence of new fantasies.

Pretending to spread the cards more evenly on the carpet, he brushed his hand against her flesh and left it lying there. He had already touched her in his delicious mind-adventures. But to do it in real life . . . These were the games he wanted to play. He wanted to stroke her skin there, in a circuit above the knee, to rub it as if cleaning steam from a window. This thought seemed connected to his loins, where he felt a surging sensation. He wanted his hand to continue moving up towards the impossible whiteness of those knickers until it reached the material. And what then? Would she clamp her thighs together, trapping his hand between her legs?

Frieda gave no sign that she'd noticed his touch. She lay Cuthbert down and switched her attention to the doll's house, pulling herself up on to her knees and taking in the configuration of the dolls. She pointed to the small boy doll in the bedroom.

'This you. This' – pointing to the doll at the piano – 'Frau Morgan. This' – indicating the dolls on the roof – 'my father and me.'

Edmund nodded. He wanted to go back to the other game, but Frieda seemed quite taken with his re-creation. She swapped the Frieda doll with the doll that represented Rachael, placing Frieda with Edmund on the first floor and Edmund's mother with Herr Lubert on the roof. Then she placed the adults together in the master bedroom. She seemed amused by this rearrangement. Edmund laughed, too, although, in truth, he wasn't sure if it was funny. The sight of the Lubert doll and the mother doll together in the bedroom gave him a strange feeling.

'Where is Edmund's father?' Frieda asked.

Edmund pointed to the car sitting on an island of clothes by the rocking horse. 'Heligoland.'

She got up and went over to the horse, stroking its shiny back, and put her foot over the car. She rolled it back and forth on the carpet.

'You can send him back,' said Edmund.

'Now?'

'Now.'

With her foot, Frieda propelled the car back across the carpet with enough force to jolt the side of the doll's house and flip the car over on its side.

Rachael could see something moving in the woods: figures tracking them in parallel, moving from the cover of one tree to the next. As she looked, she slowed and tugged Lubert's arm, forcing him to look, too. 'I think we're being followed.'

Lubert looked to the trees. '*Trümmerkinder.*'

The figures stopped and peered from behind a tree. One of them looked to be carrying a large stick resembling a spear. He could have been the same age as Edmund.

'Don't worry about them. They'll just think we're refugees, or lovers going for a walk in the park.'

The term 'lover' seemed too breezy to Rachael. Being a lover, she had discovered, required more stealth and guile, more plotting and planning than writers of romantic fiction liked to let on. They had spent many an evening in front of the fire, talking deeply, but the house was all ears and eyes, and with the cold months keeping everyone indoors it was no place for easy intimacy. Even this brief escape had required her to leave the house first and him to follow after: she 'to get some air'; he 'to look for wood'. Lewis had been gone nearly two months, and yet this was the first time they'd managed to find time to be fully alone since that Christmas night.

As they walked through the grounds of the Jenischpark, she thought that winter was the right season for an affair. Much easier for furtive bodies to find anonymity when everything was under wraps. From a distance, everyone looked the same and, today, both she and Lubert were so well swathed – she in her galoshes and black wool coat; Lubert in a ski hat and carrying a rucksack filled with fuel for the gamekeeper's hut – they could easily have passed for two displaced persons heading for the nearby camp.

The park was only fifteen minutes' walk from the house, but it felt like another country. The snow was virgin except for deer prints. Icicles hung from the architraves of the great house at the park's centre. As they walked, Lubert explained the park's history. 'It was landscaped by a man called Casper Beck. A talented man. Although something of a tragic figure. He tried to find a universal language in his work and failed. He fell into despair and took his own life.' As they approached the gamekeeper's hut, he explained how Claudia's family connections had given them a licence to shoot game in the park and private access to it. The hut was a folly of sorts, a mock log cabin in the American style, overlooking a pond that in summer was a private pool. In snow and surrounded by pines, it perfectly resembled a shack on a lonesome frontier. Lubert produced a key, brushed the snow and ice from the lock, and unlocked it.

Inside, the cabin was furnished with thick wooden chairs and rugs; a gun rack and a stag's head adorned the wall above the fireplace where a stove had been set. From his sack, Lubert produced kindling – a broken-up tea chest, a copy of *Die Welt* – and set about lighting it. The floor was covered in dried dead bugs that scrunched and popped beneath their feet. Rachael swept them under the door with the limb of a fir tree and cleaned a space in front of the fireplace, where she laid all the rugs to make a bed. She then sat and watched Lubert get the fire going. He waited for the flare of the kindling to die down then added some coals, carefully setting them one by one among the burning twigs. He then joined her on the bed of rugs and together they watched the fire do its work, sitting like scouts at a camp. Despite the significance of what she – what they – were doing, Rachael couldn't help but think that the affair still had the feel of a children's game.

The snow from their clothes began to steam around them. Lubert took off his hat and scarf, and Rachael did the same. He then kissed her and, cradling her head with one hand, lowered her on to her back. They kissed for a long time and then began to make love, this time keeping most of their clothes on. It was not the same as that first night. The temperature required haste and awkward fumblings. Despite the clothes, though, Rachael felt more exposed than when she'd first lain naked with him. She was too aware of herself this time, and too conscious of time and life pressing in. Afterwards, they lay back, looking at the cobwebs in the beams above. She wondered how long they could keep the realities of the world at bay.

'When I practise again I will design huts in the style of the American West.' Lubert stood up and started to draw something with his index finger on the steamed-up window of the hut. 'This is all people really need,' he said.

'When will you get your certificate?'

'Soon. Although that major seems determined to find something. Anything that proves I'm not clean. Imagine if he could see us now . . .'

'Don't,' she said. Neither of them was clean, but the idea of Burnham finding out about this affair made Rachael feel especially grimy.

Lubert continued to draw on the windowpane with his finger. 'One room, but with a minstrels' gallery and a bigger veranda. I think this is all we need.'

She watched him with genuine pleasure. He was at his best when imagining. What she had at first taken for cocky insolence was really an appreciative, creative enthusiasm. His willingness to talk and to get her to talk about anything – religion, marriage, art, grief, loss and death – was inexhaustible. It felt as if they had shared more in these last few weeks than she had in twenty years with Lewis. 'No more villas for millionaires. No more commissions for overfed and under-concerned Hamburgian merchants looking to outdo their neighbours. From now on, I will design buildings for the greater good.' When he was done, he stood back for her to see. 'There. What do you think?' he asked. 'Could you live in it?'

Rachael looked at his steam drawing in the window, a whole structure suggested by only a few lines. But, in truth, it was a two-dimensional impossibility, providing no answers to looming, practical questions – about Edmund. And Lewis.

'I think so.'

'With me?' He asked this with more serious intent.

A British soldier's helmet suddenly appeared in the window, in the midst of the drawn plans. Rachael sat up, pulling her covering around her. The figure tapped the window and pressed a face to the pane. It was a rapscallion face. One of the *Trümmerkinder*.

'*Weg!*' Lubert yelled, tapping the glass back.

The boy made an obscene gesture with his finger and thumb and continued to stare at them, smiling gleefully. Lubert went to the door and chased him away. A blast of cold air pierced the fuggy warmth and Rachael pulled her coat tighter. She got up and went to the window to look. Lubert had chased him a few yards and gamely hurled a snowball after him. The boy scampered away into the woods yelling words she couldn't translate.

Lubert re-entered, laughing. 'Little tyke. At least he missed the show.'

Rachael buttoned her coat, uneasy at the idea of their intimacy being a show.

'Right,' Lubert said, brushing the ice from his hands. 'Time for our picnic.'

He reached into the rucksack and produced a piece of cheese, a jar of pickles, half a loaf of bread and a porcelain jar of margarine and a small bottle of peach schnapps. Lubert had brought a gingham tablecloth and some cutlery as well as two pewter goblets. He laid everything out precisely, like a man who'd done this before.

'Did you come here with Claudia?'

A flash of annoyance crossed his features. 'Of course. Why?'

'I'm sorry. She . . . I'm just curious to know what she was like, that's all.'

'What would you like me to say?' He sounded defensive now.

'I don't know. Just be honest.'

Lubert sighed. Apparently, this reminiscing was not part of his plan.

'She was lofty. Merciless towards any stupidity. Stylish to the point of offensive. Good at getting the best from people.

Stubborn. An introvert who was a socialite. A reader but not well read. A lover of music but tone-deaf. And a better person than me.'

'Why better?'

'She would have shown . . . more self-control in a situation like mine.'

'Does that make her better than me?'

'No. I mean she would never have shared the house in the first place.'

'You still miss her, don't you?' It wasn't really a question.

'For a time – almost up until you arrived – I could think of little else. After the firestorm, I spent months searching for her. I forgot about everything else and everyone. Especially Frieda. Frieda suffered for this. I think that I lost contact with her then. And have not regained it yet. But you coming . . . you coming has changed this.' He looked at her, wanting her to accept this as the truth. 'But now I see you are thinking too much.'

'Sorry. I think it was that strange boy.'

The boy with his gargoyle face had spooked her, puncturing their idyllic bubble.

Lubert poured some schnapps into a goblet and handed it to her.

'You are thinking. Thinking about this situation, about what we are doing.'

Until today, she had not allowed herself to look clearly at what she was doing, and it had only just crept into her peripheral vision, but it was enough for him to notice.

'I have had these thoughts, too,' Lubert said. 'Your husband has been kind. And he trusted me.' He took her hand. 'But what we have is precious, no? We understand each other. You have made me feel again. And I like to think I have done the same for you.'

She leant forward and kissed him tenderly. It was easier to think such things, here, in this hut. Now, in the present.

'I almost feel I have to get away to think. Away from the house and all its ghosts. Somewhere we can talk without fear of being overheard or watched.'

'Then I will take you somewhere. I will take you to the most beautiful city in Germany. Lübeck. The city of my birth. For a few days. We can take the train from the *Hauptbahnhof*. I know a place where we can stay. A nice hotel. Heike and Greta can look after the children. We can do this, Rachael. We can go tomorrow, next week.'

She could not imagine too far ahead. To do this meant thinking of other responsibilities.

'Rachael?'

'Yes. Yes. But let's not talk about it just yet.'

12

Ozi paid Hokker the one thousand cigarettes and went to collect the gun from a man called Grün who lived in an apartment in Altona. Grün was almost the colour of his name: he had the pallor of a cheap teacup and wore a double-breasted suit and a hat like Hokker's; he had two gold teeth which he made a special effort to show off by finding everything that Ozi said tooth-flashingly funny. The gun lay wrapped like a baby in a blanket on a camp bed in the corner of his stinking hovel. Grün flicked the blanket back to show Ozi his wares.

'Mosin-Nagant 91/30 with 4x Carl Zeiss scopes. Russian practicality. German precision. And two boxes of ammunition.'

The gun was an impressive, honest-looking object and Ozi stroked the cold barrel to the muzzle, nodding knowledgeably, pretending to be a connoisseur of such things.

'Looks good enough,' he said.

Grün laughed at the boy. 'Of course it is. It's the gun that won Russia the war. You have my tip?'

Hokker had told Ozi that Grün had to be paid a tip in gold or jewellery. Berti had given Ozi a garnet necklace, and he pulled it now from his pocket and handed it to Grün, who held it up to the bare bulb.

'It's not rubies.' He bit a stone. 'But it'll do.' Satisfied, he pocketed it. He then covered the gun with the blanket and handed it to Ozi. 'What's it for then?'

Ozi was under strict instructions from Berti to say that the gun was for hunting.

'I'm going to shoot rabbits with it. I might try it on those fat crows that float down the river, too. Why let those bastards live when we're all going hungry?'

Grün looked at Ozi sceptically. 'Shouldn't you be in school or something?'

'My school is a pile of bricks. But I go to the Tommylectures. Ask me anything about the British Vay of Life. King of Vindsor. I know.'

'You do, do you?'

Ozi had brought his suitcase for the job. He opened it then laid the gun diagonally in the top compartment. He tucked the two boxes of ammunition into the corner and shut the case.

'Well, I hope you shoot yourself some nice fat pheasants with that gun. You look like you could use some meat.'

Ozi took the tram to the top of the Elbchaussee then walked along the road to Petersen's house. As he walked, he began to wonder what the gun was really for, and the more he thought about it, the heavier the case became. He had to pause every hundred yards to swap hands and rub out the red, rutted welts left by the handle. Berti was cooking up a plan to hurt Tommy. He wouldn't say what, only that it was big. Ozi had tried to explain to him that Tommy was not so bad, but Berti's mind was hard to change. It was set like stone. Wasn't that what their mother had said? That's what happened when you couldn't forget a trespass: you turned to stone. Berti couldn't forget what happened in the night raids, seeing his friend Gerhardt turned inside out. He couldn't forgive Tommy for that or for what happened to their mother, their cousins, aunts and uncles and all the others in the great firestorm. The medicine had helped, but he still had nightmares. And he didn't get enough sleep. Perhaps the stronger medicine would help.

Ozi picked up the case and continued along the road, arguing it out.

'I could throw the gun in the river and tell Berti that I was chased by some Tommies.'

'Berti will find out.'

'I could throw it away and get the hell out of Hamburg.'

'He would only come after you.'

'I could warn Edmund. Go down to the gates of his house when no one was looking.'

'Too dangerous. If Berti knew then . . .'

'Who can stop him?'

'There is only one person who can stop him.'

'Who?'

'Me.'

'He won't be able to hear you. You know that I am the only one who can hear you, Mutti.'

'He will recognize my voice. If he sees me he will think twice . . . Let me talk to him.'

'Yes. He will listen to you. To you, he is still just little Berti, who cried at night and made us laugh when he sang songs under water. Berti who hid his comics in his pants when he knew he'd get a beating. And who once had a smile like Lew Ayres. I haven't seen my brother smile for several winters, but he will smile for you, Mutti.'

Ozi found Berti snoozing in an armchair pulled to the front of the fire in the dining room. Judging from the position of his arm and his distant smile he had just injected himself with the new medicine.

'Hey, Berti.'

Albert didn't acknowledge Ozi's entrance. Ozi had preferred him when he was taking the old medicine: at least that
had made him engage with the world; this new medicine
took him far away.

'He isn't ready. Let's do this another time.'

'*It has to be now.*'

'But look at him. He has that dopey look. Trust me, Mutti,
you don't want to talk to him when he is like this.'

'*It has to be now!*'

Albert opened one eye and sat up straight.

'You have it?'

'I have it, Berti. It has Russian practicality and it has
German precision.'

'You said it was for hunting.'

'I said it was for hunting, just like you told me to.'

'Where is it?'

Ozi opened the case, lifted the gun wrapped in its blanket
and laid it at his brother's feet. Albert leant forward in his
chair to look at it. His hands were shaking and his face had a
sheen. He threw the blanket open, picked up the gun by the
stock and nestled the butt into his shoulder. He trained the
barrel on the wall, the ceiling, then on Ozi.

He won't talk now he has the gun, Ozi thought.

'*Trust me.*'

'Did anyone see you come?' Albert asked.

'He's not even heard me, Mutti. How will he hear you?'

'*Let him see me.*'

'Who are you jibber-jabbering to?' Albert asked.

'No one.'

'Yes. You were talking to yourself. Are you still talking to
our mother?'

'No.'

'You were. I heard you say her name.'

273

'*Let him see me now.*'

Albert stood up and came towards Ozi, still aiming the gun and adjusting the scopes as he did so.

'She wants to talk to you, Berti. She says she still knows that you are the same boy who used to smile and laugh and collect all the bottles in Hammerbrook. She says that she knows you saw a bad thing . . . but she thinks this plan to hurt Tommy is bad. There must be some Russki. Or a Frenchman. Or a lousy DP from Silesia.'

'She does, does she?'

'Yes. Come, Berti.' Ozi beckoned him back to the suitcase. 'Come and see.'

Albert walked towards it.

'Under the top part.'

Using the gun, Albert lifted the divider to reveal what was in the lower compartment of the case.

It contained the head and ribcage of a semi-skeletal, semi-fossilized body, the mummified and shrunken corpse of someone caught in a particular phase of the firestorm, dressed in a girl's lace christening gown, yellowed by time and confinement. The skull was brown-grey and still had some crinkled, burnt, black hair. It was shrunken like a head-hunter's trophy.

'*Bombenbrandschrumpffleisch?*' Albert said. 'Why the hell have you got this?'

'It's Mutti. Look, Berti. It's our *Mutti*. I found her outside the Wendenstrasse coffee factory. Three days after the great fireball. I had to put this dress on her. She was naked. And I felt bad. And some of her has broken off. And the Tommy-bombs made her small.'

Albert stared at the skeletal doll.

'It's just any old corpse.'

'It's her. Look. See what is around her neck.' Ozi pointed

to the silver chain and cross melted out of shape. 'She wanted to see you, Berti. And I am sure if you listen you will hear her speak . . . You can hear her. You know what she is saying? I can hear it. She is saying: "Put down your gun. Forget the trespass!" The way she used to. Can't you hear her, Berti?'

Albert looked at the appalling cadaver and his mouth started quivering with a raging disgust.

'Did you hear that?' Ozi asked. 'She really speaks.'

'You crazy fool,' Albert said. 'You crazy, fucking, firebrained freak!'

He took Ozi by the lapels of his smoking jacket and pulled his brother in close, eyeballs to eyeballs. 'You lost your head. The heat melted your brain! She is dead. Dead! Dead! Dead! Dead! Dead!'

Ozi continued to object. 'But you know that she is right.'

'No! She isn't right because she is dead! She doesn't know anything about this because she is dead. She doesn't speak because she is dead. Gone. Goodbye. Dead!'

'But she would say . . . she would say . . . this.'

'No, she wouldn't. She would want me to do it. And Gerhardt would want me to, and all my friends would want me to, too, and our cousins. And our aunts and uncles. She would listen to me . . . not you. She always listened to me. I was her favourite. You were a freak. Born in a sac!'

'She said that was good luck.'

'She did not even want you! I heard her say that to Father. You were a mistake. You were the bad plan . . .'

Albert pushed him back away from the catafalque suitcase. He then lifted the corpse – light and brittle as a wicker birdcage – from the case and carried it towards the fireplace. A rib fell to the ground as he lifted her. Ozi scrambled across the floor and grabbed it, stuffing it into his belt.

'What are you doing, Berti? Don't break her.'

Albert lifted the corpse high then dropped her into the flames. The dry fabric of the christening gown was like summer tinder, and it flared up quickly. Ozi tried to interrupt the pyre but Albert pushed him back again and stood like a fire-guard over the conflagration, and watched until the bones collapsed in and their mother turned to ash.

'You will be all right here . . . while I'm in Kiel? Seeing the Buckmans?'

'Yes, Mummy. You have asked me three times this morning.'

Rachael had discovered that an affair required a scaffolding of lies to hold it up, until – she presumed – the structure was solid enough to stand on its own. Every day seemed to demand she add another cross-plank to the construction. Her interactions with Edward tested its foundations more than anything else.

'I won't go if you don't want me to.'

'I'll be fine.'

'You will be good? Don't wander off too far. Do as Greta and Heike say, yes?'

'Yes.'

She could not stop herself from touching his face, the lovely, downy hair on his cheeks that would one day stiffen to stubble.

'Is it all right if I show Frieda the films again?' he asked. 'She told me she likes Buster Keaton best.'

'Of course. I'm pleased she's being friendlier now.'

'She was jealous before. I think it's because she doesn't have a mother.'

Rachael was relieved to hear that Edward felt a mother was still worth having.

276

'Mummy, is it true what they say? That there is going to be another war?'

'I'm sure there won't be.'

'Is Father trying to stop it happening?'

'Yes. In a way, yes.'

'Do you mind Father being away so much?'

This came out innocently enough, but Rachael had to think about the scaffolding.

'I do. Very much.' As she said it, it didn't sound like a complete lie. 'Why do you ask me that?'

'You don't seem unhappy any more.'

Rachael was sure that Edmund's uncanny perceptiveness was not simply the gift common to all children, but a kind of aberrative result of her own distractions and failings, a skill he had acquired quickly because he'd had to. It made her wonder if her neglect had been his gain.

'Mother?'

'Yes?'

'Do you think Herr Lubert is clean?'

'Yes. I'm sure of it.'

'Not like Herr Koenig.'

The front-door bell rang. 'No. Not like Herr Koenig.'

'Is it all right if I like Herr Lubert very much?'

'. . . Of course. I'd best get that.'

Rachael opened the front door to a cherubic captain clutching a box file with a parcel and some letters stacked on top of it. His Volkswagen was still chugging in the driveway. She'd not actually met him yet, but, from Lewis's many descriptions of his number two, she guessed who it was.

'Mrs Morgan?'

'Yes.'

'Captain Barker.' He offered his hand. 'Your husband's stand-in. Or stand-up, depending on who you talk to.'

277

'It's good to meet you. Lewis speaks very highly of you.'

'He won't when he sees what I've done to his department. Anyway, he's asked me to pass on this message.' The captain was too cheery to be a harbinger of bad news, but a surge of adrenalin caused her heart to fibrillate as he read from a strip telegram perched on top of the pile. 'It was dictated at the royal naval shore establishment this morning. "Delayed in Heligoland. STOP. Logistics demand stay. STOP. Expect March 1 return. STOP."'

Not so long ago, she would have gladly leapt upon the coded endearment in the date 1 March – St David's Day – the day on which Lewis had always tried to give her daffodils; now, all she could hear was what lay between the lines: STOP what you are doing. STOP while there is still time. STOP before it is too late.

Lewis back in a few days? He had been gone two months, but, to Rachael, it had felt much longer. The telegram was a rude snap back to a truer chronology.

'Thank you.'

'And I should have run these over sooner. They've been sitting in the office. Two months overdue, but better late than never . . .'

Barker handed her the letters and the brown-paper parcel, which was addressed to Edmund. It was from Lewis's sister, Kate, and, judging from the softness and the weight, she'd knitted him the cricket sweater she'd promised. Thinking of her sister-in-law brought comfort and regret. She had a special fondness for her.

'And this is for the colonel to look at when he's back.' He tapped the lid of the box file and handed it to her.

'What is it?'

'Just another nifty project he's instigated. I don't want it getting lost in the ether.'

He stepped forward to help her restack the parcel on top of it. 'Shall I carry them in for you?'

'No. Thank you. I'll manage.'

Rachael wondered if Barker could see right through the exterior of the model colonel's wife – assured, loyal, with a passing interest in her husband's work – to the inner maelstrom.

'Sorry not to swing by before. No peace for the wicked. I assume everything's all right here. You look to be coping.'

'We're . . . all managing. How are things . . . in the department?'

'Joking apart, I could actually do with your husband getting back before the whole bloody thing falls apart. He's like one of those vital cogs you notice only when they're taken out.'

The praise was hard to hear, but Barker's warm words gave her an unexpected tingle of pride.

'Anyway, I'll be off,' Barker said.

As he backed down the steps to his car, he raised a hand of praise to the sky. 'Sunshine at last!'

Rachael watched him leave, feeling warmth on her skin. The wind was blowing from the west rather than the east, lifting off the lid of grey they'd been under for weeks, leaving the sky Meissen-blue.

She went inside, carrying the post to the study. She set the box file down on Lewis's desk and opened the letters: two Christmas cards – one from Lewis's mother, and one from his sister. The card from her mother-in-law was typically spare and to the point – Lewis had inherited his mother's dislike of frills. His sister's card – depicting a robin redbreast on the branch of a tree, the sickly yellow lights of an idyllic village glowing in the thighs of hills – was knowingly tasteless.

A scrawly note inside read:

Dearest Rach, In grip of most terrible winter. Alan and I have been stranded in a Trust Houses hotel in Ross-on-Wye for four weeks! I don't know if this letter will ever get to you. Much complaining here about the state of everything. Austerity is the word. I hear life there is quite grand. Is it true you have servants? We have an agonized craving for the sun. The hotel serves dismal meals produced with a kind of bleak triumph that amounts to a hatred of humanity and humanity's needs! Anyway, a very belated Merry Christmas and Happy New Year to you all. At least this weather is good for knitting. Hope it fits! Love K and A.

Kate was the only other person in the world who called her Rach. Kate had huge affection for her brother, and that enabled her to get away with teasing him mercilessly. The first time Rachael had met Kate she'd looked at Lewis and said: 'This is the first time you've brought a girl home who doesn't have two heads and scales! What's happened, Lew?'

Rachael looked at the box file. What had Barker said? 'Just another nifty project he's instigated.' The captain's affectionate compliments seemed to go deeper than mere professional admiration. Had she imagined it, or had Barker been trying to tell her something – something Lewis was too modest ever to do – that her husband was undervalued?

Rachael lifted the lid of the box file. The document was entitled 'Missing Persons Register. Hospices and Hospitals. Kreis Pinneberg'. There was a handwritten note clipped to the top of the page: 'NB See patient file, page 27. Any relation? Maybe nothing. Barker.'

She took the document, which was some hundred pages thick, from the box file and turned to page twenty-seven.

It was a patient profile. The typed sheet had a photograph clipped to the notes. It was a grainy shot of a woman seated in a wheelchair in a walled garden in summer, staring slightly off camera, posing as though for a portrait in a magazine rather than a medical mugshot. Although the woman was thinner and unmade up, her hair unkempt, Rachael recognized her immediately as Claudia. The Claudia of the unhung portrait: the heavy eyebrows, the determined intelligence. She read the notes:

> Admitted September '44 after being released from a hospital in Buxtehude. Suffered Primary Blast injuries. Patient unable to walk for several months. Hearing damaged. Started speaking last year. Suffers from chronic amnesia but making steady progress. Patient remembers a few details of her life. Gives her name as Lubert. Says she is married. Has a daughter. And used to live by a river.

Rachael went over the detail again – to be sure, to buy time – but she couldn't get to the end of the page, and she didn't need to. It had imprinted itself in her mind with one stamp. As she looked at the photograph, she found herself touching Claudia's face.

'It's you,' she said. And then she slumped in the chair and wept bittersweet tears for the ladies of the house.

Rachael wore her hat at a steep angle and her coat collar high to minimize the possibility of being recognized. At the station, she saw traces of familiar faces in every passing stranger: the porter could have been Richard – or his twin brother; while the rotund ticket master reminded her of Captain Barker.

'Two return tickets to Lübeck, please,' she said in German as she showed her passport to claim her free travel. Her German was much improved, but not good enough to stop the inspector switching to English.

'Who is the other ticket for?'

'A friend.'

'Is your friend here?'

'Not yet. Should I come back when they get here?'

'Your friend is English?'

'German.'

The ticket inspector looked at her papers. 'What is the purpose of your trip? Business or pleasure?'

'The purpose . . .'

'Yes. The purpose?'

'Pleasure.'

'There is no carriage for Occupation personnel on this train. You will be sharing with Germans.'

'Fine.'

'Is everything all right, miss?'

'Yes . . . I have . . . a cold.'

'Here. The ticket. For your friend.'

Rachael wiped her nose and went and stood, as agreed, below the clock with no hands. She set her valise between her feet, pressing her ankles against either side to hem it in, but after a few minutes it didn't feel secure there, so she picked it up, looped her arm through the straps and held it in the crook of her arm.

She lit a cigarette. Birds were careening in and out of the glassless station roof. Smoking didn't settle her nerves at all, and after just two puffs she dropped the cigarette to the platform. A man bent to pick it up and she felt wretched at her profligacy, guiltily handing him the rest of the pack.

A group of British military personnel walked past, and she stepped back into her disguise, angling her hat brim to the ground. She caught snatches of their conversation as they passed – something about 'Brighton being grander than Travemünde'. She had no connection to, or particular nostalgia for, that particular English resort, but the name or the idea of it made her feel homesick.

Lubert appeared at the arched gate and, even from fifty yards, she could see his excitement at seeing her. He held a newspaper aloft, his arm like a periscope guiding him through the sea of people towards her. When he reached her, he kissed her without inhibition on the lips.

'Stefan . . .' She had to hold him back. 'Your ticket,' she said. 'We must take our seats.'

Everyone in Hamburg looked to be catching the train to Lübeck, many of them *Hamsterer*, with baskets and bags for whatever food they could scavenge in the countryside and store away. The platform was already three or four rows deep, and when the train came in the crowd pushed as one to try to get a seat; young men without tickets jumped between the buffers and were pulled back roughly by whistling guards. The train was in a terrible state: bullet holes pocked the carriage sides and the seats were basic. Rachael planted herself on the hard bench between two women, keeping her case with her on her knees rather than putting it in the overhead rack. Lubert took a seat opposite her and made the passengers shuffle up so that he could be close. The carriage smelt of ersatz tobacco and body odour, and Lubert sniffed the air, mischievously implying that the two ladies either side of Rachael were the source of it.

One of the two women shifted to show her displeasure. Rachael signalled with her eyes to shush him. He leant towards her.

'I have a question for you. Question 134 on the *Fragebogen*: is it all right to feel this happy?'

She had to look out of the train window to keep from having to answer him.

The skies had been clear for three days now, the sun allowed to do its work: melting snow in the fields of a subtly undulating and ancient-looking landscape that might have been Sussex or Kent rather than Schleswig-Holstein. She saw a farmhand cracking the ice in a trough with a hoe. In another field, a team of horses pulled a plough over soil that had been snow-covered for months. When the famous green spires of Lübeck came into view, Lubert got up from his seat to see it better.

'The city of my birth,' he said proudly. 'See the spires . . .'

Rachael could see them: bronze-green spires puncturing the sky.

'The spire of the Marienkirche is missing,' he said. 'But still: the loveliest church in Germany. You will soon see.'

At the station, he took her valise and, as they strode towards the city's ancient gates, she took his arm.

'Do you want to go to the hotel first, or see the city?' he asked.

'Let's make the most of the light,' she said.

Lubert was an erudite and emotional tour guide, showing her the house where he had been born and where his parents had lived, just outside the city gates.

'The outskirts have suffered badly. The Royal Air Force tested the bombs that they used on Hamburg here. The old wooden houses burnt easily.' As he took it in, he became more sombre. Memories of his old life came back to him. 'My dear friend Kosse used to live just there.' He pointed to a husk of a house. 'He was obsessed with the movies. He would sell his grandmother for a ticket.

'Now I will show you my favourite building in all of Germany.' Lubert strode on, keen to share another essential part of himself with her.

They passed beneath the Holstentor – the city's medieval entrance tower – and across the canal and up towards the red-brick Marienkirche. It was a grand but restrained struc-ture, bomb damaged and perhaps more striking for it. Its main tower had been destroyed by fire and the roof was open to the elements, a great arch transept dividing a ceiling of air. Lubert entered the nave and instantly began rebuilding it in his head then drawing plans with his hands.

'You can see how lovely it is? Even like this. A beautiful ruin. Perhaps they will rebuild the tower – in wood.'

Rachael was drawn to the two broken bells that had fallen from the tower and lay on the cracked and dented stone floor of the south chapel. The area had been sealed off and the bells left there as a memorial or, perhaps, as an apology by the British. What a sight they must have made: the silent weight of a 300-foot fall, then the mighty clanging at the shattering of crown, head and waist, and the splitting of the sound-rim. The two bells lay there side by side. They had endured a tremendous fall, but they were still somehow together.

Lubert misread her tears. 'You are moved. And rightly so. It is quite something. Quite something.'

He put a hand to her elbow to steer her onward. 'There's much more to see,' he said. 'The streets where I played as a boy; my old school, the greatest marzipan shop in all the world.'

The personalized tour continued, and the more he shared his memories the more conscious of her own she became. When she'd married Lewis, the priest had said that two biographies had become one history. Was their story over? Despite everything that had, was still, and might yet conspire to end it, she did not want it to be.

At the Hotel Alter Speicher, Lubert signed them in as 'Mr and Mrs Weiss' in anticipation of his *Persilschein* being granted soon. Their room was modest and decorated in a homely way. A sentimental depiction of a rural mountain scene in Bavaria hung over the bed. 'The picture is bad,' he said. 'But right for the room.'

Rachael took off her hat and shook out her hair, laying her disguise on the table by the window. Outside, the sun was still visible and sanguine. Lubert joined her at the window and studied her face as she studied the view. He traced the line of her jaw with two fingers.

'You know me a little better now.'

He kissed her, but she broke off and pressed her cheek against his coat and hugged him, less like a lover, more the way a sister might. She held him like this and tried to find the words with which to begin.

'This long winter is coming to an end,' she said.

'Now you are talking about the weather!' He lifted her chin with his finger to better search her thoughts. 'What is this code? What are you thinking? At this very moment now.'

'I am thinking that I am glad for you, Stefan. I am glad that you . . . that you have a future.'

He tried to kiss her again, but she held back. She needed him to come down from the heights of the day. She took his hand and looked at the lines on his palm. She saw a map of roads, forking and intersecting, abrupt terminations and fading endings.

'I think your future will be good, Stefan. You have plans. Good plans. To rebuild your life. Your city. You must realize them.'

A crinkle formed across his brow.

She went and opened her valise and took out the box file that was underneath her one change of clothes. She had never packed so badly in all her life. She'd forgotten her beauty bag and put in a book she was surely not going to read. She opened the file. Barker's handwritten note was still clipped to the top.

She turned to the relevant page and held it out for Lubert to see.

Lubert took it and looked at the photograph of Claudia. He stared at it for so long without betraying any emotion that Rachael suddenly doubted the veracity of the photograph. He continued to stand there, not moving, for a long time. And then his head moved from side to side, very slowly, and his features formed an expression of pained incomprehension. He took the photograph from the clip and held it at arm's length, eyes askance. He tried to hand it back to Rachael. 'This is a trick,' he said. 'I looked for her. For months and months. She is dead.'

Rachael refused to take the photograph back. 'Stefan. It's her . . .'

Lubert looked again, still shaking his head, trying to will the truth away. Finally, he touched the outline of Claudia's face. He still hadn't looked at the bare facts, facts she'd taken in at one glance, contained in the notes.

'Stefan. Read it. Read the notes. She is at the Franciscan Hospice in Buxtehude. She's only just started speaking again. She has lost her memory but is making steady progress, Stefan . . . steady progress.' He was still too stunned to read, so she continued: '"Gives her name as Lubert." Your name, Stefan. She remembers your name. The patient says that she used to live by a river. It's her. Your wife. She's alive.'

He looked at her.

'But . . . we were at the beginning of something.' He was already using the past tense.

'You woke me up, Stefan. You woke me up to what I had forgotten. But . . .' She paused, not wanting to intensify his suffering but needing to speak the truth. She cupped her hands around his, which were still holding the photograph. 'It was loss that brought us together. And you have refound what you lost.' And, with that, Lubert began to weep and Rachael held his hand as he bent over and crumpled in on himself.

13

Lewis woke with his face against the frame of the passenger window, his drool wetting the glass. Barker was driving the Mercedes, glancing over at him with amused concern.

'You all right, sir?'

'Bad dream,' he explained, wiping his mouth and sitting upright. 'Did I say something?'

'You shouted out a few times.'

'Not giving away any state secrets, I hope.'

'You called out your wife's name.'

After being picked up by Barker from headquarters, Lewis had been rocked to sleep by the oceanic motion of the car. In his reverie, the Villa Lubert was before him, set in a season he'd not yet seen it in: lawn lush green and everything in flower – the beds full of daffodils. But there was something too vivid in the scene, something uncanny about the way the daffodils dominated the picture.

'How long have I been out?'

'Ten minutes.'

Lewis rubbed his face and slapped his cheeks. 'It felt like hours.'

During the war, a nap like that would have revived him and allowed him to get through several nights without sleep, but he felt utterly exhausted now. In Heligoland he'd started experiencing an enervation he'd not felt before. At first, he attributed it to the insidious damp of the air and the ennui induced in him by his pointless task, overseeing preparations for the biggest non-nuclear explosion in history. But it had got worse since leaving the island. He could only describe it as an ache in the marrow, such as Rachael had complained of in the wake of Michael's death.

'Everything in order?'

'Pretty much as it was before, sir.'

'Pretty bloody terrible then.'

'Bloody awful, sir.' Barker grinned.

Lewis could have used Barker's company in Heligoland. Once Ursula had left for London, and Kutov, Ziegel and Bolon had seen what they needed to see, the days had dragged.

'CCG are easing up on fraternization. The *Fragebogen*'s being reviewed now that the Intelligence boys are having to turn their attentions east. The big news is the aid package the Americans are suggesting. Can't even remember the number it's so big. The Russians don't like it. It looks like we're heading for two Germanys. So, you still haven't told me what the general wanted.'

Lewis was still taking in the implications of what the general wanted.

'To offer me a job.'

'You see. You get more strokes for destroying things than repairing them. Berlin?'

'Berlin.'

Barker looked slightly forlorn. 'Bloody hell. The next front line. Did you accept?'

'On two conditions. That they don't ask me to share a house with a Russian, a Frenchman and an American.'

'No danger. It's all flats there.' Barker was joking, but he couldn't hide his disappointment at the prospect of Lewis moving on. 'What was the other condition?'

'That you come with me.'

Barker glanced at Lewis. 'Bloody hell.'

'You don't have to give me an answer now. Maybe in five minutes.'

'Bloody hell.'

On the back seat, Lewis noticed a substantial pile of 'pending' paperwork which Barker had brought for him to review.

'More files for me to mislay?'

'Sorry. There's one report on the illegal export of valuables which you need to see fairly urgently. Some familiar names. It's . . . an ugly read. Anyway. Something to look at in the bath.'

A bath was precisely what Lewis wanted. In a few minutes they would be at the house: the Mercedes was already passing the patrician houses on Klopstockstrasse. He patted some colour into his cheeks again and checked his hair in the mirror. By his own reckoning, he looked terrible. His hair was longer than regulations allowed and he'd failed to shave for several days. Even the smallest loss of sleep gave him saucer eyes. He'd never really cared for his looks – he thought his nose a little long, his face too thin – and he was always surprised when Rachael complimented him. Although he'd never needed the affirmation from her, looking at the fatigued face in the mirror he found himself wanting it.

The car turned on to the Elbchaussee and, on the left, Lewis could see the river through the breaks in the trees. The Elbe had been frozen for one hundred days – a record they were saying would never be matched – but some flowing water was just visible; the ice was beginning to thaw.

'You must have been sorry to see Frau Paulus go.'

'Whitehall asked if I knew of an interpreter who'd be willing to work in London. I recommended her.'

'Shame. Don't think the Berlin girls will cut it.'

Lewis could see crocuses and snowdrops at the base of a copse.

'They have daffodils in Germany?'

'Haven't seen any.'

'Stop if you do.'

A crack appeared in the windscreen and spread like a web across it. Lewis presumed that some grit or a stone had struck the glass; only when the car started to veer across the road did he notice Barker slumped, his head snapped back, a clean, crimson-black hole just above his brow. Lewis took the wheel and lifted Barker's leg off the accelerator then wrenched the handbrake on; the car juddered as it stalled, scraping a plane tree and coming to a halt half in, half out of the road.

Blood and tissue were spattered on the back seat and window directly behind Barker. Even before he felt for a pulse at his neck, Lewis knew that he was dead. He lowered himself in his seat and reached in the glove compartment for his pistol. He checked the chamber and saw the blood on his hands, bright crimson and warm. The windscreen had been shot to white, so he looked across the road through the side window. Behind him, the Elbchaussee curved out of view; ahead it ran straight, trees either side, before veering right, away from the river. The shot must have come from one of the great houses on the riverbank. He saw a figure, some hundred yards away, sprint across the road and head towards the river.

Lewis got out of the car, took off his coat, throwing it back in, and set off in pursuit. He ran hard, adrenalin veiling his fatigue and lack of fitness, until he reached the soft dog-leg that led away from the road. He followed the natural line of the land down towards the river, where the figure was still heading. The figure reached the river's edge and started walking out across the frozen Elbe until one of his legs crashed through the ice and he pulled back to the bank and moved along the river's edge, looking for a more solid section. Finding it, he set off across the river again, looking back and, perhaps for the first time, seeing Lewis coming after him. The figure picked up his pace and started to slip-slide on the ice. From the slim body and supple movements, Lewis could see that it was a young man. Not much more than a boy: seventeen, perhaps, but no more.

Lewis had slowed to a fast walk now. He had a stabbing stitch in his shoulder and could feel his heart hammering at his throat. By the time he reached the bank the young man was roughly a hundred yards across the river. Lewis bent over, resting his hands on his knees, gasping for breath. He had already checked the pistol's chamber, but he checked it again. Still six bullets. Still six chances to kill the one who had killed Barker.

The young man had stopped walking across the river and was looking tentatively at the surface ahead, testing it with his boot. The ice gave way again, and he leapt back. Then came the sound of more ice breaking in the middle of the river, like the creaking of an old door. Lewis watched as the young man searched for another way across. Another section of ice cracked ahead of him. There was no way forward.

Lewis could feel sweat chilling on his skin. He felt disembodied, and sat on the trunk of a felled tree. The young man wasn't going anywhere and had no weapon that Lewis could see. He waited to see what he would do. He was walking around on the ice, full of skittish energy. Then he started calling out in German.

'*Guten Morgen*, Morgan!' he shouted, laughing at his own joke and repeating it several times until Lewis got the implication of what he was saying. How did he know his name?

'*Here I am!*'

The young man put out his arms, offering a wider target. He'd stopped at the limit of pistol range. From here, Lewis might just be able to hit him but, if he really wanted to make sure, he could step on to a solid jetty of ice that stretched out into the river and shoot him from there. But he stayed where he was, his breathing returning to normal. He had the sensation of being a spectator at a winter sporting event.

'Come on, Colonel!'

Lewis didn't want to shoot him. But he wanted him to die.

'That bullet was for you, Colonel. But it doesn't matter. A friend of yours is an enemy of mine.'

Another creaking sound came, this time from the ice on which the young man was standing.

'The ice is breaking. It is time for you to leave Germany! This is my land! And this is my river! And this is my sky!'

The young man paced up and down the ice platform, gabbling away. It was quite a performance. He was full of maniacal laughs and gestures, his voice breaking back to boyhood in his excitement. But the more he gabbled, the more Lewis's silence seemed to annoy and frustrate him. Lewis thought he could hear fear cracking the boy's voice and he continued to say nothing and let the fear take hold. It felt good.

'Come and arrest me.'

Sounds like sonar pulses came from different parts of the river. The water below and the sun above were conspiring to break the ice apart. Lewis closed his eyes, just for a moment. The sun left imprints on his retina. He blinked them out. The young man was silhouetted for a few seconds then he suddenly started hot-stepping on the ice as the platform beneath him fragmented into a dozen pedestals, then leapt on to the largest he could see, a section of ice about the size of a door, and landed with his arms out either side to balance himself. It could not take his weight and tilted him into the ice-water, his hands grabbing at air before he plunged in. He cried out with the shock of the cold water and tried to grab at the pedestal but could not get any purchase on it. He floundered for a few seconds then swam to get to the edge of the next small iceberg. He made an attempt to pull himself up on to the little block but it kept tilting him back in. He tried again and then again to get on. After the third time, he gave up and just floated there in the black water.

'*Hey! Help!*' No bragging now, just fear. 'Use a branch. Tree!' And this last word – 'tree' – in English.

Even from here, Lewis heard the shivering in the words. He watched, feeling a vague sadness at his own lack of concern for the young man.

'Please . . . Colonel!'

In under a minute his tone had changed from defiant contempt, through to panic and pleading.

'Tree!' he shouted in English again.

The young man had now drifted to within twenty-five yards of the jetty. If Lewis wanted to save him, he needed to take the branch now. But he was paralysed by an ancient justification; a justification he'd worked hard all his life to refute. Eye for an eye. A boy for a boy. This was how the world still really worked.

With little breath, the young man's words came in bursts of one.

'Frieda! You. Know. Frieda!'

The name registered slowly.

'Frieda . . . Proper . . . German . . . Lady . . .'

Lewis watched and counted the seconds. It would be over soon. The young man had trod water for longer than seemed possible in such cold, and he now started moving very slowly with the current, away into the middle of the great river. Lewis heard powerless gasps. The young man made one last whimpering cry – the word sounded like 'Mutti' – then he sank.

Lewis stood watching the surface of the water. He watched the river and listened to the noisy forming of striations, the great melting movement as it reclaimed itself from its icy occupation. He watched, thinking that there were things to do but that he was done with doing. He could feel something inside himself breaking up. He continued to watch the horizon, feeling his own disintegration. He was like the shot-cracked glass in the car windscreen. If he could just get back to the house before someone touched it, he might avoid shattering completely.

The pain in Lewis's shoulder intensified. It was the stitch he always got after running hard, exacerbated by age and too many cigarettes. He rubbed it and rotated his arm to loosen it, but the stabbing continued. Nearly there, he said to himself. Nearly there.

He'd kept it together so far. Even when examining Barker's spiritless body and the broken capillaries in his eyes; while giving his statement to the Military Police whom he'd found at the scene upon his return. He somehow stopped himself from connecting that slumped husk with the Barker of whom he felt so fond. But now, as he arrived at the gates of the Villa Lubert, he was no longer sure what it was exactly that he was trying to keep together.

He'd left the house two months ago, pure white and picture perfect, but the snap transition from winter to spring had created ugly bald patches of grass in the snow, a mulch of browns and greys and blacks in among the white. He entered through the side door, glad that no one was there to greet him. He took off his coat and rubbed his face in a confusion about what to do next: he wanted to sit down, he wanted a cup of tea, he wanted a smoke, he wanted a drink, he wanted to see Edmund and Rachael – but not quite yet. He fixed himself a whisky and knocked it back in one, to let the sting of alcohol bring him round a little. He poured another then went upstairs.

Edmund was in his bedroom standing in front of a dressing table, admiring himself in the mirror. He was wearing a cricket sweater like Michael's, except for the turquoise stripe of the 'V' at the neck. Even in two months, his only son had grown. Lewis wanted to embrace him.

'Ed.'

'Father.'

Edmund beamed but seemed embarrassed at being caught looking at himself.

'That's a nice jumper.'

'It's from Auntie Kate. She knitted it herself.'

Lewis realized that he was using the door for support. Just climbing the stairs had made his legs ache. He had never fainted but wondered if the airy feeling in his arms was a precursor to doing so.

'Is Mummy not here?'

'I think she's coming back from Kiel today.'

'She went to see the Buckmans?'

'Yes.'

'Have things been all right?'

'Yes. Everything's been fine.'

His son was looking at him with some alarm. 'Are you all right, Father? Have you cut yourself?'

'I had ... an accident ... It's fine.' Lewis looked at the blood on his hands. It looked worse than he had thought. He had to sit down soon. Now.

'So you've been holding the fort for me?' he asked, sitting in the armchair.

'Yes.'

'And the Luberts are well?'

'Yes. But Herr Lubert is not here . . . I think he went away. Somewhere. Something to do with his clearance. I'm not sure.'

'So . . . you're here all by yourself?'

Edmund nodded.

'I'm . . . sorry that I was away for so long. I missed Christmas again.'

'It's all right. Did you blow many things up?'

'A few factories. Submarine pens. The big one is yet to happen. They're putting all the ammunition Germany had after the war in one place and then blowing it up. They will feel it as far away as London. Maybe even Aunt Kate will feel it, in Berkshire.'

Lewis pulled his cigarette case from his coat pocket. It was his first of the day, and the first drag made his head spin.

'Did Mummy give you that case?'

'Yes.'

Lewis handed it to Edmund. Edmund opened it and looked at the photograph of Michael. Michael was wearing his cricket sweater.

'Why don't you have a picture of me?' Edmund asked, quite plainly.

Lewis wasn't sure he even knew why, but he could feel himself about to lie to make it better.

'Is it because Michael died?' Edmund asked, rescuing him. 'And you needed to remember him?'

'Yes . . . That's it. I didn't need a photo of you, Ed. I have you instead.'

Edmund seemed to accept this.

Lewis began to see that the clothes on the floor had not been thrown there but formed an intentional topography. He followed the boulevard of socks between the doll's house and the island jumper and saw the Lagonda car on the road between.

'So what's happening here?' he asked.

Edmund seemed coy. 'It was just a stupid game,' he said.

'It looks fun,' he said.

'The car is meant to be your Mercedes. But Dinky don't make an actual one yet so it's just a Lagonda. And that's Heligoland.' Edmund pointed to the mound of jumpers and shirts, a solitary tin soldier standing at its peak.

'That's me over there?'

Edmund nodded.

Lewis looked back at the doll's house. He could see the two doll children in the bedroom and the male and female adult dolls leaning against the piano on the ground floor.

'So this is Mummy and Herr Lubert – playing the piano?'

'I didn't put the dolls like this. That was Frieda ... she swapped them around,' Edmund said, blushing and looking annoyed with himself for even pointing it out.

Lewis looked at the miniature Rachael and Lubert, and nodded.

'It looks like a happy home,' he said. 'It looks as if everyone's getting along. Which is the main thing.'

It was dark when Rachael arrived at the house. Three lights were visible – in the drawing room, in Frieda's bedroom on the top floor, and in her own. It looked to Rachael as if the house were narrowing its eyes at her. The dusk made a grimacing smile of the slats on the balcony. Lewis's Mercedes was not in the drive, but the thought of seeing him again stirred up butterflies.

Heike met her in the hall, the maid bowing and taking her valise. She was even more jittery than usual, glancing nervously in the direction of the drawing room. It sounded to Rachael as if someone was playing the single-noted, staccato opening of 'The Earl King'.

'Is everything all right, Heike?'

'The colonel . . .' she said. And again she looked towards the drawing room.

Rachael gave her coat to the maid.

'Is Edmund all right?'

'Yes. He is in bed.'

Rachael went to the drawing room and found Lewis at the keyboard, bent over, one arm propping his forehead. He didn't look up when she entered, he just carried on hammering and trying unsuccessfully to play the arpeggio that followed it.

'Lewis?'

He didn't look up but kept on insistently with the note.

'Lew? Why are you playing that?'

Lewis stopped playing but kept his forehead resting on his arm. He was pale, and Rachael noticed there was blood on the arms of his jacket.

'This first bit is easy,' he said. 'But then this next bit . . . I don't know how you do it.'

Rachael's first thought was that somehow he already knew – everything. She went towards him: 'Lew . . .?' She eased herself on to the double stool next to him. The score of '*Warum?*' was on the stand. Lewis's nose was running. She wanted to lift his head, to see what was in his eyes, but he kept his face angled to the ivories, his snot dropping on to the keys.

'What's happened? Something's happened . . .'

Lewis wiped his nose on his sleeve and Rachael saw the

dried blood on the back of his hand. She took his hand in hers; it was ice cold. 'Your hands. You have blood –'

'Not my blood –'

'Whose blood? Lew? You're frightening me.'

'Barker's . . . He insisted on driving . . . I shouldn't have let him . . . The bullet was meant for me.'

'What bullet?'

'The young man I let die.'

'Let who die? Which young man?'

'The young man who shot Barker. The young man . . . who said he knew Frieda . . .'

Rachael couldn't keep up with these leaps.

'I didn't see the danger. But it was there. Right under my eyes. Right in my very house.'

Rachael turned his face to hers, forcing him to look at her. This raw, broken Lewis was unsettling and mesmerizing to her.

'I chased him . . . I could have saved him. But I let him die . . . I wanted him to die . . . Not just for Barker . . . but for Michael . . . for everything.'

Lewis held out his hands, Barker's blood a red-brown constellation across their backs. 'I've chosen the wrong path, Rach. I've nailed my colours to the wrong mast. Burnham was right . . . If you trust everyone, someone will pay.'

Rachael took his face in her hands. 'Don't say this –'

'But you know it's true. Tell me . . . Rach. Tell me. Have I been too trusting?'

He looked into her eyes.

'Yes . . .' Rachael ran her fingers up the side of his face, brushing back his hair. 'But . . . I need you to . . . trust again . . . I need you to, Lew . . .' She kissed him on his forehead, holding her lips and nose to his skin, breathing him in.

'I'm sorry.'

'It's me that should be sorry. And I am. I am sorry.'

'We're a sorry pair,' he said.

Rachael pulled his head to her breast. 'Rest.'

Lewis lay his head there and she held him, rocking him slowly. She had rarely seen Lewis cry. He'd once said that she did the crying for the both of them. As she rocked him, he emitted a quiet but continuous moan; it was not a sound she thought he had in him but it was one she recognized: the sound of someone mourning their son.

Lewis could not rise from his bed, but nor could he sleep. Shock and exhaustion had paralysed him; now, self-loathing and a sort of pleasurable despair kept him awake. He could sympathize with the wisdom that said the idle and the diligent meet death alike, so why bother? He would achieve just as much by lying here as by rushing about. Indeed, given his recent efforts, it was reasonable to think that it would be better for the world if he never got up again. Putting things and people together required a degree of stamina and patience he no longer had and a system of belief he no longer trusted. It was so much easier to knock down than build up: a city raised over millennia could be razed in a day; the life of a man ended in a second's crack. In years to come, Edmund and his children would know the names of planes and tanks and battles and invasions and recall with facility the atrocities of the age, the names of those who committed them. But would any of them be able to name a single repairer of the breach or fixer of broken walls?

Lewis lay there, indulging this solipsism. It felt almost satisfying. Perhaps he'd missed his vocation. He should have been a poet or a philosopher, or perhaps a nihilist.

He could smell coal-tar soap. He held up his hand and saw that Rachael had cleaned the blood from his fingers. She had also taken off his boots and loosened his shirt buttons. At some point, she must have opened the curtains. Particles of dust danced in the light that streamed through them. He must have slept, because he could remember none of these things happening. He could recall Rachael holding him at the piano, caressing his face, studying him like a treasure refound. What had made him suddenly so appealing and precious? Was it that he had nearly been killed? She said she had made a terrible mistake. Told him that Herr Lubert's wife had been found. And then, without using code or even the cushion of an endearment, she told him she loved him, a phrase she did not use lightly; indeed, had not used since . . . he could not recall.

The door opened and Edmund entered the room carrying a tray of breakfast – a boiled egg in a silver eggcup, a slice of bread cut into soldiers, and a cup of tea on a saucer. He moved andante across the room, focusing all his efforts on not spilling a drop. Lewis sat up and pulled his legs up from the bottom of the bed to allow Edmund to lay the tray on the flat. The small of his back ached and his hamstrings were tight from the chase.

'Mother said to wake you at noon. To remind you that you have to go to headquarters.'

'It's noon? Crikey.'

Edmund watched, waiting. 'Aren't you going to eat your egg? I made it. Greta showed me how.'

Lewis took a knife to the thin end of the egg, remembered, then flipped it around to leave the fat end up.

'Mummy is a Big Ender, too. We are all Big Enders.'

Lewis cracked the top off and dipped the head of the bread soldier in the yolk that was just-runny.

'Perfect. Exactly how I like it.'

'Herr Lubert is a Little Ender. And Frieda, too. I wonder if Mrs Lubert is a Little Ender.'

'We'll find out soon enough.'

Lewis used his soldiers to soak up the yolk then picked up his spoon to get to the white.

'Father? If you think something bad, is it the same as if you actually do it?'

This felt like one of those answers he had to get right. 'It depends. You need to give me an example.'

'Well, when you were nearly killed yesterday I thought . . . I was glad . . . that Captain Barker died instead of you. Even though that is sad.'

Lewis set the tray to one side and beckoned Edmund closer. His son came forward and Lewis took his son's oval, downy face in his hands and kissed him, missing his forehead and landing on the bridge of his nose as Edmund ducked a little from embarrassment.

'Is this bad?'

'It's not bad, Ed. It's just bad that . . . you were put in a position to have to think such a thing.'

'Do you have bad thoughts?'

'Yes. I have bad thoughts. I have already had several today.'

'How bad?'

'Well, I thought that I might not get up. Because it wouldn't make any difference if I did. I didn't want to help people any more. I started to think that it didn't get me – or anyone else – anywhere. I didn't want to help Germany. Or the British. Or Herr Lubert. Or Frieda. Or Mummy. Or you. Or myself. I wanted to give up. There. Do you think that is bad?'

Edmund looked unsure. 'That isn't what you will do, is it?'

'Maybe for a few minutes.'

'It wouldn't suit you.'

'No.'

'Did you know that Frieda has been arrested?'

'I didn't.'

'Do you know what they will do to her?'

'What do you think they should do?'

Edmund thought. 'If they knew her mother was alive . . . they might let her go.'

Intelligence could use a boy like this, Lewis thought. It would save them months and mountains of paperwork. He wanted to kiss Edmund again, hug him the way he used to when he was an infant. But two kisses in one day seemed a little too much.

'Have you decided what you are going to do?' Edmund asked him.

'I think so. But you'll have to give me your hand first.'

Lewis put out his hand. Edmund took it in his two and pulled his father to his feet.

14

She was seated in an armchair, sewing a sampler. She had a new shock of white in her hair; her face was fuller, but better for it. She looked calm – calmer than Lubert remembered her ever being – and she appeared as compos mentis as the sister had described: her expression alert and thoughtful, her eyes quick-blinking, and that faint but familiar smile.

The sister in charge had accepted his request that he 'see her before she sees me', and she stood with him now as he observed Claudia through the hatch in the anteroom.

'She sews all day,' the sister said. 'She's been quite prolific. We have many samplers to frame and hang here in the wards. When she isn't sewing, she is writing: remembering.'

'She had such a keen mind,' Lubert said, to himself more than to the sister. 'She has her faculties?'

'She knows her mind – even if some parts of it are still in a process of being recovered. She's a highly intelligent woman. Witty. Creative. Quick.'

How they used to spar, Lubert thought. How he usually lost!

'She remembers some things?'

'She gets fragments of recollections – some in real detail – but then she loses them again. But a picture is building. Bit by bit. And when she gets one bit, it can lead to the finding of another. For the last few months, there's been real progress. We have encouraged her to write things down. Look. She is doing it now: remembering.'

Claudia set the sampler on her lap and picked up a notebook and pencil from the pedestal table by her chair.

'This has been happening more and more. She's writing something every day. Drawing pictures, too.'

Claudia wrote fast, without pausing.

What was she writing? Lubert wondered. What was she remembering? Was he a part of it? Would she remember him? The best of him? Or the worst? Would he live up to what she remembered?

'Does she recall what happened to her? The night of the firestorm?'

'She has not talked of it. Or yet written about it. But I believe she's not ready to remember it. So far, she remembers things that are good – anything that involves relationships. Family. Friends. Home. This is common with cases like this. The mind remembers what the soul can bear. It's all in God's time.'

He envied her: to begin again and build only on good soil. There was a kind of purity in this. She looked content. Perhaps he should leave her in this state. With her clean slate. With this *Stunde Null* of the soul. Why sully things with his messy complications?

'I'm not the same person. I have not . . . I have not been true to her memory.'

The sister studied Lubert's face. He wanted to look away from her benevolence, he felt so unworthy of it, but her kindliness drew further confession. 'I thought she was gone. I tried to start again. With someone else. Someone whom I thought I loved.'

She took Lubert's hands, quite unperturbed by this admission.

'You still love your wife, Herr Lubert. Start with this.' She squeezed his hands, conducting her certainties. 'Come. Let me show you something. Come.'

She led him to a table where three finished samplers had been laid. One was abstract, all zigzags and flower motifs; the second a schoolroom cross-stitch alphabet; the third was figurative. 'When we can, we will frame them,' she said, then picked out the figurative sampler and laid the fabric across the span of Lubert's hands.

'It was the first she made.'

The sampler depicted a house with colonnades, a long, tree-lined drive, a garden leading to a river with a sailboat. In front of the house stood three figures: a man in traditional German dress holding an architect's rule, a woman in hat and old-fashioned skirts, and a girl with plaited hair between them.

'She said it is a copy of a picture she has made before. She wasn't sure if it was her house or her family. All she could tell us was that the ship was a symbol of hope. But you recognize it . . .'

Lubert had never really paid much attention to the original – and he'd lost the right to comment after mercilessly ridiculing Claudia for her 'folksy hobby' – but he did recognize it. It was an exact replica of the sampler that now hung in Frieda's new bedroom.

'This house is yours?'

Lubert nodded.

'And this man is you?'

'Yes.'

'And the girl? This is your daughter?'

'Frieda.'

'And your wife.'

He nodded.

'Is anything missing?'

He shook his head. 'No. It's . . . all there.'

*

'Take a seat, Colonel.'

Lewis took the one and only chair on the other side of the desk from Donnell and Burnham. It was still warm from its previous occupant. The two men were both standing and looked in need of stretching their legs and fresh air after a long day's questioning. In this interrogation tag team, it was clearly Donnell's role to supply the preamble and perform the niceties; Burnham's to watch and wait.

'We're sorry about Barker,' Donnell said. 'We're obviously doing all we can to find his killer. We've got some leads. We've arrested a number of insurgents, including Frieda Lubert.'

'You've interviewed her?'

'We've made a start,' Donnell responded. 'Although we had to abandon the session. She complained of stomach cramps. The MO is with her now.'

They must have done a number on her, Lewis thought. Burnham had his instruments of torture spread across the table: the photographs of Nazi atrocities – camps, lynchings, experiments. Lewis could see one of the pictures: a girl, naked and terrified, Frieda's age, staring off at an unseen assailant whose invisibility made the photograph even more chilling.

'We found her in one of the requisitioned houses on the Elbchaussee. The insurgents were obviously using it as some kind of operational base.'

'Did you find her guilty?' Lewis asked.

'Guilty?' Donnell asked.

'Of all this.' Lewis nodded to the grotesque collage.

Burnham took this as his cue.

'You think it crude, Colonel, but it is still a very simple and effective litmus: there are those who can't look; those who look and then look away; those who look and linger.

Some look and weep. Some look and enjoy it. Some even look and laugh. And there are many shades of reaction in between. You, I noted, looked then quickly looked away, a reaction that suggests an understandable weariness with the subject but perhaps an unwillingness to confront the evil presented – or a tendency to pretend that it isn't there.'

Burnham delivered this neutrally, as though it were an empirical fact. Captain Donnell, who had presumably heard it all before, dutifully nodded.

'And what was Fräulein Lubert's reaction?' Lewis asked, reaching for his cigarette case. He was more nervous than he should be, a little afraid of the coming confrontation.

'She wouldn't look at them. She insisted on staring at me.'

'Who blinked first?'

'Come again?'

'Don't worry. So, you think she is connected to all this?'

'We know she is,' Donnell said. 'Here. This was found in the house.' Donnell produced the demontage file that Lewis thought he had mislaid and pushed it across the table. 'It was found along with plenty of other incriminating evidence.' Donnell checked his notes. 'It was a regular little Boots the Chemist. Ration cards, chewing gum, penicillin, quinine, saccharine, salt, matches, lighter flints, condoms. They had everything. Even a suitcase full of sugar tongs.'

Lewis looked at the file but didn't touch it. He clicked his cigarette case open, tapped out a cigarette and lit it.

'And this proves what?'

'She confessed to stealing the file,' Burnham explained. 'But to quite a lot more besides.'

Burnham's modus was interesting. Like a player in a game of cards, the stillness of his expression increased with the certainty of his advantage.

'Frieda Lubert was part of a group led by your would-be

assassin. Judging from the way she talked about him, they were close. She claims she knew nothing about his plan to assassinate you, but this seems unlikely. His name is Albert Leitman,' Donnell said. He passed Lewis a photograph. 'She was carrying this in her purse when we arrested her. At the end of the war he was stationed with the Alster anti-aircraft battery in Schwanenwik.'

Lewis looked at the photograph and felt wretched. Albert was dressed in the uniform of an anti-aircraft gunner, hair slicked with brilliantine, smiling proudly atop a firing platform. A proud, handsome young man, ready to defend his country.

'It's the only photograph that elicited an emotional response from Fräulein Lubert,' Donnell added.

'I see you recognize him, Colonel,' Burnham observed. 'You know this man?'

'He's looks more like a boy to me,' Lewis said.

'Man or boy, he shot your second-in-command. And we believe he and his gang are responsible for the hijackings of trucks and the stealing of CCG property. Their group matches the profile of other Werwolf-inspired insurgent groups in the zone.'

'What profile is that, Major? Malnourished? Orphaned? Under sixteen? She's just a girl with a grievance. She was manipulated by someone more powerful than her, someone who also had a grievance.'

'The story of the entire nation: "We were manipulated, your honour!"' Donnell joked.

'She shows a remarkable lack of gratitude for someone who's been shown so much kindness,' Burnham said. 'She blames us for destroying her country, her city, her mother. Stealing her house. She complained about everything – even your wife.'

'Rachael's made a great effort to be friendly.'

'A little too friendly, according to the girl. Let's see.' Burnham looked for his interview notes. '"Frau Morgan tried to steal my father."'

Lewis held his eyes on Burnham, waiting to see if the major knew anything more than he knew himself.

'Obviously, she's angry and delusional and her views are not to be taken too seriously,' Burnham continued. 'But it seems you have failed to win her over, Colonel.'

'She's fifteen.'

'You and I both know that her age is no defence. The mark on her arm is enough to have her shot.' He looked at his notes again. '"I can't tell you where he is. Even if you kept me here for a thousand years I couldn't tell you!" Have you noticed how fanatics always think in blocks of a thousand years?'

Lewis's heart was pounding with anticipation.

'Am I to assume from your silence, Colonel, that you have no interest in Leitman's capture? In seeing him brought to justice?'

'Tell me, Major. If you captured him, what would your sentence be?'

'The law would sentence him to death.'

'I mean, would that satisfy *you*?'

'When caught, he will be executed.'

'Albert Leitman has already been executed.'

Burnham's smooth surface was finally disturbed: a ruffled forehead; an odd, sideways look at Donnell; a weary sigh.

'I chased him on to the Elbe. He tried to get across but the ice began to break up. He fell in. I watched him die.'

'You shot him?'

'He drowned.'

Donnell stopped scribbling. 'Let me get this clear, Colonel:

you saw him die? You are certain of this? He didn't somehow escape, or swim to the other side?'

'I let him die. I'm not going to forget that.'

'You forgot it when you reported the incident to the police.'

'I was ... in shock.' Lewis found Burnham's reaction to this – a contemptuous wince – oddly reassuring. He pressed on. 'I recall you once said something about wanting to reconstruct the psyche of this brutalized people, Major. Wasn't that what you said? The speech to Shaw? "Twelve years of ignorance and illiteracy has turned them into animals."'

Burnham didn't answer. He feigned a kind of boredom, which Lewis didn't believe.

'I take it you are still committed to this.'

'In the case of Fräulein Lubert, there won't be time.'

'There's time.'

'Don't be preposterous, Colonel,' Donnell protested. 'She assisted the assassin. We have proof.'

'You will have her shot for stealing a file? Look. I'd like to propose a deal. If you let her go, I'll reconstruct her psyche in a day.' Lewis didn't wait for a response. 'I have two reports here that I have to submit to de Billier. Barker was working on both of them. They concern different things, but they are connected. This first is a register of missing patients in all the hospitals and hospices who have yet to be reunited with their families. It's a substantial work, for which I claim only the credit of instigation. But it has led to the discovery that Herr Lubert's wife is alive and in a Franciscan hospice in Buxtehude. Information I am sure you would not want to keep from a girl who thinks her mother is dead and who has set out on a course of action motivated by that belief. I'd like to show this to Frieda and then take her to see her mother.'

'This is all very interesting,' Burnham said. 'But it doesn't change the fact that Fräulein Lubert is an accessory to a crime, Colonel.'

It was time to play his full hand.

'The other report is of more direct interest.'

Lewis produced a blue folder from his briefcase and pushed it across the desk. Burnham looked at the title: 'The Unauthorized Export of Valuables from German Properties'. He opened the report, showing nothing of his inner reaction. He began to scan the relevant pages – helpfully highlighted by Barker. Lewis had been staggered by the quantities. The Burnhams hadn't squirrelled away a discreet amount of goods; they'd plundered the lot. He waited for Burnham to say something.

The major kept his eyes down as he closed the report and, although his expression gave little away, Lewis felt the balance of power shift to his side of the desk. After a long silence, the major blinked. He then looked at Lewis. It was a curious look, one of genuine enquiry and bafflement. Burnham held the report in the palm of his hand, as though trying to guess its weight.

'Your capacity to ... overlook ... the wrongdoing of others knows no bounds. You really are ... a mystery to me, Colonel.'

Fifteen minutes later, Lewis stood outside the heavy grille door of the detention-centre cell, looking at Frieda through the eye-gate. She was crouched on a bench, her knees pulled to her chest. She looked unscathed but utterly crushed; more fifteen-year-old girl than deadly insurgent. The medical officer had examined her and said he could not find any symptoms of malnutrition, oedema, TB, or any of the other ailments that beset her countrymen. But the stomach cramps he could explain.

'It's nothing to worry about, sir, although her parents might have other ideas,' he said. 'She's pregnant.'

When Lewis entered the cell, Frieda flinched and cowered. To reassure her, he stayed in the doorway and held out his hand. Frieda moved back against the wall and pulled in her knees tighter. Her outer defiance and resentment peeled back to reveal a core of simple, animal fear.

'I didn't know . . . I didn't know what he was planning.'

'It's all right. Come.'

'Come where?'

'Home.'

'Why?'

'Why? Well, because that is where you should be.'

'It is not my home any more.'

'It's better than this.'

'But that man said I was going to prison.'

'My car is parked on the Ballindamm. I'll wait outside for you.'

Lewis left Frieda staring at the open door. He told the guard to let the girl leave in her own time and went outside. On the steps of the detention centre, he lit a cigarette and waited, watching two young men launch a sailboat out on to the thawed waters of the Binnenalster. The Jungfernstieg was alive with pedestrians, all of them going somewhere, moving with purpose. A hundred lives making decisions, mistakes, bargains, deals, trysts, promises.

A cigarette later, Frieda appeared at the entrance. She stopped a few yards away from him. Lewis heeled his stub, indicated to her where he was going, and set off. He walked a few yards ahead, checking that she was following him but letting her keep her distance, playing the game of pretending that they were not together so that she would not feel any more ashamed than she must already.

314

At the end of the Jungfernstieg there was a brand-new, white-painted wooden shop with a corrugated-iron roof selling sweets and newspapers. Lewis stopped and bought a bag of peppermints for the journey and a copy of *Die Welt*. The front cover showed an aerial shot of Heligoland under the headline 'Island Prepares for Great Explosion.' He scanned the first paragraph: 'Remains of Nazi war machine to be destroyed in one mighty blast.'

Frieda had paused a few feet away. Lewis held on to the sweets, knowing that she would refuse them if he offered them in the open. A great convoy of trucks carrying rubble crocodiled back up the street. Flying dust and grit made little tinkling sounds on the road. They waited for the trucks to pass and crossed over to Lewis's mud-brown Volkswagen. He held the door open for Frieda and handed her the sweets.

'These are for you.'

She took them and got in.

They drove south then east, passing the mighty ware-houses of HafenCity, following the waters of the Nordelbe until they reached the wasteland of Hammerbrook.

Frieda remained silent, curled up and facing away from Lewis. When they joined the autobahn to Buxtehude, she sat up.

'This isn't the way.'

'I know.'

'You're going in the opposite direction. My home's back that way.'

'I know,' Lewis said. 'But we're going to go a different way.'

'But this is the wrong way. It'll take longer.'

'Trust me. It's a better way.'

15

On his way to the certification office, Lubert passed the one remaining wall of the old art museum – the 'Have-You-Seen-Wall' – still crammed with requests, many overlapping earlier requests, for information concerning missing loved ones. A section of photographs had now been added, comprising lost children seeking their parents. A man and woman were bending down over it, painstakingly looking at each photo. In the months after The Catastrophe, when people were finally allowed back into the city, Lubert had come here nearly every day. Although it was autumn at the time, something strange had happened to the vegetation: trees and bushes that had been burnt in the summer raids suddenly bloomed again and, completely out of season, lilac and chestnut produced blossom. The new tolerance of the soil subjected to heat allowed for a freakish colonization of the ruins by plants and flowers: bulbous buttercup, chickweed, dwarf mallow and rosebay willowherbs were everywhere, growing from the ashes of loved ones. Lubert had refused to believe the eyewitness account of Claudia's companion, Trudi, that she had perished in the fire-hurricane, and had insisted on adding a notice to the collage of a thousand similar notices. Today was the first time he'd walked past the wall without needing to look.

'I hope you find them,' he said to the searching couple then walked on to the office at the bottom of Steindamm.

Lubert's own hopes were now focused on the granting of his clearance so that he might practise again. He tried hard to rein in his expectations. Not everyone who came to collect a certificate left happy; many were sent away empty-handed and told to come back for further questioning, often without knowing the reason why. Since Claudia's return, though, he had started having ideas, fully formed visions of buildings arising out of the rubble: a new Rathaus, a bridge spanning the Elbe, a concert hall in the docks. They were fanciful and overambitious ideas, probably just the visual laments of a failed and frustrated architect, but they kept coming. Claudia told him to get out his old plans. He'd not looked at them since before the war and his juvenilia made him both smile and wince. The idealism and arrogance of his student days – it was a little like reading an old love letter. He found his plan for his 'House Without History', the workers' village with gardens and canals, fountains and recreational spaces. The name was a youthful vanity: who had ever designed, let alone built, a house without reference to the past? Professor Kramer, his tutor at the institute, had dismissed his plans as ideologically tainted and too bourgeois. Lubert had been too green to argue with such a sophisticate, but now, twenty years on, he thought he saw something in the plans that seemed urgently relevant.

There were two people in the waiting room: a woman biting her nails and a man reading a novel. He took a space on the bench opposite them and, as he sat there, he tried to work out which of them was going to get their certificate and which wasn't. He guessed that the woman, who kept looking at her feet to make sure they were in perfect parallel, was, despite her nerves, an acceptable shade of grey; whereas the man reading his book and turning the pages with his gloved hands looked too calm to be innocent. Lubert could easily imagine him in the immaculate strip of the SS, shining his death's head every morning. He was surely dressing down from his former life. What was he even doing in the same room as this man?

'How long have you been waiting?' Lubert asked him, fishing for some biography that might confirm his suspicions.

'I forget.'

The man didn't even look up from his book.

'What about you?' Lubert asked the woman.

'This is my third time here,' she said, not answering his question. 'I can only tell them so many times what they already know. We weren't even married. We weren't even lovers! I just went to the theatre with him a few times. And now they want to throw me into an internment camp.'

Lubert could guess the details for himself: the man must have been a Somebody in the Party, and she had been his innocent floozie. It was a common enough story.

'Calm yourself, woman,' said Death's Head. 'The more you bang on, the less I believe you. Save your energy. Stick to your story. You have nothing to fear if you stick to your story.' He went back to his book. Lubert was sure of it: this fellow was as black as his shoes.

The wait to be called dragged on. Perhaps it was part of the ploy: give them long enough for doubts to surface; let them sit in this fetid room with others who are tainted and wait for them to start accusing each other.

'Rosa Turnweg?'

The woman hurriedly approached the counter, which resembled a bank till, with a window and a hole beneath it, through which the good or bad news was pushed. Lubert tried to listen to what was being said, but it was hard to hear. Something was passed across the counter to her.

'What is this?' the woman asked. She suddenly erupted with a shriek, slamming her hand on the counter. 'No! No more interviews! Please God! There is nothing more. I have told you everything I can. I need this certificate! Let me live my life!'

No solace came from the official on the other side of the glass. Only silence. When the woman continued to protest, the duty guard stepped forward and ushered her away before she made more of a scene. Despite her triple rejection, Lubert felt sure the woman had been maligned.

Minutes later, the hidden official called Death's Head.

'Herr Brück.'

A sure-fire Party name if ever there was one. Herr Brück looks so very sure of himself. The bastard is in for a shock.

Death's Head stepped up to the counter. The same muffled voice came from behind the glass, and something was pushed across the counter. Herr Brück looked at it and held it up. It was a certificate: a lovely pure-white certificate.

Claudia was right: he was too impulsive. Too quick to decide. It was – as Kramer had always told him – what made him both a very good architect and a very bad one.

Lubert had not contemplated being denied – he believed in his innocence and even in a nebulous concept of British justice – but now new doubts pressed in. Perhaps they had found something he wasn't even aware of, made a connection to someone in the family somewhere, traced a cousin to Bormann, an uncle to Himmler. Perhaps they had discovered his adultery with Rachael.

'Stefan Lubert?'

A bad start. The British official pronounced his name the French way, with a silent 'T'. When he stood, Lubert's legs were weak with pins and needles. The clerk behind the glass wore the navy-blue CCG uniform and had one of those toothbrush moustaches the Führer had made his signature. Lubert had never liked any kind of moustache, and had secretly thought the Führer's a silly affectation. It was odd

319

that so many British servicemen still opted for this style. Didn't they see who they resembled! To think that he might have his freedom denied by an English Hitler lookalike!

'Your certificate.'

A white card with 'Certificate of Clearance, Control Commission for Germany' written on it came across the counter. Lubert stared at it. It had hardly any text. Half of it was taken up by a CCG stamp and the signature of the Intelligence officer. The signature was precise and controlled but for the extravagantly looping first letter of the surname. Burnham.

Lubert stroked the certificate, smelt it and even pressed it to his chest as though it were a billet-doux. He had a *Persilschein*! He wanted to kiss the Hitler lookalike and wave his certificate in the air and tell the whole of Hamburg: 'I am clean! I am free to work! Free to travel! Free to live!'

Lubert left the building and stepped into the street. He breathed in deeply and crossed the road, to stand at the very edge of the ruins. Steindamm marked the outer limit of the firestorm's reach and, even four years on, this was still plain to see: on one side of the street stood six-storey buildings; on the other an area of flattened ruination stretching south to Hammerbrook, like a great plain meeting sheer, jagged cliffs. It was lifeless except for black redstarts looking for food in the snow melt and homes in the rubble.

He watched the birds and started to imagine: all the rubble cleared and the foundations for new buildings dug, the roots of future buildings flowering out of the ground; a library with a loggia overlooking a courtyard, a hospital with an arcade, a school that has gadrooning and bossage! A new cinema with his signature minstrels' gallery for outdoor projections. Roads for cars. Paths for bicycles. Pavements for people. Trees planted in lovely boulevards. Boat houses on the lake. Trains on raised tracks running over the roofs of the houses. Fountains firing water in patterns like flowers. Parks and gardens to think and talk and play and dispute and share in. He could see a whole new city growing out of the desolation. A fine city fit for children, parents and grandparents, lovers and seekers, for the broken and the fixed, the missing and the missed, the lost and the refound.

Epilogue

Ozi and Ernst walked along the banks of the Elbe, taking the back route to the good Tommy's house.

'Why didn't you kill him?' Ernst asked. 'You had the chance.'

It was true. Ozi had had the Beast in the cross-hairs of his x4 Zeiss, his finger on the trigger of the Mosin-Nagant, butt hard to his shoulder the way Berti had showed him. They had been walking like hunters through the park, feet pointing out, knees bent, looking to shoot a pheasant, when there, right in front of them, they'd found a black panther with his head inside the guts of a deer, his neck muscles twitching as he pulled the meat off the bones. Ozi could see the teeth like piano keys, the black fur like a fancy lady's coat, the eyes like emeralds. 'Go on!' Ernst had whispered. 'What are you waiting for?' Ozi could have taken him there and then, but he couldn't do it, and in the moment of his uncertainty the great cat looked up, winked his emerald eyes and slinked away.

Ozi shrugged. 'I don't know. I can't explain it.'

As they walked on, Ozi swatted away the squadron of flies that had engulfed his head.

'I swear we're in for a thousand years of flies. The little bastards have taken over the city. They're not choosy. A fly would requisition a turd, invite his whole family and all his cousins to stay, and call it home.'

'I miss the snow now,' Ernst said. 'At least it was keeping a lid on the stink.'

They came to the bend in the river, the point where Ozi had

thrown his mother's ashes off the end of the jetty. He wondered where she was now. There was no telling where a river might take you if you let it. She could be in Cuxhaven. Heligoland. Sylt. Just as long as she hadn't got caught in the mudbanks of Grünendeich, only for those bastard-fat crows to have her for breakfast. There was a moment, when the wind blew her ashes back over his boots and into his mouth, when he thought he really should have scattered her over the ruins of Hammerbrook or sprinkled her on the lawns of the Jenischpark. But then he remembered what she had always said: 'I'd like to live by the river.' So he waited for the wind to die down then scooped her up from the cake tin in one handful and threw her ashes out, and this time they'd settled like snowflakes over the waters of the Elbe and floated off west to the sea.

As they got closer to the house, Ernst started to get twitchy.

'I'm not sure we should be doing this. You think we should be doing this?'

'Edmund's our friend. He always gave us ciggies.'

'The police might still be looking for us.'

'We'll move between the trees, sly as the Beast himself.'

They turned in from the river, traversed the gardens and crossed the road, moving from tree to tree until they were opposite the gates of the house. They climbed a tree to get a better look over the garden fence. Ozi had taken the Zeiss sights from the Mosin. He pulled them from his pocket and started to scan.

'See him?' Ernst asked.

The colonel's old car was no longer in the drive and the Tommy flag was no longer flying on the pole. There was no sign of Edmund or the colonel or the colonel's wife. Not a trace.

'I can't see the Tommies.'

'Maybe they've gone back home.' Ernst offered. 'They're probably sitting by the White Cliffs of Vindsor, making jokes about Hitler's balls.'

Ozi felt a tremendous sadness at the thought of this, and not just because he needed cigarettes. He continued to scan the house and grounds, hoping to catch sight of his friend – or any of the good Tommies.

Through a downstairs window of the house, Ozi saw something move. He adjusted the sights and saw the legs of a man standing on a ladder. The father of Berti's girl was fixing something: a picture on the wall. Ozi watched this for a while then continued tracking: window–wall–window–garden. He saw a lady sitting in a chair facing the river. She was working at something with a needle and thread, but he couldn't make out what.

'What can you see now?'

'There's a lady. But it's not Edmund's *Mutti*. I've never seen her before. She looks nice enough. Though she's no Marlene D.'

'Someone's crossing the garden,' Ernst said. 'A fat girl.'

Ozi drew back from the sights and saw a girl walk across the garden towards the lady in the chair.

'It's Berti's girl.' He looked through the sights again. 'Someone's put a medicine ball down her skirt.'

'What?'

Ozi lowered the sights. 'Berti's girl is going to be a *Mutti*.' He handed the Zeiss to Ernst and continued to watch the scene with his naked eye. He thought about his brother. He should know about something like this.

'There's a man coming now,' Ernst said.

Ozi saw the father of Berti's girl walk across the garden towards the others with a tray of coffee and cake. He laid it on the garden table and pulled up a chair next to the lady. He said something to her and took her hand.

324

'Shall we come back later?' Ernst asked. 'Ozi? What do you want to do?'

'Let's watch for a bit longer,' he said. 'I just want to see what happens.'

Acknowledgements

My father for telling me how, in 1946, my grandfather Walter Brook requisitioned a house in Hamburg for his family and did something unique in allowing the owners to remain in their property, thus leading to a German and British family sharing a house for five years, starting one year after the Second World War. A situation that gave me the inspiration for this novel.

My uncle Colin Brook who, along with my father, provided essential background detail, memories and texture (as well as photographs) from that time. Without this, I would not have been able to construct my own picture or story.

My agent, Caroline Wood, who for years badgered me into writing the story, insisting that it should be a novel (as well as screenplay) and didn't stop badgering me until I gave her enough words for her to get a publisher interested.

Jack Arbuthnot, film producer at Scott Free, who, after hearing my pitch, commissioned a script, an act that galvanized my agent into badgering me even more into writing the novel.

My editors, Will Hammond at Penguin and Diana Coglianese at Knopf, for taking a leap of faith on a book that was only one sixth written then helping me sculpt the slab of putty I eventually delivered into something worth reading.

Various friends who have, over the years, encouraged me

to write another novel when I wasn't sure if I would or should or could again. You know who you are.

My wife and editor-in-chief, Nicola, who has put up with me trying to write while she has been teaching truly great literature for the last twenty years.

The Author Of All Things.